BAPTISM OF FIRE

Any other Wais would have already fainted dead away, but Lalelelang was better prepared for viewing combat than any other of her species. She sensed movement nearby and retracted her neck. The Human Umeki would be relieved to see how well she had done in her absence.

But it was not Umeki who stumbled around the base of the tree. The Mazvec warrior was huge, its bright orange ruff dyed a camouflage green. Lalelelang began to shake violently.

Then a mountain fell on the Mazvec from behind—a Human much bigger than Umeki. There was a sharp *crack*, and the Mazvec crumpled. The Human lifted the alien warrior and dashed its rounded skull against a log.

Lalelelang blinked. Then she spat out her recorder from her beak and added the contents of her crop to the mess.

By Alan Dean Foster
Published by Ballantine Books:

THE BLACK HOLE

CACHALOT

DARK STAR

THE METROGNOME AND OTHER STORIES

MIDWORLD

NOR CRYSTAL TEARS

SENTENCED TO PRISM

SPLINTER OF THE MIND'S EYE

STAR TREK LOGS ONE–TEN

VOYAGE TO THE CITY OF THE DEAD

. . . WHO NEEDS ENEMIES?

WITH FRIENDS LIKE THESE . . .

The Icerigger Trilogy:
ICERIGGER
MISSION TO MOULOKIN
THE DELUGE DRIVERS

The Adventures of Flinx of the Commonwealth:
FOR LOVE OF MOTHER-NOT
THE TAR-AIYM KRANG
ORPHAN STAR
THE END OF THE MATTER
BLOODHYPE
FLINX IN FLUX

The Damned:
Book One: A CALL TO ARMS
Book Two: THE FALSE MIRROR
Book Three: THE SPOILS OF WAR

THE SPOILS OF WAR

Book Three of *The Damned*

Alan Dean Foster

A Del Rey Book

BALLANTINE BOOKS • NEW YORK

A Del Rey Book
Published by Ballantine Books

Library of Congress Catalog Card Number: 92-90403

ISBN 0-345-37576-9

Manufactured in the United States of America

First Hardcover Edition: April 1993
First Mass Market Edition: January 1994

For John Soderberg: sculptor
Fellow shaper of the aether
Fellow explorer.

"I wish that you would not do this thing. You know that we all do."

They reposed on the slightly raised dining platform on the external lip of the restaurant. From their present height they could see much of the city spread out before them, an urbanized extravagance that covered a vast amount of territory. Mahmahar was not that heavily populated, but since by law no structure could be more than four stories tall, expansion was predominantly horizontal. The vast number of gardens and parks demanded by custom and aesthetics further contributed to the large areas occupied by even modest conurbations.

Not that the city had the slightest overtone of urban sprawl. On the contrary, it barely resembled a city at all, much less the kinds of metastacizing metropolises one found on the Hivistahm or O'o'yan worlds. Architecture that emphasized the harmonious while intertwining with gardens and parks made sure of that. In such a setting it was the larger structures that looked like interlopers and not the other way around.

Home to slightly more than two million, the community of Turatreyy was one of the larger on Mahmahar, and its inhabitants were proud to call it home. Where possible the Wais preferred to restrict the size of their cities to less than five million but more than one. In socialization as in everything else, the Wais found beauty in definition.

Sometimes this engendered a mixture of contempt and envy among the other members of the Weave, who would

1

deride the Wais for their manners and formalities while secretly admiring their ability to develop or find beauty in everything. Even among their detractors there was no denying that Wais society and civilization represented the zenith of Weave culture, one that other species could only aspire to emulate even when Wais action (or lack of it) proved exasperating. It was a responsibility the Wais took seriously.

Like every other member race of the Weave, they had sponsored the war against the Amplitur from the beginning, over a thousand years ago. It was a support that had never wavered, one as strong as their desire to shun actual combat. In that they were no different from the majority of their allies.

Lalelelang's mother toyed with the three traditional drinking utensils in front of her. One for the aperitif, one for the main course, a third filled with a lightly citrus-flavored spring water for ceremonial clearings of the palate between bites. Like every other aspect of Wais society, dining had been raised to a fine art.

As the dominant surviving representative of their matrilineal line, her mother had to say such things; it was her place. Her grandmother would have been even more forceful in her objections, but that honored life-giver was two years deceased, clipped, embalmed, and reverently ensconced in the family mausoleum. So the disagreeable task was left to her mother. Her father would be informed of the results only when the females saw fit.

"You could be so many things," her mother was saying. "Among your age and study group your potential gradient is by far the highest, as it is among the family. You show flashes of brilliance in narrative poetry as well as industrial design. Engineering is wide open to you, as is the entire range of organic architecture." Gold-tipped lashes fluttered above wide, blue-green eyes. "You could even be, dare I venture the notion, a landscaper!"

"I have made my choice. The proper venues have been notified." Lalelelang's tone was deferential but firm.

Her mother inclined forward, sipping through her beak

delicately and with perfect grace from the damascened aperitif container.

"I still do not understand why you felt it necessary to choose such a dangerous and uncertain occupation."

"Someone has to do it, Mother." With the prehensile, featherless tips of her left wing Lalelelang nervously fingered the four small plates of food arranged in the standard midday meal pattern before her. "History is a respected and valued profession."

Her intricate body language conveying unyielding parental concern, the senior female ruffled her feathers as she straightened in her chair. Her movements signified frustration rather than anger. There was disapproval in the delicate tilt of her head, remorse in the slight arching of her feathery cranial crest. Her father's, Lalelang mused, would by now have been twinkling iridescent crimson. Lacking such colors, a female had to make do with subtlety of movement.

She got the message nonetheless. Her mother had been flashing it in various guises throughout the meal.

"You choose to be a historian, by which amusing quirk of nature I cannot begin to imagine." Lengthy eyelashes fanned the air between them. "Eclectic enough, but not in itself objectionable. It is your fascination with the war that confounds and distresses me. The obsession is unWais."

"However much we may dislike it, it remains the single most important component of our modern history as well as of our daily lives." Lalelclang picked up a clutch of perfect, tiny, bright green berries from the dish nearest to her and used (as was proper) just the tip of her beak to neatly nip them one at a time from their black stems. When she'd finished she placed the stripped stems back on the empty plate, carefully positioning them so that neither end pointed either at her or at her mother. A perverse profession she might have chosen, but she still remembered her manners, of which there were intricacies even those representatives of other species who had worked intimately among the Wais for years did not suspect. After a while they ceased to care, which helped greatly to ease tension between them and their hosts.

In the midst of difficult times it struck some, like the Massood, as a waste of time and energy, not to mention an overemphasis on foolishness, but to the Wais manners were the very lifeblood of meaningful existence. It was a principle reason why they had contributed so much for so long to defeat the enemy: if imposed, the Amplitur Purpose would have wreaked havoc with traditional etiquette, without which, the Wais were convinced, there could be no true civilization. Other species did not disagree with this tenet so much as they did the emphasis the Wais placed upon it.

"Even if I grant your thesis, daughter, I still do not see why you could not have left this work to someone else." Her eyes swept worriedly across the nearest garden, a dense paving of six-petaled yellow and orange *Narstrunia* that were just coming into glorious full bloom. They were edged with tiny violet *Yunguliu*, a touch the senior female was not sure she wholly approved of. Black and white Wessh would have provided more contrast, and they were in season.

We are all of us critics, she thought, *as I am now in criticizing my offspring.* It was a principle reason why within the Weave the Wais were greatly admired but less than universally popular.

An empty package marring the soft floral perfection of the garden path caught her eye. Doubtless dropped by a visiting alien, she knew, for no Wais would be so careless with the visual aesthetic. Possibly a S'van, though they were no more or less crude than any of the other Weave races. Their irreverent attitude toward life, however, bordered on the regressive. It was with some difficulty that she repressed her instinctive urge to leap over the ornate railing and spring across the lawn to snatch up the debris before it offended another passerby's sensibilities. She forced herself to concentrate her attention on her patiently waiting daughter.

"Because I believe that I am best suited to the task, Mother." Politely Lalelelang searched the remaining three plates of food in front of her for something appropriate with which to chase the green berries. "The same attitudinal approach which would make me a good engineer or landscaper will stand me in good stead in my chosen field of endeavor.''

''Aberrant behavior,'' her mother whispered in the most inoffensive dulcet tones imaginable.

''No. Just a talent . . . and a calling.''

''So say you. Aberrant proclivity, then.'' She sipped from the container of spring water and picked at her own meal, sufficiently upset to ignore dining protocol by selecting directly from the fourth dish. Her concern for her daughter outweighed any hunger, but it would have been unforgivable to have ordered food and not eaten.

She leaned across the table, the narrow head protruding gracefully from the half-meter-long neck. ''You grade out top of your age group. You already speak fourteen Weave languages fluently when the norm for your educational cluster is five and for matriculated adults ten. I grant you your choice. I grant you your determination.'' The head drew back and the senior female gazed into the distance.

''But this area of specialization you have settled upon, like a stone sinking down through the darkest waters: that I cannot give my approval to.'' Her crest was absolutely flat against the back of her head and neck as she spoke. ''Why, of all the subjects available, must you choose this?''

''Because no one else has,'' her daughter replied.

''And with good reason.'' She shifted dialects effortlessly, from one of admonition to one indicative of deep concern. ''Your very health and future are at stake. Even the males in the family are concerned.''

''Everyone is worrying themselves needlessly.'' Lalelelang's reply was strong, but she could not meet her mother's gaze. She focused instead on the other midday diners, careful not to stare at any one group or individual for too long.

Her mother's neck contracted. ''I do not understand you. I do not understand how you can cope.'' She reached for one of the half-dozen lightly broiled *Hapuli* grubs on her second plate, hesitated, and withdrew her wingtips. Distress had ruined her appetite.

''I have trained myself,'' Lalelelang explained. ''When

dealing with extremes I use the special medication that has been devised for such purposes.''

Her mother whistled soft derision. ''Who ever heard of embarking on a career that requires periodic ingestion of strong medication merely to enable one to maintain one's normal equilibrium? What sane Wais would voluntarily subject themselves to such a prospect?''

''There have been one or two,'' Lalelelang protested. ''Not here on Mahmahar, but off-world. Careerists of the diplomatic service.''

''They had no choice. You do. Yet even they did not opt for this peculiar . . . specialization . . . that so perversely attracts you.'' She adjusted her posture significantly. ''I concede you the honors you have won, but surely you must have noticed with what distaste they have been granted?''

''Someone must do the distasteful work,'' Lalelelang countered.

Her mother's beak clicked regretfully. ''Yes, but why you? Why the brightest of my offspring?''

''Because I am the best suited, and additionally the only one so inclined.''

''So you continue to insist.'' She straightened formally in her chair. ''It is clear you are obsessed by this and intend to pursue it, no matter the dangers.''

''It is not an obsession. It is simply what I have chosen. Or as certain poets say, for reasons unfathomable it has chosen me. I am already regarded as one of the top three in the field.''

''Easy enough to excel at something everyone else avoids.'' An uncomfortable pause followed this observation, which neither mother nor daughter knew how to gracefully break. As the younger, Lalelelang finally felt it incumbent on her to speak out.

''Then you won't come to the presentation tomorrow?''

''Do you really think I could cope with it?''

''I do not know, but I would like you to see some of my work instead of condemning it solely on the basis of second- and third-hand knowledge.''

The senior 'lang's feathers quivered. ''I am sorry. The

mere thought unsettles my insides. It is difficult enough just to sit here and discuss the subject with you. But to actually observe your work . . . no, I cannot. Of course, your father will not be present, either."

"Because you refuse him permission?"

"Don't speak ill of your father. As males go he is exceptional. Your genes speak to that. It is simply that he has no more stomach for your choice of subject matter than do I. The same is true of your brother and sisters."

Lalelelang considered the remnants of what had been a less than serene meal. "I expected no more. I'm sorry you will not be present. It is fascinating material, when you consider that in the first instance—"

"Please, daughter." Both wings rose at just the precise angle to emphasize unease. "I have heard quite enough already. Remember that though as a good parent I tolerate your fixation, that does not mean I am required to share in it. It astonishes me that any in your department can do so. Tell me: Prior to such presentations, do they also take medication?"

"I am sure there are some who do, as a precautionary measure if for no other reason. You may not believe it, but there are others besides myself who can examine everything without special preparation. It's like working with any toxin; the more you are exposed to it, the greater the immunity you build up. Though there are always surprises."

"And this is the life you have chosen." Her mother steadied herself. "To scholar the war is one thing. But to focus on the *Human* quotient?" Her eyelids flicked eloquently. "If you had not graded out so remarkably on all the standard tests, I would have recommended you for advanced adolescent therapy."

Rising from the table, they commenced the ritual of parting suitable for female parents and second daughters. "I know that you love me, Mother." Wingtips, eyelashes, feathers, and beaks all bobbed and swayed in eloquent, intricate rhythm as she spoke.

"I do indeed, despite the repulsive avocation you have selected." Wingtips danced and lightly caressed.

* * *

The following day Lalelelang strove to put her mother's words and deep concern out of her mind as she checked the equipment in the tiny auditorium. Given the light attendance expected, there was no reason to request a larger facility. Besides, it was convenient to her office and relatively isolated from the main body of the university. No one should be offended.

Attendance was restricted to those qualified either by membership in the department or dual recommendation from a senior scholar. This was as much for the protection of unwary students as anything else. Should an unprepared innocent expecting a normal lecture happen to wander into one of Lalelelang's presentations, the resultant emotional and mental damage could be serious.

She wasn't worried about that. Security was the responsibility of others, and she gave herself over wholly to the upcoming presentation.

The audience consisted of a dozen expectant observers, each occupying a cradling individual rest pad. Like everything else on Mahmahar, or any Wais world, the presentation chamber had been constructed with an eye for beauty as well as function. Each pad had its own lighting and reproductive screen, as well as remote terminals for recording and observing.

The holo projector stood quiescent off to one side, and a simple flat screen had been secured to the depth wall. Lalelelang had learned early on in Human Studies that the usual life-simulating three-dimensional projections were too unsettling for even experienced researchers to handle. Displaying Humans in flat, obviously artificial two dimensions, particularly when combat was involved, made it much easier for novitiates to take and was about all most Wais could handle.

She lit the slightly curved flat screen and checked the projector, adjusting the speech amplifier clipped to her lower beak. Most of those in attendance were known to her, though her heart jumped slightly when she noticed Fasacicing among them. He was accompanied by the two other males of his bonding trio, probably for moral support.

All three worked in the sociohistory department, though

only Fasacicing had shown any interest in Human Studies. For the most part they preferred to specialize in the easy prewar Golden Period of Waisisill itself. It was a mildly rewarding and decidedly unchallenging field of endeavor. Fasacicing was taking her lectures as a subspecialty. He was a handsome and extremely colorful specimen, gratifyingly flamboyant in his plumage and manner of dress. They had exchanged more than pleasantries on several occasions, advancing as far as fifth-stage verbal-physical interaction. Try as she had, she'd been unable to stimulate him to further action. He remained interested, however.

She had to concentrate on her presentation, though that didn't mean she couldn't spare him an occasional glance. She'd acknowledged his arrival with a semiformal wave of one wing, and his triumvirate had responded synchronously, acknowledging as three the greeting intended for one. She admired his stride, almost a prance, as the trio entered and settled into adjoining pads.

After allowing a decent amount of time for late arrivals, she launched into her presentation, beginning with a verbal overview of her most recent work, reading from her next report, and finally dimming the lights and initiating visuals. Immediately those peripheral attendees began to squirm and fidget uncontrollably. She made no concessions for them. The subject of her presentation was clearly described in the university overprogram and it was incumbent upon everyone present to know what to expect.

Though life-size and sharply defined, the images displayed on screen were reassuringly flat, rendering them considerably less intimidating than they would have been in three dimensions. Even so, a few distressed murmurs were audible from the back row, close by the entry portal. This was normal. Lalelelang ignored them and continued with her erudite explication.

"As I mentioned earlier, today we will be examining social interaction between Human fighting forces and various noncombative representatives of the Weave. In this particular case study, the Hivistahm."

Lalelelang culled her visuals and related information from multiple sources, distilling those items of interest to her from numerous nonmilitary as well as military venues. Given the length of time Humans had been in the alliance, there were a fair number of sources to choose from. Such had not been the case hundreds of years ago, when contact with the Weave's erstwhile Human allies had been restricted for safety's sake.

Still, it was difficult to find usable recordings that illustrated specific instances of social interaction between Human soldiers and representatives of other Weave species, since the latter did their best to avoid the former even in noncombat situations. When such contact did occur, it was usually accidental. Lalelelang spent a good deal of her time scouring otherwise uninformative media reportage in search of the occasional useful nugget.

Sometimes representatives of logistical support teams, be they Hivistahm, O'o'yan, or S'van, would find themselves accidentally caught up in a flurry of fighting. More rarely a media or military reporter would be present. Out of this exotic combination of circumstances came what little material she could use.

She began with updated diagrams, giving the preoccupied a final opportunity to ingest any personal medication. As for herself, she'd been able to dispense with most of it two years ago, scientific detachment and experience having combined to inure her to even the most shocking sights. As she delved more deeply into the presentation and Massood, Humans, and others began to appear on screen in abnormal proximity to one another and to actual fighting, the usual outbreak of involuntary chirpings and whistlings began in the audience. Personal recorders took down everything that was shown, everything she said.

When the first detailed combat footage appeared, the shuffling sounds from the rear of the auditorium grew more pronounced. Even several of her regular students looked a little queasy. But no one left.

As she elucidated, the projector flashed a particularly graphic sequence showing Human soldiers taking apart a slightly larger number of attacking Crigolit. An isolated incidence of unsuppressible regurgitation from somewhere in the auditorium failed to interrupt the flow of either words or images. Courteous or not, she didn't have time to coddle the unprepared.

It was normal for several visitors to throw up during the course of her presentations, and so she was anything but shocked when it happened.

There was the usual palpable whistle of relief when she concluded the visual exhibition and resumed unsupported speaking. Her gestures, she knew, were not as refined as those of more experienced scholars, her movements not as polished by the winds of academic discourse. In her presentations information took precedence over skill of delivery. No doubt this would slow her professional advancement, but it in no way abrogated the efficacy of the material she was imparting, and she was content with that.

As she shut down the equipment and pocketed the storage bead in her shoulder pouch, she took a moment to study the faces of her departing audience. It was smaller than when she'd begun, several visitors having left—or fled—prior to completion. This was not unprecedented. She might have smiled had her inflexible upper beak permitted such an expression. Not being so endowed, the Wais instead made do with a bewildering variety of gestures, eye movements, and vocal inflections. It was not a deficiency they felt keenly.

Crossing the auditorium, she intercepted Fis and his companions. He seemed to have handled the presentation all right, his expression being only slightly queasy. Though his companions looked less well, they still ritually interposed themselves between the oncoming mature female and her obvious quarry. Either of them would readily have mated with her to cover for a less adventurous member of their triumvirate.

While there was nothing wrong with either young male, it was Fis who attracted her. As usual he did not respond to her elegantly convoluted request for a private meeting—a date, the Humans would have called it, though for a Wais the social implications were far more subtle—with the result that the rest of the four-way conversation was politely formal if somewhat stilted.

As they departed, however, one of his companions returned with the message that Fis would be pleased to meet with her in two weeks, if only to mute her persistence. Naturally she professed indifference even as she acknowledged the acquiescence. Colleagues had worried and even quietly criticized her lack of a normal social life. Perhaps evidence of this ritually scheduled assignation would mollify them for a while. Societal politics were the lifeblood of Wais culture, but sacrificing valuable research time to meet one's minimum expected social obligations could sometimes be a pain.

It was a blunt observation for a Wais to make, but one couldn't spend months studying Humans without being influenced, however slightly, by the subject of one's studies. She knew that among the university hierarchy her unusual straightforwardness was not always appreciated.

Two weeks, then. If they could finalize a casual assignation, it would go a long way toward silencing her critics. Nor was she totally averse to such a liaison. Fis was mature enough and his companions respectable. There was also that streak of iridescent lavender that ran from his neck down onto his chest . . .

She made a last check of the auditorium equipment. Sometimes it was hard to be a female, she thought. You were always expected to make the first moves. That derived from ancient days when male body chemistry was governed by hormones that fired only several times in a year. Science had since homogenized that biocurve, but social conventions had proven far harder to change.

What must it be like for Humans, she wondered, where the male was usually expected to be the aggressive one? Or for the Massood, whose minimal biological and social differentiations allowed sexual courtship to proceed in an atmosphere of genteel ease? She could envision both from an academic standpoint, but not a personal one.

By now the auditorium was deserted except for herself and one remaining visitor. She blinked in surprise, wondering what Kicucachen wanted. She hadn't noticed the presence of her departmental superior earlier and decided that he must have entered while her presentation was still in progress.

While it wasn't like him to drop in on scheduled lectures, neither was it unprecedented. She observed that despite the loss of color in his crest and chest feathers he was still handsome. Not in Fis's class, but still a viable mate. It was a compliment for someone of his advanced years. She did not voice it, of course. Given the difference in their respective scholarly positions that would have been a serious breach of academic etiquette.

There was nothing wrong with her speaking first, however.

"Are you all right, Senior?"

"I believe so." His reply was strong despite undisguised overtones of discomfort. "I hadn't been to one of your infamous Human Studies presentations in some time and had forgotten how graphic they can be." He glanced involuntarily in the direction of the now blank screen, as if something alien and lethal might still be lurking there just waiting to pounce on the next unwary passerby and tear him beak from limb.

"You certainly haven't moderated your subject matter."

"I study Human activities in war and how they relate to the rest of Weave culture, particularly our own." She made a show of adjusting the projector. "The actions of Human beings do not easily lend themselves to moderation. It is not something that can be adequately studied through indirection."

Seeing that the brusqueness of her response had taken him aback, she hastened to soften it with appropriate follow-up gestures. It was an awkward attempt and she made a bad job of it, but he showed no offense.

"You are a very unusual individual, Lalelelang. It is a continual surprise to many in the administration that someone of your background and ability should have settled on so gruesome a specialty."

She chose not to comment. There was no specific reason to do so, as she'd been hearing the same thing for many years.

"Might I inquire if you have found time in your busy schedule to make arrangements to mate?"

For a change, a comfortable coincidence. She relaxed. "There is someone I am interested in, but it is difficult. My work keeps me so occupied."

"Yes, your dedication is frequently remarked upon." The senior strove, not entirely successfully, to conceal his impatience. "May I accompany you back to your office?"

"I delight in your company," she said, knowing she was hardly in a position to refuse. Her crest erected proportionately.

As they walked, scholars and students, visitors and researchers swirled around them, a brilliantly chromatic academic conflagration of dialects and whistles, chirps and dips and bobs, that wonderfully poised social interaction of gregarious Wais on a mass scale which would have appeared to some outsider as a carefully and exquisitely choreographed dance. Among the sweeping gestures and strides, the arch of feathery crests and flashes of male iridescence, the luster of clothing and jewelry, the occasional exchange student or scholar representing some other species stood out like a chunk of weathered debris drifting across the surface of an otherwise mirror-still lake.

Here a bright green Hivistahm, all scales and polish. Alongside a coiffured stream, a clannish pair of even smaller O'o'yan murmuring to one another.

"Don't tell me administration is complaining again?"

"No." The senior's eyelids barely flickered. "They recognize the significance of your work and know that someone has to do it. Since they do not dare appoint anyone, they are silently grateful for your enthusiasm. In the final analysis it affords them more relief than distress."

"I am glad." She did little to hide her sarcasm. "It does my spirit good to know that because of my efforts the administrators can sleep soundly at night."

"There is no call for that tone. You have had ample administrative support."

"Ample but reluctant, as though I were researching some dreaded disease." When the senior did not attempt to dispute this analogy, she continued. "I am sure no one would be terribly disappointed if my entire body of work were to evaporate and I were to be reassigned to something less . . . discomfiting.''

They walked down a glideway lined with stained glass and planted in pink *finushia.* ''No doubt there is some truth to that observation,'' he admitted. ''Yet they also realize that there will be a place for your efforts until the war ends.''

''Afterward as well, though they do not see it.''

He glanced sideways at her. ''How do you mean?''

''The end of the war will not mean the disappearance of Humankind. At the Weave's encouragement they have settled and populated many worlds in order to provide the alliance with more and more soldiers. The war's conclusion will not make them go away. We will still have to interact with them socially. That is why my studies are so important.''

The senior was silent for a while. ''I am not so sure that will be necessary,'' he said finally. ''Many believe that with a little appropriate assistance Humans would be glad to resume their original isolation.''

''That's nonsense,'' she replied, ''or wishful thinking. You cannot keep offspring from revisiting the nest once they've matured. They can't be swept out and forgotten like old droppings. No matter how much Weave society might wish it, they will not go away. So in order to live with them we must understand them better, and in order to understand them we must study them.'' Her eyes flashed. ''Under *all* conditions.''

''Pray me no polemics, for I am on your side,'' said the department head. ''Were it not so, I would not have supported funding of your work thus far, I say only that there are others less farseeing . . . or tolerant.''

''I am not alone in my studies.''

''I know. There is Wunenenmil at the University Siet and Davivivin on Koosooniu.''

''I know them well, from their work. As they know me. We are a small bonding; an unlikely triad, scholarly in intent rather than sexual.''

They turned beneath a waterfall, along the winding path that led to the residences. ''This reluctance to study Humankind in combat is not limited to the Wais,'' the senior remarked. "It is a distaste common to all our allies, from the S'van to the Chirinaldo. The result is a lamentable gap in the history of the war. The Massood could fill it in well but are too busy fighting, the S'van too happy-go-lucky, the Lepar obviously out of the question. The Hivistahm and O'o'yan and Sspari are too intent on logistics." A soft whistle escaped his beak. "Sometimes I think only the Wais are interested in serious scholarship."

"The Humans claim they are."

The senior glanced at her in surprise.

"What do you mean?"

"They have their own institutions of higher learning, in which they actually, believe it or not, study something other than the mastery of war."

"Yes, I've heard such stories." The feathers on the back of his neck quivered visibly but his crest did not erect. "A Human university seems almost a contradiction in terms. It must be a terrifying place."

"I do not know. Someday I hope to experience it for myself."

"It is a true scholar you are, to be so dedicated to your work."

"No more so than any of my honored colleagues," she unassumingly assured him.

"Perhaps, but they are driven by respect and love for their subject matter. Surely it must be different for you."

"It is true I have no more love for Humankind than any other thinking Wais. I would not, could not deny that. My affection is for the vast gap in an important field that must be filled in. I am glad that despite their personal feelings the membership of the administration can see this."

"Rest confident that they do."

"Then they will understand how urgent it is that they fill the grant that I am going to formally request as of tomorrow."

"Grant?" His eyelids closed halfway. "For what? Additional memory storage? Some exotic research materials? Perhaps an off-world leave to journey to Koosooniu to confer with colleagues in person. I see no difficulty. We are at present adequately funded.''

"Nothing so prosaic, I am afraid. It concerns something which has been troubling me for some time."

He halted abruptly. "You are not ill?" His concern was genuine. She'd sensed for some time that the department head's interest in her was more than merely professional. Not that she in any way resented such attention: it was simply that he did not intrigue her as a potential mating partner. Her lack of interest kept his attentions at a distance without wholly discouraging him. She knew that it was a purely male thing over which he, even at his advanced age, had no control.

"I feel strongly that I have progressed as far as possible given the materials available and must therefore take whatever steps are necessary to broaden the scope of my research activities."

"Of course; certainly. An in-person conference . . ."

"No, you don't understand. I have exhausted the literature going back to the first contact between Humankind and the Weave. My own work has already moved beyond anything being done anywhere else. I need—" She hesitated as she tried to couch her comments in the most persuasive possible dialect. "—to do some fieldwork."

The senior didn't react immediately. When he did it was to chirp uncertainly, "Fieldwork?"

"Yes. I feel I can no longer advance by means of impersonal study. I have gone as far as I can. You've seen my reports."

"Brilliant. Highly original work. One might almost say ingratiating despite the unpleasant nature of the subject matter. You have brought much credit to the department and the entire university."

"And I intend to bring even more, by pursuing my studies in the field. I need this grant in order that I may visit, in person, a combat site. The battlefield. After examining the most recent media reports, I have settled on Tiofa as a good place to begin."

"Tiofa is a disputed world, on which actual fighting is

taking place.'' The true meaning of her request had still to sink in.

"Correct. Where else can I personally observe Humans interacting with other species in a combat situation?''

Forgetting courtesy, he gaped at her as they entered the spiraling *Gucheria* garden. "You cannot be serious! You are Wais. I do not care how much you think you have hardened yourself to such horrors. Academic proximity is not the same as actual experience.''

"Precisely why I must go,'' she contended.

"You know from your own work that we are emotionally and mentally unable to cope with such conditions.''

"Over the years I have developed a number of exercises, mental as well as physical, that I believe will enable me to do so. There are also updates of the standard medication.'' Her neck bobbed sharply, a fluid punctuation mark. "I *must* do this. Otherwise my research comes to a dead end.''

"Yet you are still comparatively young.'' The department head sounded regretful.

"I will not stunt my intellectual growth any more than I would the physical. Fieldwork is the next step for me.''

"I don't know . . . the administration might consider itself responsible if anything were to happen to you in the course of work they had funded.''

"I have already prepared the necessary waivers. As far as the legalities are concerned I could as readily die here as on the battlefield.'' She used the approximate phonetic equivalent for the term, there being no word for "battlefield'' in any of the Wais dialects.

"Have you considered that in the course of this work you might at times be the only non-Human present?''

A slight involuntary shiver ran down her legs but not enough, she was certain, for the department head to notice. "I think I have thought of everything, though naturally there is no way to tell how one is going to react to an unprecedented situation without actually experiencing it. I would not propose the prospect if I felt I could not survive it.

"This is more than a matter of simple academic research," she added intently. "I have partially formulated certain hypotheses which trouble me deeply. I am convinced that this proposed fieldwork will eventually allow me to solidify or, preferably, discard them."

"If you are so troubled, you would be better off taking a pill for it," the department head murmured.

She halted on the trail and faced him demandingly. "Will you recommend that funding be appropriated?"

He hesitated, having trouble reconciling impartiality with personal concern. "You put a burden on me."

"If anything happens to me, it will be on myself and no one else. This is a simple matter of academic propriety. There is no guilt attached."

"If you should survive this and return with even a minimal amount of original material, it would be a triumph for the university. Personally I think your mental state is questionable. Professionally I can only proffer my abject admiration." Several minor crest feathers erected appropriately.

"I will put through your request and recommend that it be granted promptly. To what I hope is not my everlasting regret, I will not do so anonymously." He shifted smoothly to a much more personal dialect. "And I will certainly think of you fondly while you are engaged in this extraordinary enterprise."

"You will not be disappointed, nor will the university." His approval sent a little thrill of elation through her. "I will bring such credit to the university that—"

"Yes, yes," he said, interrupting her as the delicately curved and etched doorway parted to admit them to the temperature-controlled interior of the next building. "If you survive."

She'd never been off-world. There wasn't much reason for a Wais historian to leave his or her beads and scanners. Except for individuals who chose to serve in the diplomatic service, Wais tended to stay close to home, supporting the war effort in other ways. This was due as much to personal preference as to practicalities. They invariably found all other worlds, no matter how supposedly sophisticated and advanced, a comedown culturally and in most other ways from their own homes. Besides, there was no need for academics to travel between worlds when it was far easier, simpler, cheaper, and faster to shuttle requested information through Underspace.

As the shuttle lifted her orbitward to rendezvous with the Underspace transport, she had her first view of her home planet, and found it most exhilarating. Her personal as well as academic voyage of discovery had truly begun.

Other inhabitable worlds must be equally glorious sights, she thought. Great glowing spheres surrounded by lambent halos of cloud-painted atmosphere, their single landmasses adrift in all-encompassing oceans of burnished blue.

Except for Earth. Alone among the inhabited worlds, Earth was different. Home to Humankind and a perversely active geology. Font of weirdness and uniquely regressive but highly useful sapient behavior, not to mention her career.

What a wonderful and shocking place it must be, she mused. Perhaps someday she would get there as well.

She found herself starting to shake and immediately began

one of the numerous mental and breathing exercises she had developed. The shaking went away. To imagine actually being on Earth, a possibility traditionally employed to frighten unruly children, was something few other Wais would dare to voluntarily contemplate. To the best of her knowledge no Wais had ever visited that distant sphere of mystery and horror, or any other Human-settled world. Such contacts were better left to the more resilient Massood, or even the S'van.

At J'kooufa she had to transfer to a smaller vessel, far less luxurious and equipped with fewer amenities. There were only a handful of Wais aboard, and they clustered together for the duration of the voyage. Fearing misunderstanding if not outright isolation, she kept the purpose of her journey to herself as she socialized with them.

After stopping at two other worlds she had to transfer again at Woura IV, to a ship filled with S'van and Hivistahm. There was also a contingent of Massood soldiers aboard. She saw her first weapons—simple sidearms. But no Humans. Not until she found herself aboard the armed military shuttle dropping like a stone toward the contested surface of Tiofa.

Like many advance worlds of the Purpose, Tiofa had been erratically settled by farming T'returia protected, in this instance, mostly by fighting Mazvec. Traditionally, Weave forces would first establish a foothold and then push the defenders back toward their planetary strongholds, from whence they would eventually surrender.

But resistance on Tiofa had been unusually robust. Not only had the Weave assault been enjoined, but in places actually reversed by counterattack. Weave Command was in danger of having to seriously consider abandoning the entire effort and withdrawing all forces.

Prior to that it was decided to send a much larger than usual contingent of Human warriors into the fray. With the introduction of these reinforcements, the tide of battle began to turn, but the future of Tiofa was still very much in doubt. The fluidity of the situation appealed greatly to Lalelelang.

The shuttle was not attacked as it descended, the enemy instead concentrating its efforts on resupplying its own troops on the surface rather than wasting resources on the difficult and dangerous task of attempting to interdict Weave vessels as they emerged from Underspace. Weave forces mimicked this approach, for which Lalelelang was grateful. When antagonistic vessels actually managed to synchronize—usually accidentally—their emergence from Underspace, one or the other invariably vanished in a silent flash of debonding atoms as overwhelming weaponry controlled by electronics operating faster than thought was instantly brought to bear. Such rare, isolated encounters generally concluded before either side had a chance to reflect on whether it had won or lost.

Down on the surface, where the great majority of fighting took place, the opportunities for surviving a combat situation were considerably better, particularly for nonparticipants.

Military consultants unhappy about her journey had warned her about the facilities she was likely to have to deal with. She shrugged them off, believing she was prepared for anything. Besides which, a Wais having to live anywhere besides a Wais world was by definition roughing it. Nor had she traveled this far to sample civilized verities.

She was prepared not to see or encounter another Wais for the duration of her stay. The impending social isolation did not trouble her the way it would have an ordinary citizen. Serious researchers spend the majority of their time working in solitude anyway, while historians in particular tend to stumble awkwardly through reality, their minds constantly adrift in other times and places.

As soon as it set down, the shuttle was guided into a heavily shielded and camouflaged shelter set in a valley among modest, round-topped mountains. It docked alongside a number of other similar craft. Several were in the process of being serviced while large, malicious shapes were being carefully unloaded from the largest.

Only the setting was utterly unfamiliar. The rest she had noted and committed to the experience of memory from numerous studies. She felt disoriented but not alienated. Her research stood her in good stead.

Tall, angular, and lethally armed, a no-nonsense Massood

directed her and the few other nonmilitary passengers to a waiting lounge where crude but adequate multispecies facilities had been installed. She folded herself elegantly into an appropriate chair and prepared to wait. Medication as yet unsampled weighed heavily in her shoulder pouch.

It was an excellent vantage point from which to observe a fascinating and constantly changing consortium of visitors. Ferocious-looking Massood strode purposefully in and out of the lounge, towering over everyone else. Stocky, hirsute S'van bumped into one another, exchanging volatile fusillades of conversation and laughter before moving on. Reptilian Hivistahm in an infinite variety of electric green skin-tones rushed hurriedly to and fro, occasionally pausing to exchange greetings with their more high-strung but less loquacious distant relations, the O'o'yan. She even saw a bulky, massively built Chirinaldo looking unusually thoughtful behind the mask of its heliox helmet.

But no Wais. Nor Bir'rimor or Sspari or numerous other Weave allies. No doubt the mix would narrow radically the nearer she moved to the front lines.

It was then that she saw her first Humans.

After so many years of intimate study, their appearance, the way they moved their heads and eyes, their limbs and bodies, was as familiar to her as that of her own family. There were three of them, coming down the central concourse toward her. Two males and a female, the latter recognizable by the characteristic mammalian generalities. As was usual, the males were slightly taller and more muscular, though there was considerable variation among the sexes within the species.

They were talking animatedly, their conversation occasionally punctuated by loud bursts of raucous and utterly undisciplined Human laughter. This extraordinary noise, approximated within the Weave only by the S'van, caused heads to turn among the Hivistahm and other strollers, who gave the trio a wide berth.

Lalelelang's recorder seemed to have materialized magically in the grasp of one wingtip, and she was annotating her observations almost before she realized it. A thrill of excitement raced through her. Here were, after all, in the flesh, representatives of the species which formed the basis of her life's work. They appeared to be typical specimens, which . . .

No, she reminded herself. Uncivilized they might be, but it wouldn't do to think of them in that fashion, even if they were only associate members of the Weave itself. That was as much their choice as that of the other allied species. She would have to be careful to adjust her perspectives accordingly.

One of the males was comparatively tall, but none of the three was especially massive. All were larger than any Wais, or Hivistahm, or S'van, but the Massood were generally taller and the Chirinaldo bulkier. Their fluid lope was familiar to her from years of intimate study. Primitive muscular bulk made their uniforms bulge in numerous unexpected places, and she fancied she could hear the grinding of their heavy, dense skeletons. Hunter-killers with intelligence. She started to tremble ever so slightly and immediately steadied herself by reciting an appropriate mnemonic.

Nervousness gave way to expectation as she aimed her recorder. Her entire career had been spent in preparation for this moment. If her colleagues could see her now, they would be shuddering with fear.

One of the Humans noticed her, stopping to point. They conversed briefly among themselves. Then the two males departed down a side concourse. The sole female headed in her direction.

From an academic standpoint she would have preferred one of the males and so was slightly disappointed. Conversely, the female was little taller than herself and therefore far less physically intimidating. Coincidence, she wondered, or diplomatic foresight?

The female halted at a politic distance and spoke through her translator. "You're the historian Lalelelang. I'm to be your liaison while you're here on Tiofa. My name's Lieutenant Umeki."

A naked, smooth-skinned, five-digited hand was thrust toward Lalelelang. Aware that it could smash right through her rib cage, she flinched instinctively, her carefully prepared greeting completely forgotten. Immediately apologetic, the human retracted the gesture.

"Sorry! I forgot that you Wais are a little less . . . direct." She proceeded to bestow on her charge an excellent example of the wide, feral Human grin. No doubt it was intended to be reassuring.

Fighting to steady herself, Lalelelang ignored the unutterably uncultured, blatant display of cutting teeth and extended the flexible tips of her right wing. "It's all right," she said in perfectly inflected Huma. "My fault."

Fingers brushed against her gripping quills. The bare skin was warm and the flesh beneath deceptively flexible. This time a determined Lalelelang did not so much as twitch. Suddenly she was glad that neither of the males had been assigned to greet her.

She fluffed her feathers, those on her head and the back of her neck erecting to the proper height. It was a cultivated automatic response to the handshake, and completely lost on the Human.

"If you'll come with me?" The officer turned and started back down the concourse. As she complied, Lalelelang observed the easy, rolling gait, perfectly fluid despite the taut internal bracing of thick ligaments and heavy tendons. The shuttle hangar, her last tenuous link with real civilization, receded rapidly behind them.

"I've been looking forward to meeting you." The Human Umeki's speech was utterly devoid of the civilized overtones and inflections that so graced even the baser Wais dialects. "I've done a fair amount of liaison work, but it's always been with Hivistahm or S'van. Techs and logistics specialists. We've never had a Wais here before." She glanced in friendly, reassuring fashion at her guest, blissfully unaware that her eyes burned. Like any number of inherent disconcerting characteristics, it was something Humans couldn't help.

"I understand that you've been studying us?"

"For some time." Lalelelang explained carefully. "It is my field of specialization."

Umeki chuckled. "I know something about Wais society. Your friends must think you're slightly daft."

"More than slightly. Your unpopularity among us does not trouble you?"

"Nah. We're pretty much used to it. Most of the time it's just amusing."

"Knowing as much as I do about your kind," Lalelelang replied, "I expect to get along quite well." She'd already discarded the rituals of greeting she'd prepared and had slipped into the Human conversational mode, which favored directness and brutal familiarity above all else. There was precious little room in such uncouth interaction for even minimal interjections of appreciation and courtesy.

For all that, the Human seemed eager to relax and reassure her. Lalelelang listened politely, discarding the clumsy conversational chaff while retaining that information which might later prove useful.

"Your Huma's better than mine," Umeki said in a bumbling attempt at flattery, "but of course linguistics are your people's specialty. It's nice not to have to use the translator. Last Hivistahm I squired around needed two minutes to figure out anything and five to reply."

"I also dislike the distance mechanical devices interpose between individuals," the Wais replied politely. The Human was deliberately shortening her stride and slowing her pace to enable Lalelelang to keep up with her. But then, Lalelelang reminded herself, this individual was experienced at liaison work. The average Human would not have been so thoughtful.

She turned off her recorder. Umeki was not a useful subject for detailed study.

"I am also familiar with the majority of current Human colloquialisms."

"You don't say?" Umeki led the way around a corner. "Is that important in your work?"

"It can be. I am a social historian. I study not only how Humans interact with other species but with each other."

"Same thing our own sociologists do. Everybody wants to know something about everybody else, don't they?"

At ease now with the Human conversational mode, Lalelelang was able to overlook the casual, unthinking insult. "In the crudest sense, yes."

"We'll check on your luggage. I understand you Wais like to travel with a lot of luggage."

"You will find me difficult. I came prepared for my destination as well as my work."

"So much the better." She stared at Lalelelang appraisingly until she became aware that her guest was starting to fidget uneasily. "You know, you people are the most beautiful little things. Your personal decoration, your natural coloring . . . makes one want to take you out in the sunshine and just admire you."

Realizing that the comment was intended as a compliment and not an unforgivable breach of behavior, Lalelelang was able to accept it as such. The more time she spent in this Human's company, the more at ease she felt. Years of intense study were paying off. The combination of offhand affronts, verbal and physical directness, threatening gestures, and unsympathetic posture—not to mention body odor—would have by now reduced any unprepared Wais to a quivering wreck.

Perhaps her visit wasn't going to be such a debilitating proposition after all. She felt a socially acceptable quotient of pride.

They drew plenty of stares as they penetrated farther into the complex. She saw no other Wais, nor did she expect to. The attention she was receiving came not only from the increasing number of Humans, but from Massood, Hivistahm, and even dull-visaged Lepar, who wondered at the presence of a fragile Wais in such company.

They must be speculating furiously on my intentions, she mused. In that respect their reactions were no different from those of her friends back home.

"I'll show you around the complex once we get you settled," Umeki was saying. "Won't take long. It's pretty compact. After that and at your leisure, I'm directed to take you any place you want to go. The storage facilities here are extensive, and weapons upgrading and repair is interesting. Lot of O'o'yan and Hivistahm at work there. There are also the R-and-R facilities."

"I want to visit the front lines."

The Human halted with an abruptness that nearly caused Lalelelang to trip over her own feet. Though she was intimately familiar with such acute gestures from her studies, it was still something to experience it in person.

"You want to do *what*?" Umeki gawked at her.

The sudden shift in tone, the overwhelming aura of accusation, the implication of possible attack inherent in both timbre and movement finally set Lalelelang to shaking violently. To her credit Umeki recognized what she'd done and hastened to rectify the mistake.

"Sorry, take it easy. I didn't mean to spook you. I know you're easily startled."

The exercises began to work their magic. "Yes. We certainly . . . are," Lalelelang replied.

"It's just that your request startled *me*. I can't take you to the front."

Lalelelang mustered her reserves. "You just stated that you have been ordered to escort me anywhere I wish."

"That's true, sure. But a Wais in a combat situation . . . you're serious, aren't you?"

"Entirely. It goes to the heart of my research." She was astonished to find herself speaking forcefully to a Human. An untrained Wais would not even have been able to respond. "It is what I came here for and it is what I want to do."

Accusation crept back into the Human's tone. "I don't like this. I'm personally responsible for you while you're here. If anything should happen to you . . ."

"I do not intend that it should. I am only here to observe and record. You do not need to worry about me picking up a weapon and charging off to rage among the enemy." The comment, much less the attendant dark humor, would have been impossible to execute in any of the genteel Wais dialects.

Umeki considered the unexpectedly obstinate ornithorp. "You sure as hell have prepared yourself. No wonder your request to come here was approved. I'll have to double-clear this with my superiors, but if it's what you want, and you'll sign the appropriate waivers, I guess I'll have to take you."

"I think you will find that all the necessary forms are already on file. I do not want to waste time dealing with the bureaucracy."

"Oh, I think you'll have enough time." The lieutenant looked thoughtful. "There's constant skirmishing on the Kii Plateau. Secondary theater of operation. We're pushing them back there, but it's slow going. That should do for you." She paused as if waiting for an objection. When none was forthcoming, she added, "If you're sure this is what you want?"

"Quite sure."

Umeki looked her up and down, merely another breach of courtesy in a list grown long. By now the historian had become adept at ignoring them.

"We're going to have a helluva time finding proper field dress for you."

"Do not trouble yourself. There is no military gear for Wais. Even if we could improvise functioning equipment I would not be able to make use of it. It would be wasted on me."

"That's true." This observation, at least, was a statement of fact and therefore not insulting. "We'll have to devise something in the way of attire, though. Nothing confining. You've got feathers, you don't need much in the way of insulation. Get rid of your jewelry, for a start." She waved into the distance. "You're not gonna be very comfortable out there."

"I do not expect to be. If I wished to be 'comfortable,' I would not have come to this world. If I wished to be comfortable, I would not be talking to you now."

Umeki was nodding slightly to herself. "Yeah, you know

the language, all right. Everything you say sounds like it's coming out of a musical instrument.''

Lalelelang accepted the crude compliment, knowing that there were less than a dozen individuals on all the Wais worlds who would even have considered trading places with her.

''You also seem to know what you want.'' The lieutenant started to put a guiding arm around the historian's thin shoulders but thought better of it, and rightly so. ''I promise you you're going to find it.''

They draped her with some cursory, loosely secured folds of the most flexible protective weave they could find and put her in a heavily armored air-suspension vehicle heading north. She had an ill-fitting seat forward, right next to the pilot and away from the Human soldiers clustered in back.

To see them in full battle armor, dripping weaponry and related means of destruction, would have been for an ordinary Wais something out of a particularly bad nightmare. Lalelelang was not only familiar with their appearance; her studies enabled her to identify by name and function many of the destructive devices they carried. Even so, she found proximity to so many of them more than daunting. As usual, the exercises helped.

Every soldier in the transport was larger than Lieutenant Umeki, and some were truly massive. She kept her distance from them while they ignored the fluttery alien dropped in their midst.

Strange to see the comparatively diminutive female Umeki decked out in similar gear, with less armor to allow for more freedom of movement but wearing fully functional double sidearms and a brace of concussion darts. Lalelelang recorded it all for posterity and future study.

Before leaving the base she'd dosed herself with a duet of stabilizing drugs, knowing that exercises alone would be insufficient to protect her stability should she find herself in an actual combat situation. It was entirely possible she was the first of her kind to *intentionally* place herself in such inimical surroundings.

From a social standpoint the information she expected to gain by being a part of the experiment instead of merely an observer ought to prove invaluable. Already she had secured enough data to have made the long, difficult journey from Mahmahar worthwhile. In her mind's eye she could envision the reaction of her professional colleagues.

Hopefully she might even see enough to allow her to retire the unpleasant theories that had from the very beginning served as the main impetus behind the expedition and indeed, behind her choice of career.

The terrain visible through the armored transparency that fronted the troop carrier changed from grassland to scrub-covered hill country as they advanced. Occasionally she saw other vehicles accelerating past them or whizzing by in the opposite direction. Some were considerably larger than the transport in which she rode, and boasted frightful arrays of destructive technology. Once, one of them fired repeatedly at a target out of her range of vision, and later something deadly and unseen sent a fountain of soil and gravel blossoming skyward not far to port.

A terse shiver ruffled her feathers. So this was combat, she thought. This was the tactile actualization of one intelligent species attempting to destroy another: what the Amplitur had finally resorted to in their attempt to bring the members of the Weave into their all-encompassing Purpose. The unnatural act the representative species of the Weave had been compelled to embrace in order to preserve their independence.

Praise to all Elevated Spirits for the existence of the prolific Massood, who had been one of the founding members of the Weave and who had carried the burden of actual fighting for so long. Praise also to the legendary Massood explorer Caldaq, whose team had first made contact with the disagreeable but invaluable Humans, who were at long last turning the tide of battle against the enemy.

The single enemy miss did not upset her as much as she

thought that kind of encounter might. Easy enough to mentally classify it as kin to a natural calamity, like a bolt of lightning or a meteor falling from the sky. Terrible to contemplate but relatively simple to abstract.

The transport slowed as it entered a forest of taller trees, flora different from that of home. Tall and straight-boled, their branches were dense with long, pointed shapes instead of leaves. Surprisingly few bushes sought the shelter of large, glacially polished boulders.

Umeki materialized next to her, flipping a coppery colored visor down over her face. "Get ready."

Anxious but excited, Lalelelang rose from her seat, awkwardly adjusting her own modified visor. Umeki helped her with the improvised face shield, grumbling as she did so.

"You're not fully protected, but this is better than nothing. Try to keep your head down."

"I am somewhat familiar with the conventions from my studies. I will be careful." Lalelelang checked her recorder and its backup, far more concerned with their condition than with something as peripheral to her desires as body armor.

Umeki took a step back. "You don't look like you're very comfortable in that getup."

"I am not, but I will manage." She considered upping the level of medication in her bloodstream but decided against it. Higher concentrations posed the possibility of debilitating side effects, which could affect her work. Besides, she felt as much exhilaration as fear.

"You really are remarkable, for a Wais." In full light field armor the Human female looked quite intimidating. "Not that I've dealt with that many."

"I am only doing what is necessary to fulfill my work."

Umeki nodded, a typically brusque and unsophisticated Human gesture. "You ought to get plenty of that out here." She drew a sidearm, a compact and thoroughly wicked-looking contrivance of plastic and metallic glass.

"As soon as the squad has taken up its assigned position we'll follow. This is a standard reconnaissance-and-destroy sortie in an area that's already been partly secured. Shouldn't be any serious trouble.''

She nodded in the direction of the Massood pilot, who was folded intently over his instrumentation. ''He can't hang around too long. The transport's too big a target. This plateau's full of patrolling shapeseeker drones.''

''I understand.'' It meant that she would be stuck in this place for the duration of the sortie with nothing but Massood and Humans for company, until such time as it was deemed strategically viable for the group to be withdrawn.

She checked to make sure her equipment was running as she recorded the squad's efficient and rapid deployment, looked on admiringly as they took up positions between trees and rocks. Her aural resonator was full of closed-channel communications. The soldiers were conversing in clipped, professional tones, and she had no trouble deciphering their sometimes slang-filled exchanges, whether they took place in guttural Huma or the more sophisticated high and low Massood.

Language was a matter of sorted sounds, of which there were always a finite number. Translating was simply a cataloging problem. For reasons the Wais had never been able to quite comprehend, all other species seemed to find this difficult. Like the rest of her kind she felt sorry for those who were forced to rely for communication on simple, primitive systems—which meant every species that was not Wais.

''It's time.''

Umeki led her outside and down the shielded disembarking ramp, lightly resting one gloved hand protectively on the base of Lalelelang's long neck as they ran from the transport. Breathless, recorder running, she hunkered down next to the Human's reassuring bulk as they entered the woods and took up a position behind a massive chunk of oblate granite.

There were two other Humans there. One spoke into his suit communicator while the other gave orders. Save for a quick glance they ignored the presence of the two female observers, enabling Lalelelang to study them at her leisure.

Their activity level, both verbal and physical, was daunting. She'd anticipated as much, but it was still impressive to observe it in person as opposed to via a holo reproduction, no matter how accurate the latter. The speed and suppleness of their movements, their coordination though burdened with armor and weapons, was as stylish as that of the finest Wais dancers, possessed though it was of a terrible alien beauty.

She made notes in a steady stream, pausing only to take throat-soothing sips from the service tube built into her makeshift suit. Every minute, every second was fraught with new and invaluable insights. Information garnered on this single excursion would provide material for a year's study. She was immensely grateful for the unique opportunity, and proud of the intestinal fortitude which enabled her to take advantage of it.

So intent was she on her observations that she hardly noticed the heavy hum of the troop transport as it rose from the forest floor and pivoted in midair before retracing its path back through the trees.

"I have seen enough here." She addressed her guide through the visor's voice membrane. "Can we move on?"

Umeki's face was hidden by her own visor, but there was no mistaking the amazement in her voice. "You really are something, you know?" She pointed. "Let's try that hollow over there."

Lalelelang followed the crouching Human as they entered a dip in a dry ravine dominated by a particularly impressive specimen of the local growth. She played her recorder up and down the burly, rough-skinned trunk, marveling at its stature. What a centerpiece this would make for a formal Wais garden, she thought! Great gnarled roots snaked into and out of the surrounding rock, supporting and nourishing the venerable forest giant.

Such fantasizing helped to calm her. She wasn't trembling at all when she turned to see that Umeki was peering cautiously over the rim of the ravine. Lalelelang adjusted the recorder, taking close-ups of each of the Human's limbs.

"What happens next?"

"We wait. The squad's moved forward, toward a rumored

Mazvec bunker. If they find one, they'll try to clean it out. Either way, we stay here until we're told it's safe to advance."

"But I came to witness combat, to see Humans fighting."

Umeki looked down at her. "One step at a time. Don't overreach yourself."

Beneath the composite armor Lalelelang's feathers fluffed. "I have made the study of such matters my life's work. I assure you there is little to be encountered here that would surprise me."

"You think so? I've seen others who thought they could handle it. Hivistahm and one time a S'van. They couldn't. Some things you can't quantify."

As if to reinforce her warning something whispered over their heads, silent as a gliding seabird. An instant later Lalelelang felt herself crushed to the ground as Umeki flung herself atop the startled Wais. The incredible density of the Human skeletal and muscular system impressed itself on the historian in a way no amount of study could have done. She felt like a leaf stomped by a falling stone.

Even so, Umeki took most of the shock on her hands. A second later the ground heaved as the deceptively sedate humming gave way to an explosion of deafening proportions. Gobs of seared soil and carbonized plant life vomited skyward before raining down on them.

Sidearm in hand, the Human rolled off her. A dazed Lalelelang fumbled with her recorder. Secondary explosions reverberated around inside her shocked skull. Thankfully they were farther off.

" 'u∧li∧i∗' . . . what . . . ?" she mumbled, hurriedly translating.

"A cute little new toy the Mazvec have deployed. Sounds like a big bug, doesn't it?"

Lalelelang nodded, utilizing the simplified Human gesture instead of the far more elaborate Wais response the query called for. It could not have been adequately executed in the suit and would have meant nothing to her guide anyway.

"It just comes floating in, unobtrusive as you please, and

you're tempted to ignore it." Umeki's eyes were as active as her lips. "As soon as it senses any number of preprogrammed target shapes—like us—it swerves and tries to land on your head."

"But . . . we are all right." Lalelelang kept her stunned legs tucked tightly beneath her.

"The squad has decoy shapes out. It went for one of those. Too close by half, though." A voice hailed Umeki and she responded to her helmet pickup. "Here, dammit!"

For the third time Lalelelang lowered the volume in her earset as she listened absently to the conversation. It was thick with military jargon she couldn't quite translate.

"Shit." Umeki broke off and skidded back down to the bottom of the ravine. Slipping an arm beneath Lalelelang's left wing, she raised her bodily to a standing position, fairly flinging the ornithorp to her feet.

"What is it, what is wrong?" Lalelelang looked around uncertainly. Explosions continued to echo nearby.

"The Mazvec are coming out. Either they were waiting for the transport to unload or else they're less surprised than we hoped they would be. They're coming this way, and in greater numbers than we anticipated. Bunker must have shielded sections our detectors didn't pick up." She started up the ravine, back the way they'd originally come.

"Let's go. We've got to get out of here and join up with the others." A hand reached back and locked around a wing, yanking Lalelelang forward.

"I do not understand." Once clear of the ravine she saw other armored figures, Human and Massood, backpedaling through the woods. Those farthest away would occasionally stop to aim and fire before resuming their retreat. Smaller explosions ripped the ground not far from where they were standing. Something unseen snapped a tree in half a body length above the ground. It toppled majestically, splintering half a dozen lesser versions of itself. Colorful energy beams, bright lances of destruction, severed branches and split smaller boulders. The smells of scorched vegetation reached her nostrils through the selective visor membrane.

"You wanted to see combat!" Umeki shouted, pulling her along so that her feet barely skimmed the ground.

"This was not how I . . . envisioned things," Lalelelang gasped breathlessly.

"You ain't alone."

They scrambled over small ravines and protruding roots, dodging trees and rocks determined to intercept them. Once they splashed violently through a wide, shallow stream running dark with tannin. Except for the inexorable grip Umeki maintained on her wing, Lalelelang knew that the Human could outdistance her in seconds. But her guide would not abandon her to the mercy of the battlefield and the oncoming Mazvec.

Trying to keep up as best she could, Lalelelang felt a fiery pain lance through her lower right leg as her broad but fragile foot struck a rock. The delicate ankle twisted and she went down in a heap.

"Hell!" Umeki slid behind a huge fallen log carpeted with some dense blue-green mosslike growth, dragging Lalelelang down with her. The upturned confusion of exposed roots at the dead tree's base provided some protection from above.

A visored face thrust into her own. "You stay here," the Human hissed.

"Stay here?" Lalelelang lay uncomfortably on her belly, her right ankle throbbing. Her flexible neck enabled her to raise her head and gain some idea of their immediate surroundings, but smoke from burning foliage and continuing explosions reduced visibility in all directions. "But where are you going?"

Umeki was already on her feet and moving around the base of the fallen forest giant, a weapon gripped tightly in each hand. "Orders. Forming counterattack. That includes me. You should be okay here."

Painfully Lalelelang sat up. She was shaking so badly it took several moments before she could focus on the readouts on her recorder. It was still running. Umeki's voice echoed in her ear.

"Sector control knows what's going on. They're sending

out some heavy weapons, but they won't get here for a while."

"I am coming with you." Bracing herself on her wingtips, she fought to rise.

Umeki turned back toward her. Her posture, her whole attitude indicated that the Human battle drive had taken over her system completely.

"You . . . stay . . . here."

Lalelelang froze. It was the peculiar, distinctive inflection Humans utilized only in combat: edgy and confrontational, charged with all manner of primeval hormones. She knew it intimately from her studies.

But none of the recordings she had analyzed so dispassionately had ever been directed at *her*.

She found herself paralyzed by the combination of tone and attitude, rooted to the spot. If Umeki had ordered her to bury her head in the dirt and cover it up, she was convinced she would have complied. Her trembling redoubled.

A wingtip fluttered over a control on her belt, missing several times before striking home. The injector it activated hissed imperceptibly, and a piercing but not painful heat spread through her left side. As the medication took hold she relaxed. The uncontrollable trembling gave way to a less debilitating quiver. She sat back down as her guide vanished around the upturned base of the tree.

Time passed inconclusively. When the last of the disconcerting palpitating had ceased, she rose and walked over to the massive log. Beyond she could see Humans and Massood moving slowly away from her.

Holding the recorder in her beak, which could reach higher than her prehensile wingtips, she extended her neck to the limit and peered over the mossy barrier, panning slowly from left to right. Sheer excitement kept her going. This was what she had come for, this was what she had come to see.

Any other Wais would have long since fainted dead away. Better prepared for the situation than any member of her species before or since, she was determined not to waste a single moment. Any psychological damage could be dealt with later. Right now she was coping, thanks to her extensive preparations and studies.

This isn't so bad, she thought. *With proper training others of my kind could do this.*

She sensed movement near the dead log's exposed roots and retracted her neck. The Human Umeki would be relieved and perhaps a little surprised to see how well her charge had done in her absence.

It was not Umeki who stumbled around the base of the tree.

The ruff of bright orange fur that framed the short neck had been dyed a dull camouflage green. The neck emerged from a tubular, tanklike torso—squat, unlovely, and not much bigger than her own—which was clad in flexible forest-brown armor. Two double-jointed arms emerged from the upper body. They were tipped with four fingers apiece, all of which currently occupied themselves with the manipulation of a long, narrow-barreled weapon of alien origin and unknown potentiality.

The Mazvec advanced on broad, splayed feet, each toe individually padded and protected. The exposed skull was small and rounded. Tufts of dyed fur ran in lines down from the top of the head to lose themselves among the denser drifts of the neck ruff. Behind the narrow snout filled with flat crushing teeth, bright green eyes turned to focus on her.

The mouth beneath the snout parted and a rasping squeak emerged as the alien aimed its weapon. It didn't look like much: a cluster of thin metal tubes atop a small plastic sphere. One of the alien's long fingers began to contract on what was obviously some sort of trigger mechanism.

Without her ever becoming aware of the actual moment, she realized numbly, events had passed beyond the stage of philosophical speculation.

She thought of all the reports she wasn't going to get to write, all the marvelous lectures it would never be her privilege to deliver. Hopefully her recordings would survive to be an inspiration to other, less reckless scholars who would acquire much credit for dissertations based on her notes.

Here I am about to die a brutal and unnatural death at the hands of another intelligent being and all I can think of is my work, she found herself musing. *Scholar is as scholar was to the end.* She began to shake violently.

A mountain fell on the Mazvec from behind as her assailant's weapon emitted an incongruously soft *bang.* Something supersonic whizzed past her to strike the edge of the boulder against which she'd been leaning. There was a pause following which half a dozen tiny explosions shattered the solid granite as the shell's independent burrowing fragments dispersed prior to detonation. The concussion knocked her to her knees.

She looked up, fearful of what she might see but unable to keep herself from doing so. Still locked convulsively in her clenched beak, her recorder continued to hum softly.

A Human had fallen on her attacker from behind, just as it had been about to terminate her unfulfilled life. It was much, much bigger than Umcki, the massively muscular Human male build clearly apparent beneath the flexible armor. She was glad she couldn't see its face because she knew from extensive study the kind of contortions it must be undergoing.

The Mazvec let out a despairing screech as it tried to swing its weapon to bear. Before the muzzle of the long gun could be brought halfway around there was a sharp, distinctive snap. The Human unlocked its thick fingers and the enemy alien crumpled to the ground, no longer a thinking, breathing creature. A single quick, unimaginably savage gesture had reduced it to dead meat, its neck broken.

To make certain, the Human lifted the Mazvec by its limp splayed feet and dashed the rounded skull against the unyielding log. Lalelelang blinked. Then she spat out the recorder and added the contents of her crop to the mess.

Breathing hard but evenly, the oversized, highly efficient lungs sucking air, the massive Human stood over the body of her would-be assassin. It straightened, towering above her. It was at least four times her mass, completely encased in light, color-adaptive chameleon armor, its head concealed by a helmet and visor more elaborate than the one Umeki wore. A rifle the size of a small field-artillery piece was slung across its back, while the broad chest was draped with a variety of unidentifiable equipment. Holstered sidearms protruded from either hip.

A gloved hand rose to push back the protective visor, and for the first time she had a glimpse of the naked face. It was streaked with sweat and one thin line of blood. No fur or feathers disguised the naked skin, no brightly hued scales threw back the diffuse forest light. Still gasping sickly, she fumbled for her recorder.

It growled at her in friendly fashion.

"I'll be damned . . . a canary!"

★ IV ★

Obviously unversed in appropriate diplomatic procedure, it took a giant step toward her. "What the hell are you doing out here?"

Trembling violently, she tried to scrabble away. Her legs gave out and she collapsed in a quivering heap, staring at nothing, both feet kicking convulsively at the moist ground.

The Human halted. "Hey, take it easy! I didn't mean—" In one smooth movement he dropped to a crouch and whipped the huge rifle off his back, aiming it to his left as another figure hove into view. A second of observation and then he straightened again, relaxing.

Umeki noted the condition of her charge, flipped up her visor to glare at the much bigger male. "Ah, hell. What happened here? What did you do?"

"Saved its life, Lieutenant." The soldier grunted and stepped aside, allowing Umeki a view of the dead Mazvec.

"Hopefully there isn't any serious emotional damage." She bent worriedly over the prone form of the ornithorp, folding back the makeshift visor. "You know how sensitive Wais are."

"Who me?" The soldier craned his neck for a better look at the recumbent alien form. "I'm just a grunt, Lieutenant. First canary I've ever seen . . . in person. Not much to them, is there? 'Feathers and frivolity' it says in the handbook. Still, an ally's an ally."

"Your uniform was probably made on one of their

43

worlds.'' Umeki's voice fell. ''Lousy luck. I was hoping for a commendation out of this. Didn't want the job. Taking a Wais out to the front lines. Knew something like this might happen.'' Gently she cradled the limp, blank-eyed avian head. ''She said she was prepared, that she could handle it.''

A distant explosion brought the soldier's eyes up and around. He fingered the trigger of the rifle nervously. ''Yeah, well, at least she ain't dead. Woulda been if I hadn't come along.''

''I know.'' Umeki fumbled with her service pack. ''If anyone gets a commendation out of this it'll be you, soldier.'' She adjusted a knurled knob on a short, thick wand-like instrument and applied it to Lalelelang's shoulder. The twitching moderated. ''Your appearance may have stunned her more than the Mazvec.''

''She's better off stunned than shot. I'd better get back to my unit.''

''Yes, go ahead.'' Umeki spoke absently, without looking up from her patient. There was no need to exchange details. Their respective suit recorders had already taken care of that.

She slipped the wand smoothly into her pack and rocked back on her heels. While the trembling had slowed, the wide-eyed Wais was still unresponsive.

''I'm going to catch hell for this, you know,'' she muttered at the prone form. ''Knew you were going to be trouble. Of course, it isn't your fault. You can't help what you are.'' She glanced up, toward the woods from which the sounds of ongoing battle were beginning to fade. ''Not your fault that the Mazvec chose the occasion of your visit to launch a counterattack, either.''

She sat back against the base of the fallen log and put in a call for evacuation. Unless the enemy had brought in heavy weapons they ought to be able to get a medevac in and out immediately, provided one was in the area and available. Not that those on board would know anything about Wais physiology, but their resident medical computer would.

Once she'd made contact and given their position, she verbally disengaged the communicator built into her helmet and returned her attention to her catatonic charge.

"You wanted to see combat. Why didn't you stay home? Patrol your gardens and listen to your cantatas? But no. You had to stick your beak where it didn't belong, where it's not historically or culturally designed to go. Next time listen to Nature. You're not made for this." A long-range enemy shot snapped a nearby tree in half ten meters above the ground. Umeki eyed the smoking bole casually.

"I'm wasting my time here with you, you know that? Baby-sitting an alien academic when I should be doing something useful and constructive . . . like killing Mazvec."

She awoke to a pale green sky and walls dense with holoed flowers. Someone had improvised a traditional heavily padded nest in the midst of a large bed designed to comfort a different kind of body. Sheets were piled around her, supporting her weakened form in a correct upright position, legs carefully folded underneath her abdomen. She straightened her neck, bringing her head off her back where it had been resting in the feathers between her folded wings, and surveyed her surroundings. Trouble had been taken to insure her comfort.

"Good to see you awake." Umeki stood near a chair. "I was told you've been showing signs of coming around."

Memories came flooding back to Lalelelang, and with them the trembling. But the room was quiet, the sight of the lightly ruffled flowers soothing. She recalled her training and steadied herself. Her eyebrows flexed decorously.

"I remember now. Everything. I fear I have become the vessel for more apologies than I can adequately convey." She concluded with an elaborate trill, a kind of running whistle with three distinct glottal stops. Tradition demanded it even though Lalelelang knew it would mean little to the Human female who stood before her.

"There's nothing to be sorry for," Umeki replied with straightforward superficiality. "It wasn't like you asked to be attacked."

Lalelelang studied the guide. The transformation was remarkable, as if when putting off her armor Umeki had simultaneously doffed an attitude. She no longer looked threatening and deadly, as she had out in the field. Now she was no more than a flat-faced, clumsy primate waiting dumbly for conversation to resume.

What a species, Lalelelang thought.

"You're lucky to be alive," the guide ventured unnecessarily.

"I know." There was a great tiredness in her. "How long?"

"Couple of days. You scared the hell out of me out there. My career could've died with you."

What a primitive, adamantly impolitic thing to say, Lalelelang mused. No doubt another Human would have thought it reasonable, perhaps even amusing. Naturally she did not comment.

"But you're okay, so no harm done." Umeki smiled, displaying sharp incisors and canines. It did not last long, for which Lalelelang was grateful. "You're not, uh, thinking of going back out again, are you?"

"I think I've gained enough firsthand information for a while."

The human relaxed visibly, laughing softly. "You Wais. Always understanding."

"What about my recorder?" she asked suddenly.

"In better shape than you." Umeki gestured toward a cabinet. "It's in there, with the rest of your gear. You'll have some interesting images to relive. You'll be going home now, I presume?" Her tone was ripe with expectation.

"I imagine so. I hope my leaving early will not displease you?"

"Do you expect me to lie? You'd see through it anyway. You people master languages too well." She turned to the door. "There's someone who wants to say good-bye. He doesn't have much time . . . not that I think the two of you would miss the opportunity for lengthy conversation."

She opened the door and spoke to someone out of Lalelelang's range of vision. A moment later the portal opened wider to admit the soldier who'd saved her. He looked just as massive in his duty uniform as he had in armor.

Reciting silently and rapidly kept her from shaking.

Now that circumstances were different she was able to view him in light of numerous studies and saw that he was no more than slightly above average in height and mass for a Human male. He towered over her as he approached the bed. This time she did not flinch.

There was contrition in his voice. ''They tell me my appearance upset you pretty bad. I didn't mean for it to.''

''You saved my life.'' Lalelelang spoke rapidly, trying to forestall any additional embarrassment on the soldier's part. Most Humans had only their inadequate words with which to try and elucidate interpersonal relationships. Under such primitive conditions it was a wonder any matings at all survived long enough to produce offspring.

She forced herself to extend the tips of her right wing. Surprised, the Human reached out to grip them in his powerful fingers. She tensed, but he was careful and did not bruise her.

The hand withdrew.

''I just wanted to say that I'm glad you're feeling better.'' The soldier held his duty cap in his other fingers. As she watched, he latched onto it with his second hand and began kneading it absently, as if he didn't know what to do with his limbs. This kind of undirected motor activity was quite common among Humans. ''The lieutenant told me that you're some kind of professor and that you're studying us.'' He smiled almost shyly. ''I wouldn't want to think that you'd got some kind of wrong impression from me.''

''Actually I am a historian and no, the impression you gave me was . . . no more than what I expected.''

He seemed relieved. ''Glad to hear it. Hey, I guess this means I'm gonna be in a history book or something, right?''

''Or something,'' she murmured noncommittally.

''My name's Kuzca.'' He whispered the name, as if delivering himself of some confidential information of consequence. "K-u . . . I guess you being a Wais, you won't have any trouble with the spelling."

"I do not think so."

"Michael Kuzca. Homeworld's Tokugawa Four."

"I will remember. I have a good memory for names."

"Better than me, I'm sure. I'm just a grunt." Lalelelang recognized the application of an ancient term Human soldiers liked to apply to themselves. Its true meaning was difficult to divine, overlain as it was with the conflagrative psychosocial detritus of thousands of years of unrelenting warfare.

"You take it easy now. You canar . . . you Wais don't heal so fast."

"No," she murmured. "We do not have your recuperative powers. But then, neither does any other intelligent species."

He left with a parting wave of one huge hand, an ineloquent but nonetheless affecting gesture . . . in its crude, primitive fashion.

"He didn't want you to leave with the wrong impression." Umeki approached the bed-nest. "Because of the special circumstances he was able to get leave long enough to look in on you."

"I am touched. Where he is going now?"

"To rejoin his unit. Back to the fighting."

"Of course," Lalelelang murmured. "Where he will be happy."

Umeki studied with interest the makeshift nest in the center of the bed. "You're pretty exceptional, to have survived what you went through. Any other Wais would still be catatonic. Maybe never come out of it."

Lalelelang shifted her body into a more comfortable position. "I have made this my area of expertise for many years. And I have developed my own training exercises, both physical and mental, to enable me to cope with extremes."

"Still." Umeki was silent for a moment. "I may or may not have the chance to talk to you again before you're taken to your shuttle. I just want to say that I hope you got what you came for.''

''More than I hoped for in my dreams.''

''I'll bet.'' Umeki chuckled softly to herself as she moved away from the bed. Halfway to the door she turned to bow slightly in its direction.

''I am not familiar with your gesture in the context of our present situation.''

''It's tribal instead of species-specific,'' Umeki explained. ''A gesture of respect among my familial ancestors. A lot of them were fighters and would have understood.''

''All of your ancestors were fighters,'' Lalelelang responded. ''That *is* something that is species specific.''

''Well, I guess what I meant to say was that a lot of them were professional soldiers.''

Lalelelang acknowledged the correction with a gesture. There was much more she could have said, could have discussed with this useful Human, but she was too tired, exhausted in both mind and body.

She was ready to leave, yes. Ready to return to the peace and sophistication and familiar surroundings of Mahmahar. For all that, a perverse, irrational part of her was ready to do it all over again.

The difference between dedication and fanaticism, she reminded herself, *is measurable as the diameter of one's pupils.* She did not ask for a mirror.

She feigned sleep but kept one eye half-open until the Human officer had departed. Guide and savior Umeki might be, but she was still Human, and Lalelelang could not relax until she was once again alone in the room. Her caution caused her no guilt. You couldn't trust a Human, not even those who seemed completely reliable.

How could you, when for the entire stretch of their recorded history they'd been unable to trust themselves?

No fanfares, no celebrations stood poised to acknowledge her return home. Nor would she have responded favorably to any such overtly tasteless display. Not that she was ostracized. As a representative of her species to have actually experienced combat her status was unique. This meant that a special social subniche had to be created for her, with the result that she was simultaneously sought out and ignored.

This did not trouble her. She'd always been something of a loner, even within the requisite sisters triad to which she belonged. Her triad siblings were at once regretful that she participated in so few social gatherings and proud of her accomplishments. Lalelelang hoped they balanced out.

One immediate result of her expedition was that attendance at her presentations tripled in numbers if not enthusiasm. As the novelty of her journey faded, so did attendance. She thought this as inevitable as she did amusing, realizing that many of the newcomers were driven by perverse curiosity rather than serious scholarship. Yet not even the dilettantes could help but depart enriched.

It did not trouble her, since research and publication rather than education had become her primary focus. Fortuitously, this coincided with the administration's goals. Anyone could teach, but the experiences on which she alone could expatiate were singular and deserving of a wider audience.

By virtue of a single journey she had become the leading expert in her field.

There existed a small coterie of specialists with whom she regularly exchanged information: Hivistahm and O'o'yan and one Yula, as well as fellow Wais. Many shared her concerns, though none were as yet sufficiently bold or committed to subscribe to her most radical hypotheses. Lalelelang knew she at times entered dangerous theoretical ground: places where even brilliant fellow academics feared to tread. Her report on ''Irreversible Bloodlust in Traditional Entertainment,'' for example, was not merely controversial but simply beyond the realm of comprehensibility for many scholars. They tended to try and deal with such propositions in the abstract, which correspondingly reduced the effectiveness of her formulations.

Lalelelang was working from a historian's viewpoint toward a comprehensive theory of Human behavior, and many of her colleagues and contacts did not much care for the direction she was taking. This she could not help. As a dedicated empiricist she had no choice but to plunge helplessly on down the path she had chosen.

The deeper she delved and the harder she studied the more she was convinced she was on to something of critical importance not only to her own people but to the entire Weave. Something so obvious and yet so elusive that the rest of the Weave had elected to overlook it rather than probe too deeply.

Another combat experience might have crystallized everything, but she wasn't ready for that. The memories of her previous encounter with the battlefield were still too fresh, too readily brought to mind. She briefly considered actually applying to visit the speciocentrically named Earth, but decided there were limits to what even she, with her specialized training and experience, could stand. The thought of being isolated on an entire world full of Humans, all of whom were potentially unstable, and where she would invariably become an object of curiosity and attention, was sufficiently daunting even in the abstract to kill the notion aborning. She felt herself beginning to tremble whenever she considered it and hastened to recite a calming mnemonic.

She was convinced she needed to further observe Human soldiers, preferably in more intimate circumstances, but was not prepared again to go through the suffering she'd experienced on Tiofa. By now her academic reputation was such that she could make use of proportionate funds without having to go through administration.

What were her alternatives?

Ideally she should attach herself to one of the primates as closely as possible in order to make the exhaustive observations she felt her ongoing work required. Much of the difficulty would lie in finding a Human soldier willing to put up with a Wais underfoot while it went about its waking activities. Her brief interaction with the Human Umeki had hinted at the difficulty of establishing such a relationship.

She felt it was something she had to do, that she could not fully know or understand the species until she had lived with one of them, shared its daily experiences, observed how it interacted not only with representatives of other species but with its own kind. It meant not only putting her proposal before administration but personally applying to Human authority. Her experiences on Tiofa should count for something with the latter.

They would be concerned that she not inhibit the combat readiness of whomever she was attached to. She doubted that was anything to worry about. Among all the intelligent species only a Human could peacefully discuss dance, or cooking, or luminescence sculpture, and at an instant's notice be ready to fight and kill. The presence of a single Wais in such company was unlikely to cause much in the way of interference.

If she was fortunate, she might make contact with a soldier conversant with Wais as well as Weave culture. It would make her work much easier, not to mention more comfortable, if all the requisite cultural condescension did not devolve upon her. Yet, if necessary, she was prepared to deal even with that.

She framed her proposal carefully. There was a good chance the preparation would be wasted and all would come to nothing. After all, what Human soldier would want to have a Wais, traditionally ready to go unpredictably comatose or spasmodic at the first difficult moment, for company while it was trying to carry out its assigned duties?

Excitement and apprehension followed the dissemination of her application. In many ways this was more extreme than her request to visit a battlefield. She was applying not merely to observe but for an extended period of interspecies cohabitation—with a Human soldier, no less.

She knew that she had to try. For the sake of critical theories not proven fact as well as for personal feelings that ran deeper still, to the core of what she believed, she had to try. In so doing she hoped for revelation, but was willing to settle for understanding.

Among the Wais there were few as powerfully driven by their convictions.

What she wanted more than anything else, of course, was for experience and study to prove her wrong. If she was right, then the occupation of future historians would be simply as annotators of footnotes to the potential cataclysm only she seemed able to see. Barring the triumph of the Amplitur and their Purpose, of course, in which case all history would become, in the grip of that singular race, merely another of their manifold clever fictions.

What truly terrified her was that the steadier the edifice of her principle theory became, the less sure she was that an Amplitur victory would be the greater of the two evils.

★ V ★

Straat-ien and his beloved drifted in a blue mist softly illuminated by stars flung like glitter across a palette of black velvet. About them puffy white cumulus clouds floated: ambient cotton. In the distance lay rugged mountains decked out in brown and green and capped with brighter white, a more intense absence of color.

Proximate details were easier to resolve. Strange trees and vines bound the land together in a vibrant network of intertwined life. Harmless huge insects drifted among the vines on iridescent wings that were shards of soap bubble. They scattered on languorous hums as the nearly nude couple drifted down through them.

At precisely the right moment the man and woman came to placid rest on a beach of ruby sand that had been formed by millions of years of wave action on a shelf of solid corundum. A translucent emerald sea sang joyously against the reef just offshore as they consummated their journey.

Afterward they rolled onto their backs, the woman's fingers lightly gripping the man's wrist. Naomi inclined her eyes to her companion. Sweat lightly beaded her forehead, and her pale blond hair formed golden veins against the deep red sand. She smiled.

"You've got to hand it to the Hivistahm. For a race whose lovemaking is pretty damn prosaic they really know how to create a dazzling enviromood for us nonreptilians."

Nevan Straat-ien saw no reason to disagree as he lay on

his back searching the simulated sky. It was a perfect sky, devoid of pollution, speckled with just the right number and kind of clouds. Exactly as had been requested. The rate of their imaginary descent to the beach had been controlled by their respective degrees of arousal, all monitored by the Hivistahm's remote foreplay software, everything combining to insure that they landed on the opulent sands at the truly perfect moment.

He had no complaints.

Other simulations allowed them to tumble together down an icy mountain slope, or glide beneath the sea surrounded by choreographed piscine inhabitants. Such enviromoods served to take the participants' minds off the battle raging for Chemadii, to which they would soon have to return.

Base Atilla was the most advanced of the three hardened bastions that the Weave expeditionary force to Chemadii had succeeded in establishing on that contested world. By coincidence it was located on the shore of the western sea, a far bleaker and less stimulating coast than the one that had been conjured up by the Hivi sensorial. The sands of the beaches that backed onto the military complex were dirty white and profligate with decaying oceanic flora, while the ambient temperature was anything but tropic.

As the thin, slightly metallic headband he wore monitored internal hormonal shifts, the sky above faded and the sand beneath him grew dull. They were lying on a utilitarian platform bed beneath a four-meter high dome the color of fresh milk. Flattering lighting came from indirect sources. He blinked and sat up, hooking his knees with his forearms. The sensorial had concluded.

''It's a shame that having invented something this sumptuous, the Hivis can't enjoy the full effect themselves,'' she opined.

''They get something out of it,'' he replied. ''It's just that their hormones don't rage like ours.'' Memories of shimmering insects and ruby sands were already waning.

There was nothing synthetic about Naomi, however. She lay next to him, open and unself-conscious. The length of her hair was a dead giveaway that she wasn't a combat participant. Her actual duties lay in Supply and Replenishment, a classification that provided them with a considerable source of amusement.

They lingered beneath the dome because his leave ended tomorrow. It was the first time since they'd met that they'd had more than two consecutive days together and both had intended to make the most of it. In this they had been successful.

He knew they missed him in Planning. Chemadii was one of the frontline worlds on which the Amplitur and their allies had recently been able to muster real strength. It was a place where there had not been and were not likely to be any quick, decisive victories. The enemy was deeply entrenched and had thus far given every indication of remaining so.

Which would make the triumph all the greater when the minions of the Purpose were finally thrown out, he mused. After that, after Chemadii, there would be another world, another confrontation. It was the way of the war. Perhaps the Weave would try to take another semisettlement, or even the nearby, important agricultural Segunian-dominated system of Jwo. He'd heard rumors. There were always rumors, to which officers were no more immune than the lower ranks.

It didn't matter. He went where they sent him, took it one world, one battle at a time. That was how the war had gone for hundreds of years.

He felt fingers lightly caressing his lower back. His relationship with Naomi had grown into more than a diversion. He hadn't planned it that way, but such things rarely happened according to plan. Much easier to develop a strategy for dealing with the enemy.

She was intelligent and attractive, understanding and thoughtful. Her mental net did not cast as wide as his, but that was no drawback. Oftentimes her perception exceeded his. She was much better with people, for example. She squirmed a little nearer and he felt her warmth.

"You're planning again. We don't have much time left. Can't you just relax?"

"Sorry. I can't help myself."

"No, I don't suppose you can." She grinned. "You weren't planning a little while ago. You were extemporizing like mad."

He smiled the boyish, almost bashful smile that women seemed to find so endearing. It was the only innocent thing about him.

He was short, a little below her own height, but it hadn't caused them any problems. Combined with his smooth, easily depilated face it gave him the appearance of someone ten years younger, though he was nearly forty. He had the build of a gymnast, slight and limber but extremely muscular. The latter was the result of fortuitous genetics and a great deal of hard work. His hazel-colored hair was cut in a short brush, a single jagged slash shaved into each side above the ear. It was a style he found both comfortable and defining.

Occasionally his appearance and stature gave him trouble, since he looked more like an orderly than a colonel. On more than one occasion he'd had to produce proof for other Humans as well as aliens attesting to his actual rank. As a child he'd hated always being mistaken for someone younger, but as he aged he'd come to appreciate the advantages and no longer cursed that particular aspect of his heritage.

Though like any Human he missed the thrill of actual combat, he'd resigned himself to working in Planning. He seemed to have a knack for spotting enemy weak points, a talent that resulted in quick promotion if not personal fulfillment. He soon came to realize that Planning was an ideal place from which to best utilize his other talent, the one none of his colleagues suspected. The one that allowed him to forcefully suggest occasional changes in tactics to even the most tentative Massood officer.

Nevan's genes were inherited from his Cossuutian parents. He was one of the Core.

Like any normal Human, Naomi suspected nothing. His abilities had no effect on other Humans, and she never saw him at work. To her he was only Nev, her confidant and lover.

Now he had to face the possibility of her becoming rather

more than that. It was something he both wanted and dreaded. Marriage outside the Core was possible, but very difficult. Keeping a great secret from friends and acquaintances was comparatively easy. Concealing it forever from a wife and life-partner was another matter entirely.

They genuinely liked one another. She was a good talker, and he liked to listen. Her enthusiasm complemented his natural reticence. They were good together.

He'd never married and had nearly reconciled himself to the likelihood that he might never do so, though the Core encouraged marriage among its members. Not outside, though. Maintaining the Core gene pool had priority over mere love.

Naomi had lost one husband to the war. There were no children, which would help in the event that . . .

He stopped himself, surprised at how far down a difficult path he'd already traveled.

"You look happy." She sat up next to him.

"I am. It's just that there's work to do."

She sighed. "Always working. Sometimes I'm tempted to drug you, but I'm not sure it would make any difference."

He slid off the platform and started to dress. "I'll keep in touch. Get back as soon as I can beg off active duty. Maybe in a couple of weeks." He stepped into his off-duty jumpsuit.

She lay back on the bed, watching him, enjoying the play of sharply defined muscles in his back and legs. "You have an overdeveloped sense of responsibility. I wish I could have it surgically removed."

"The next couple of months are going to be critical." He turned to face the bed, running a finger up the front of his suit to seal it. "I'll try to arrange a private line out. We can talk."

She stretched enticingly. "My private line's always open to you."

"Stop that or I'll never get out of here. They'll knock me down a grade if I'm late."

"I doubt it. You're invaluable. And not just to those deadheads in Planning. How are we doing, anyway? Everyone sees the reports and wonders."

"The Amplitur are fighting like hell for this world. There are so many transports on both sides arriving from Underspace that the orbital shell is getting crowded." He looked down at himself, then back at the woman with whom he was more or less in love. "I've got to go, Naomi."

"I know." She sighed resignedly. "That club of yours."

"We're just touching bases before we have to get back down to business."

"I wish you'd drop it. That would leave more time for us."

"It's only an occasional get-together. Friends and cronies from the homeworld. Don't you go to the Barnard's socials?"

She shook her head. "I don't know many of those people. I guess Cossuutians link tighter."

"We do. It's our background."

"I know the history of the Restorees. A miserable business all around. But it's over and done with. Their descendants are all normal folk. Like you."

He forced a grin. "And all this time I thought you considered me exceptional. It's nothing special, Naomi. Just a few hellos and some sharing of memories. There aren't a lot of us. It's not like an Earth or Carry-on get-together, where you can always find a few hundred people to chat with." It was different in many other ways, he knew, but he couldn't tell her about that. There were many things he couldn't tell her about.

Exposure was what the members of the Core feared most, and they guarded their privacy dearly: even from loved ones who suffered from normalcy.

He could dream about a permanent relationship, though. He could fantasize having Naomi by his side forever. There were no strictures against that.

"Go on, Colonel." Her despair was transparently and intentionally specious. "Go to your damn meeting. I know what's really important to you." She softened. "At least we have tonight."

Maybe, he thought. It depended on timing . . . and other things over which neither he nor she had any control. He leaned over the bed and kissed her good-bye. It was awkward, but neither of them protested.

When he finally managed to pull away, she said unexpectedly, ''Maybe sometime I could go to one of these soirees with you?''

He tensed slightly, hoping it didn't show. ''You'd find it boring as hell.''

''Oh, I don't know. It would give me a chance to meet some of your friends from back home.''

''They're just regular people. Just like you said, Cossuutians are no different from anybody else. Not since the Hivistahm and O'o'yan straightened out our ancestors' anatomy and fixed the damage the Amplitur had done.'' He strove to change the subject. ''Or is there something still screwy about me?''

''Absolutely.'' She laughed. ''You turned out better than average.''

We all did, he mused, but neither you nor anyone else can be allowed to know that.

He couldn't marry her. She was too perceptive, and it would be impossible to keep the secret of the Core from her forever. If that was discovered, then greater concerns would take over. It would be impossible for him to protect, to shield her from inevitable consequences. Better never to let it get that far, to stop it now before the danger to her became too great.

It wasn't going to be easy.

She was sitting on the other side of the bed slipping into her overblouse. ''You Cossuutians.''

Could anything be read into so bland a statement? Did she somehow suspect something? He prayed she did not.

If the Massood or any of the other member species that comprised the Weave suspected that certain Humans could influence their thought processes in the same fashion as did the Amplitur, the revelation could destroy the alliance. It was a great secret, one that had to be preserved at all costs. If

Naomi or anyone else learned the truth, they would have to be dealt with as necessary. Nevan knew that if it came to that he would do what was necessary himself.

Paranoid fantasies, he murmured silently. She knew nothing, and he'd see to it that it stayed that way.

Half-dressed, she came around the foot of the bed to put her arms around him. "I am most reluctant, Colonel, to let you go. I hope it shows."

"It's not the only thing," he responded playfully, kissing her again.

"How far from me are they sending you this time?"

"The Circassian Delta."

"Damn. No night leaves, then?"

" 'Fraid not."

"You'll get in touch as soon as you win the battle?"

"If we win the battle. Nothing on Chemadii is certain."

"It seems like this world means a great deal to them."

He stepped back. "These days everything seems to mean a great deal to them. I suppose that's a good sign."

She sat down on the foot of the bed and fingered her pants. "I don't suppose the end of the war is in view?"

"The end of the war?" He found he'd never really pondered so outrageous a notion. "The Weave's made a lot of advances since Humanity sided with them, but I don't see any indication that the Amplitur and their alliance are falling apart."

"I suppose not." She shrugged. "Still, it's a nice thought."

Like most Humans, he'd been trained to be a soldier from the time he was old enough to press his first fire-control button. He'd never thought about an end to the war, nor to the best of his knowledge had any of his friends. But Naomi was different. It was one reason why he loved her.

Later, when acceleration pressed him into the back of a speeding, dodging courier skimmer as it raced up the coast from Base Atilla toward his field assignment, he found himself wondering if, no matter the desperation of the circumstances and the need to do so, he really could kill her.

Ranji-aar could have done it, but he'd been the first; a legendary figure in Cossuutian history. Nevan knew he was no Ranji-aar. He was just an ordinary soldier with a talent for strategy.

If only we could suggest other Humans the way we can the Massood or S'van or Hivistahm, he thought as he stared out the window at the gray, alien sea. It would make one's personal life so very much easier.

★ VI ★

The regional command module lay four-fifths submerged in the dark waters offshore from the delta. As the skimmer drew near and began to slow, a shapeseeking Crigolit concussion dart changed course to intercept. VR projectors on the skimmer went to work to confuse the incoming threat, striving to rattle its sensors. Electronically, the skimmer seemed to change into a large, low-flying waterfowl of a type common to this part of Chemadii. The biobit mappers had done their work well. The dart's shape-recognition circuitry was forced to pause and reanalyze lest it spend itself uselessly against an example of harmless local fauna instead of the enemy.

It quickly saw through the deception, but the delay had allowed the skimmer's own weaponry to lock on and respond. It flung a cloud of subsonic lenticular shells in the attacker's direction. The dart took evasive action of its own, but one small shell struck near the engine and the self-contained weapon was forced to retire, wobbling back inland in the general direction of the delta.

There were no other attacks, and the skimmer arrived safely, docking with one of the subsurface ports in the module's ventral side without further interference. Humans in rebreathing dive gear attended the arrival, one looking up from her work to wave at the skimmer's pilot. He smiled through the foreport.

A Lepar crew would have done the work better and faster, Nevan thought as he disembarked, but like so many of the Weave's inhabitants no Lepar could function efficiently this close to actual combat. Among all the species of the Weave, only the slow-witted amphibians and Human beings were comfortable with underwater work. While this ability only enhanced humanity's reputation for differentness among the rest of the Weave, it rather endeared them to the slow-moving, slow-thinking Lepar.

Nevan was one of the most respected Planners on Chemadii. He had a flair for laying out the means to take enemy positions with a minimum amount of risk and casualties. Troops aware of his reputation felt better when they knew he was among those preparing the battle plans they would be required to carry out.

Field planning and strategy were directed from a crowded chamber located in the center of the floating, mobile command station. While special stabilizers kept it steady, the module could shift its position in the bay to react to changing conditions. It could not fly, like a plane or skimmer; it could not completely submerge; nor could it make much speed, but neither was it rooted to one place and therefore correspondingly vulnerable to enemy detection and attack.

Fresh water from the delta mixed with the saline body of the ocean to create a habitat that was rich in native Chemadiian fauna. It would have been a treasure trove for avid xenologists had not the air and water been filled with agile, eager weapons of destruction looking for targets against which to expend themselves. The delta had been home to intensive if infrequent fighting for several months, with neither side as yet able to claim a strategic advantage.

Local combat forces contained a higher proportion of Human soldiers than was usual, Nevan knew. This was because of the Massood aversion to water. The delta was notably lacking in stable, solid ground of which to contest ownership, which left most of the actual fighting to Humans.

It also gave them an advantage over the equally water-shy Crigolit, who compensated by means of superior numbers and constant aerial patrolling. Now, if the Lepar could have participated, Nevan mused . . . but that was a ludicrous thought. A Lepar wouldn't have brains enough to make use of a complex weapon, much less the inclination.

It was left to Humans to fight for control of the vital delta region.

There was plenty of cover for individual troops moving through the aqueous terrain. Lots of trees and bushes. But anything big, like a floating battery, was sure to be spotted and destroyed. Weave command was faced with the problem of trying to secure the area with light firepower only. It was a contradiction they had thus far been unable to solve.

Though the regionally assigned Massood were reluctant to participate in the actual fighting within the soggy deltan landscape, they had no problem staffing the module, thereby freeing up the Human contingent for combat. Nevan was discussing strategy with one other Human officer and four Massood when the first explosions shook the deck beneath them.

One of the Massood reacted with a distinctive twitch of whiskers and an accompanying observation via his translator. "Long-range sensing detonation. I recognize the vibration. It should not have made it through our defenses."

As if in confirmation, the first explosion was soon followed by the simultaneous activation of multiple alarms. Lights flickered uncertainly A junior officer burst into the chamber.

"We are under attack!" he shouted in vibrant Massoodai.

"Control yourself!" The field colonel in charge of the module was a wizened old Massood who'd survived several theaters of operation. She glanced sharply at a screen set in the east wall. "I see no evidence of enemy skids or floaters in our vicinity." The module shook again. "Explain your conclusions."

The junior officer was not reluctant to do so. "I know it seems impossible, honored Colonel, but the Crigolit are attacking without the aid of aerial transport . . . from underwater."

"Impossible!" declared another of the Massood. At that moment the lights went out.

Self-powered screens and fluorescent wall coatings flickered to life, restoring interior illumination. A quick check with the rest of the module confirmed the implausible report. The Crigolit were indeed mounting an unprecedented subsurface assault, which explained how they had been able to approach the module so closely without exposing themselves to early detection. The module's defense systems were designed to hunt for incoming vehicles or self-propelled weapons, not for individuals quietly approaching below the surface.

As he raced from the command chamber, Nevan found himself wondering at the daring of it all. The Crigolit had the same healthy fear of watery submersion as other intelligent species on both sides. Somehow a group of them had been persuaded to overcome that fear.

Sensors provided video that showed Crigolit soldiers advancing by means of small, self-contained rebreathers attached to their chests and backs. Wraparound masks allowed them to see underwater. Since the notion of swimming—not to mention the mechanics of the process—was as alien to them as it was to the Massood or Hivistahm, each attacking soldier had been provided with a small propulsion pack fitted to his or her rear legs. Arms held weapons while the second set of legs hung free.

The Amplitur, Nevan reflected, must have worked long and hard with this particular assault group to enable them to mount such an unnatural offensive. Repeated suggestion sessions would have been required to overcome deeply ingrained Crigolit fears. Whatever the eventual outcome of the battle, such radical alteration of natural instincts would inevitably result in some severe psychological damage among the survivors. That would not trouble the Amplitur, Nevan thought grimly. Wasn't it all in the service of the Purpose and therefore self-justifying?

Scooting forward singly instead of en masse, they had succeeded in fooling the module's detection systems until well within attacking range. Now the unnerved defenders hastened to try and organize a defense against a kind of offensive they'd felt sure could never happen.

While some of the Crigolit went to work on the stabilizers and propulsion system, others attacked surface-mounted weapons from below. Still more broke in through the landing and service ports just above water level. They swarmed into the module's corridors, discarding their rebreathing equipment as they advanced.

Nevan found himself retreating, using his sidearm as he dodged incoming fire. The Crigolit were familiar with Hivistahm engineering and so concentrated their efforts on the module's communications and fire-control rooms. That left Nevan and a few others room to maneuver, but only temporarily. As soon as they had secured communications and rendered the module's defenses helpless, the enemy would begin a methodical search of the remaining chambers.

The defending Massood and Humans fought back ferociously, but they had nowhere to retreat and no room in the narrow corridors in which to maneuver. With the Crigolit jamming internal communications, there was no way to make use of the two large sleds docked in the module's service ports. Furthermore, the bulk of the module's combat contingent was updelta, fighting to drive the Crigolit inland. Not only was the enemy on the verge of taking control of the floating base, but if they did so, those troops fighting upriver would be cut off.

The module's crew had been caught seriously unprepared, having made the assumption that since the enemy had never attacked underwater before, it was a possibility that could safely be ignored. They had been fooled as well as taken off guard. Perhaps the Amplitur had lifted the idea from the many times Humans had attacked their own installations utilizing a similar approach.

Explosions and loss of illumination came more frequently as the Crigolit continued to advance. In hastily rigged defensive positions, isolated clusters of Massood or Humans tried to make a stand. The interior of the module had not been

designed for internal defense, however, and one by one the
defenders were killed or captured.

One other Core member was part of the module's regular
operating staff. Sergeant Conner came rushing around a bend
in a corridor, splashing through the salt water that had entered through a breach in the outer base wall, and pulled up
next to Nevan. Blood ran down his face from a cut in his
forehead, making him blink. He was breathing hard.

"Glad I found you, sir!" Though all Core members were
on a first name basis with one another, it was important to
maintain appearances in case others might be watching or
listening. As such, it would not do in a combat situation for
a noncom to address a superior in too familiar a fashion.
"We're losing it."

Nevan glanced around the corner, drew back. The corridor
ahead was still deserted. "What's the word on reinforcements?"

"Mostly unprintable, sir. Not much likelihood. The bugs
got to communications fast. Several of us sent out a quick
report over field units, but chances are they don't have sufficient range to reach our people upriver. Even if they did
there's not going to be enough time for them to get back
here." The sergeant paused, wheezing. "I'm open to suggestions, sir."

Nevan considered. "If they've taken communications,
they'll go for engineering next. Let's keep moving in the
opposite direction."

Once they nearly stumbled into a pair of Crigolit skittering
down a corridor. Milky eyes gazed back into their own, followed by a startled exchange of oaths and fire. Nevan found
himself dropping and rolling to avoid the neural beams which
sought his spine. One struck nearby and his right foot went
numb.

His own weapon was less sophisticated. The Crigolit's
head exploded on contact with the tiny expanding shell as
Nevan's pistol flared. The other insectoid carried a rifle,
which took a small chunk out of the sergeant's shoulder.
Conner's return fire snapped his assailant in two.

Ignoring his tingling foot, Nevan struggled erect and examined his companion's wound. It was messy but superficial. They resumed their desperate odyssey.

It was clear that the Crigolit were in complete control and there was little chance of driving them off. Their unprecedented assault had been a complete success. With any reinforcements or relief questionable at best, there was no thought of organizing any kind of counterattack.

"This way, sir." Conner was leading him toward the emergency lifeboat bay. The corridor heading toward it was depressingly deserted.

The lifeboats had been included to provide a means of escape in the event that the delta region was struck by a severe storm. They contained no weapons or armor, but neither Straat-ien or Conner much cared. Right now they constituted a possible way out; maybe the only way out.

Unfortunately, the same idea had also occurred to the Crigolit.

There were half a dozen of them assembled near the entrance to the bay. It looked as if they'd only recently arrived. Several were in the process of removing their bulky underwater rebreathers. Behind a makeshift barrier of jumbled furniture and equipment, the others were trying to calibrate a large and nasty-looking automated weapon for close-quarter work.

Whoever had planned this assault knew what he was doing, Nevan thought in frustration.

They crouched behind the last bend in the corridor. "I don't think they saw us," he whispered. "They're too busy setting up their position. I think I saw five."

"Six." Conner continued to bleed from the shoulder, but the gash in his forehead was clotting reassuringly. "Maybe more, but I don't think so." He was about twenty-five, Nevan guessed. Already an experienced soldier, scared and hardened all at once. "If we wait till they get that big gun on auto, we'll never get past them."

"Too many to rush." Nevan considered, eyeing his young

companion. "You know how to suggest." It was not a question.

Conner gazed back at him uncertainly. "I've only done it a couple of times, sir. Each time it involved an allied individual I was close to. Never an enemy, and never in numbers."

"Time you tried." Nevan loosened the grip on his sidearm's trigger. "I want you to pretend that you're a Crigolit officer. A High Unifer. Believe that you're in command. We're going to order them to search the next corridor. We're going to present the edict in such a way that they won't even think of questioning its logic."

Conner looked doubtful. The young sergeant had to do his part, Nevan knew. There was no way he could successfully suggest half a dozen Crigolit on his own. If they were merely confused instead of immediately convinced, they would open up with their weapons as a matter of training. And that would be that.

They would have one chance to do it right.

"Don't use your translator. Don't even open your mouth. Just make the suggestion. You're a Crigolit Unifer giving an order to troops in the field. They have to listen."

They rose. When Conner nodded, Straat-ien stepped around the corner and started boldly up the passageway. They'd had one good look at the enemy soldiers; sufficient to visualize them.

Two of the Crigolit glanced up immediately. Nevan stared right back at them, feeling the sweat start down his ribs. He reiterated the directive in his mind, tensing with the strain. Conner marched next to him, staring straight ahead.

The four other quadrupeds edged away from the formidable gun to stand alongside their brethren. A moment flickered away; heavy time. Then they simultaneously pulled their sidearms. Nevan heard the sergeant suck air but he couldn't spare the energy to admonish him. His own sidearm hung uselessly at his side.

Fortunately, the Crigolit could not be counted among the enemy's mental giants. They traditionally thought and did things as a group. If one complied, others tended to follow. Brandishing their weapons, the six Crigolit started down the corridor. One brushed close enough to Nevan to make contact. It hesitated, the tiny black pupil shifting, but lurched on in pursuit of its comrades. It was clearly confused but while operating under a direct order from a High Unifer couldn't spare thought for reflection.

That would come soon enough, Nevan knew, as the powerful mental suggestion he and Conner had applied wore off. Then the six would slow, blink, and gaze at one another in search of explanation. They would remember, and hurry to return to their former position. By which time the two Humans needed to be gone.

The Crigolit rushed into the next passageway. They had been ordered to challenge a possible counterattack. It was easy to see that no such assault was in progress or even in evidence, but they scoured their surroundings nonetheless. Gradually their efforts slackened. An edict was an edict, but none of them could recall precisely when or how they had received it, or the name of the commanding Unifer in whose name it had been issued.

Two paused to confront one another. Mass delusion was not unknown in combat situations. Had there even been an order? It was time to ask some questions.

Avoiding the eerily pulsating but uncalibrated big gun, Conner vaulted over the makeshift barrier into the lifeboat bay. Straat-icn was close behind. As they passed it, both men looked longingly at the almost operational weapon; at the narrow barrel and attached magazine of explosive armorpiercing flechettes. If they hung around, there was a good chance they could wreak some serious havoc . . . before they were killed.

Conner energized the nearest lifeboat tube. A watertight door slid aside to reveal a craft far larger than they required. It would hold up to forty Humans and Massood.

Nevan glanced back up the corridor, saw only smoke and haze. If there were other survivors who hadn't yet been captured, they would have to make their own way down to the bay. It was important that someone escape to provide Base Command with a firsthand report of the disaster.

They piled into the compact craft. Conner slid into the pilot's chair and initiated the console. As soon as the watertight door shut behind them, the external cover rolled aside. As it did so they were greeted by a view through the foreport of several startled Crigolit chugging clumsily past. In their bulky rebreathers and individual propulsion units they looked distinctly unhydrodynamic.

That hadn't hampered their activities, Nevan reminded himself.

One of the swimming Crigolit awkwardly managed to twist out of the way. Its companions were less fortunate as Conner gunned the engine and the lifeboat smashed into both of them. Looking back Nevan could see the pair fumbling weakly at their damaged rebreathers. The fumbling quickly ceased.

Conner flicked the switch that would return them to Base Attila. The lifeboat rose to the surface and raced southward. A rearward-facing viewer showed smoke and occasional flame rising from the islandlike exterior of the captured command module. With the module's defenses now disabled, a Crigolit skid had pulled up and docked alongside to unload fresh troops unencumbered by unnatural rebreathing apparatus. The battle was all but over.

Not overconfidence but oversight had doomed the station, Nevan reflected disconsolately. Fatal oversight. Because the enemy had never before done such a thing it had been blithely assumed they never could. Some long-term strategic assumptions were going to have to be reevaluated.

Amphibious Crigolit. What would the Amplitur come up with next?

One step back, two steps forward. That was how you won a war, he thought. This was a decided step back. Gripping the back of the seat he was leaning against until his fingers hurt, he envisioned the number of dead and dying Massood and Humans who remained behind, trapped in the module, which had been turned into a giant spherical coffin. There was nothing he could do about that, nothing he could do for them.

He looked away from the viewer. Conner was trying to get his attention.

"I've got movement onshore, sir. Range about a hundred meters." As it fled, the lifeboat hugged the coast for protection. "Doesn't look like Crigolit, but it's hard to tell. These on-board sensors weren't designed for combat use and don't have battlefield resolution. They're pretty basic."

"Could be an Ashregan signature." Nevan sat down next to him, studying the readout.

"Possible." The sergeant glanced up from the board. "Or some of our own people. Maybe one of those hand-unit generated distress calls got through."

As an important field officer, Nevan knew it was his duty to save himself for further combat, not to mention so that he could report in person on what had happened here at the mouth of the Circassian delta. He thought swiftly. The lifeboat was empty. Only two lives were at stake, and one of them was his own.

"Let's take a quick look. Make as fast a pass as you can, evasive approach. Just get us in close enough for one glimpse and then take us out as fast as this thing can scoot. Use a multiple-field-frequency scan."

The latter wasn't necessary. They had visual confirmation before a responding voice shouted at them over the console speaker. Conner nudged a switch and the lifeboat slowed as it approached the tree-lined shore.

"Identify yourselves," he said, addressing the pickup.

"Who the blazes are you? Identify your own damn self! What the hell's going on out in the bay?"

Nevan smiled slightly as he leaned forward. "This is Colonel Nevan Straat-ien, Strategy and Planning. Delta module has been taken by enemy amphibious assault. As far as I know only myself and Sergeant Conner managed to get out."

"Amphibious Crigolit? Who're you trying to kid?"

"I don't know. You tell me."

There was a pause before the voice replied, only slightly

more under control than before. "I'm Lieutenant Mogen, Second Alphan Biodiv Corps. We hit the bugs hard upriver, sir, and were on our way back for requip when we heard the fireworks start. My noncoms and I caucused and decided a roundabout return might be a good idea."

"Better than you know, Lieutenant. I'm not kidding about the amphibious Crigolit assault. I wish I were. It looks like the squids have been working overtime on minds as well as machines lately."

Conner eased the lifeboat closer to the cluster of anxious, confused soldiers waiting inshore, negotiating a path between shattered tree stumps and mud banks. Nevan studied them through the foreport. Sixty to seventy heavily armed men and women, all wearing recently acquired dirt and muck in addition to standard camouflage. They were accompanied by perhaps fifty Massood. He saw few wounded. Their sliders idled beneath overhanging vegetation, hot and ready to run.

The lieutenant was a stocky, powerfully built man with dark skin and straight black hair. He wore a seeasy over his wounded right eye. It would help him make out shapes and changes in the light while the damaged organ beneath healed. Behind him a Massood junior officer stood at semiattention. A distant explosion drew everyone's attention back to the bay.

"I still can't believe it," the junior officer muttered.

"Neither could we. It's real enough, all right."

"What do we do now?" The lieutenant indicated his distraught troops and the double rank of two-person sliders parked in a semicircle beneath the trees on the highest patch of boggy ground. A combat seat clung to each side of the battle units' drive frames.

"We've been fighting for days. There isn't a slider in the bunch with enough of a charge left to reach Attilla even if they take one soldier per unit."

Conner stood patiently next to Nevan. "We could probably fit most of them in the lifeboat, sir. At the very least we could evacuate all the wounded and many of the rest."

That was what they should do, Nevan knew. That would be the eminently sensible course of action. It was also diametrically opposed to what he was feeling. Judging by the expression on the lieutenant's face, he felt similarly, and said so as he nodded in the direction of the bay.

"Most of us have friends, buddies back there. We could try and give 'em a hand."

"The attack was made in strength," Nevan informed him. "The Crigolit continue to bring additional firepower to bear." He was aware that the nearest cluster of soldiers was staring at him intently, listening hard.

"Anything else . . . sir?" The lieutenant's tone was coldly correct.

Nevan nodded absently. "I was just thinking that, if anyone was so inclined, we could slip back to the main river channel, using the jungle as cover. Try and hit their reinforcements in the shallows as they come downriver."

"Your pardon, honored Colonel," said the Massood junior officer who stood behind the lieutenant, "but our unit is not equipped with underwater breathing apparatus."

The lieutenant glanced back up at her. "We're Human, Sholdid. We don't need any."

"I am aware of that, but if what the colonel has told us is true, then the Crigolit will still retain the advantage. They will have full underwater breathing capability for the duration of any confrontation. I know that breath-holding capability varies among Humans, but if I recall correctly it is in no wise time-intensive."

"The bugs are operating in an unfamiliar and to them frightful environment," Nevan pointed out. "I suspect only some kind of extensive Amplitur conditioning is enabling them to function at all. I doubt that they've been training for or are prepared to engage in any kind of underwater combat. I've seen the propulsion systems they're using. They're crude and improvised, not representative of the kind of highly refined Mazvec or Korath engineering we usually encounter in these kinds of situations. I have a feeling everything they're using today was thrown together for this one tentative attack, to see if it works. Their weapons systems aren't designed for underwater combat either.''

''Neither are ours.'' The Massood's expression was grave.

''That's right.'' The lieutenant bared his teeth, causing the Massood to twitch a little more sharply than usual as she dug at a persistent substernal itch. ''There are many ways to terminate an opponent underwater.'' He indicated his assembled, restive troops, turned back to Straat-ien.

''As you suggest, sir, I think we might be 'so inclined.' ''

Nevan considered. If the Crigolit reacted boldly, he'd do well not to return to Base Attila. On the other hand, if they could catch them off guard, particularly now, when they doubtless thought victory inevitable . . .

He nodded once, sharply, to the younger officer. ''Let's do some damage, Lieutenant.''

''I have to voice concern.'' The Massood was more than uneasy. ''The risk and danger involved are . . .''

''We don't expect your people to deal with water,'' Nevan assured her. ''Someone needs to take charge of this lifeboat. You can lie in ambush along shore and pick off every non-Human head that shows itself above the surface.''

The Massood's ears flicked uncertainly back and forth, and her long lower lip curled downward slightly. She was outranked by this Human but could still call on interspecies protocol to argue further. Trouble was, she couldn't think of any more objections. Nor was she sure she wanted to. Out in the bay, friends were dying.

''Gratefulness for that,'' she muttered.

''It's settled, then.'' Nevan turned on his heel and led the way back to the lifeboat.

★ VII ★

It was very crowded, with the tall, nervous Massood packed in tight among the squat, more muscular Humans, even though most of the latter had sped off riverward on their battered sliders. Clinging to the dense undergrowth, the lifeboat followed at a more leisurely pace. It was not armored and would offer little protection against heavy enemy weaponry in the event its presence was discovered.

It was not. The hastily organized counterattack hit the startled Crigolit all up and down the delta. Weapons at the ready, the Massood watched in astonishment as their Human companions, stripped of their familiar battlefield armor, dove from the lifeboat and idling sliders to challenge the enemy in the depths of the clear, unpolluted river.

Caught by surprise in an element alien to them, the Crigolit were no match for the agile, breath-holding Humans. Their hastily engineered motorized propulsion units were designed to push them from point of embarkation to a chosen destination. They had not been constructed with maneuverability in mind.

Bereft of mechanized aids, the Crigolit could not swim. Devoid of clumsy rebreathing units, they could not survive more than a few seconds underwater. They drowned in large numbers, flailing madly with thin, useless legs and arms. As their respiratory systems were unable to generate sufficient buoyancy in proportion to their body weight, they sank instead of rising naturally to the surface.

"I've got something big moving in, sir." Conner spoke from his position next to the more experienced Massood pilot who had assumed control of the lifeboat.

Straat-ien had just returned from a series of dives. Dripping wet, he moved to stand by the sergeant's shoulder. Nearby Massood eyed him surreptitiously, fascinated by the way in which the furless, naked skin, more like that of a primitive Lepar than their own, shed river water.

He studied the console screen. A pair of large skids was coming downriver, moving fast. They would mount heavy weapons. The fight for the command module was coming to an end.

"Get everyone back on board," he growled tersely. "We can't stand up to field equipment. We've done all we can here."

Conner nodded understandingly.

One by one the divers were informed of the deteriorating battlefield situation as they returned to the lifeboat. Even so, they were understandably reluctant to leave. So were the Massood, who from the air-conditioned comfort of the compact craft had taken their time obliterating those Crigolit who had managed to make it to the surface with the aid of their propulsion units.

As soon as the last soldier was back on board, the Massood pilot gunned the lifeboat's engine and sent them racing back toward the open sea. Their actions had not prevented an Amplitur victory, but the swift and unexpected—if modest—counterattack had certainly tarnished the enemy's triumph.

Now that it was all over, the Massood officer wondered at her ready compliance with the Human colonel's tactics. By nature a cautious individual, she was surprised that she hadn't haggled more strongly for restraint. Her puzzlement quickly faded in the afterglow of a job well done. There was no way they could have retaken the module, but at least they had made the enemy pay for its victory.

Among the other Human–Massood patrols that had been working the upper delta at the time of the unprecedented underwater Crigolit assault, some escaped untouched through the surrounding swamps to be picked up by special small, superfast rescue and reconnaissance craft hastily dispatched from Base Attila for that purpose. Others were not so fortunate. Losses were heavy. There was no way of glossing over the severity of the defeat.

Not only was Straat-ien absolved of any responsibility, he was awarded a commendation for his quick thinking in organizing the lightning if ultimately inadequate counterattack. Having only just arrived at the command module when the enemy assault began, he could hardly be saddled with a portion of the blame for its loss.

There were misgivings but few recriminations at the base. No one had imagined the possibility of an underwater attack by Crigolit; therefore no defense had been designed to cope with it. Planners and Scopers immediately set to making sure it would not be repeated elsewhere. The Weave prided itself on suffering the effects of such shocks only once, and the Amplitur were fast running out of surprises. Eventually they would run out entirely.

Neither that knowledge nor his commendation left Straat-ien feeling any better as he awaited reassignment. It was the first time in his career that he'd been involved in anything so close to a rout, and it continued to weigh heavily on him as the weeks passed. He didn't even have Naomi around to console him, since she was off on assignment elsewhere on Chemadii. Therapy helped some. It could ease his days, but not his memories.

He was glad when the call finally came.

The presence of the female Wais in the base commandant's office did not surprise him. Despite the ornithorp's finery he hardly spared the visitor a glance. For a Wais to make planetfall on a contested world like Chemadii was unusual but not unprecedented. No doubt this one had been assigned to deal with some problems of translation or protocol. Nothing to do with him.

Krensky leaned back in his own chair and acknowledged Straat-ien's arrival with a desultory wave of his real hand.

The other was prosthetic all the way up to the shoulder, a flesh-toned marvel of Hivistahm design and O'o'yan manufacture. When too much of the original body part was lost for regeneration to have a chance of working, a Hivoo replacement was the next best option. This was not necessarily a comedown. In many instances the artifice exceeded the efficiency of the natural.

There was no desk and no window; just seats and benches suitable for life-forms of varying physiognomy, a waveform soholo on the curved rear wall, and in the center of the room, a large metallic glass vase of exquisite design, which served as home and frame to a clutch of pale pink and blue blossoming clover. It was real clover, from Earth. He could smell it. The incongruity of its location was matched only by the cost of its maintenance.

A base commandant could barely afford such luxury.

The clover might have been able to survive on the surface: Chemadii was not an inhospitable world. But the room lay beneath fifty meters of solid basalt and two intervening layers of compression-injected shielding. Under such conditions the healthy deep green of the clover was a testament to the skill of a dedicated, if displaced, horticulturist. No doubt the garden-loving Wais had a greater appreciation for it than did any of the commandant's human visitors.

"Good day, Colonel Nevan." For someone with a tough reputation Krensky had a disarmingly delicate voice. "I've got a special assignment for you." As any experienced soldier would, upon hearing this declaration Straat-ien immediately tensed.

Not that the details mattered. Something to do, at last. Something to take his mind off the catastrophe in which he had been an ineluctable, if peripheral, participant.

"About time, sir. I've been going slowly crazy waiting."

"Apparently the psychs think otherwise or they wouldn't have released you to Command. You've no right to be impatient. None of the delta survivors has been released for return to duty until they've been double-cleared. You know that."

"I know that, sir, but I don't have to like it."

Krensky snorted approvingly. "That's pretty much what they've all said. Well, you can relax now. You've been passed. As of this morning. Still, I would've given it another few days except that I need you for something special."

"I'm ready for anything, sir." Straat-ien waited expectantly.

"Are you? I wonder." Krensky's gaze shifted to the heretofore silent alien.

"Hello," it said. It took Nevan a second to realize that the greeting was directed at him.

The Wais spoke in sweet, ethereal tones. It sounded as if her words were being voiced through panpipes. In addition to being superb linguists they were perfect mimics. In a darkened room it would be difficult even for an expert to tell one from a Human. Or a Lepar, or a Hivistahm, or whomever the Wais would choose to sound like.

This one, at least, was not as severely overdressed as were most of her kind. He knew it was a female from the slightly duller natural coloring, the marginally less florid plumage.

Krensky introduced them. "This is Lalelelang of Mahmahar. She's a historian. Or something like that."

A supple susurration of perfectly matched feathers and attire rose to extend a prehensile wingtip. "Colonel Straat-ien, I am very pleased to meet you."

He gripped the proffered limb carefully, feeling the resilience in the modified quills beneath the feathery covering while wondering at the alien's presence. At the same time it occurred to him that he had never before seen a Wais initiate such contact. Like other Weave species they preferred to avoid physical interaction with Humans unless it was absolutely unavoidable. Clearly this Lalelelang was an exception, that rare example of her kind who was comfortable—if not entirely at ease—among the big, contentious primates. Perhaps her demeanor was a function of her work.

He turned back to Krensky. "About my assignment, sir?"

The commandant nodded toward the Wais. "Our distinguished visitor *is* your assignment, Colonel."

Nevan blinked. "I don't understand."

"Consider her profession." Krensky steepled his fingers and regarded Straat-ien out of hard eyes.

Nevan didn't blink. "You already mentioned that . . . sir. What has that to do with me?"

"Our guest's particular area of interest centers on how different species relate to one another under battlefield conditions. Obviously, she needs a guide."

Straat-ien had tensed anew. He found himself glaring involuntarily in the direction of the patient Wais. She flinched under his gaze, but less than he expected.

A sudden unnerving thought struck him. Did she know or suspect something about the existence of the Core? He forced himself to relax. Just because she was a historian who had apparently worked among Humans didn't mean she knew anything of the secrets of Cossuut's genetically altered offspring.

He told Krensky in no uncertain terms that he wanted no part of such an assignment. Krensky was equally adamant.

"I'm sorry, Colonel, but this determination was approved at the regional level. They wanted someone of substantial rank who is also intimate with field activities. Like it or not, you qualify, you're presently unassigned and available: you're elected."

"It's crazy. I can't have some"—he nearly used several terms he would have regretted—"*Wais* trailing me around out in the field. There's unfinished business I need to take care of. I was hoping to be sent back to the delta."

"The revenge motif," said the Wais unexpectedly. He turned sharply.

"What are you talking about?"

"I've always been fascinated by the intricate contortions of logic your species invents to justify its actions, even as you simultaneously recognize their illogicality. Such complex mental-emotional-physical rationalizations are unique to Humankind, and constitute an important stimulus for my studies."

It was not the kind of reply he'd been expecting. Though

it was easy to generalize about any alien species, he found himself more than a little intrigued by the individual who stood before him, staring up out of bright blue, heavily lashed eyes, unafraid to meet his feral Human gaze. He tried to envision her trailing along in his wake, tiptoeing through the swamps out in the field while trying to keep her perfect plumage pristine.

The image was ludicrous, the notion absurd. He so informed Krensky. The commandant listened patiently, smiling and quite unshakable.

"What happens to her if she's my responsibility," Nevan asked finally, "and I find myself in a combat situation?"

"You needn't worry about me, Colonel Straat-ien. I have been in combat before."

"Say again?" Nevan's tone shifted from accusatory to curious. "No Wais goes into combat. The Hivistahm and S'van rarely, but never Lepar, or O'o'yan. Or Wais."

"I am an exception. To the best of my knowledge, the only exception. I was in combat on Tiofa. In the company of Humans and Massood."

Krensky was nodding confirmation. "She's telling the truth, Nevan. I saw her dossier. She was very nearly killed in action. Mazvec."

Nevan hesitated, his gaze narrowing. He was now on completely unfamiliar territory. "You didn't . . . you didn't carry a *weapon*?"

"No." She didn't tremble at the thought, and took pride in her equilibrium. "Of course not. Not that I couldn't have *carried* one," she added with sudden boldness, "but I naturally could not have used it."

"Right." Nevan felt a little more confident. The universe had not turned inside out after all. "You really have experienced actual fighting?"

"Quite so."

He looked thoughtful. "That doesn't necessarily mean anything. Combat isn't like a poison. Repeated exposure doesn't make you immune."

"I'm quite aware of the psychological ramifications, Col-

onel Straat-ien. I would have to be in order to successfully
pursue my interests. I have devoted my life to the study of
how Humans interact with other species in combat situations. While I agree that I personally am not exempt from
the mental danger posed by being placed in such a position,
I can state unequivocally that I am better prepared to cope
with it than any other representative of my kind. Over the
years I have developed and refined a number of highly effective pharmacological and psychological prophylactics to
insulate me from the danger.''

"You can't insulate yourself from combat," Nevan argued. "If someone's shooting at you, it's necessary to shoot
back.''

The image thus conjured caused her to quiver slightly. She
hoped they wouldn't correctly interpret the sudden slight
fluffing of the feathers on her neck and spine. It was doubtful
that they would. The two males before her were, after all,
only Human soldiers, albeit of enhanced status. Such types
were usually not attuned to the subtleties of interspecies expression.

"I will rely on you to do any shooting, Colonel Straat-
ien.''

Nevan discovered he was smiling in spite of himself.
Though still disgusted with the situation, he had to admire
the alien. "You've got guts; I'll give you that.''

" 'Guts.' '' Her Huma was superb, but Human colloquialisms followed no formal rules of gestation, being as hap-
hazard and unpredictable in their development as the species
that propounded them. So she hesitated slightly before replying. "Yes, to your way of thinking, I suppose that I do.
You might be interested to know that my colleagues think I
am borderline irrational. As I do not regard it as a prereq-
uisite for my job, I naturally disagree with them.''

Listening to her talk was like listening to music, Nevan
mused, though the effect was less when she spoke in an alien
tongue like Huma instead of their own. It was seductive. He
found himself being persuaded.

It helped that he had no choice in the matter.

He spoke slowly, for emphasis. "If I agree to this, when we're out in the field you'll do exactly as I say. I don't give a shit how many degrees, or honors, or delegations of prestige you hold among your own kind. When I say jump, you jump. When I say shut up, you shut up. If I tell you to roll yourself into a ball of feathers and lock yourself in a chest, you comply. Instantly and without question."

"So long as you don't ask me to fly," the Wais replied dryly. "As you know, we lost the ability to do that millions of years ago, although we can still glide for short distances. We traded the power of flight for intelligence. However, if you order me to fly, I will endeavor to try to the best of my ability. I must warn you, though, that sports were never a favorite activity of mine." While the Wais did not share the ready, raucous sense of humor of the S'van or the cavalier boisterousness of Humans, the concept was not utterly alien to them. Their trenchant subtlety was usually lost on other species.

Having immersed herself in the study of Humans, Lalelelang had perforce been required to investigate their sense of humor as well, and as such was able to modify her own sufficiently to make it comprehensible to the two men standing before her.

"Well, you're without question the most unusual specimen of your kind *I've* ever met," Nevan told her.

From his posture and expression she deduced that he'd accepted her. Human attributes in those areas were so blunt and unequivocal that even an adolescent Wais could be trained to interpret them.

"I have simply prepared myself to do my job," she explained. "I don't expect to be welcomed, but I promise you that I will not encumber your movements or interfere in any way with your normal daily activities, whatever they may involve. Think of me, if you will, as nothing more than an ambulatory recording device."

He recognized the self-effacement for what it was: a ploy to ingratiate herself into his confidence. Not that it mattered. "All right. There's nothing I can do about it anyway."

"That's right, Colonel." Krensky looked satisfied, a difficult task accomplished. "I hope you two will get along. Anything that contributes to good interspecies relations benefits the war effort."

"Yeah, right," Nevan muttered. An "ambulatory recording device"? Why not? His thoughts switched to business, which involved reassignment to the field. Preferably to the strike force that was being assembled to try and retake control of the Delta.

He had to admit that she did a good job of keeping in the background as preparations were made.

It had been decided soon after the disaster that there was no point in trying to recover the captured command module. The intention was to hit the enemy hard and fast, before they had time to establish themselves too securely. In an attempt to do exactly that, artillery and self-guided missiles had been pounding the region ever since the defeat, complicating the enemy's efforts to install permanent facilities in the area.

Overall command of the strike force was given to a general officer. Humans and Massood would go in on fast sliders, bypassing the outer fringes of the delta, where the old command module had been located, and striking boldly for the enemy's main bastion of supply, which was located farther upriver. If they could take that, then the Crigolit forces that had established themselves throughout the delta would be forced to rely on aerial resupply while attempting to fight off the Weave attackers. A successful first strike would also cut them off from active reinforcement.

Of course, the strike force might also find itself cut off, behind enemy lines, once again leaving the enemy in control of the region with their position stronger than ever before. Boldness always entailed risk.

Lalelelang observed all the preparations intently. Humans handled the requisite logistics with a forcefulness and precision that was comparably lacking in their social and personal relationships. It was not unreasonable to contend that they spent their entire lives in one kind of combat situation or another.

Only with the Massood, their companions in combat, could they ever truly relax. The Massood appeared to reciprocate, but non-Humans could see this supposed familiarity for the sham it was. The Massood were nearer in temperament to the Wais or S'van or any of the other Weave races than they would ever be to Humankind. Even among the tall fighters, distaste remained for a species that actually enjoyed combat instead of treating it for what it was: a necessary evil that went against every tenet of civilized society.

She found all of it fascinating. Filling up bead after storage bead, she realized she was accumulating more material than any one individual could annotate in a lifetime. Her best students would have to carry on in her wake. It bothered her that she was acquiring material that she personally would not have the opportunity to analyze in detail. There was little glory in fieldwork, and the eventual accolades would go to others, those who would be fortunate enough to collate, explicate, and publish. Such thoughts troubled her only occasionally.

After all, she was not in it for glory.

★ VIII ★

Weave forces struck the delta just before sunrise on a day when the morning mist was thick on the river and its tributaries. Straat-ien's troops sped up a chosen byway on glistening, camouflaged sliders and a single command sled, advancing on a heavy, monotonous hum that would be difficult for enemy aural sensors to pick up. Somnolent wildlife barely had time to flap or splash out of their path.

His group was equally divided between Humans and Massood. Noting the unease of the latter at traveling for so long in such close proximity to open water, Lalelelang hardly had time to be nervous herself.

The sliders rendezvoused at a long, low island, one of dozens that split the main river into the hundred channels which constituted the delta. They overwhelmed the installation that the Crigolit were in the process of constructing in the island's center.

Lalelelang heard but did not see any actual fighting, for which she was grateful. Centered on the big air-repulsion sled, the command post that Straat-ien had established was responsible for directing fire and lines of assault, not for forcing the enemy front. She encountered both Massood and Humans who had been injured, but her training and medicine kept her own endocrine system in balance and allowed her to continue work unabated.

As ordered, she stayed close to Straat-ien. She felt that in the days leading up to the attack she'd come to know him fairly well. He struck her as in no wise exceptional: simply another competent Human officer, highly efficient and effective in concocting battlefield strategy in concert with his Human and Massood subofficers. Though she did not have an opportunity to observe him in combat, she had no doubt he could handle an actual weapon as efficiently as any of his more lethally equipped brethren.

He was shorter and more muscular than most. Though he still towered over her comparatively diminutive form, she was more comfortable speaking to him than to the average Human, who stood taller still. Even during combat, in moments of uncertainty and tension, he was invariably polite to her, having lost his embarrassment at having a Wais dogging his heels much of the waking day. She thought she detected a grudging admiration for the manner in which she was comporting herself in conditions that would have reduced any other Wais to a shivering, immobile clump of feathers cowering in the nearest available dark corner.

Despite that, there were moments when he seemed inordinately suspicious of her, wary beyond reason. She tried but failed to find reasons for these occasional, unpredictable shifts in attitude. It was as if there was something quite intimate he was desperately trying to hide. Some personal failing, perhaps. She was not particularly interested in how this affected him, her interest being wholly professional.

Intrigued, she tried venturing casual questions whenever he manifested overt suspicion. This only made him warier, to the extent of threatening the excellent working relationship she had patiently built up out of her detailed knowledge of human psychology. She promptly backed off, deciding to wait for openings rather than trying to force them. It wasn't as if she had nothing else to record, nothing else to study or occupy her time.

Watching Straat-ien as he directed forces and propounded strategy was quite fascinating. Not once did she ever see him, or for that matter any other Human, express concern over arrangements designed to ultimately result in the deaths of a large number of intelligent beings. That was the terrible Human gift, of course: that this they could do which no other species could. Every day she was presented with astonishing and often appalling new perspectives.

Sometimes the Humans displayed impatience with their more cautious Massood colleagues. The tall, slit-eyed warriors accepted these spirited admonitions gracefully, but only, she knew, because in matters of combat it was the Humans who usually made the right decisions.

Once the offensive was under way, Nevan pretty much forgot about his Wais charge. He was suddenly too busy to worry about her, and she kept her promise to keep out of his way.

Halfway into the assault, the Crigolit counterattacked in strength, flooding the delta with floaters and skids. Gouts of flame and the destructive colors of coherent energy beams sliced through the swamp growth and roiled the water at the fringes of the pseudo-mangroves. Self-seeking missiles of intentions nefarious waited just beneath the surface of the water or hid behind trees, poised for some suitable target to stumble unaware into range. The rapid pace of engagement quickly rendered untenable the prospect of either side calling in heavy air support.

Single- and double-piloted floaters and sliders darted through the forest and across narrow ponds and tributaries, seeking confrontation. Larger skids and sleds utilized on-board VR projection systems to blend as closely as possible into the swamps.

Within the armored, camouflaged confines of Straat-ien's command sled, Lalelelang was somewhat divorced from the actual fighting, though she was surrounded by plenty of confusion and shouting if not blood. Massood and Humans rushed about, the Humans exhibiting the usual facial and skin-color changes, the Massood displaying more frantic twitching and scratching than usual.

The sled was the largest craft that could be utilized in such an attack. Anything more commodious was apt to make an easy target for long-range enemy ordnance. It could carry command electronics, a substantial crew, and some heavy-weapons systems of its own. Such vehicles were the nerve centers of any fast-moving offensive. Lalelelang thought it crowded and uncomfortable but admirably efficient.

At least, it so appeared until the undetected explosive charge, which probably executed its stealthy approach entirely underwater, erupted from the river beneath them.

Automatic sensors assumed control of the sled's engines and reacted evasively. The Korath-designed, Acarian-built weapon detected the incipient escape effort of its chosen target and immediately engaged a proximity trigger. The result was a powerful, shaped-charge explosion just below and to the right of the dodging craft. Glassine and metal and flesh disintegrated as the sled lurched.

Alerted by the weapon, several dozen Crigolit riding individual floaters arrived subsequent to the blast. They swarmed the sled from all sides, attempting to capture and take control rather than simply exterminate the wounded inhabitants.

Anyone not directly responsible for flight operations drew arms and rushed to confront the attackers. That included suddenly superfluous order-givers like Nevan, who pulled his sidearm and joined a group of Massood hurrying toward the point of attack. Unnoticed and ignored, recorder humming imperceptibly, Lalelelang trailed close behind.

She never saw the Crigolit who dropped from the ceiling. With their sextupal limbs they were capable of utilizing surfaces denied even to the agile Humans. Twisting in midair, it landed on its four feet just to her left and aimed two hand weapons in her direction . . . and hesitated. Startled by her appearance, which conformed neither to Human nor Massood, it took a few seconds to determine whether she was friend or foe.

That was long enough to allow a hand to reach over the front of the Crigolit's visored skull and yank sharply backward. The slender neck snapped like a twig, releasing a small, narrow fountain of green, copper-tinged blood from the quivering torso. It splattered Lalelelang, the sticky wetness matting her feathers and staining her attire, dripping cloyingly from her beak and neck. Finding that she was beginning to shake violently, she fought to calm herself by focusing on the necessary and immediate task of cleaning the small lens of her recorder.

The decapitated body before her trembled for a moment longer on its quadrupedal appendages before collapsing like a broken child's toy. Stepping out from behind the corpse was Nevan, the Human she had in preceding days come to think of as relatively sophisticated and progressive for his kind. His eyes were dilated and his breath was coming in short, sharp gasps as his highly efficient respiratory system supercharged his muscles with fresh oxygen.

The Crigolit's head hung from five remarkable, powerful digits. Nevan flung it aside and it bounced several times on the deck. Though fighting swirled around them, she kept her attention on her protector, wishing she could retreat somewhere long enough to take some additional medication. She was afraid that if she did she might miss something of value.

Though she continued to shake, she did not, somewhat to her surprise, go catatonic. Years of training and conditioning were paying off. Straat-ien kept staring at her. His stance and expression hinted at approval, appraisal . . . and something more, something she couldn't quite define.

Then he was gone, whirling to rejoin the fight.

The Massood had a difficult time with their assailants. Not only was it important for the command sled to maintain its position and function in the greater conflict that was roiling the delta, those on board had to fight off the harassing Crigolit as well.

It occurred to Lalelelang that if the sled's defenders were unable to defeat the attacking enemy, it wouldn't matter whether she lost her shakes or not. No doubt the Amplitur would be delighted to have her: they didn't see many Wais prisoners.

The efficiency of the Humans in repelling the attackers was appalling to observe. The distancing exercises she had devised received a strenuous workout. Repeated checks of the recorder helped her to half convince herself that she was not witnessing actual fighting; merely recording a demonstration. Lives were being lost all around her only in the abstract. Such practiced self-delusion enabled her to maintain her emotional equilibrium amid hellish conditions.

Halfway through the battle to retain control of the sled, a singular incident ensued.

An entire squad of Massood, some limping, some otherwise wounded, was retreating down the corridor in which she found herself when they were confronted by a single Human noncommissioned officer: a slightly built, dark-haired individual who addressed them sharply via his translator unit. Being almost as fluent in Massoodai as she was in Huma, she understood both his comments and the sibilant replies they provoked.

The Human's argument did not strike her as especially persuasive in light of the apparent injuries several members of the squad had suffered. They halted before him, staring rather vacuously. Then, one by one, they turned to retrace their path. Clutching his own sidearm, the Human noncom started to follow, when he suddenly noticed Lalelelang staring in his direction. Amid the chaos and confusion of battle their eyes locked for an instant: hers wide and blue, his small and black-pupiled. She wanted to look away but found that she couldn't.

Then the Human was gone, back down the corridor.

Doing her best to ignore the deafening screams and echoing explosions all around she struggled to analyze what had just happened. The conversation she had overheard had contained no semantic surprises that she could recall. It had been straightforward, uncomplicated, and brief, and her knowledge of the languages involved was at least the equal of that of any of the participants.

Nevertheless, the six Massood, hell-bent on retreating, had been convinced by a single unimpressive Human to put aside all concern for their injuries and return to combat. Their expressions had cogently reflected the fear and panic they'd been feeling. Yet a single Human had somehow helped them to brush all that aside.

Something screamed past her head and she half ducked, quivering violently. The incident was for pondering later, in surroundings more conducive to analytical thought. It was all there on her recorder. That was the task of the moment: to record, not to dissect.

Under the direction of Nevan, the sled's captain, and the Massood officers and Human noncoms, the invading Crigolit were driven from the craft. Thus repulsed, the surviving attackers stood clear on their floaters and resumed their assault on the vehicle itself. At this critical moment, when the enemy had finally decided that the taking of prisoners was not worth further sacrifice and destruction therefore had become the order of the hour, a dozen sliders crewed by fresh Massood arrived on the scene in response to the command sled's ongoing omnidirectional cry for help.

Suddenly the Crigolit had their claws full defending themselves from attack from behind. Battered and oozing smoke but still airworthy, the sled was able to drift off into the meager but very welcome cover of a cluster of forest emergents.

Despite her pledge to stay near in the confusion of battle, Lalelelang had become separated from Nevan. It took her a while to find him. He'd returned to the damaged but still functional central command room.

At her arrival he smiled, carefully keeping his teeth concealed so as not to offend. The expression of recognition was brief, and he returned rapidly to his work. This she observed, her recorder still humming softly. Though she carried spares, she was glad it had not failed on her. The material it now contained was quite irreplaceable.

When at last he stood back from the consoles and his fellow soldiers she was sufficiently emboldened to step forward and ask, "How are we doing?"

An exhausted Nevan nearly replied as he would have to another Human, so exacting was her speech. As it was he bowdlerized his response only slightly.

"We're beating the excreta out of them, kicking their chitonous butts all up and down the river. This sled's right in the middle of it and that's why we got hit so hard.'' He squinted at a console. ''The attack on their principal base of supply started slowly, but it's picking up now. Before this is over we'll push them out of this whole region.''

''Turn previous defeat into victory?'' she opined undiplomatically.

He took no offense. ''You bet your feathery crest. Look there.'' He gestured toward the uppermost of a rectangle of small, oval screens.

The feed from the remote airborne eye was presently relaying a visual record of the assault on the target in question. As they watched, an enormous gout of flame erupted from somewhere on the ground and the eye briefly displayed blank sky as the drone dodged to avoid the aftershock. Other screens showed the telltale airstreaks of sliders and floaters engaging in low-level aerial combat.

Out there, she knew, dozens, perhaps hundreds of supposedly civilized, intelligent beings were in the process of being eviscerated, dismembered, killed. The muscular trembling resumed despite her most efficient and agile mental gymnastics. Everything had happened so fast. To make things worse, she was sure her medication was starting to wear off.

''You okay?'' Nevan's gaze and tone narrowed simultaneously.

''I will be fine. I told you not to worry about me.''

''That you did. Still, I don't think you'll miss anything critical if you decide to take a breather. Why don't you spend a few minutes in the medical cubicle and give yourself a rest? You've earned it. A Massood would have earned it.''

She fought to keep a tremor from invading her reply. ''Thank you for your concern, but if you don't object, I would just as soon remain here. If I black out completely, I would appreciate it if you could move me to a corner where I am less likely to be trampled upon in the course of battle.''

He nodded approvingly. ''You know, for a Wais you're really something.''

''So another Human soldier told me not so very long ago.

I am only doing my job. This is my life. *You* are my life. Or rather, your species is.''

A Massood tech seated nearby begged Nevan's attention for a few moments. When he again had time for his charge, he told her, ''Other Weave researchers have tried to make a career out of studying us, but to the best of my admittedly limited knowledge none of them have been able to do so under combat conditions. After a few cursory attempts they all give it up.''

''I suspect none of them were historians.''

''What does that give you that they didn't have? A bigger picture?''

''Something of the sort is my goal,'' she acknowledged. Such conversation helped to steady her nerves, except when he yelled. Not at her but at his colleagues. She still found the sound of the sharp, concussive human voice, its harsh syllables detonating against her finer sensibilities, disconcerting.

As the battle continued, Nevan forgot her afresh. Only later did he notice that she had disappeared. Perhaps she'd taken his suggestion and had chosen to get some rest. As tired as he was he worried that the Wais, with her far less resilient neuromuscular system, might be near collapse.

By nightfall the Crigolit and their allies were retreating all across the region, taking what equipment they could, fighting as they fled but fleeing nonetheless. Mopping up continued throughout the night, the methodical butchery of resisters and taking of prisoners proceeding according to time-honored precedents. During that time he saw her only once, ambling through a corridor intersection, her recorder operating as quietly as ever.

Conner confronted him the following afternoon.

They were standing on the badly marred surface of an enemy floater hangar near the southern edge of the captured enemy base. Below, Crigolit and a few Mazvec and Acarian prisoners were being assembled in a hastily erected temporary enclosure. They offered no resistance. Having been defeated, enemy prisoners were naturally passive, as were those representatives of the Weave who were taken by the other side. Only Humans regularly rebelled in captivity. It was one more puzzlement to the Amplitur.

There were no Amplitur among them. It was not certain any were on Chemadii, and if they were, they would remain traditionally distant from the scene of actual combat. To capture an Amplitur was a feat every soldier of the Weave aspired to. The fact that this had but rarely been done in the entire history of the war did not dissuade the dreamers from their individually vainglorious moments of hopeful anticipation.

As cleanup efforts continued, flames belched intermittently from ruined storage facilities and underground bunkers. The Crigolit base was extensive and had been heavily fortified and protected. Its loss would cripple enemy efforts far beyond the delta. Taking it more than made up for the destruction of the floating command module.

"What can I do for you, Sergeant?" Despite the fact that they were alone he was careful to maintain the appearance of a normal officer–noncom relationship. "Your squad come through okay?"

"One wounded, sir. The Massood took the brunt of this one. Many of them had friends or clan members on the delta module. That's not what I need to talk to you about."

Nevan kicked at a fragment of charred, twisted ceramic armor. "What then?"

"It's that canary you've been squiring around." Human soldiers had pet nicknames for all non-Human species, friend and foe alike. Even though they resembled emus far more than diminutive bright yellow songbirds, all Wais were "canaries," just as the Massood were "rats" and the Amplitur "squids," and so on into the depths of Human inventiveness. Such terms were rarely employed in the presence of the species so labeled, all of whom were nonetheless aware of this particular primate penchant. Most took no umbrage.

After all, they had their own distinctive, secret names for Humankind.

"What about her?" At present the Wais historian was back

on board the sled, perusing her records and checking her equipment.

"She saw me."

Nevan turned from his examination of the captured base. "What do you mean, she saw you?"

"During the fight for the sled I ran into a squad of retreating Massood. Five or six, as I recall. They were pretty well shot up, but not so bad that they couldn't hold a position or serve as backup. They'd had a communal lapse of guts and were looking for a place to sit out some fire while they collected themselves. As you know, sir, at that time the hull had been breached and we needed every hand we could muster."

"You're saying they were running away?" Nevan watched a sled loaded with supplies and reinforcements set down delicately on the partly repaired landing platform.

"I wouldn't go that far, sir. More like they were retreating in disorder. They were all field rank, not a subofficer in the bunch. I could see they still had plenty of fight left in them. They just needed someone to give them some direction."

Nevan nodded slowly. "Which you decided to provide."

"I made a suggestion. First to all of them collectively, which was hard, and then when I had their attention, to each one individually. That was easier. It went smoothly." He glanced around, feigning indifference. They were still alone.

"That's good. They all responded well?" The wind changed and both men turned away from it. Acrid smoke stung Nevan's eyes.

Conner nodded. "Conditions made it kind of hard to concentrate, but I think I did pretty well. After the first two turned back that half persuaded the others. No problem there. The trouble is," he added quietly, "that *she* saw the whole thing. I know she did, because when it was finished and I started to head back to my own station, she was looking right at me."

"So, what did she see?" Nevan was nonchalant. "One Human noncom talking to a bunch of Massood. You said they had no subofficer among them. That means you ranked them. What more natural then for you to give them orders, especially under combat conditions?''

"You don't understand, sir." Conner licked his lips. "She had that damn recorder of hers going. The whole time.''

That made Nevan look up sharply. "She *recorded* you persuading the Massood?''

The sergeant nodded. "Not that anything conclusive will show up on the recording. But I just know, I feel, that she felt something, suspected something. Maybe I'm being paranoid, but when she has time in the peace and quiet of a study somewhere to go over that piece of information in detail, to look closely at the visuals and listen to the audio, it just might strike her, sir, that there was something out of the ordinary taking place.

"I could sense it. She didn't understand why the Massood were returning to combat, why they were listening to me like that.''

"Are you trying to tell me that you read her mind?''

"You know we can't do that, sir." Conner looked into the distance. "Like I said, maybe it's all in *my* mind. But you know that we're taught from adolescence, from as soon as we're made aware of our talent, to err on the side of caution in order to protect ourselves, to protect the Core. You can't blame me for that." He shrugged. "You're probably right, though. I'd know a lot more one way or the other if I had any experience interpreting Wais posture or expressions.''

"Few people have, except a few specialists. Everything the Wais do is elaborate and subtle.''

"Maybe I shouldn't have said anything. It's just that it was a difficult moment and I was, well, I was being very sensitive to everything going on around me. In combat you get jumpy.''

"Don't get down on yourself, Sergeant. You were right to tell me.''

"I just thought, sir, that since you're in charge of her, maybe you could sneak around the subject. Ask some questions, watch for reactions. Try to find out if she does suspect anything from the experience. You'd be a lot better at that sort of thing than I would."

"Don't count on it. How do you ask questions about something that's not supposed to exist without bringing it up? Asking questions, no matter how vague, could be more dangerous than simply ignoring the whole business."

"That's just it, sir." Conner turned his gaze back on his superior. "Can we ignore it?"

Nevan was quiet for a while. "Go back to your duties, Sergeant. Leave this to me. I'll take it from here."

"Whatever you say, sir." The sergeant didn't hesitate. "And if you make a decision that requires the problem be resolved, I'm available to help." He didn't need to elaborate.

The two men parted, Nevan heading toward the command sled, the sergeant jogging off in the direction of an armed group which was combing the rubble in search of survivors or resistance.

★ IX ★

Nevan remained at the captured Crigolit installation for several days, helping to coordinate consolidation strategy before he received orders to return to Base Attila and a certain amount of acclaim.

On the return journey he encountered Lalelelang in the control cabin. She was recording the activities of the sled crew, which consisted of Massood and one lone Hivistahm. Armor ports of transparent Bullerene showed swampy islets and open tropical ocean speeding past beneath the field-repaired craft.

She was squatting in typical Wais resting posture; legs folded beneath her, against a rear wall, as unobtrusive and out of the way as possible. He started to take a seat nearby, then changed his mind and sat down on the floor next to her. A Human lieutenant walked in, conversed with one of the Massood operators, and was turning to leave when he spotted the colonel sprawled on the deck, his back propped comfortably against the wall. The junior officer started to say something, thought better of it, and exited without comment.

"Well, did you get what you came for?"

The large beaked skull pivoted easily on the long supple neck to regard him out of oversized, alien blue eyes. Tight curlicues of iridescent gold and purple glitter framed each eye. The Wais were ever conscious of their appearance, even under unnatural conditions.

Lashes fluttered. "All that and more, Colonel Straat-ien. More than I could have hoped for."

"I think we can drop the military appellation. Just call me Nevan."

"Very well. And you may address me by the familiar phonemic syllable."

"I'll try to remember that, whatever it is. Ready for the next battle?"

"I must decide." She dipped her head to examine the compact recorder that Nevan had yet to see absent from her wingtips, it being easier for a Wais to move its eyes close to a subject to be studied than to raise it up for a better look. "I have gathered so much material over the past days that I am considering returning home to examine what I have acquired."

The importunate concern that Sergeant Conner had planted in Nevan's mind like a permanent itch flared a little more brightly. It was impossible, of course. There was no way she could have divined any truths from watching Conner work on the Massood. Under leisurely examination the confrontation, should she choose to fixate on it, might strike her as odd, but it was an unimaginable jump from that to presuming heretofore unsuspected mental abilities on the part of any Human being. The incident flaunted no raised flags, nothing overt to provoke suspicion.

Still, Conner insisted he'd sensed something. She'd stared at him. Did that mean anything except that the sergeant was overcautious? Nevan was not heir to the same degree of paranoia that affected many Core members.

Only to a lesser degree.

Did she suspect anything at all? If so, given the Wais penchant for discretion, would he be able to detect it no matter how clever and carefully thought-out his queries?

"You really are fascinated by how we interact with other representatives of the Weave. The Massood, for example."

"Particularly the Massood, since they are the only other intelligent Weave species that has overcome their conventional state of civilized behavior sufficiently to wield arms."

"Have you come to any conclusions?" He smiled encouragingly. "Propounded any hypotheses?"

She didn't reply immediately. Had there been something in his voice? He reminded himself that she was an expert in Human language and expression. He was going to have to tread as lightly with his questions as if walking on eggshells.

"I haven't even begun to collate my research, much less postulate conclusions."

He was unwilling to let it go at that. "Surely there must be some things that you've found of more interest than others? Some observations or revelations that have particularly intrigued you?"

"There always are." He tensed a little, hoping it didn't show. "You sitting down next to me, for example."

He was able to relax. "How do you mean?"

"It demonstrates a degree of politeness and courtesy not normally associated with your kind. Being aware of how your stature intimidates all but the Massood and the Chirinaldo, you voluntarily chose to reduce your inherent physical advantage by taking a seat on the floor. Or did you think I would not notice?"

"I didn't really think about it. It's just that you're my responsibility and it's my duty to make you feel as comfortable while you're here as possible."

"Really? What a shame. I would have preferred to have ascribed your action to higher motives. I shall adjust my commentary accordingly."

He felt as if he'd just been offered an easy opportunity to double his money and had instead chosen to throw it away on a particularly dumb bet.

"Anything else?" he inquired, with less interest than before. "What have you decided about how we interact with the Massood?"

"The relationship is less abrasive than I would have expected." He thought she was being slightly defensive, but then with a Wais you couldn't tell.

"That's all?" A Mazvec tracking weapon exploded somewhere nearby, momentarily jolting the high-speed sled. A fleeting strike from some distant enemy position, launched at extreme range more out of hope than expectation of doing any real damage.

"There is the undeniable fact that the Massood seem to fight with greater determination when they go into battle in the company of corresponding Human forces."

"That's not news. Why do you think that is?"

"Although it is a phenomenon which has been studied extensively, no one has yet produced a completely satisfactory explanation, including the Massood themselves. It has something do with the Human ability to forget civilization entirely and revert to a purely primal carnivore mode." There was no hint of accusation or disapproval in her voice, he noted. Her approach was purely academic. She was simply reciting cold facts.

Without being prompted she added, "There was one incident among many in the recent conflict which stands out in my memory."

He went cold as she accurately described the encounter between Conner and the retreating Massood squad.

"At the time, those Massood soldiers seemed quite determined to avoid battle. Yet with very few words one of your soldiers succeeded in convincing them to return to combat."

"You recorded the encounter, of course."

"Naturally." Lashes bobbed, and the long feathery neck flexed expressively. "There is little I wished to record that I did not. Without wanting to appear boastful, I am not ashamed to say that I am good at what I do."

Straat-ien feigned indifference. "That sort of thing happens all the time. The Massood often need a little psychological boost to help them overcome their natural 'civilized' reticence. It's one of the services we Humans provide."

"I do not doubt it. It is just that I hadn't had the opportunity to witness such an encounter previously. I found it but one memorable incident among many. It puts me sadly in mind of all that I have yet to learn." She blinked at him. "You remark on it at length. Do you find it in some way unusual?"

"No," he said, perhaps a little too quickly. "It's only that I had the chance to chat with the noncommissioned officer in question, a Sergeant Conner, and in the course of general conversation on other subjects he happened to mention it to me. Not because of the encounter, which is common enough, but because he happened to notice you off to one side recording it."

"My presence did not compromise his behavior at a sensitive moment, I hope?"

"Not at all. But you know that your presence in such surroundings is unprecedented. You have to expect that it will be noted."

She sounded relieved. "I understand. As a researcher I am naturally always concerned that my presence may influence and thereby alter the very situation I am attempting to study."

"If a tree falls in the forest and there's no one around to hear," he muttered.

"Your pardon?"

"Nothing. I'm rambling. So your work is in good shape?"

"Better than I. Exhaustion has become my constant companion."

"Never know it to look at you."

"You flatter promisingly. It is something Humans are transparent at, even to one another. But I appreciate the concern." She let out a long, trilling whistle that finished in a descending coda. "When I return home I am sure I will require several months' rest before I can even begin to think of dealing with the mountain of material I have accumulated. It will be work enough simply to see to its proper replication and storage."

"Yes," Nevan murmured absently, "it would be terrible if any of it were lost." Bracing himself against the wall, he straightened and stood towering over her. Despite her conditioning she flinched at the nearness of his bulk. It was an instinctive reaction she could not completely shroud. And Straat-ien was one of the smaller Humans on the sled.

"So you'll have plenty to keep you busy back at the main base."

"Assuredly. I have recorded and observed. Now it is time to systematize. If possible I should also like to obtain more material on Human interaction with Weave species other than the Massood."

He inclined his head. "If you need anything, don't hesitate to ask."

"I am sure that by now you have observed that where my work is concerned I am anything but reticent." The lashes fluttered again.

"You've been very straightforward," he admitted.

"I know. Among my kind that would be a serious criticism."

Sensing that he was making her increasingly nervous, he retreated several steps. "You're damned unique, Lalelelang."

"How would you know?" She made it sound almost playful. "How many Wais had you met before me, Colonel Nevan Straat-ien?"

"Well, two." He laughed and quickly dampened the reaction when he saw her flinch at the sight of his exposed teeth.

"I hope your opinion of my kind has not suffered from our relationship."

"Likewise."

"I can say confidently at this point that you are less than a revelation, but more than a confirmation. You aspire to civilized behavior. It is not your fault that the nuances of proper behavior escape your species."

Though he knew there was no malice in her comments, he couldn't keep himself from bridling slightly. "We've got other things to do. There are no nuances on the battlefield."

"The propoundment of hasty absolutes are the conclusions of the insecure," she replied, rather more enigmatically than he would have preferred.

Back at Base Attila a week later he found himself traversing the main service concourse in the company of Mai Pauk

Conner. In addition to other Humans and Massood, the serviceway was thronged with Hivistahm and O'o'yan, S'van and Lepar, all operating on Chemadii in important support capacities. Enclosing bubbles of Bullerene armor let in sunlight to nourish the native plants that grew in profusion in the free-form planters that lined walls and floor.

The two men were discussing the matter of a Massood captain who had noted the frequency with which his own troops often disregarded his orders in favor of those issued in the field by lower-ranking Humans. It had been discovered by a soldier with Core connections to Conner that this officer had begun keeping a personal file on such incidents. Thus alerted, the young woman had quietly brought the situation to the sergeant's attention.

This was not unprecedented. Core members found themselves having to deal with such potentially dangerous attention throughout the Weave, with far more frequency than they would have liked.

If the officer in question had eventually submitted his data to an analytical computer and had happened to ask it the correct, discomfiting questions, it might possibly have informed him that the presence at such times of citizens whose ancestry could without exception be traced back to Cossuutian Restorees suggested an unreasonable coincidence that might bear further investigation.

Conner was informing Straat-ien that the worthy Massood officer in question had died tragically in the battle for the great strategic peninsula known as Jac II. It was not an isolated death. Other Massood and Humans had also perished in the fight. Under such circumstances the loss of one more Massood would neither be remarked upon nor investigated.

It would be reported that the captain had died bravely, a credit to his clan. It was the first time that Nevan had been involved even tangentially in the essential death of an ally to preserve the secrecy of the Core. It did not sit well with him. It did not sit any better with those more immediately involved, but all knew that such regrettable measures were sometimes necessary. Their continued survival, as well as that of their spouses and offspring, depended upon keeping themselves and their peculiar abilities out of the light.

The need for such preventative social surgery was extremely rare. That it might have to be carried out so soon again, and on the same world, was troubling. The fact that the individual so marked for possible excision was a representative of one of the Weave's least offensive species made it that much more uncomfortable to contemplate.

"How much do you think she suspects?" the sergeant asked him.

"Nothing, yet. She may never. Dammit, Conner, you're the one who got me started on this."

Conner shook his head sadly. "I didn't call her. I didn't tell her to be there when I was suggesting those Massood. I didn't remind her to use her recorder. You're just as worried as I am or you wouldn't be talking to me about it now."

Straat-ien stopped to peer over a tubular metal railing at the level immediately below the main concourse. "I still don't believe she's onto anything. But in the unlikely event that she is, and something were to happen to me, it's important that a relative knows. Just in case. You know the Law."

Conner nodded. "You're worried about what she might think when she gets back to her homeworld and starts deciphering her material."

"Not really. I just wanted someone else to know."

"You're being sanguine, sir." Conner was now speaking to his companion not as a junior, but as a distant relative. They were all related, of course. All the Core members. Through ancestry. Through Amplitur genetic manipulation. Through need.

"The Wais are persistent. Their minds are the equal of any, and there's nothing wrong with this female's. Sure, she may skip right over the encounter. It's buried in the mass of data that she's accumulated. But sir—Nevan—can we take that chance? If she divines anything it's going to be a lot harder to correct the situation on her homeworld than it would be here."

Straat-ien considered the tree climbing from the lower level before him. It had multiple entwined trunks and long, pale yellow leaves. "What're you getting at, Conner? That when the opportunity presents itself I 'suggest' she forget all about the incident?"

Conner didn't hesitate. "We both know that won't work in this case, sir. If she'd just witnessed it, sure. But she made a recording. As soon as she saw it again it would wipe out the effects of the strongest suggestion you or I could make. That would be worse than doing nothing at all because it would start her thinking about why she forgot it in the first place. Nor would suggesting her and trying to isolate and erase the recording be enough. She might have had it duped and stored elsewhere."

"All right. What's your 'suggestion'?"

The sergeant didn't hesitate. "Take her out on another combat pass. From what you've told me about her I'm sure she'd jump at the chance." The younger, taller man put closed fists together and twisted them in opposite directions. "Wais are fragile."

"This case isn't that simple." Nevan found displeasing the image so dynamically envisioned by his companion. "She's not a combatant, she's an important individual on her own world, and she's been made my personal responsibility. If she dies here, under any circumstances, it's going to reflect badly on me."

"Better for you to become bad news for a while than for her to find anything out. You know that."

A squad of Massood strode past beneath them. Nevan knew what the reaction of their kind would be to the revelation that certain select Humans could mentally manipulate them as effectively as the Amplitur.

He glanced up, through the Bullerenc glazing. Beyond the deep-sea cove in which the base had been constructed, ascending cliffs forged a towering bluff that formed a distinctive cream-colored landmark against the sky. For most of their length the cliffs were sheer and unclimbable except by experts fitted with special equipment. The western ocean of

Chemadii crashed eternally against the granitic escarpment, throwing showers of spray over fifty meters into the air even in calm weather. Deep inside the base he was effectively insulated from their thunder.

It was a splendid panorama, as profoundly stark as any he'd encountered in his travels.

"Naturally it has to look like an accident." Conner rambled on, placidly homicidal. "I imagine the easiest way will be to get her out into another battlefield situation. If she's had her fill of that there are other ways. If you're worried about your involvement, I can take care of it."

"I can't distance myself that easily." Straat-ien allowed his gaze to wander away from the view and back to the strolling inhabitants of the concourse. The attack siren whined once, causing a number of pedestrians to glance moodily upward, but the electronic exclamation was not repeated. False alarm, he mused, or an asymmetrical test.

"I don't see why you're so worried about problems that don't yet exist, Nevan. Whatever the reaction we can deal with it. Accidents happen. Especially in combat. And she's no soldier, hasn't had any training. If she were to go proto during her visit here, her fellow Wais would probably be less surprised at her fate than anyone else. They'd all bob their heads knowingly, or whatever the hell it is they do."

"I know all that." Straat-ien's reply was tinged with irritation. "All I'm saying is that I'm not sure it's necessary. Just because she saw you suggesting a bunch of Massood doesn't mean she'll ever divine anything deeper than that. Remember, she's swamped with information."

"That's today," the sergeant argued. "Who knows what she'll see in it a year from now, or five, after she's had time for cerebration?"

"She may skip right through it. Mark it down as just another unremarkable Human–otherspecies encounter."

Conner considered a moment before replying, somewhat quizzically. "This isn't just a matter of professional respect anymore, is it? You really like this canary."

"You have to admire her. Put the average Wais through

what she's experienced and it would go cataleptic inside a minute.''

"Shit, man, I admire her, too. The trouble is, every time you turn around that damn recorder of hers is up in your face.''

"That's her job,'' Nevan reminded his companion.

"Her guts are what make her dangerous. Look, Cossucousin; you rank me, both in the corps and in the Core. The decision's up to you.''

"I need to be certain the danger is real before we throw away a mind like that. Even a non-Human one. Give me a few more days.''

Conner shrugged. "I don't see what the big deal is. In the great scheme of things what's one Wais historian more or less?''

Straat-ien stiffened slightly. "Obviously my feelings in the matter differ from yours, Sergeant. If there's truth in your sentiment then we're no better than the Hivistahm and the S'van and the others think we are.''

"I'm just letting you know how I feel, sir. As for how the Weave sees us, I personally think it's a little late to try and collectively convince them that we're the pastoral, benevolent type.'' He took a step backward.

Straat-ien hastened to reassure him. "If I don't think the problem can be resolved any other way, I promise you I'll take care of it myself.''

"What about your concerns about being responsible for her?''

"I'll take care of that. I can be unobtrusive. There's the advantage that she won't suspect me, and when it's over neither will anyone else.''

Conner hesitated. "You know best, Nevan. But if you change your mind and decide you need help . . .''

"I can get ahold of you through the system. I'll keep in touch.''

"That's good enough for me.'' Conner saluted smartly, grinned, and headed off down the corridor, leaving Straat-ien alone with his thoughts.

* * *

That night Naomi found his repeated mention of Lalelelang puzzling. "Why are you so interested in this alien, anyway? When she first got here all you could do was gripe about how she was complicating your daily routine, getting in your way, and generally making life difficult for you. Not to mention endangering herself and those around her."

"Opinions change." Straat-ien rolled away from her and lay on his back, hands behind his head as he considered the ceiling. "For a Wais she's shown extraordinary courage."

"Good for her. That doesn't mean you have to get obsessive about it."

Submerging the distress he felt, he turned his head slightly. "Who says she's becoming an obsession?" Was he going to have to arrange for his lovely consensual companion on Chemadii to have an accident as well? Once one was forced to embark on a program of excising a problem, it wouldn't do to leave potentially embarrassing complications lying around.

He smiled and rolled over to face her, letting his left arm drape itself over her waist. "She *has* been a concern, but hardly an obsession. Because of what she's voluntarily subjected herself to, her motivations intrigue me."

"She's a historian." Naomi snuggled closer. "She's just doing her job. Nothing amazing about that."

"There is if you know much about the Wais." Considering how best to defuse her unhealthy curiosity, he had a sudden inspiration. "Would you like to meet her?"

Naomi looked thoughtful. Eventually she gave him an indifferent smile. "Naw. I've met Wais before. They're uppity, standoffish, look-down-their-beak-at-you snobs. No matter how brainy she is I'm sure that at heart this one's no different. Maybe she seems friendlier, but I bet that's just part of her job. She can't very well go around offending the very Humans she wants to study. She has to be part professional diplomat. So she keeps the proverbial grip on her olfactory organs while smiling verbally at her stinky subjects. She's certainly charmed you."

"I said that I was impressed by her dedication. I'd hardly say that I was charmed."

Naomi was obviously enjoying herself now. "She probably talks about you behind your back, makes snide remarks about Humans in general when she's communicating with other Wais. They're like that, you know. Gossipy. Not that the rest of the Weave doesn't do likewise, from the Massood right on down to the Lepar."

"The Lepar aren't smart enough to be snide," he argued.

"You know what I mean. They all quietly look down on us. And that's okay, as long as they respect us. But the Wais, they're just so damn supercilious about it. It makes you want to put a hand over their beaks until they start to turn blue."

"The Wais look down on everyone, not just Humankind." Nevan's hand moved, distracting her. "It's their culture: form over substance."

Her lower jaw dropped slightly and her eyes slitted. "Speaking of form over substance, Colonel . . ." She drew him closer and for a while he gladly put aside the problems posed by the dangerously persistent alien historian.

★ X ★

"Why did you bring me up here?" Lalelelang had her recorder out and operating, dutifully tracking her surroundings.

They stood near the edge of the point that formed the northernmost end of the penetrating cove whose fulcrum was occupied by the hardened Weave base. A single sled could be seen approaching a landing platform. It hugged the cliffs, using them for cover. Seventy meters below, the green sea of Chemadii smashed against the pale granite cliff face. Spray broke away from the crest of the angry surf to rise up and over the top, dampening her feathers. She knew it probably didn't bother her companion. Humans could tolerate remarkable extremes of climate.

A double-seated slider sat parked behind them, waiting to carry them back to the base. Colonel Nevan Straat-ien moved closer, and she could sense his bulk. The proximity made her uneasy but she held her ground.

"I thought it might be helpful for you to have an overview of the entire base. Sort of framing information for the rest of your material. Besides, it's pretty up here."

"I agree, but my interests lie in individual interactions." She gestured with a dank wingtip. "This is textbook background. As for its aesthetics, I can only admire abstractly the undisciplined ruggedness you Humans seem to find so attractive. As a Wais I prefer scenery that has been tastefully imbued with the order of civilization."

They were quite alone. The base had been in operation for some time, and the view from the point was no longer a novelty. Toward the horizon he thought he could make out several of the monstrous cephalopods who this time of year could regularly be observed on their southward migration. They swam in stops and starts with contractions of their massive split tails, short tentacles thrust downward like the centerboards of ancient sailing vessels.

Surf thundered against the cliff base far below.

For all that his motives in coming to this place were entirely prosaic, he thought his present position morbidly akin to that of certain protagonists in highly melodramatic tales of love and revenge. He found himself staring fixedly at the back of the Wais; at the long, lightly clad legs ending in sandal-clad three-toed feet; the highly decorated feathered body; the slim, flexible neck. She, too, was gazing at the migrating leviathans, the compact recorder clutched firmly in the flexible quill-tips of her right wing. He would be surprised if she weighed more than thirty kilos.

The Wais had lost the power of flight millions of years ago. If she were to topple over the edge, her residual feathers could conceivably slow her fall to the point where striking the rocks at the base of the cliff might not kill her. She'd referred half-jokingly to some minimal gliding capability. But she would certainly be stunned. And the Wais, like so many Weave races, could not swim. A single massive surge of water against granite would finish it quickly. No one would expect her to survive. The body would be pulverized, its fragments scattered.

There were no protective railings on the cliff point, no marked trails. A slip, a gust of wind could easily make a difference in the fate of so fragile a creature. It would be understood that he had tried and failed to save her. There would be censure, but no investigation.

If she resisted, which was almost inconceivable, a single twist of both hands could snap the frail neck as easily as a plastic tube. The all-concealing sea would obliterate the actual cause of death.

He glanced behind him. They were as alone as when they'd first arrived. His fingers flexed. Despite their physical proximity she hadn't moved away from him. After all, she trusted him completely. Why shouldn't she? What conceivable reason could there be for a human officer to want to do harm to a Wais historian?

The rationale was fixed in his mind; indeed, was an inseparable part of it. A part of whose existence and function she could not be allowed to suspect.

He knew that her triumviral sisters would miss her, but she'd told him that she was not mated and had no offspring. She lived on the fringe of Wais society. Far more professional than personal mourning would greet the news of her demise.

He took another step toward her. Far below, unrelenting waves crashed devouringly against naked rock. It wasn't necessary to try and disguise the sudden movement, and he was expecting it when her head pivoted on her neck to look back at him. The large blue eyes started to widen and feathers quivered, a gesture no doubt full of meaning to another Wais.

His hands stayed tight at his sides. He had to know for certain.

"You've told me a lot about your work." He sensed her nervousness and pressed on, using that part of his mind the secret of which he was simultaneously striving to preserve. "But I have this feeling that there's something of particular interest you suspect or have discovered. Something you haven't felt free to discuss with me despite all the talking we've done and all the time we've spent together."

She wavered slightly on her feet, no more able to resist his mental probe than a Massood or S'van would have been.

"No, I . . ." She blinked, inhaling as if a timed-release injection of some powerful drug had suddenly dispersed into her system. "You are right, Colonel Nevan: there is."

Here it comes, he thought tensely. It would be a simple matter to snap the slim neck, pick up the crumpled form and heave it over the cliff. A quick flash of iridescent plumage and sparkling beadwork and she would be gone. It would all be over within an instant, his fears and doubts swallowed along with her body by the all-embracing sea. Both he and Conner could relax.

But he wanted to hear it from her first.

"Well," he prompted relentlessly, "what is it?" He loomed over her.

She was afraid now but somehow unable to move. It was as if her feet had suddenly melted into the stone, fastening her to the spot. She was dimly conscious of responding to his question. This was most peculiar because she hadn't intended to tell anyone of her suspicions. They were potentially too dangerous, too portentous to reveal even to her own kind. If she told a Human she had a pretty good idea of what the consequences might be.

It didn't matter that she was unburdening herself to Colonel Nevan. Despite the genuine concern he had shown for her welfare, something in his eyes, in his posture, still marked him for what he was. She could no more deny his ancestry than could he.

"My studies," she heard another person saying clearly while realizing it was herself, "have led me to some very unsettling conclusions." She tried to leave it at that.

He would have none of it. "Continue." She wondered vaguely why she couldn't ignore him.

Like water through a shattered earthen dam the old fears poured out of her. "It is something I came to realize only after repeated perusing of my accumulated research."

"After you witnessed the encounter during the battle for control of the delta between Sergeant Conner and the squad of retreating Massood," he offered with bleak helpfulness.

"That is certainly part of it."

"Probably it all ties in with what you've learned from watching me," he added fatalistically.

"Naturally." He was standing so close to her, she realized, blocking out the sun. And he wasn't even particularly big, for a Human. Powerful, flexible, killing digits flexed at the ends of his wrists. "Also with everything I've learned from observing Humans in combat, both here and on Tiofa."

Uncertainty entered his voice. To a Wais it was as blatant as a change of color. "With everything?"

"What else?"

He took a step back, clearly confused. For whatever reason, she was grateful for his partial retreat. "I guess I don't understand. Are you saying you found nothing exceptional or remarkable about Sergeant Conner's encounter with the Massood, or in your observation of me?"

"They only confirm what I have augured from watching other Humans. Should it be otherwise?" Her own confusion increased.

"No. No, of course not," he agreed, rather expeditiously. "Forget it. It's not important. Not important at all. No more or less so than any of the rest of your observations."

She took the suggestion. Naturally.

"Tell me about your conclusions, then," he urged her, in a most peculiar tone of voice. "About what you've learned from examining us."

She found herself rambling with an openness she did not suspect she possessed.

"Everything I've seen, everything I've witnessed, only confirms the hypotheses I had formulated before beginning my fieldwork." Salt-laden wind ruffled her feathers. It was growing cold on the edge of the cliff. "Using my own personal observations of Human–otherspecies interactivity as a springboard, I devised a computer program to carry out some experimental extrapolations into which I also incorporated the work of others, both contemporaries and predecessors."

It was as if she were lecturing a seminar consisting of a single student. She knew she was being entirely too revealing, both of herself and her information, but she couldn't help it. Something was compelling her to unburden herself.

"I set myself to this fieldwork in the hopes not of confirming my conclusions but of disproving them."

"You mean you've been looking for something here on Chemadii and before on Tiofa that would invalidate your life's work?"

"Precisely." She discovered that she could move after all.

She was not fastened in place physically; only mentally. "I began to wonder what would happen if the Amplitur were finally defeated."

"Not if: *when.*" Straat-ien spoke the good-soldier speak.

"Whatever," she said impatiently. "Certainly it is coming. The tides of war turned significantly about two hundred years ago. Before that they were always able to develop some new weapon, some new strategy, with which to counterattack. With which to once more press upon the Weave.

"Two hundred years ago the Weave gained a new ally: Humankind. That has made the difference."

"We've done what we could." A by now thoroughly bemused Straat-ien wondered what she was getting at.

"What happens when the Amplitur have been utterly defeated? What happens when they can no longer wage this war of the Purpose against us or any other species? When all their subject races have been freed from the insidious genetic and mental manipulation to which they have been subjected?"

"I don't want to sound simple," Nevan replied carefully, "but I'd think that would mean that the war would end and there would be peace."

"If I am correct then the two may be mutually exclusive," she commented cryptically.

"Why wouldn't there be peace if there's no longer any war? Everyone will quit fighting and go home."

"Everyone?" She was staring straight at him. For a moment he felt as if he were the one subject to mental paralysis.

"If you're talking about my species, we'll return to peaceable pursuits just like everyone else. And maybe apply for full membership in the Weave. We'll go back to what we were doing on Earth before the Weave discovered us and involved us in this war."

"You confirm my worst fears."

"Come on, now!" he argued. "I've studied my own history. There was hardly any serious fighting taking place on Earth when the first Weave ship arrived there."

"By whose standards? There has never been peace on

Earth, just as Humans have only played at 'peaceable pursuits.' Before you began to fight the Amplitur and their allies you contested continuously among yourselves, the only 'intelligent' species to do so. These were aberrations of natural law engendered by your unique planet and your own evolutionary development.''

''We've outgrown that,'' Straat-ien argued. ''We've mastered our ancient history. You talk of early Humans making early mistakes. Our long association with the civilized species of the Weave has changed our society forever.''

''Yes, but has it changed it enough? Grant me a moment my thesis. When the Amplitur capitulate, who will you fight?''

''No one. There'll be no one to fight.''

''I'm not so sure. I think there will be a brief period of peace, like a long exhalation, and then you will have to find someone new to confront. This isn't a question of something in your society; it's a matter of what is in your DNA. You enjoy conflict too much. There is a saying: 'One human is a civilization, two an army, three a war.' ''

By now Nevan had nearly forgotten the reason for their presence on the cliffs. He realized that she didn't suspect a damn thing about Conner, about himself, about the Core, or about the particular talent the unwitting Amplitur had released in the minds of perverted Cossuut's genetically altered human offspring. Instead, she had been carefully shielding a discreditable theory that she'd formulated long before she'd even arrived on Chemadii.

On the other hand, he was slowly coming to realize, if provable, her own suppositions could cause tremendous damage in an entirely different direction from the one he had been concerned with.

''You'll turn on us, on the Weave.'' This she declared with the certainty of the utterly convinced. ''That is what my projections show. Because you now have other species to bicker with besides just yourselves, you will end up picking a conflict with the Wais, or the S'van, or perhaps even the Massood.''

"Why should we want to do that?" He was honestly baffled. "Why would we want to start a war with those who've been our allies for hundreds of years?"

"Because you can't help yourselves. Development of your civilization has always been geared to and propelled forward by conflict. You've made your greatest technological strides in times of war. It's all there in your history.

"It will not take much. A suspicion here, an imagined threat there. I predict you will battle the Massood first. That would be more satisfying for you than picking a fight with, say, the Hivistahm."

"I think your conclusions are addled," he told her firmly. "Remember: You're deducing all this from the perspective of a Wais, a preternaturally sensitive species."

"There's nothing sensitive, preternaturally or otherwise, about the computer models I set up."

"The equipment you're using was designed by Wais or Hivi techs."

"Now you're being self-deceptively facile." She chided him from behind the haze that still enveloped her thoughts. "Believe me, nothing would please me more than to see my theories demolished. Unfortunately, the evidence to date tends to accumulate in the opposite nest."

He looked thoughtful. "I can see why you've been reluctant to tell anyone."

Yes, and why am I now telling you? a part of her wondered. *Why should I trust you? You're not even an academic.*

"What do your colleagues think of your theory?" he asked.

"I have yet to share my data with anyone else. I still have thoughts of disproving the constructed model. But I am less hopeful."

Was he going to hurt her? she wondered suddenly. Perhaps even kill her? Was that why he had brought her to this isolated place? She started to shiver. She'd shepherded her research carefully. It was impossible to imagine that he'd suspected. She'd told no one, not even her two companions in triad. But he didn't have to suspect, she realized. She'd just told him everything. *Why?* What had come over her? What had prompted his battery of irresistible questions?

If her theories were made public and subsequently confirmed by independent sources it could seriously damage Human–Weave relations. That would delight only the Amplitur, who would rush to exploit the internal divisions that had always threatened Weave unity.

The same thought occurred independently to Straat-ien. "Could the Amplitur have planted this idea in your mind in hopes of sowing dissension in the Weave? You know how they can 'suggest' anyone but Humans."

"I have never been anywhere near an Amplitur, either alive or dead." Her response was prompt and confident. "Certainly one has never visited my homeworld."

"If one had, it could have 'suggested' that knowledge out of your memory," he countered.

"Then why would I be telling you all this now?"

He couldn't very well answer that one. Better to change his line of inquiry. "One theory at a time. I accept that your work isn't Amplitur-inspired. You're only one historian. Why should you be the only one to have reached these radical conclusions?"

"What makes you think that I'm the only one?" she replied demurely.

That took him aback. "You know of others who've come to the same conclusion on their own?"

"I didn't say that. I merely suggest that others, perhaps working in different disciplines, may have reached identical ends via a different route and are maintaining their silence for reasons similar to mine."

He picked up a rock and juggled it in his palm, finally tossing it over the cliff. It vanished into the mist and foam boiling up from below. "You know," he told her softly, "ever since that first encounter the Weave has encouraged us to become better warriors than we ever were when we were isolated on our one world."

She blinked then and swayed slightly before recovering her balance. "I suddenly feel rather dizzy."

"It'll pass," he assured her absently. "You're just not used to the combination of sea air and wind."

"Yes." The fog that had been hovering thick and confusing in her thoughts abruptly dissipated. "You have a saying, unsubtle as with most Huma but descriptive nonetheless. About having 'a tiger by the tail.' "

He turned to face her, his hands jammed into the slit pockets of his thin jacket. "That's right. And the Weave went out and found itself a tiger cub and force-fed it steroids so it could take on the Amplitur."

"Just so. Soon we will have no more meat to throw at this tiger. I am firmly convinced that everyone is naive to believe that it will willingly and easily switch its diet to vegetables."

"Anything can learn to change its diet," Straat-ien muttered.

She executed an elaborate Wais gesture of negativity. "Theoretically. But will it be willing to allow claws and teeth to atrophy? Or want them to?"

He had no reply.

"My greatest pleasure in life would be to disprove this hypothesis," she told him.

He nodded. Just to be absolutely certain in his own mind he said bluntly, "Those of us who trace our ancestry to Cossuut have had even more reason than most of our kind to want to make use of our fighting skills." He was watching her carefully.

Insofar as he could tell there was neither hesitation nor artifice in her reply. "I can understand that. As a historian specializing in Human affairs I am familiar with the actions of the Amplitur on that unfortunate world, though after a hundred years I would think that lingering hostility would have faded somewhat."

"We have long memories," he told her. He was convinced now. She neither knew nor suspected anything of the Core's existence or the talents of its individual members.

He'd been on the verge of committing murder, of killing an ally and, indeed, a personal friend, for nothing.

Except that now she could as easily be slain to suppress

the theory she had developed, for it threatened not only him and his relations but the entire Human–Weave relationship.

"Do you intend to disburse your theory?"

"Not yet. I am quite aware of the dangers inherent in doing so, and as I have said, I am still willing to be persuaded of its inaccuracy. Having devoted many years to its construction I do not think it will be easily demolished."

In a half-wild moment he found himself saying, "Maybe I can help you."

"Why should you help me? I would think . . . I would think you would want to stop me." She shook her head. "I don't know why I've even told you any of this after keeping it a secret for so long, even from my own colleagues."

"You can't keep it hidden forever," he told her. "If you don't put it forward someone else eventually will. Better to disprove it now. As for telling me, I'm amazed that you haven't shared your thoughts before this. Maybe it's easier to tell a member of another species." It wasn't an elegant rationalization, he mused, but it would have to do for the moment.

"I do not mean to offend, Nevan, but I'd think to trust my colleagues before I would an alien."

"I'm not offended. I guess something within you decided now was the time to get it out and that I was a reasonably safe receptacle. Maybe the isolation had something to do with it." He indicated the sweeping panorama of sea and stone. "In any event you don't have to worry about me running off to the nearest media rep. I can see the potential for disruption and I'll keep your secret."

"How can I be certain of that?"

"You have my word as an officer and a Human. You argue that your data corroborates the inevitability of Human–Weave conflict. I claim otherwise and I'll do anything I can to prove you wrong."

She made a gesture he was unfamiliar with. "I accept your offer. Perhaps the interposition of a Human viewpoint will expose flaws in my work that I would otherwise not be able to see." She turned and started back toward the waiting slider. He paced alongside, his long stride slowing to match her much shorter one.

"How can you assist me?" She let the slider seat adjust itself to her body type. "You're a field soldier assigned to an active theater of combat."

"I have some leave time accumulated that I never got around to applying for. With the delta and the upriver region now under our control Command should be able to do without me for a while."

"Won't you miss the butchery? It has been my experience that if Humans are deprived of participation in conflict for too long they begin to suffer from disorienting psychological phenomena."

"Naturally I disagree with that observation also. Fighting is just what we're trained for." He switched on the slider's engine. A low whine rose beneath their feet.

"It is what you are genetically disposed toward. There was a Human, an individual who from my studies of your history I gather did not want to be as famous as he became, who was an intimate part of the first meetings between the Weave and your species."

"Sure." Straat-ien had to talk through a pickup as the slider rose from the ground, kicking up dust and noise. "The musician-contact William Dulac. Learning about him is part of normal adolescent matriculation, along with Caldaq and Jaruselka and all the rest. Those are names you can never forget."

"Did you know that for many years after contact Will Dulac attempted to prove that Humans were not naturally inclined to combat?"

"Seems to me I read something along those lines a long time ago. Dulac was brilliant in many ways but he was way off on that one. We know better now." He chuckled. "It's the sort of thing you might expect from a musician. But just because we like to fight and are good at it doesn't mean we *have* to fight all the time. When the war's over it'll be over for good." He increased speed as he headed downslope toward the base. "We're intelligent, rational beings, Lalelelang, even if by Wais standards we're not entirely civilized. We're not some runaway machine everyone else has to fear.''

''Your intelligence is what makes you so dangerous.''

''Well, right now it's going to make me helpful. I have access to military files and facilities that are denied to you, and we can use the Underspace links to libraries elsewhere. You have access to Wais and maybe other sources. Let's try cross-correlating some information and feeding it to your analytical programs and see what we come up with.''

''That is something I have long wanted to do but could not acquire the appropriate authorization for.'' She was nodding, the Human gesture perfectly executed.

He was feeling upbeat about the future. First he'd discovered that she had no inkling whatsoever of the Core's existence, and now by bringing to bear information she'd heretofore been denied they were going to disprove this preposterous subversive theory of hers. Nor had he been forced to commit murder there out on the point.

''You have entry to everything?'' she inquired.

''Not all of it. I don't rate a universal clearance. But I can certainly access material you'd never be allowed to see. That's where your studies have been lacking: no Human input. You've been forced to base all your work only on personal observations and those reported by other aliens. We can change that.'' He nudged the steering bar and the compact, superbly engineered air-repulsion vehicle plunged down an otherwise impassable slope.

''If you think you can work with me, that is.''

''On Tiofa I worked closely with a Human female. I have devoted my life to the study of your kind. Why would I find your presence inhibiting?''

''No deprecation intended. It's just that it's hard to get used to the idea of a Wais who isn't afraid of Humans. Your kind usually run when they see one of us coming. Or at least move to the far side of the walkway. But then you're not your average Wais.''

''So everyone keeps telling me.''

Straat-ien was warming to the prospect before them, planning his assault on the various libraries. "We're going to choke that analytical program of yours on facts and make it change its tune. We'll ram some Human realities right down its processor."

"Listen to yourself. You approach research exactly as you would a raid on a Crigolit position. It is the Human approach. Even your most casual analogies are conflict-based."

"It's only a manner of speaking," he replied defensively. "You can't read overarching social evaluations into that."

They slid off the mountainside and skimmed toward the base, racing along several meters above the waves that marched shoreward into the narrow cove. A large piscine predator snapped at the slider, missing badly.

"What if we do all this and the new information you obtain confirms instead of contravenes my work?"

"I don't think it will." He tried to sound confident. "Your work has been preprejudiced by your source materials. It needs balance, and I'm going to provide it."

And if not, he thought, I can always make you forget it.

His superiors were not especially surprised by his request for leave. The loss of the delta command module and the subsequent heavy action involved in retaking the delta was enough to tire any soldier, particularly one saddled with the responsibilities of a field command. His request was granted without comment.

Only Conner wondered, but there was nothing the sergeant could say. Despite their distant family relationship Straat-ien was still a colonel and Conner only a noncom. He accepted Straat-ien's explanation that the Wais was ignorant of the Core's existence because there was no reason to doubt him, and for a time they went their separate ways.

Straat-ien asked for and received permission to spend his leave at Base Tamerlane. The original Weave installation on Chemadii, it was now far from any areas of actual combat and comparatively isolated from danger. He and Lalelelang could pursue their intentions there in comparative comfort. Base Tamerlane was also home to more support personnel than Attila. The Wais historian found comfort in the occasional company of Hivistahm, O'o'yan, and S'van.

Responding to her requests and under her direction he initiated inquiries via various entry links as well as putting through a number of Underspace connections to research resources on other worlds. His high clearance allowed him access to facilities that would have been denied someone farther down the chain of command. Conner, for example, would have gotten nowhere with many of the queries.

Their activities centered around the base library: a modest and underpopulated annex to the central command structure. As sensitive material she would never otherwise have been able to examine came pouring into the files she and Straat-ien jointly established, Lalelelang forgot her initial hesitation in the joy of dissecting a remarkable succession of documentation. So involved in their research were she and her Human associate that they had long since come to ignore the stares and comments of those who couldn't help but remark, often in their very presence, on the highly unusual working relationship.

Nothing in the flood of new material that Straat-ien was able to obtain weakened Lalelelang's hypothesis. Every fact and report they fed into her analytical program only seemed to confirm what she had initially propounded. Nevan began to worry . . . and to contemplate alternative resolutions.

It was in the middle of the second week after the information had begun pouring in that Straat-ien found something that intrigued him. If nothing else, it was a diversion. Sensitive to Human emotions and reactions, Lalelelang quickly sensed his preoccupation. She didn't probe. That would have been unforgivably impolite, if not downright Human. If it was something he intended to share with her, she knew he would mention it eventually. Meanwhile she attended to her own business, of which there was presently a delicious surfeit.

Another week passed before he chose to confide in her. Since her Huma was a match for his own and better than that of many Humans, he let her take control of the voice-activated annex unit he'd been working with.

"See this here?" He directed her attention to a portion of the material currently visible on screen.

Her neck bent forward; a supple muscular curve. "It is a spin-off of one of my programs, but I do not recognize the correlations."

"Keep looking. I didn't fabricate it to confuse you. Cross-check if you want. It's for real."

She guided the unit efficiently, superimposing a central processor of her own over his program. She was much better at it than he was, but that was to be expected.

When she was finished, everything lined up as before. Her finely boned skull turned to face him. "It is certainly interesting. Perhaps even revolutionary. But I fail to see how it bears on our current work."

"Try again. Don't you find it sufficiently provocative to pursue?"

"I just said as much, but it's a dead end. There is no way to track it further. At least, no way for us."

He was grimly pleased. "On the contrary. There is a representative of the projected distortion right here on Chemadii."

She stared at him. "I did not know."

"Why should you? For that matter why should I? I'm not privy to the inner workings of the central command team."

"I assume," she said quietly, "that its presence here is intended as a check and supplement to Human–Massood strategy."

"Yes. At least, that's what they're expected to do. That's what they've supposed to have been doing all along." He indicated the screen. "It's just that until now no one suspected they might also be up to something else. No one would. There was no way to guess at it or even imagine it— except that if you ask the right questions it shows up as a blip on your program, a nugget buried in your research. In searching for a resolution to one anomaly it seems we've stumbled onto another. Maybe one nearly as important."

"You are quite serious about this, aren't you?"

He gestured violently at the screen. "Look at the data. You're the one who's been insisting ever since we started in on this that so long as the material being fed to it is accurate your program can't lie."

"That is so. But the results can always be misinterpreted."

"Granted. So how do you interpret this?"

She eyed the readout uncomfortably. "I told you: I cannot. It does not make any sense."

"That's because you're thinking like a representative of the civilization of the Weave. If you look at it from a Human point of view the discrepancies and inconsistencies jump right out." He told the unit to flick off and it dutifully complied.

"I'm going to set up an appointment with the individual in question. Not necessarily a confrontation, because at this point all we have is abstract data. But this is too important to ignore, even if it means neglecting our other work. There's no need or reason for you to come along."

"Nonsense." She fluffed her feathers. "Of course I must come, however exomorphically this bears on my research."

"If I'm right, if my interpretation of the results is correct, there could be some risk involved."

She emitted the trilling chirp that constituted a Wais laugh. "That is absurd."

"Sure it is. As absurd as your own program's conclusions."

"Your interpretation of those conclusions," she shot back.

"My," he commented amusedly, "that tone was nearly hostile. Almost Human."

"Entreat but do not insult me."

"S'van humor, too. Maybe the Weave is more integrated than its own participants think."

"I will go with you," she said, aware that she had demonstrated a momentary but nonetheless inexcusable lack of manners, "provided that you promise not to venture any unfounded accusations. What we are seeing here is no more than your personal interpretation of some highly contestable conclusions.''

"I know, and I'm probably wrong. It's too extraordinary. But it *has* to be followed up, so that we'll know for certain. The implications are profound.'' Seeing that any further attempts to dissuade her would only intrigue her further and even make her suspicious, he reluctantly acquiesced to her request.

"We've spent a lot of time trying to disprove one theory,'' he concluded. "Hopefully it'll only take a few minutes to disprove this new one.''

★ XI ★

Lalelelang was far more uncomfortable than Straat-ien as the lift descended to the lowest inhabited level of Base Tamerlane. Perhaps because of their avian ancestry they were comfortable in high places whereas subterranean venues made them distinctly uneasy. Nevertheless, she said nothing as the lift finally slowed and the single door slid upward to allow egress.

She stayed close to him, however, marveling at his indifference to their claustrophobic, dimly lit surroundings.

"You Humans," she murmured. "You can run and jump, travel temporarily beneath water, crawl through caverns, do everything *but* fly. You're so ridiculously adaptable."

"We had to be." Straat-ien spoke while consulting the schematic he held. "As a specialist in Human affairs you must be familiar with the geologic and meteorologic caprices of our eccentric planet. It's not exactly benign, like the others which gave rise to independent intelligences. Your own homeworld, for example, is a temperate garden compared to most of Earth."

"I know. Multiple continents, multiple seas. Tectonically active. An absurd state of affairs. It explains much about your particular evolution."

"Our ancestors had to learn how to fill diverse ecological niches." He paused to briefly scan the schematic before heading down a right-hand branch. "According to this, most of the space down here is used for storage, especially sensitive or little-used items.''

That anyone would prefer to be billeted in such a wan, dank place seemed implausible. It reminded Straat-ien of pictures he'd seen of ancient dungeons on Earth. Only one species, one resident race of the Weave, found such surroundings congenial.

''Had a hell of a time setting up this appointment,'' he grumbled. ''Rank helped. We're not supposed to stay very long. Either way this shouldn't take much time to resolve.''

She remembered his cautionary words to the effect that the encounter could prove dangerous and found herself shivering. Her companion took no notice of it. The delicate Wais shivered much of the time, for reasons others could not fathom. The short feathers that formed her neck crest flexed and relaxed.

They halted before an unprepossessing door. Nevan announced himself to the small speaker set in the wall, knowing even as he did so that it was unnecessary. The visual pickup set just above the portal exposed him to the apartment's interior. A moment passed before the doorframe was suffused by a pale violet light. Somewhere within, a locktight clicked a soft electronic greeting. The barrier slid aside.

''Let me do the talking,'' he whispered to his companion.

''Why would I want it otherwise?''

They found themselves in a domed chamber. Walls and floor melted into each other. The total absence of straight angles and the patterned texture of the walls gave the room a soft, ductile feel, as though they were standing inside the organ of some vast dead animorph. Furniture—if such it was—was low and massive.

The far side of the chamber was all window; not Bullerene—there was no need for armor down here—but some other transparent material sufficiently tough to resist the modest pressure of the seawater that ebbed and surged against it. They were below the surface of the Chemadiian sea and tangent to its euphotic wonders.

Piscines with exuberantly attenuated fins migrated lazily

back and forth in small schools while a pair of long eel-like creatures chased each other in and out of the muddy bottom. Small soft-bodied things made tracks in the ooze, wending their way around spiky growths of pale green and yellow.

It was an expensive habitat, but the single occupant of the chamber had specific requirements. Its presence was considered important enough for personal whims to be indulged.

Nor were concessions made for visitors. Both Human and Wais were forced to squint to make out shapes in the gloom. Compared to the temperate climate above, these reapportioned depths were cold and clammy.

Nevan checked his translator prior to addressing the shadows. "Colonel Nevan Straat-ien and Honored Scholar Historian Lalelelang present themselves as scheduled."

"I know who you are or I would not have let you in." Despite the heroic efforts of another, unseen translator, the words emerged garbled and vague, difficult to understand.

A large shape that Nevan had initially taken to be part of the furniture detached itself from the floor and edged closer to the window, where it pivoted with patient awkwardness to confront them. Air whistled from Lalelelang.

It was the first time she'd ever encountered a Turlog in person, though she was intimately familiar with the bulky, slow-moving shape from holomages and recordings. It settled onto its multiple squat legs and gazed coolly at them out of eyes extended on thick stalks.

A hand or foot reached out to caress a nearby mound, which turned out to contain several mage screens. Straat-ien knew that it was through these that the Turlog tactician communicated its thoughts and advice to Weave command. The Turlog were not fond of exchanging ideas in person. In fact, they were not fond of company of any kind, including that of their own species, this being a principal reason why the population of the highly regarded, long-lived creatures remained always at dangerously low levels.

"I do not know why you wished so strongly to meet with me." Eyestalks bobbed and the stressed translator hissed and rumbled. "As this encounter must be as uncomfortable for you as it is for me, I ask that you state your business so that we may quickly put an end to it. While we attempt to converse I lose time of contemplation. There is strategy to be devised and reviewed and I am alone here.''

"I realize that," Nevan responded, "and we apologize."

The Turlog did nothing to contradict its kind's reputation for brusqueness. "Do not waste more time attempting to give body to the refuse of social niceties. State your business."

"You should have been informed that my Wais companion is a historian of note. Were you made aware of her area of expertise?"

"Something was mentioned about ongoing attempts to record and analyze Human–otherspecies interactions."

"That's correct." While Nevan spoke, a fascinated Lalelelang examined the remarkable creature. It resembled nothing else she'd ever encountered, Weave or foe, being in form and development more alien even than the heliox-breathing Chirinaldo.

"I've been helping her with her research," Straat-ien was saying. "She has propounded an interesting hypothesis." Startled, Lalelelang put a wingtip on his forearm. None of her colleagues could have followed through with the gesture, but it didn't matter anyway. He shrugged her off. "She suggests that when the Amplitur and their supporters have finally been defeated, we Humans will turn on our former allies out of a desperate need to continue fighting."

"Colonel Nevan!"

He smiled reassuringly. "It's all right, Lalelelang. It's only a theory. Sometimes you have to be provocative in order to get a reaction." He eyed the Turlog. "What do you think of that?"

"Interesting, as you state. I do not believe it has much validity. Of course, I have not been exposed to the data on which this theory is based. If your intention in coming here is to seek an opinion you will depart without one. I do not render unsupported analysis."

"You mean you're not even slightly interested in a hypothesis of such import even though if true it might adversely affect your own kind?''

"Why would it do that?" The creature's feet made scraping noises on the floor. "We have had only the most tenuous contact with your uncivilized people."

"Uncivilized but useful," Straat-ien responded.

"Do not feel singled out. Because of our solitary natures we choose to have as little contact as possible with all other beings. We regard this, as you would say, as a necessary evil. We regard life itself as a necessary evil."

Straat-ien was nodding. "Yet from the very start of the war the Turlog have been involved in structuring many of the classic battles against the Amplitur, long before Earth was drawn into the fray."

"You have absorbed some history yourself. This is irrelevant and untimeworthy. If you have nothing more to say, leave."

Straat-ien shifted his weight. "Not sufficiently intrigued? Then try this. I recently learned that there were three Turlog involved in the fight for a world called Houcilat."

There was no immediate response. The transparent external wall was completely noise-proofed and the only sounds in the chamber were those of three entirely different organisms processing oxygen.

"What of that?" declared the sexapodian finally.

"It seems that they survived the attack and even managed to escape the Crigolit onslaught which devastated that unlucky colony."

"So did numerous Humans, Hivistahm, and Massood."

"You Turlog have broad interests but as you say, it's rare to find two of you in the same place at any one time."

The translator choked and struggled. "You find it remarkable that three of my kind were present on that unfortunate world. It has not been so remarked upon by anyone else."

"I've recently had the chance to study some interesting correlational data. My personal motivation also happens to be rather less distanced than that of your average historian. You see, I'm fourth-generation Cossuutian Restoree."

Eyestalks rose and fell. The inflexibly carapaced face was incapable of expression, the bulbous eyes blandly unrevealing.

"That explains your interest in Houcilat. If your intention in coming here is to seek new information based on the presence there of three of my relations at the time of the Crigolit massacre I am afraid I have nothing to add to that sad piece of history that is not already available from the usual sources."

"Wait. I'm just getting started. There were also Turlog present on Coban, Eirrosad, and other Weave worlds where my genetically modified ancestors were first compelled to fight against the Weave on behalf of their then Amplitur masters."

"I do not see an end to your striving. Turlog have been present on most contested worlds, helping to devise strategy and tactics on behalf of the Weave. Human commands have benefited as much from our efforts as have any other."

"I don't deny that. Just as it can't be denied that Turlog are rarely taken prisoner on contested worlds, usually because you stay safe in places like this. It's only happened a few times. Houcilat was one of those times. So was Coban. So was Eirrosad. In each case those captured Turlog were later swapped back for Crigolit or Mazvec or other enemy prisoners of war."

"We are grateful that our value is recognized and appreciated," replied the Turlog slowly.

"Oh it is, it is." Now Lalelelang was eyeing her companion with as much puzzlement as the Turlog. Was he rambling sardonically to see what kind of reaction he could provoke, or did he have something more substantial in mind? Doubtless their host was wondering that as well.

"I'm sure your demonstrated usefulness was why the Weave was so anxious to repatriate those of you who'd been captured on Houcilat, and Eirrosad, and Coban. And the other couple of worlds in question.

"I find it fascinating that like the Amplitur, the Turlog are also ambisexual."

Legs scratched. "To what purpose do you now digress into mention of reproductive habits?"

"I'm not sure. I'm trying to make some difficult, unpleasant connections and it isn't easy. I also find it fascinating that your people were taken by the Amplitur from worlds on which my ancestors fought before they were freed from the squids' genetic machinations, and that all were subsequently repatriated."

"We have suffered our share of prisoners taken on worlds unknown to your ancestors for hundreds of years before there were Humans on Cossuut, or Houcilat, or anywhere in the Weave. We accept the possibility of capture as must any who are actively involved in contesting the mastery of a disputed world."

"How noble of you. Let's take a moment to review. Three Turlog are present on Houcilat when the Crigolit attack. Three Turlog are captured, yet survive to be repatriated even though hundreds of Humans and Massood are slaughtered. Two Turlog are taken on Coban and subsequently returned, and the process is repeated again later on Eirrosad."

"You repeat yourself now. Finish and depart. I lose contemplation."

"Contemplate this: It seems that ever since the restoration of the Humans who were modified by the Amplitur to look like Ashregan began, certain Turlog have been taking a good deal of interest in the reintegration of such individuals into normal Human society."

"Such observations are relational to the overall war effort."

Straat-ien was shaking his head slowly for no discernible reason. "None of this would have gone remarked upon if I hadn't been exposed to Lalelelang's research. Without her programs the correlations between Cossuutian and Turlog activity would've remained undetected. I wouldn't even have known what kinds of questions to ask. The funny thing is, we've been working on something else entirely. My stumbling across all these unrelated coincidences was pure accident. We call that serendipity."

"You are implying something," the translator moaned.

"The one thing I still don't understand," said Straat-ien, "is what the Turlog hoped to gain by orchestrating strategy for the Weave at the same time as they were aiding the Amplitur in their experiments on captured Humans. It strikes me that some of you people have been working at cross-purposes."

Lalelelang looked up at him in shock. There was no immediate reaction from the Turlog.

"That is a very peculiar observation," the alien said finally. "In one respect you are correct. What would we have to gain from such a contradiction? Why would anyone take both sides in a conflict?"

"Well, I have to admit that I don't know of another species that would. I suspect it has something to do with the fact that the Turlog are the only known intelligent species who can think about two distinctly different subjects at once. Not even the Amplitur can manage that."

"There are no Turlog fighting for the Amplitur. You know that we despise their grand Purpose as heartily as any member of the Weave. Your most basic research should have unequivocally shown you that." The Turlog did not sound angry or upset. From the time the conversation had begun its tone had not changed in the slightest.

"What my research has shown me," Nevan went on, "is that of all the member races of the Weave, the Turlog are the most likely to have their own agenda. I was hoping that in light of what I've found out you might be able to explain it to me. What do the Turlog actually want out of the Great War? Come on: prove to me the absurdity of my suppositions. Show me where my statistics are wrong. Convince me that my thesis is invalid."

"Many questions." The Turlog's dim silhouette shifted. "You could never convince the Weave high command of anything."

"Maybe not, but I think the Human high command would be a lot more receptive. Remember: We're basically uncivilized. Much more suspicious and untrusting than the S'van would be, or the Hivistahm.''

The Turlog settled itself atop what looked like a large block of wood fastened to the floor, but which was in actuality a far more complex structure. ''You are right when you observe that none would take such assertions seriously save your own paranoid kind. And only a few Humans could have made the unfortunate connections or would have had reason to: you unpredictable offspring of the Cossuutian Restorees.'' It made an untranslatable sound: a deep, benthic gargle. ''Always there was the potential for you to make trouble.''

''What is it talking about?'' Lalelelang turned sharply to her companion. ''What is going on here, Colonel Nevan?''

''Wheels within wheels. Take it easy.''

''I will satisfy your damnable Human curiosity,'' the Turlog was saying, ''after which it will be necessary, as I am sure you will understand, to kill you.''

Lalelelang was too stunned to shake. ''You can't do that. The Turlog are a civilized species. Among the Weave only Humans and Massood can kill.''

''You have no idea what the crabs can do.'' Straat-ien was very still. ''It's well known that our friends the Turlog are not a very gregarious bunch, like the S'van or even the O'o'yan. Are you?'' He stared at the large, flattened shape.

''You know well we dislike the company even of others of our own kind. Were it not for the need to occasionally exchange information we would all gladly exist in a state of delectable hermitage.'' Eyestalks inclined toward Lalelelang. ''You are correct in your assumption that I cannot kill in the manner of a berserker Human. I could not bring myself to utilize a gun, or a sharpened stake, or a large blunt object.''

Lalelelang responded in high-pitched but comprehensible Turl. ''I still do not understand what is happening here. If you are certain no one will believe my friend's thesis, why speak of killing us?''

''A precautionary measure. We are a meticulous species,

though it appears not as much as we might have believed.'' It shifted one eye to Nevan. ''It is difficult to conceal everything; to hide every fact, every statistic. Historical coincidence is hard to bury. I regret that your conclusions must vanish with you.''

Lalclelang had been slowly shifting her position until the heavy, muscular form of her Human companion stood between her and the Turlog. ''You said you would satisfy my companion's curiosity. I have yet to see any evidence of that.''

She was trying to stall, Nevan saw. How piquant.

''To say, as the Human does, that we are not gregarious is to grievously understate our psychology.'' The Turlog examined Straat-ien closely. ''Your revelation was an accident.''

''Many great discoveries are made accidentally,'' Nevan replied.

''Many more are never made. It would have been better for you to have overlooked this one. Did you really think you could come down here, confront me with this, and then depart quietly to tell others?''

''I had to have confirmation. Exposing myself along with what I've learned seemed the best way to draw you out.''

''And now you will rely on your skills as a Human warrior to extricate you.'' A heavy, clawed limb gestured. ''You Humans are the finest fighters the Weave has ever known, but you are not gods. You are not omnipotent. We both know that you will not leave this chamber alive.''

''What if I told you there was a whole squad of Humans stationed on the level just above us, and that if I don't contact them within a specified time they'll storm this room?''

''And do what? Kill me? I have lived several hundred of your years and have no fear of death. We regard life as a burden, an experience to be tolerated rather than savored. Perhaps this is because we are compelled to suffer so much of it trapped in physical equipment ill-suited to its enjoyment.

''In any event your ploy is futile. I have the means with which to monitor the area immediately surrounding my chambers. No cluster of ravening Humans waits to dismember me at your command.''

Straat-ien shrugged. ''All right; a bluff. But I wouldn't have done this if I didn't think I could get away.''

''Bluffs within bluffs,'' the Turlog murmured. ''Keys within keys. Strange things, keys. When they go missing they are often very close to you.'' An eyestalk sought the cowering Lalelelang.

''None of this is very complicated, historian. One of the few things the Turlog like and struggle to preserve is our privacy.''

''No one who can avoid it visits your homeworld,'' she responded, ''and you have never demonstrated any interest in colonization. Contacts between Turlog and other beings are at best minimal.''

''No, you do not understand. It is your tall companion who has puzzled it out. We like our *privacy*. Few as we are, we find our one world too crowded. The galaxy is too crowded . . . and too hostile, and too noisy. A blazing, cacophonous, febrile place in which we have been forced by sapience to share residence. Only in unimaginably vast reaches of emptiness and silence do we find the individual solace we seek. It has always been a great regret of ours that we cannot survive in a vacuum, for if we could we would surely flee to the great void between galaxies.

''Ours swarms with other intelligent beings. Constantly procreating, they spill out in all directions to fill up the pristine empty worlds, denying their solitude to those who might truly appreciate it, polluting the pure ether with their Underspace conversations and vessels. Trillions and trillions of them, all breathing and eating and reproducing.'' The Turlog's voice grew erratic. ''A vast heaving monstrosity of fleshy consciousness.''

It was an outburst Straat-ien had not expected. ''You're not saying that the Turlog had anything to do with provoking the Great War?''

''No. That would have been an uncivilized gesture. We support the war because, like every other thinking species, we have no wish to be coopted into this metaphysical Purpose of the Amplitur. Conversely, we were not disappointed by their appearance.''

"That is wicked." Lalelelang's outrage overcame her fear.

"Our perspective, as your companion has quite accurately pointed out, is different. Consider that of all the intelligent species only the Turlog can think on two subjects simultaneously. The war seemed to us a very useful way of slowing and perhaps even contracting the unbridled expansion of noxious life-forms. An extensive interspecies conflict would reduce population growth and divert resources from the settlement of blissfully empty worlds. It would, in brief, enhance privacy.

"This it has done, and we are correspondingly pleased. We welcome the demise of thousands on both sides. It would be much better if weapons of mass destruction were being employed, and we try where possible to encourage their use, but the Amplitur wish to convert the living, and the Weave to secure a civilized peace. This is regrettable. Only on one occasion did we succeed in overcoming the reluctance of attackers to exterminate on a satisfactory scale.''

"Houcilat!" said Straat-ien. "You were responsible for Houcilat.''

"No. Addled Crigolit were responsible for Houcilat. Our recommendations reached only so far. In the end those who exceeded their combat mandate were disciplined by the Amplitur. A pity they are so civilized.''

Nevan studied the Turlog. "So you advise the Weave on strategy and tactics and then pass the information on to the Amplitur so they can take appropriate countermeasures? My research led me to realize that's what happened at Houcilat, but I didn't have access to sufficient statistics to indicate how widespread the practice was.''

"It is what we do whenever possible. Regrettably we cannot be involved in every battle, every skirmish. We must also work unobtrusively so that it will not be noticed that we are playing both sides against one another. We never would have guessed that a Human would be the first to take note of it.

"We were delighted when your kind joined the war effort. Prior to that we had to work hard to insure that the Amplitur did not actually win. You have subsequently helped to rid the plenum of a great many swarming beings.

"The problem now is that as your own species multiplies, it is the Weave that is in danger of becoming ascendant. We are having trouble impeding you, but we will think of something. As the war continues it will eventually enfeeble both sides. Your overpopulated so-called civilizations will falter and collapse. It is with fondness that we anticipate your mutual annihilation. We seek not dominance but the demise of those who would dominate. Only then will the Turlog once more know true privacy. Only then can we once again be peacefully alone."

"I think you're pretty alone right now," Straat-ien told him. "You're more isolated than you can imagine."

"I sense sarcasm in place of empathy." The Turlog displaced its bulk slightly. "It is time for this conversation to come to an end."

Nevan flexed his fingers. "You're bulky and slow. I have no weapon, but I can still take you apart."

"Beneath my plastron is a switch which I can activate simply by slumping. I will point out that we are presently within a sealed environment. You may be aware of the fact that because of our very slow metabolism Turlog can survive, albeit only for a short time, at a reduced atmospheric pressure which would be fatal to most other higher forms of oxygen-breathing creatures. I do not regard the implementation of such a condition in the same light as I would wielding an article designed expressly to cause physical harm to another creature, such as a gun or knife.

"If you gesture in my direction, I will relax. This will activate the control I mentioned, simultaneously sealing the door through which you entered and exhausting the air to a degree which will be uncomfortable for me but fatal to you."

"But you're not going to do that." Straat-ien stared at the bulbous optics.

"I am not?" The heavy-shelled body drooped a little and Lalelelang inhaled sharply. "Why not?"

Nevan's gaze was unblinking, his tone even and cold. "Because I'm *telling* you that you can't."

The Turlog quivered ever so slightly. Its translator rasped. "I . . . am . . . going to."

"No you are *not*." As Nevan took a step forward Lalelelang looked on with wide eyes. "What you *are* going to do is raise yourself very carefully off the object you are straddling and move to your left, so that you're standing next to the viewport. Then you're going to *stay there* until I tell you otherwise."

"I am . . . not." Eyestalks weaving in obvious agitation, the Turlog rose and ponderously scuttled over to the ceiling-high port as reluctantly as a sumo wrestler banished from the ring by a referee's decision. Ripples of diffuse sunlight slanting down through the water mottled its dorsal plates.

Lalelelang's crest was fully erect, the iridescent feathers flashing in the sickly light. "It did exactly as you ordered, Nevan. *Why?*"

"Not now," he replied absently as he started toward the Turlog. It awaited him by the window, unable to move away. "Are all Turlog party to this duplicity? Answer me!"

The rumbling reply was hesitant. The Turlog was speaking against its will. "No. Those who choose to participate try to operate in concert. Others opt for traditional isolation, preferring to have as little contact as possible with either side."

Straat-ien emitted a grunt of satisfaction. "So the entire species isn't indictable. That's something, anyway." He redoubled his concentration.

"Stop . . . that," the Turlog murmured.

"I have to." Nevan stared, utterly focused on their host.

"It is like . . . the *Amplitur*."

"Shut *up*." Having had all his suspicions and fears confirmed, Nevan was in no mood to be gentle. He knew Lalelelang was gawking at him in astonishment but he couldn't spare her even a glance. What he was doing was delicate and required his complete attention.

Memories and knowledge helped to focus his efforts. Houcilat, his great-grandparents, the lost relations he would never know, would never know of. Much of that anguish the fault of duplicitous Turlog. But if there had been no Houcilat there would have been no Restorees, no estimable Ranji-aar, no exposition of the great dormant Human talent that was the equal of the Amplitur's. Perhaps it would have been better that way. He would never know. No one would. The talent was revealed, was real, had been passed on down through the generations and had to be dealt with by those who now possessed it. Benign or inimical, neither it nor the conditions it created could be ignored.

He decided to start with the eyestalks and work his way down to the vital organs. There would be questions, of course. A lot of questions. The Turlog were highly regarded. But he would find a way out, invent plausible excuses.

A flexible wingtip clutched at him, able to jog his conscience if not his arm. "You can't. This is a Turlog, a civilized being."

"A traitor to you, me, and the entire Weave. No better than a Crigolit or Mazvec," he responded tightly. She saw the killing look in his eyes and backed away. "It has to die."

"There will be questions."

"I'll deal with them if and when they arise. This must be dealt with. There's no other way."

He leaned forward. The paralyzed Turlog quivered but did not try to escape. It could not. The compulsion Straat-ien had placed in its mind was too compelling. "Unless . . ."

He could spare her the violence, he realized. He straightened and addressed his helpless quarry forcefully. "It's been a very interesting meeting. We value your views and I'm sure you value ours. Don't you *agree*."

The Turlog did not hesitate. "Yes. Most . . . interesting."

"It's useful sometimes for representatives of different species to exchange opinions, even on the most inconsequential matters. Isn't it?"

"Inconsequential matters." The Turlog swayed slightly. "This is manifest."

"We're going to leave now." Straat-ien turned and headed toward the entrance. Dumbfounded but alert, Lalelelang trailed alongside. "After we have departed, you will find that this existence no longer has any meaning for you, and you will take appropriate correctional measures. Thank you for your time."

"You are welcome."

The Turlog moved back to the hump in the floor. Lalelelang tensed as it shifted a heavy limb toward unseen controls, but it was only to open the door.

It closed behind them with equal efficiency. They were back in the access corridor.

She waited until the lift was within sight. "How can you be sure?"

"Sure of what?" He strode along next to her; eyes front, expression grim, thoughts elsewhere. The Core would have to be notified of the invidious duplicity of certain Turlog. Those particular antisocial aliens would have to be dealt with, as he had just dealt with their representative on Chemadii. People would have to be moved or transferred into position. The operation would be tricky and would take time, but it was less risky than trying to take out the traitors all at the same time. Physical violence on such a scale would draw to the Core far too much awkward attention.

Besides, it wasn't necessary. Those Turlog operating with Weave forces could be individually approached and queried. Then, if necessary, they could be dealt with. Merely adjusting by means of mental suggestion the attitudes of those singled out would be worse than inadequate: it would be dangerous to allow an Amplitur to make contact with a former ally who had been so treated. The entire ancient conspiracy had to be eliminated without its existence ever being revealed to the Weave at large.

All that was necessary was for a few Core members to make the right suggestions.

Lalelelang was looking back down the corridor. "How

can you be sure now that we have left that it will not revert to its original thoughts and continue as before?''

"Because I know from previous experience. It will comply with my directions."

"It won't remember what you did to it and take counter-measures?''

He shook his head curtly, knowing that she was familiar with and would recognize the gesture. "If it tries to recall our visit it will sense vague and unspecified thoughts of nothing in particular. Eventually it will stop trying to remember altogether." His tone was grim. "Then it will comply with the last of my instructions.''

The lift doors parted to admit them. "You forced its mind.''

He nudged the control for the level they wanted. The doors closed and the car began to rise. "No. I simply made a suggestion, which was accepted."

She was acutely aware of their isolation in the rising car. Yet he'd made no move toward her. "Just as you 'suggested' that it move away from the atmosphere switch it was threatening us with and stand motionless by the viewport? It was much more than a suggestion. It could not resist you. It was helpless.''

"I can be very persuasive," he told her, aware that nothing he could say would destroy what she'd seen with her own eyes.

"More than facile words were involved. The Turlog had just enough sense left to recognize that. It commented that you were having the same effect on its mind that an Amplitur would have had. You persuaded it as effectively as an Amplitur would have.'' Considering her situation, she was keeping herself remarkably under control. He could only admire her for it.

"Colonel Nevan, what are you?''

He sighed. "It's a talent very few of us possess. All who do are descendants of the Cossuutian Restorees. You remember the gist of the Amplitur experiment: to modify captured Human children to fight for them by convincing them through genetic alteration of their minds and bodies to believe they were Ashregan.

"When the great Ranji-aar, the first Ashregan-Human the Weave captured, had his Humanity surgically restored, a change neither they nor the restoring Hivistahm surgeons could have foreseen took place. The Amplitur had inserted an artificially engineered organic neural nexus into the brain of each Ashregan-reared Human child. This was designed to block the ability of the Human nervous system to defend itself against Amplitur mind probing. The Hivistahm surgeons surgically severed the connections between these introduced nexuses and the rest of the brain. They thought their work was permanent, but they underestimated the built-in resilience of Amplitur organic engineering.

"Unbeknownst to the surgeons or to anyone else, the neural connections spontaneously regenerated. But rather than following the original neuronic paths laid down by the Amplitur, the regenerated neurons instead penetrated and linked with a portion of the Human brain that is normally not in use. In so doing a previously unsuspected Human talent was activated. This turned out to be the same kind of ability to 'suggest' other intelligent beings that the Amplitur have always possessed. In our case, their careful genetic manipulation has backfired on them.

"As with the Amplitur, we cannot suggest our own kind. Nor can we communicate telepathically as they do. But as near as we can tell, our ability to withstand their probing has been fully restored. In that sense we are more complete, and therefore more dangerous, than they are. But only to them and their allies.

"We're very selective when and where we use the talent. Very selective. You witnessed an example of it that day during the battle to retake the delta from Crigolit control when you saw Sergeant Conner persuade that squad of Massood to return to the fighting."

"Ah. That explains your subsequent questioning of me."

Straat-ien nodded. "I told him you suspected nothing, which was true. At the time." He eyed her speculatively. "I didn't expect the Turlog to threaten two of us in a manner that would prevent me from dealing with it physically. When it did so I had no choice but to suggest. There was no time to try anything else.''

Calmly, he nudged the *stop* control. The lift halted between levels. She watched him turn to face her fully. ''Unfortunately, you saw more than enough to realize what was happening, even if the Turlog hadn't clued you to the truth. Now that you've had it all explained so that you understand everything, what do you think I should do with you?'' His fingers contracted, his muscles tensing expectantly. There was nothing she could do now.

She was silent but her mind was racing. Her response was not what he expected. But then, having traveled in her company and observed her for so long, he ought to have anticipated something out of the ordinary.

She did not plead for her life, nor did she try to rationalize her position. She did not attempt to argue with him.

What she said was ''Let me study you!''

''Pardon?''

''Study you. Your people, these modified Humans, they *need* a historian. Someone they can trust implicitly to watch them and record their activities, but not another Human who might clumsily expose them to the rest of the Weave, not to mention their own unmodified kind. An outsider with special training who can analyze and observe and make suggestions . . . albeit of a less forceful kind.''

''We can study ourselves,'' he murmured.

''Not in the manner of a non-Human. I can bring a perspective to your condition you cannot otherwise obtain. For another thing, I would be willing to wager that you have not a single trained sociohistorian among you.''

''I'm not aware of any,'' he sputtered, ''but that doesn't mean—''

''Of course it does,'' she said quickly. ''You have all trained to be soldiers, to fight. That is what all Humans train for initially. And that is as it should be. You do not have the expertise or the time to monitor yourselves properly. Don't you see? There is much to be learned here.''

''And I suppose you're the one to do it.''

''Who else is better trained? Who among non-Humans has spent more time studying you than I?'' Abruptly he realized that her agitation was caused by excitement rather than fear. ''I see this simply as an extension of work already begun. A fascinating adjunct.''

''A lethal adjunct.''

''Think how valuable this could be to your people,'' she argued fervently. ''I can be there; watching, recording, analyzing. It would give you a completely different purview on your development.''

He leaned against the side of the lift car. ''And when you decide you've accumulated enough data you disappear one day and reveal your findings to the Weave, thus initiating a pogrom against us.''

''No!'' The violence of her response startled him. It also startled her, but she neither apologized nor backed down. This was one instance, she mused, where it was useful to be able to assume some of the Human characteristics she'd inventoried. ''This is something I do for me as well as for you. I will place everything, all records, under your direct control.

''Besides,'' she added inexorably, ''so long as I am working in your company, you can kill me at any time. I think that I am the one taking on the greater risk here; not you.''

For a long moment he could only stare at her, so profound was his admiration.

''Records are easy to copy,'' he finally managed to comment.

''I will give all the originals into your keeping the instant they are made.''

''You bargain to save your life.''

''I argue on behalf of a unique scientific opportunity,'' she countered. Try as he might he could not convince himself that she was speaking anything other than the truth. ''If the former, why would I offer to remain at all times in close proximity to you?'' Her crest finally relaxed. ''This would be the grandest achievement of my professional career. Something eminently useful to leave behind. In your keeping, of course.''

"I don't . . .''

Seeing that he was wavering, she ventured what she hoped would be a conclusive argument. "Remember that at any time you can suggest I forget all about what happened here today. You can suggest I forget everything I have learned. You can even suggest that I kill myself, as you did with the Turlog.'' Her languorous, trilling voice grew soft. "For all that I know you may have planted such a suggestion in my mind already. Yet I still stand here offering you my help and my trust.''

She was anticipating everything, from possible objections to viable alternatives. He was having a hard time keeping up with her. For the first time he realized what a truly extraordinary mind lay behind the pale blue alien eyes, the birdlike head, the deceptively decorative feathers.

"You could kill me,'' he muttered, "and be safe, together with what you've learned.''

She emitted a whistling laugh. "I am Wais. Can you honestly see me, even with what I have experienced, planning and carrying out the murder of a Human? Even if I were insane enough to attempt it, do you really think you could not stop me?''

"Sorry. There's a lot at stake here and I have to consider every possibility.''

"I know.'' She was openly sympathetic, which only made it harder. "Let me tell you how you are presently feeling. You perceive isolation, both from normal Humans and from your own special kind. You are unique. So, in my own fashion, am I. We are both isolated, Colonel Nevan. You by an accident of genetics, I by professional choice. Each being able to appreciate the other's situation allows us to work together to mutual benefit.''

"You're crazy, you know that?'' he mumbled.

"No. I am simply one who is completely dedicated to her vocation and who sees before her the opportunity to record and study one of the most important interspecies developments of the past thousand years. I do not think that qualifies me for the tiara of madness.

"It may even be that your kind represent the heretofore undetected fulcrum on which my pessimistic hypothesis may be tipped."

He blinked. "How is that possible? I told you that we can't influence other Humans."

"Who is to say what you can or cannot do, how your people could or could not influence the course of galactic evolution? At the moment your presence on the social stage of the Weave is meager and restricted. Who is to say how and when and where that might change? You represent an entirely new component of social development. No one can say what direction your influence might take in the future, much less when the war ends.

"With each succeeding generation your talent may strengthen or weaken. You cannot predict. You can only record and study and analyze so that you will be as well prepared as possible for whatever may happen. Allow me, who can offer something none of your own kind can, to be a part of that. You need me, Colonel Nevan. You and your people need my perspective."

The slim, feathered, ebulliently attired figure gazed back at him expectantly. He knew he could wring the hollow-boned, flexible neck with one hand, just as he could suggest that once back on the surface she walk into the sea or step off the top of a high building. She was physically and mentally helpless before him.

Except . . . what she said made sense.

And he could always kill her later, choosing an even more efficacious venue.

"You're not afraid to remain in my company knowing that I could dispose of you at any time, or suggest that you do so yourself?"

"Of course I am afraid. I am dedicated, not numb. But my whole life has consisted of taking risks on behalf of my work. I am not about to change now.'' Straat-ien thought it almost a Human thing to say.

''I'll be watching you every minute. If I sense that you're going to run on me, or reveal even a hint of what you've learned—''

Her head bobbed as she interrupted. ''I know. You would be a fool to do otherwise.''

He extended a hand and she flinched instinctively.

''Honored Scholar Historian Lalelelang of Mahmahar: welcome to the Core.''

Her inflexible beak did not allow her to mimic the Human smile, nor would she have wished to. Wings and body, neck and eyes, feathers and lashes gyrated in the most refined gestures of elation.

Most of them were quite wasted on the unperceptive Human, of course.

★ XII ★

Disappointment and shock suffused the base when it was discovered that the resident Turlog had deliberately cracked the wall which sealed its chambers off from the cove, allowing seawater to pour in and drown the single occupant. Everyone was reminded that the Turlog were an incomparably morose species whose general disillusionment with life was well known. Although suicides among their kind were infrequent, they were not unprecedented. Weave command dutifully bemoaned the loss of strategic advice.

For their part, the Amplitur deplored the demise of one of their highly valuable dual operatives inside the Weave military structure, and thought no more on it. Though regrettable, such losses were insignificant to the overall conduct of the great conflict.

Straat-ien had to continually reassure himself that he'd made the right decision. Because of all they had been through together he trusted Lalelelang as much as it was possible for one of the Core to trust an outsider. In some ways it was easier than it would have been with a non-Core Human. But he watched her constantly, and was never entirely comfortable with the choice he had made.

Still, as she had pointed out, he could rectify the situation any time he wanted to if ever he found himself so inclined.

She was careful to do nothing to arouse any suspicion, working in close proximity to him at all times. As well as having her occasional off-world Underspace transmissions

carefully monitored, he had them run through extensive ci-
phernetic programming without her knowledge. Everything
always came back clean. She was not trying to secretly send
any information to her homeworld. Much of what she trans-
mitted consisted of generalities and greetings to her triadic
sisters.

Additionally, he had suspicions other than his own to deal
with.

It was inevitable that he eventually introduce her to the
other Core members on Chemadii. They were four in number: Lance Corpsman McConnell, a field captain named
Inez, and the redoubtable Sergeant Conner, who was participating in active operations and could not be present. Together they constituted the entire representation of the Core
on Chemadii.

Seated on the narrow recreational beach that fronted the
only shallow part of the cove, they regarded their squat, muscular colleague with almost as much suspicion as the diminutive, gaudy Wais who sat off to one side fiddling with her
sophisticated attire.

"I still can't believe you told her everything." Though not
much bigger than Lalelelang, Captain Magdelena Mariah
Inez could have eviscerated the Wais without working up a
sweat. As she spoke she gazed unapologetically at the historian. Lalelelang had perfected the technique of half closing
her eyes while still appearing to give her full attention to
Human acquaintances. This enabled her to better tolerate the
daunting, nerve-fraying, homicidal Human stare.

"She was there," he explained. "She asked questions.
Eventually she would have figured out much if not all of it.
And as I've explained I had reasons for filling her in on the
rest. I think her argument is sound. She can be useful to us."

"You could have tried to cover it up. Told her something
else, tried to rationalize it another way. Explained that only
you had the talent." McConnell was by far the youngest of
the trio, but his opinion was no less worthy than that of his
elders.

Straat-ien shook his head slowly. "She would've found out

for herself sooner or later. She's too good at making connections. I told you: Conner was worried that she'd eventually have seen something in his encounter with the Massood. It's better this way.''

"Unless we kill her," Inez added quietly.

Lalelelang remained calm. Straat-ien had prepared her for this and there was nothing she could do about it in any event.

He held his companions' attention. "I think that would be wasteful. I've already mentioned her own thesis, which I happen to disagree with."

"Imagine us turning on the Massood, or the Hivis, or any of the others." McConnell let out a snort of disbelief.

"She makes a good case. That's what I mean by having an external perspective. It would be very useful to the Core. I can assure you that her interest in us is purely professional." He glanced at Lalelelang. "Look at her. Do you think she's standing there wondering if we're going to vote to execute her?" In spite of themselves McConnell and Inez both found themselves turning to the inoffensive Wais. "No. She's lamenting the fact that I told her she couldn't bring out her equipment to record this meeting. And if we did vote to have her killed she'd want to record that, too. There's nothing there but an independent spirit of inquiry wrapped in a bundle of feathers."

"I don't know . . ." Inez remained unconvinced.

"She even thinks our existence might act as a moderating influence on what she sees as our inevitable postwar hostile tendencies."

Inez blinked, looked back to the colonel. "Assuming there's any validity to her crazy theory in the first place, how could we do that? You must have told her we can't influence other Humans."

"She insists we don't know everything there is to know about ourselves and the talent. You can't argue with that. Nobody can. The Restoration is only a few generations old. Who's to say what may or may not eventually evolve? We're all still learning as we go. I can think of a lot of instances in which it would be safer and more useful to have a non-Human opinion on Core matters than that of, say, a non-Restoree Human.''

McConnell was nodding. ''My experience is subordinate here, sir, but I see your point. *If* she's telling the truth and if she's completely trustworthy.''

''I've explained the safeguards I've put in place,'' Straat-ien responded. ''She knows that I can kill her whenever I wish, or have her kill herself. She knows that either of you could kill her or suggest that she do away with herself independent of anything I could do to stop you.''

''That's true enough,'' Inez murmured diffidently.

Lalelelang heard and quantified the implied threat as abstract data. If you could mentally reduce every aspect of uncivilized Human activity to mere data you could somewhat distance yourself emotionally from their maniacal behavior. It was a survival skill she had mastered out of necessity.

''Yet there she sits, silent and composed, while a trio of Humans calmly debates her possible termination. Does she plead for her life or try to flee? No. You know why?'' Straat-ien smiled. ''Because all she wants to do is help, and because even though we insisted she leave her equipment behind, she's still working, still observing. She's not interested in giving us away. Because if she did, it would mean she'd lose the chance to study us.''

Inez and McConnell exchanged a glance. The captain faced her superior. ''You're senior here, Colonel, both in age and experience. I won't deny that I'm less than entirely comfortable with this development, but I can see the points behind your argument. If you vouch for her cooperation, if you're that sure of this alien, then I defer to your judgment.''

''Same here,'' McConnell added readily.

Lalelelang said nothing, betrayed nothing outwardly, but inside she untensed. On this peaceful, cool beach in the company of unarmed, discursive Humans she knew she'd come nearer to dying than at any time on either of the battlefields she'd visited.

Straat-ien, too, allowed himself to relax. ''I'm glad you

agree. I don't think this is a decision any of us or any of our relatives will ever have occasion to regret.''

"This business of the Turlog." Inez's expression mixed bitterness and disbelief. "To think that they've been playing both sides; developing tactics for us and then relaying those same tactical decisions to the enemy, just to try and reduce the general population of intelligent beings and give themselves a little more 'privacy.' It's as perfidious as anything the Amplitur have ever done.''

"They can't help themselves," Straat-ien explained. "It's the way they've evolved. Fortunately the number involved seems to be small. I've been able to do some follow-up checking already, thanks to Lalelelang's help.'' McConnell and Inez glanced approvingly at the Wais. "Because of that intense love of isolation only a small portion of the species are active participants in planning Weave strategy, and not all of those are working in a dual capacity. Remember: They like to operate independently of one another.''

"According to what you've told us the number involved is big enough to have caused a lot of trouble,'' Inez commented.

McConnell was nodding in agreement. "What do we do about it?''

Straat-ien was scooping up fine gravel with his right hand, letting the wave-polished nodules trickle out between his fingers. Most of it was jade or jasper, with some agate and moonstones scattered throughout the mix. A beach of semiprecious gems.

"We'll pass the word along to Core members on those worlds where Turlog are active in military matters. They can arrange to have a private conversation with each participant. Those who are in contact with the Amplitur will be dealt with on an individual basis. Some coordination will be necessary: we can't have a dozen or more Turlog simultaneously involved in fatal accidents.''

"If you'll design the overall program, sir, I'll take care of the necessary transmissions,'' Inez declared.

"Done. Just keep me posted, Captain.''

Lalelelang listened and despite her experiences was dazed. The Humans discussed the possible termination of so many intelligent beings as dispassionately as if they had been planning to fumigate their living quarters. There was no hesitation in their speech, no regret in their manner. Not once did they mention possible alternatives, no doubt having in their own minds already dispensed with the unviable option of civilized behavior.

As they went about their planning they ignored her completely, for which she was grateful. Despite her medication and exercises she could not possibly have participated in the discussion. Merely being present and having to overhear was a daunting experience.

Inez rose. "You know, Nevan, that we can't keep this development to ourselves." She eyed the silent, elegant Wais. "Higher authorities within the Core will have to be notified."

"I intend to take care of that myself. I'm confident they'll agree with me, too." He gestured in Lalelelang's direction. "She knows we can't keep this meeting a secret, nor does she want to do so. The more Core members who know about her, the better her access to research opportunities."

"Very brave or very stupid," Inez muttered.

"I am neither." Now that her fate—for the immediate future, at least—had been decided, Lalelelang felt no compunction against speaking. "I am simply dedicated to my work. I have always been thus."

"Admirable," Inez declared. "In this instance, also foolhardy."

"Please. If you wish to belittle me, use forethought before speaking."

Wais, the captain thought. Even if one's life was at stake it could not help but be overbearing.

"I'm glad you trust her so implicitly, Nevan," Inez whispered later as together with McConnell they walked toward Underspace communications, "but if I were you I still wouldn't let her out of my sight any more than absolutely necessary. No matter how much she insists she wants to study us, wants to help, she's still non-Human. Still a *Wais*."

"Yes and no. She's advanced beyond speciesism. She's pure scientist."

"I hope you're right," Inez mused as they turned a corner. "I hope to God you're right. Because it's a hell of a chance you're taking on a bundle of easily rattled, overornamented alien fluff."

Not to mention the burden she's placing on herself, he added silently.

His inner turmoil played out on his countenance like the shifting patterns on the face of a dune subjected to a hot and relentless wind. Lalelelang marveled at the range of expressions of which the highly flexible Human face was capable. The inflexible Wais beak precluded such facial eloquence, but Lalelelang's people more than made up for the deficiency with a breathtaking range of physical gestures unmatched in depth and detail by any other intelligent species.

"You are still not sure of this, are you? Or of me."

They were on their way to a morning briefing. He glanced down sharply. "What do you mean?"

"I heard everything you told your two friends, but in your own mind you are still not so convinced. You are not sure whether to try and help me with my own work, try to make use of me, or kill me. These thoughts circulate continually in your mind and try as you might you cannot be rid of them. The result is that your spirit is unsettled."

"Not hard to tell that you've been studying us for a long time." He was a bit overwhelmed by her perception.

Even as she responded with a reflexive gesture she knew he would not understand it. "As I have so often stated, it is my work. No other intelligent species suffers such internal torment, over the meaning of existence or anything else. Your runaway racial angst is a product of your bizarre endocrine system."

"We realized that a long time ago," he told her.

"But you have not yet learned how to cope with it. No wonder you are so abnormally violent. No wonder you throw yourselves into fighting with such desperate delight. You suffer from a traitorous body chemistry.''

He could sense the pity and empathy in her tone.

"Don't disparage it. If we were 'normal' we wouldn't be half so useful to the Weave.''

"That is so, and happens to be an area of study of particular interest to me. But it cannot prevent myself or others from feeling sorry for you. A pity you talented Restorees cannot suggest other Humans.''

"I agree, but why?''

"You could probably work a therapy deep enough to make some real improvements.''

They turned up a narrow corridor. "Happy Humans won't help defeat the Amplitur.''

"Sadly so.''

The process of weeding out the duplicitous Turlog proceeded efficiently and unobtrusively. Core members passed information to relatives on other worlds, usually by means of Underspace-transmitted special codes, more rarely in person. By and by, certain Turlog met with unfortunate accidents. Their demise provoked no special curiosity among their brethren, who had no more interest in the individual doings of their own kind than in the activities of other species.

It did somewhat reduce the Weave's ability to develop and master complex new strategies. That was nothing compared to the intelligence loss suffered by the Amplitur. Hard as those persistent and patient adversaries sought an explanation for the hemorrhaging, they could find nothing.

The retaking of the delta and a host of additional bases and fortifications farther up the great river broke the back of enemy resistance on Chemadii. Thereafter, enemy actions were reduced to a stubborn but steady retreat as Weave forces reduced or removed them all across the planet. What reinforcements the Amplitur managed to divert Chemadii-way proved insufficient and ineffectual in the face of the remorseless, Human-spearheaded Weave assault.

When finally their planetary headquarters itself came under attack, they launched the usual convulsive final counterattack. Doomed to failure, it did allow the enemy command staff time to escape to an Underspace transport waiting in orbit. Ships winked in and out of Underspace and, as usual, the Weave failed to interdict the refugees.

This failure was mitigated by the official capture of the last enemy resistance on Chemadii. Another world had been freed from Amplitur control, released from involuntary submission to an alien and inflexible Purpose.

So extensive had Lalelelang's store of information become that she knew there were whole areas of specialization she would never live long enough to study in anything other than the most cursory manner. Those Wais who came after her and who chose to make use of it would have material enough to keep them profitably occupied for a decade.

Yet she was reluctant to stop. Such an opportunity might never come again, to her or any Wais. So she continued to trail Straat-ien even to the most boring gatherings, observing and recording and making notes about the most routine activities.

He ignored her, having grown so used to her being virtually underfoot that his daily routine would have seemed incomplete without her inquisitive presence. This was also true of those he worked with. The early flood of jokes and snide remarks had dried up. No one remarked anymore on her attendance at meetings or the questions she eagerly posed to startled soldiers in corridors or the recreation hall.

Despite the pullout of the enemy command unit, mopping up of isolated Crigolit outposts continued even as permanent ground-based defense systems were installed. The latter was necessary to forestall any enemy attempts to reestablish themselves on Chemadii. In the early centuries of the war the Weave had been caught out several times when it had been lulled into believing it had won control of a disputed world, only to have the Amplitur counterattack in force and regain dominance, at severe cost to the Weave in personnel and material.

That was long before Humans had entered the conflict.

Being highly civilized, the Amplitur were not mentally geared to designing combat strategy. Like the Massood and the Ashregan and the Hivistahm and all the other civilized races, they had to learn through an awkward combination of trial and error. This was a process with which Humans had no such difficulty. In the combat that was natural to them they never hesitated. Even as this facility remained a great conundrum to the rest of the Weave, they recognized it for the advantage it was and made use of it at every opportunity. The Amplitur and their minions were slow to react.

It was no wonder the tide of battle had taken a distinct and measurable turn.

Lalelelang squatted on the porch of her room, which overlooked one of several armored atriums that connected the multiple wings of the base. It was as comfortable to sit on the flat, bare extruded plastic as anywhere within because none of the furniture had been designed with Wais in mind. A Wais presence was neither required nor expected on a disputed world, therefore no facilities for them were included in construction schematics. She had to make do with a room intended for the occasional visiting S'van advisor. The S'van were squat and stocky while the Wais were slim and fragile, except in the middle. So the apartment was not comfortable. Worse, it was not even decorated. Wais and S'van living priorities were very different.

She coped. It was better than sleeping outside the complex, in the field. And S'van facilities were easier to deal with than their prodigious Human equivalents. At least she could reach certain vital components.

She let her gaze rise to the transparent roof of the covered corridor. Now that Chemadii had been freed, the armor shielding had been drawn back permanently, letting in the warm coastal sunshine. The several local plants she had adopted in an attempt to give the stark domicile a dash of Wais-inspired color strained upward.

The door chuckled, in the preferred manner of a S'van announcement, and she rose to acknowledge her visitor. She was mildly surprised to see Straat-ien. It was unusual for him to seek her out.

She stepped aside to admit him, and he had to duck to clear the low S'van doorway and ceiling. Ignoring the useless, too-small furniture, he made himself as comfortable as he could on the padded floor, wedging his bulky anthropoid frame against the wall.

"Refreshment?" she ventured. "Drink or food?"

"No thanks." He glanced briefly toward the open porch.

"Not that you avoid me," she continued, "but it is not like you to seek me out. I take pleasure in your company."

"You don't have to run the usual Wais politeness at me," he replied. "We've worked together long enough not to need to pretend. I know that like any Wais you find my physical presence unpleasant, especially in an enclosed space. You just tolerate it better."

His brief reply contained more violations of simple etiquette than the average Wais would commit in a year, she knew. She ignored it, as she ignored all such Human bumbling. You could not work with them otherwise.

"There's something I think you should know." It struck her that he was wrestling with some inner torment. "I've come to trust you, Lalelelang. No, I mean really trust you."

She half shut her eyes against that penetrating, unconsciously feral stare. "I know that. Were it otherwise I certainly would have met with an unfortunate accident some time ago."

"That's right." He made not the slightest attempt to disguise the fact, diplomatically or otherwise. "I trust you because I'm convinced that you're utterly wedded to your work. To studying us, and to proving or disproving your long-held thesis about how my species is going to react once the war is ended." He glanced toward the porch again.

"I've spent a lot of time thinking about that myself. We've discussed it so often I can't help but think about it."

"I know that." He seemed to need prompting.

"Lalelelang, among my suggestive relations far and near, I hold one of the highest ranks within the military. I've acquired substantial rank in a comparatively short time. Within the Core there are only three who outrank me. One of them is a General Couvier, who's presently stationed on Ascej.''

''I do not know the name.''

''No reason you should,'' he grunted. ''He doesn't travel in academic circles. I've just received a personal communication from him. So have all other high-ranking Core members. There's normal chain-of-command and then there's Core chain-of-command.''

She indicated her understanding. ''The latter being utilized to deal with such matters as the occasional turncoat Turlog.''

He nodded. ''Over the years we've developed our own extended family code and other clandestine methods of exchanging information. We had to. You know what would happen if our talent became common knowledge.''

''You did not seek me out in this cramped room to remind me of that which I already know.''

''No, I didn't.'' He hesitated, obviously gathering his thoughts. ''It seems that the chance to make a final determination of the validity of your life's work may not lie so far in the future as you thought. For that matter, as anyone has thought.''

She slid off the uncomfortable curved S'van lounge. ''What are you talking about, Nevan?''

''Couvier has informed me that Chemadii was apparently the last step in a long ongoing strategy, the last link in a chain of preparation that Weave command has been struggling to forge for several hundred years. But that's not the kicker. The real secret concerns something that's been known for the past half-century but has only recently been revealed to soldiers of Couvier's rank. That tells you a lot right there.'' He looked around. ''I *would* have something to drink but you wouldn't have anything here I'd find strong enough to be useful.''

''My apologies.''

''Couvier is notifying those Core members who rank immediately below him. We're to take it from there. But I've decided to inform you also, because it bears on your work. Heavily.'' He leaned toward her.

''We now know the location of the Amplitur homeworlds.''

Her crest erected as she fully digested his announcement. ''Can that be true? Captured Mazvec and Korath and others have always said that the Amplitur homeworlds were impossibly distant.''

''Distant, apparently. Impossibly, no. There are two, in the same system. Both fairly unexceptional, with oxynitro atmospheres and conventional gravity. The third and fifth worlds from their sun. Apparently there's no doubt that they're the original Amplitur homeworlds and not early colonies. As you know, the Amplitur were not active colonizers. They've tried to take control of everything else instead.''

''I am impressed.''

''That's just the ribbon on the package. Consider this: In the last decade a lot of troops and ships and material has been positioned. Quietly and carefully, so as not to provoke questions either among the enemy or the Weave population itself. I'm sure you never noticed it or thought about it. Neither did I or anyone else I know. Only the top level of Command knew what it was all really for.

''There's been a vast accumulation of forces in an otherwise relatively tranquil sector. Sources have been alluding vaguely for years to preparations for a major assault on Chi'Khi, the Crigolit home system. Well, an assault is in the works, all right, but when it comes it'll be in another direction, and through a much bigger chunk of Underspace.

''The intent is to attack the fifth world, Eil, and then move on quickly to hit Ail before the Amplitur have time to regroup and mount a significant defense of either world. If it's successful you know what that'll mean.''

Lalelelang thought back, considering the hundreds of years of intermittent but endless conflict that had existed between the Weave and the Amplitur ever since some Massood had first gone to the aid of a race called the Sspari. A thousand years of resistance to the all-dominating Amplitur Purpose, a millennium of fighting and dying.

If the secret Amplitur homeworlds had indeed been found, if they could be attacked and taken, it would mean the End of the War.

How did one contemplate such a prospect? Generation upon generation had lived and died without giving it a passing thought, ever cognizant of its impossibility. Now a killing Human sat hunched over in her living quarters telling her in its intolerably brusque, straightforward fashion that such a thing was within reach.

"The Amplitur homeworlds," she found herself whispering. "It *would* mean the end, wouldn't it?"

"A thousand years and more of war finished, over," Straatien mused aloud. "The genetically and mentally altered subject races of the Amplitur, freed. There would be a grand realignment of alliances and agreements. Maybe a true galactic civilization, something less forced by circumstance or exigency than the Weave. In a word, peace. If not contentment."

Odd, she thought, to hear a Human speculating on a state his species had never known.

"It also means that your theories will be put to the practical test," he went on, "possibly in your own lifetime. If surprise can be maintained and the attack succeeds, there'll be no more Mazvec or Crigolit or Ashregan or Amplitur for my kind to do battle with. We and the Massood will disarm, to the thanks of a grateful Weave. My people will be expected to return quietly to Earth, there to resume prewar pursuits." He shifted his position on the floor.

"Except that we can't all return to Earth. There are too many of us now, scattered in large concentrations across many worlds besides those we've begun to colonize. Human procreation was encouraged and supported by the Weave. We were urged to produce as many soldiers as possible to assist the Massood in combating the subject Amplitur races. Those men and women will be looking for new occupations, which can only be found within the greater commercial alignment of the Weave. We'll at last have to be invited in because being left out is not a viable alternative."

Isn't it? she wondered.

"You don't think that's going to happen. Your hypothesis says that we won't be able to handle the peace, that we'll pick a fight with the S'van or some other species."

"As I have wished all along, I hope that I am proven wrong," she said sedately. "A new war, between Humankind and the Weave, would be to no one's benefit."

"We'd win any such conflict," he murmured. "You know that."

"With the Massood once again fighting on behalf of the Weave, and with all the logistical support that implies? I am not so certain. I am sure only of the unnecessary destruction that would ensue. Devastation would be the only victor in such a confrontation." She gazed at him out of wide blue eyes. "It was admirable of you to confide this in me."

He rose, bending slightly to avoid the ceiling. "I didn't do it on impulse or because of my good nature. I had to think about it long and hard. But I know from experience how good you are at keeping secrets. Your work's become an important part of my life. I thought it was time to give something back."

She performed an intricate seated dance of deliberation, which Straat-ien admired without understanding. "It may still remain something for our descendants to deal with. The attack may fail, or the fight continue for many years."

He nodded. "That's right. But if nothing else, the discovery shortens the war. The Amplitur will throw everything into defending their homeworlds, which means they'll have to draw resources away from other theaters of operation. The fall of the Mazvec and their other allied races will be accelerated."

She saw him to the door, trailing his bulk. "That may yet take hundreds of years."

He turned in the corridor, bending to face her. "There was a time when that might've been true. But not anymore. Remember: *We're* involved."

She closed the door behind him, knowing he spoke the truth, wishing he did not. His revelation of forthcoming Weave military intentions cast a radical new perspective on

her own work. It was unsettling enough to have to deal with
it as theory.

Was it selfish of her to want to live out her life span before
she or any of her kind had to deal with it as fact?

"I thought we had something special, Nevan."

He continued with his packing, feeling her eyes on his
back.

"You could request that I travel with you," she went on
earnestly, "as an aide or . . . I don't know. You're clever, you'd
think of something. You've got enough rank to pull it off."

He shut and sealed the travel case. "It's no good, Naomi.
Your rating doesn't qualify you. It would look like just what
it is. Someone would notice and there'd be trouble. Trouble
no amount of rank could make disappear." He fingered the
lock on the case, tuning it to the specific electrical output of
his own body, then moved to its nearby waiting mate.

He smiled inwardly as he thought of Lal. She would think
his luggage impossibly utilitarian. Her equivalent was exquisitely contoured and embellished, reflective of traditional
Wais design.

Naomi was persistent. Maybe she had a right to be, Nevan
thought bleakly, but it couldn't be helped.

"Are you going to just walk out of here, out of my life,
and pretend that you don't feel anything between us anymore? I know better, Nevan. You can lie to me, but you can't
lie to yourself." Her tone was starting to crack around the
edges, like a stressed recording.

He was packed. Suddenly there was no more reason to
fool with the cases. So he turned. "Chemadii's been a lonely
and dangerous posting. I had certain needs, you had certain
needs. I think we complemented each other very well.

"I'd like to keep in touch, Naomi. I'd like that very much."
He reached out to lightly stroke her cheek. "But asking me
to break rules and regulations so that you can come with me,
that I can't do. Our work doesn't overlap, doesn't even brush
against each other. I'm not risking my career for you, or even
for us. Hell, I'm not going to risk *your* career.

"If we were simultaneously posted to Earth, or some diplomatic station, it might be different. But that isn't going to happen. Unfortunately, this is the way the Service works. Believe me, this isn't easy for me, either. It's just something we're going to have to deal with. Both of us."

Eyes moist, she pulled away from his hand. "Where are you being sent?"

"I can't tell you. You know that."

She nodded, then looked back at him so sharply he blinked. "I'll bet *she's* going."

"Going? Who?" Her intensity momentarily stunned him.

"The canary you're always running around with. That damned Wais."

It took a moment for the implausibility of the situation to sink in. When it finally did he could only gape at her in disbelief.

"Naomi, you're not jealous of an alien? You're not implying that historian Lal, a Wais of Mahmahar, and I have some kind of relationship other than professional?" He shook his head in astonishment. "What other kind of relationship *could* we have?"

Naomi was equally conscious of how inane it sounded. That didn't stop her. "You see her almost every day. You work together by yourselves. When she requires your presence you respond, when you have something to say to her she appears instantly at your side. You confide in her, you've told me that yourself." She folded her arms defiantly across her chest. "I'd call that a relationship. You don't have to define it any further."

"I don't *confide* in her."

"No? You share secrets. I know you do, because when I've asked you about certain things the two of you talk about you've refused to tell me about them."

"That's part of my job. Work, strictly work." This was becoming irritating.

"Is it? One hears stories, tales. I always took them for sleazy jokes, but if you're out in the field long enough you find yourself starting to wonder about everything."

"Naomi," he said tightly, "you're letting your remorse, not to mention your imagination, run away with you."

"Am I? I'd like to think so. You're the one who's running away, Nevan."

He inhaled deeply. "I am not 'running' anywhere. As you're perfectly aware, I've been transferred. You're being impossibly—"

"What?" she interrupted him. "Romantic? Maybe. Isn't it the Wais who say we have no notion of true romance, of real beauty? That our conception of romance is nothing more than a flaccid derivative of our antagonistic nature? Maybe they're right." She managed a weak shrug. "I'd like to prove them wrong, right now, right here. But I guess I can't, can I?"

"Historian Lal and I respect each other for the ability each of us brings to our respective professions."

"Of course you do." Her voice fell as her interest waned. "All I know is that that ornithorp sees you ten times as much as I do. For all I know—"

Angry now, he cut her off. "You don't know anything!"

"No. No, I guess I don't." Eyes forward, back straight, she strode stiffly past him, not looking back. The door sensed her approach and obediently slid aside, closing behind her.

He stood silently at the foot of the bed, knowing that going after her would only make things worse. If she'd been Core, now—but if she'd been Core the whole confrontation wouldn't have been necessary, would never have happened.

A painful end to a nurturing relationship, as ludicrous as it was unnecessary. He sighed wearily. With Chemadii secured, Naomi would be receiving her own transfer orders soon enough. If the general was right, and there was no reason to doubt his information, the entire armed forces of the Weave were soon going to be so busy that there would be little time to explore personal relationships of any kind. He couldn't very well have told Naomi that, of course. Somehow he suspected it wouldn't have made any difference.

He knew they'd grown close. Combat assignations were frequent, even necessary for the psychological health of those involved. Evidently Naomi had been seeking something more. As busy and self-absorbed as he'd been it wasn't surprising that he'd missed the signs.

Naturally he and Lal had become good friends; confidants, even. That was for reasons he couldn't enumerate to anyone else, much less the talkative Naomi. He and the Wais respected each other's knowledge and expertise. If that constituted a ''relationship,'' then so be it. To reach beyond that far enough to suspect improprieties of a type reserved for the more outrageous forms of fiction was the consequence of an unhealthy mind.

As he prioritized his personal effects for pickup he tried to be charitable. Naomi was obviously disappointed, maybe even devastated. That was unfortunate. He was convinced he'd done nothing to encourage her to expect anything beyond mutual comfort and succor. She would get over it, just as he would. Did she think he felt no sense of loss himself?

He forced himself to shunt personal concerns aside. They'd located the Amplitur homeworlds. What must it be like for members of the Weave, to have lived with the burden of a thousand years of war, to suddenly see a possible end in sight? It was an achievement Humankind would be able to share only in comparative moderation. To those Massood and S'van who had been informed, whose people had been among the first to resist the Amplitur, it must seem as if the universe had turned inside out.

He took a last look around the compact, comfortable room that had been his home on Chemadii. That wasn't quite accurate, he reminded himself. A soldier had no home: only duty postings. Another planet recovered for the Weave, another world liberated from the suffocating grip of the Purpose. Years of effort and sacrifice validated. Now as before, it was on to the next.

Only this time, for the first time, it was not inconceivable that the next could also be the last.

★ XIII ★

Discouragement and despair hung over the Council like a toxic fog, poisoning thoughts and polluting the atmosphere. This was not entirely metaphor, as the members could not help but project what they were feeling.

The Council was not a permanently constituted organizational body. Individuals came and went according to appointment and caprice, out of a desire to contribute or a need to depart. Whether long in tenure or brief in participation, all were renowned for their skill, their learning, their experience.

All that and more would now be required of them if the apocalypse was to be avoided.

They lounged in a shallow, steaming pool of sulfurous salt water, the informality of the surroundings belying the seriousness of the occasion. Painstakingly cultivated growths of dark green and rust red thrust through the murk, adding color to the amphitheater and perfume to the air.

The water helped to support the soft-bodied masses of the participants. Tentacles shifted from bodies to controls as squarish mouths sipped at the water or sucked at the air. The information provided by the instrumentation was extensive without being reassuring. Yellow-green light emanated from the milky, translucent overhead dome, from which dangled additional devices, each ready to respond to a voiced command or specific physical gesture.

The members of the Council did not face each other because they had no need to. They lay scattered randomly like a primordial herd, their turgid, sluglike bodies flashing silver-orange or orange-gold in the hazy, subdued light, their four stumpy legs gathered beneath them. Plate-sized eyes of slitted gold and black regarded respectively the landscaped flora, the pungent water, or a lolling neighbor. Each occupied whatever position happened to most suit it at the moment.

The extensive instrumentation was needed for education and external communication only, since all present were far more intimately linked by their remarkable projective minds. As a result, the atmosphere in the Council chamber was as thick with disillusionment as it was with solemn, cloying moisture.

In keeping with the ancient and redoubtable tenets of the Purpose there was no Supreme Leader, no Grand Potentate. All present were more or less equal, though individual accomplishments and abilities were recognized and respected. Whoever happened to be discoursing was at that moment the one in charge. When it concluded, control would be passed to another of its lugubrious brethren. It was a system to which lesser races, only dimly versed in the depths of the Purpose, could but dimly aspire to.

There were no representatives of those eager species in attendance; no Mazvec, no Ashregan, no Crigolit or Acaria or Korath. This was the Grand Council of the Amplitur. From it suggestions, and suggestions only, would be issued to those most worthy allied life-forms. Suggestions which were invariably acted upon.

In spite of strenuous efforts on the part of those present as well as their advisors, there existed a serious dearth of suggestions, a lack of laudable ideas on how to proceed. Even the Purpose itself no longer gave the kind of inspiration which had buoyed the Amplitur in their great work down through the centuries. This plagued sorely the members of the Council, who knew it was incumbent upon them to decide when, how, and what to do next.

"We must face reality." It was Nigh-cold-Singing who formulated the thought. "We are losing." That no protesting thoughts arose to contradict showed how somber was the mood within the chamber. "We have been losing ground for more than a hundred years."

"Ever since," supplemented Bulk-holds-Tree, "the species Human allied itself with the Weave."

"What a pity," noted Sand-sits-Green plangently, "that they could not first have been contacted by us and brought joyfully into the Purpose."

"I have long studied what we know of them and their evolution." Takes-short-Thinking was among the most learned present. When it ventured a thought, all paid attention. "They believe among themselves that they could never have been convinced of and brought into the Purpose. Sadly we had not the opportunity to persuade them of the folly of their own self-deception."

Takes-short-Thinking was preparing to give birth. The tumescent bud on its back had matured into a miniature version of itself and was on the verge of separating from the parent body. Its presence in the Council chamber at such a delicate and sensitive moment was due only to the extreme nature of the current crisis.

"We cannot change history." Places-change-Distant was senior among the assemblage. Mottled orange skin had faded to a deep rust hue, and the penetrating eyes no longer gleamed as brightly. But within the puffy mass of rippling flesh floated a mind as keen as ever.

"Those with us in the Purpose—the Mazvec and Crigolit, the Ashregan and Segunians and the others—are doing the best they can." Tepid water sucked at High-run-Seeking's lower body as it shifted its position. "But Human-Massood forces supported by Weave technology and supplies now defeat us at every turn. We have had some success at imitating enemy tactics, but an imitator can never ultimately defeat an originator. I fear we have reached the point of only postponing the inevitable."

"There must be something we can do." Sand-sits-Green's tentacles traced brooding patterns in the humid air.

"Not as long as Humans continue to dominate in critical

battles,'' said Bulk-holds-Tree. ''Since they joined with the Weave, our enemies have pushed us back, taking one world after another, sometimes with impunity. We hurt them, and sometimes we win back lost minds, but these creatures are dangerously prolific, moreso even than the Massood. Amazingly, the more losses they suffer, the harder they fight.''

''They are unique and could not have been anticipated.'' Nigh-cold-Singing stirred the air with both tentacles. ''Defeat strengthens their resolve, loss intensifies their efforts. They are an infernal paradox. Naturally the Weave is careful to do nothing that might influence their behavior, such as trying to civilize them.''

''They are no more than cognitive organics, like ourselves,'' the somewhat reticent Red-sky-Thinking asserted. ''There must be a way they can be overcome.''

''We have tried one new strategy after another.'' Bulk-holds-Tree slapped at the water. ''None work for long. This species is too adaptive. And unlike us or any of our allies, they are naturally warlike.''

''There must be a way,'' Sand-sits-Green insisted. ''New weapons are under development, additional ships under construction.'' Damp eyes probed the others. ''It has even been suggested that we employ orbital devices of mass destruction.'' Shocked exclamations arose from every mind present, and Sand-sits-Green hastened to explain.

''I said that this was suggested. It was naturally not countenanced.''

Places-change-Distant stirred uncomfortably. ''Millions slain are millions lost to the Purpose. Besides which the Weave, and certainly the Humans, would respond in kind. The result would be devastated worlds, obliterated populations: a vast gap in the onward march of the Purpose.''

''And yet,'' Sand-sits-Green continued, ''if the Weave is ultimately triumphant, the Purpose goes out of the universe forever. Of what use then civilized behavior?''

''Scaling up the level of annihilation might destroy but could never defeat them.'' Takes-short-Thinking snapped out the thought, clean and crisp. ''As Places-change-Distant points out, the Weave will match or surpass anything we instigate militarily. What is wanting is a new approach, perhaps even a new way of thinking. Age inevitably admits ossification. We need to reexamine ancient tenets and traditional approaches.'' Specular eyes blinked at the ends of stubby eyestalks. ''It is time to entertain antitheses.''

Glean-blue-Saying was younger than many on the Council. It had participated previously, dropped out to pursue other tasks, and only recently been readmitted. It was noted for a certain skewed manner of thinking, and its contributions were highly regarded among those for whom eclecticism was considered an attribute. Though not famed for deep analysis, Glean-blue-Saying was frequently cited as an innovator whose ideas were sifted intently for kernels of usefulness by others with more experience. Among the dozens of often dubious proposals it proffered there came forth the occasional gem.

So when that worthy finally sallied thoughts into the general pool of contemplation, all paid attention. Whatever Glean-blue-Saying had to contribute might not prove useful, but was certain to be entertaining.

''I agree with Takes-short-Thinking. We must do something radical and unprecedented. I agree also with Nigh-cold-Singing: we are losing, and will continue to lose, because we cannot defeat the Humans. To triumph ultimately we must assay something else.'' The rest of the Council listened patiently, if not hopefully.

''Let us consider what we know. Humankind is the only semi-intelligent naturally warlike species ever discovered. They are defined by their aggressiveness, their combativeness, and the adaptation of their bodies as well as their minds to warfare.'' Glean-blue-Saying paused significantly.

''In fact, it is not unreasonable to assume that the only beings who can ultimately defeat Humans are other Humans.''

''All this is known,'' said Places-change-Distant impatiently. ''Our forbears attempted a practical adaptation of that hypothesis by modifying captured Humans to look and think like Ashregan.''

''The Houcilat-Cossuut project.'' Red-sky-Thinking's remembrance was tinged with regret. ''A concept turgid with promise but ultimately a costly failure.''

''We have in the Molitar allies who are individually stronger than Humans but far less mobile, intelligent, or, one might say, predatory. Work continues on modifying them, but genetic structures are far less malleable than recalcitrant thoughts. Progress is slow.'' Places-change-Distant saw the meeting going nowhere and was anxious to return to more useful work. A challenge was issued to Glean-blue-Saying. ''What is your point?''

The individual so addressed hung motionless in the pool. ''All of us are aware of the rumor that the Weave has discovered the location of sacrosanct Ail and Eil and that they are preparing, despite elaborate efforts to deceive us as to their actual target, to attack massively. It would seem that even here, on the hallowed twin worlds that gave birth to the Purpose, we are no longer safe. If there is any truth to this intelligence it means that not only must we do something different and effective, we must do it quickly.''

No one argued with this assessment. The stunning import of the recent intelligence reports had still not sunk in completely among all the members. That the homeworlds themselves should come under Weave attack was a concept scarce to be believed. So concerned had the Amplitur been with preserving the thrust of the Purpose that they had given little thought to protecting themselves.

''If that information is confirmed,'' said Sand-sits-Green, ''then we must prepare to defend with everything at our command.''

''If we bring in sufficient forces to do that,'' Takes-short-Thinking countered, ''we risk weakening the alliance to the point of collapse. One species after another will fall under Weave authority and be lost to us forever. Of what use to save ourselves and sacrifice the Purpose?''

''Envision it.'' Bulk-holds-Tree shifted uneasily. ''Humans, here. Wading through the birthing waters of Eil.'' It shuddered, and agitated endothelial chromophores sent waves of dull silver rippling down the length of the pliant mass.

Places-change-Distant lurched in the direction of the exiting ramp even as its attention was directed at Glean-blue-Saying. ''If no one has anything specific to add, I have heavy responsibilities that must be attended to.''

Thus addressed, that individual continued. ''As Sand-sits-Green says, we must prepare to protect the homeworlds. I agree that we should assemble a large defensive force, and fortify the twin worlds impressively. Yet it is generally conceded that we cannot forever resist Human-led attacks. What then should be done? Given that assumption, how can we most usefully proceed? I have a notion.

''The Weave forces will transpose from Underspace and prepare for landings. When battle is about to be enjoined, when the first bloated transport shuttles with their loads of heavily armed Massood and Human fighters are about to descend to strike at us, when the entire enemy force is tuned to fever pitch, then and only then do we embark on what must be our final, our ultimate stratagem for defeating our enemies.''

''What stratagem is this?'' The skeptical Places-change-Distant was ambulating ponderously toward the egress. ''There is no magic, mystical means for resolving the unpleasant reality. If we draw back sufficient forces to defend the homeworlds we sacrifice the alliance. If we do not, then we ourselves are lost.''

''There is in your observation nothing I disagree with,'' Glean-blue-Saying declared.

''Your intentions are obscure.'' Takes-short-Thinking allied itself mentally with Places-change-Distant.

''I had not intended that it be so.'' Green-blue-Saying's eyestalks rose. ''Somehow we must preserve the homeworlds and the font of the Purpose. Furthermore, we can only recover what we have lost to the Weave and ultimately defeat them by stopping the Humans. After devoting much thought and contemplation to this formidable situation I see but one way of accomplishing all this.

"As soon as the enemy is about to attack, we announce our surrender."

Even Places-change-Distant stopped moving.

The members of the Council stirred uncomfortably. As they were a species not much given to joking, it was assumed that Glean-blue-Saying was being straightforward. Truthfulness did not enter into the equation. The Amplitur did not lie.

It was left to Takes-short-Thinking to seek clarification. "Even though it is not partial to our evolutionary makeup, we understand humor in the abstract. The mood today has been grim. Are you attempting in making this suggestion to lighten our dispositions?"

"Not in the sense you suggest. I am without qualification saying that we should surrender prior to the inevitable final attack. Give up, capitulate, acquiesce. Announce that we have abjured promulgating the Purpose, release those peoples who have allied themselves to our cause from their promises, submit the majority of our weapons systems and Underspace proficiency to Weave supervision, and return to an existence circumscribed by social development and solitary contemplation such as we pursued prior to that time when we were first infused with the light of the Purpose."

Places-change-Distant spoke for the others. "An interesting approach to victory. I, for one, fail to see how your proposal aids us in obtaining the objectives you so carefully enumerate. Personally I am not quite ready to put aside the Purpose, nor to turn over to the enemy without a fight control of the homeworlds."

"I said nothing about relinquishing the Purpose," Glean-blue-Saying replied. "I spoke only of announcing that we were doing so as a consequence of surrender. As for turning over the homeworlds to the enemy, they will not wish to spend time and effort administering that which is no longer a threat to them. I am convinced that we will retain full local control, which would hardly be the case subsequent to a devastating military defeat.''

"The Weave will spread false philosophies and propaganda among our allies. All who have been brought within the Purpose will be lost," Sand-sits-Green opined.

"Not all, I think." Glean-blue-Saying regarded his colleagues. "Surely we have done our work better than that? Many will remain bound through free choice and preference. Others can always be reconvinced. Work neglected can another day be restored.

"Meanwhile we will be left alone; to talk and to try and persuade, for all that the Weave will be watching, that we do not make too many suggestions to the easily susceptible. They will complain, and we will protest our innocence, and meanwhile we shall make progress where it is most critical. *Without* having to use that part of our minds which has aided us so heavily in our work in the past.

"Humankind is the key to everything. Not only are they the Weave's most effective fighters, they are also the only species capable of resisting our most heartfelt suggestions. They came raging out of the far reaches on behalf of the Weave and we did not have sufficient time to diagnose how to deal with them. If we can acquire that time, I believe that the means to undo them and the danger they represent can eventually be found.''

"And you propose to procure this time by surrendering to them.'' The opposing horny plates of Nigh-cold-Singing's mouth ground together as they nibbled on a nearby plant. "Do you think that peace will weaken the victors? They will remain powerful, while we will have disarmed. Or perhaps you believe we should have long conversations with them and try to convince them of the error of their ways?''

"Not long conversations, no.'' Glean-blue-Saying was unintentionally cryptic. "I have studied what we know of Humankind. They have devoted themselves utterly to the war, putting aside their attempts at art, at urban enhancement, at everything except turning out fighters for the Weave. They have geared their existence to defeating us, to preparing for a great, climactic battle at the conclusion of which they can celebrate in triumph.'' The Amplitur could comprehend such a notion only in the abstract. To them each victory was also a loss, for it meant the death of many intelligent beings who might otherwise have been brought into the Purpose.

''By surrendering we will deny them that triumph. They will experience not exaltation but frustration.''

''They will have won the war,'' said Red-sky-Thinking. ''How is that not a triumph?''

''They will not have *won*. The war will simply have ended. To understand the difference you must first understand the workings of that near-impenetrable organ, the Human mind. They will not have defeated us; we will have given up. To Humans there is a measurable difference. A difference which will pain them. You will see. They will realize but temporary gratification from our capitulation.'' The tips of both tentacles flexed emphatically.

''If they are indeed heir to this frustration you denote,'' wondered Sand-sits-Green, ''might they not take it out on us, by attacking the homeworlds anyway?''

''There is some small risk of that,'' Glean-blue-Saying admitted, ''but I think not. Their ability to act should be sufficiently circumscribed by their Weave allies, who traditionally control combat logistics. Without enthusiastic support on the part of other species there is little that companies of Humans can do on their own. If the Weave accepts our surrender, all combatants should be removed to their respective worlds. Humans may protest, but they do not control the transports. Not in sufficient volume to cause us any serious concern. Their own commands are too tightly interwoven with those of the Massood and others to act in dangerous independence.''

''This unseemly notion of yours may preserve the homeworlds,'' agreed Red-sky-Thinking, ''but I fail to see how it ameliorates the Purpose.''

''The Humans will react as do individuals of all species which reproduce by sexual means when confronted with an anticipated but unconsummated union, except that in the case of Humans this frustration results in unimaginably heightened aggression. Individuals trained for battle from childhood will soon seek other outlets for their store of pent-up emotion."

"With an end to the war they will have no outlet," said Red-sky-Thinking. "You admit yourself that the rest of the Weave will see to that."

"There is an exception the Weave cannot and will not try to control. There will still remain to Humans the original outlet for their frustrations and aggression."

"You mean they will seek someone else besides us and our allies to fight?" wondered Bulk-holds-Tree. "They will attack the Hivistahm, perhaps, or even the Massood?"

"No. I fear that even though they have never been offered formal Weave membership, Humankind has been a part of Weave society too long for that to take place. When I state that I believe Humans will return to the original outlet for their aggression, I mean that in its absolute sense. Having no other species to fight, I think they will once again turn upon themselves."

Excited thoughts crowded the chamber. "Surely their association with the civilized races of the Weave has matured them beyond that," said Takes-short-Thinking.

"I do not think so. The first Human the Weave contacted would not have thought so. Recall my original tenet: that only Humans can defeat Humans. By removing ourselves as a threat to them, we force them to change the focus of their hormones. I believe strongly that they are still far from fully civilized, and that left alone without anyone else to contest, they will turn back upon themselves. Their history shows that when not confronted by a perceived external enemy, they are forced to seek dominance within and among their own kind."

"Would not the members of the Weave, seeing what was taking place, seek to intervene?" wondered Places-change-Distant.

"Intervene betwixt fighting Humans? I doubt it. Among them only the Massood might have an impact, and I do not see the Massood stepping in of their own volition. They will return to their own worlds and resume a peaceful way of life. Remember: Humans fight because they enjoy it, the Massood because they are compelled to.

"The Weave will shun any such conflict lest such internecine Human fighting spread to their own worlds. Eventually the Humans will weaken themselves to the point where they are no longer a threat to our goals. It may take some time, but we have always been patient. We have waited thousands of years. The Purpose will not perish: it will simply rest.

"Our surrender will be an honest one. We will give up our weapons systems. We will retire to the sacred twin worlds. And here we will bide our time. We will not urge the Purpose on the Mazvec, the Copavi, the Korath, and the Vandir, as we have in the past. But that does not mean we cannot move among them and retain their friendship. We can always use the excuse that we are afraid of the Humans. The members of the Weave will understand that.

"We will admit defeat in this war. Concerning future wars we need say nothing."

Contemplative silence lay over the chamber as the Council members caucused. The proposal was beyond radical, not to mention risky in the extreme. Most obviously, what if Glean-blue-Saying was wrong? What if in spite of Weave restraints the outraged, cheated Humans mustered enough vessels to mount an attack? Even in small numbers they could wreak intense damage to the twin worlds.

If, however, the assumptions of Glean-blue-Saying were correct, and Humans resumed fighting among themselves, the future, albeit a distant future, was much brightened. Given a chance to confront a Weave devoid of Humans, the members of the Council knew that the Purpose could not fail.

Perilous, they thought. Perilous in the extreme. Yet the considered alternatives were hardly promising.

"We could, in taking this course of action, concede everything." Glean-blue-Saying regarded his colleagues.

"Conversely, our offspring's offspring could gain the galaxy. Alternatively, we can try to smash the force the Weave is gathering to send against us. Does anyone present believe we have a realistic chance of doing that?"

Idle thoughts filled the ensuing silence. Somewhere someone munched on a leaf. "I thought not," said Glean-blue-Saying. "Believe me, if anyone were to posit a better way, I would gladly subscribe to it myself. As for me, I can think of nothing else.

"Treated properly, Humankind will eventually prove not the undoing of the Purpose, but its salvation."

Places-change-Distant proposed quietly, "What if the Humans do not start fighting among themselves, but simply put down their arms and begin to comport themselves in a civilized manner?"

"That is a chance we take. Of course, being thoroughly pacified, none should raise objection if we choose to counsel with them; to offer a thought here, a notion there. Their history indicates that they will slaughter and kill on the least pretext, over the most ephemeral perceived slight. At one time they nearly turned primitive weapons of mass destruction on themselves, on their own homeworld."

Astonishment and disbelief at this revelation arose from those on the Council who were not so well versed in Human history.

"It is a true thing," Glean-blue-Saying reiterated.

"Lastly, I ask you to consider that this plan is fully in keeping with all Purposeful tenets. By surrendering we will preserve thousands of lives or those of their offspring for possible future integration into the Purpose."

There was no need for a verbal vote. Agreement was universal and unspoken. Glean-blue-Saying experienced much internal satisfaction.

When it was over, speculation flowed as freely as before.

"How long do you think it will take for internecine fighting among the Humans to weaken them severely?" Sand-sits-Green wondered.

"I do not know. Their history provides no adequate

stonemarks for speculation. As representatives of the humbly defeated we will naturally do our best to encourage them in the mutual suspicions which will flower subsequent to the outbreak of peace.''

''You do not think they will be leery of such activities on our part?''

''Perhaps. We must proceed carefully. But there is much in our favor. Humans are both credulous and arrogant, a potentially suicidal combination which we will exploit to the utmost. It may be that with a few considered and well-placed words and phrases we may do more to defeat them than ever we did with energy beams and explosives.''

''This is good.'' Takes-short-Thinking was finally convinced. ''It will mean an end to fighting, an end to the wasteful demise of intelligences. The peace will resonate within the Purpose. We shall fight on without weapons.

''Meanwhile we will continue to study as well as prod the Humans. We will learn and remember. It may be that some among the Amplitur will discover chemical or neurological means that may be eventually used to defeat them utterly.''

''I will inform the military.'' Places-change-Distant was appropriately grave. ''We will prepare to announce the surrender.''

''Not yet,'' Glean-blue-Saying gently reminded his colleagues. ''To achieve the greatest benefit we must wait until the last moment. Let them assemble their forces. Let them plunge through Underspace in imagined secrecy. Only when they are actually in orbit about the twin worlds do we capitulate.''

In the end, many of the Council members were surprised only in that they had not thought of such a solution themselves. The placid brilliance of it led each and every one of them to rededicate itself anew to the ultimate clarity of the Purpose.

★ XIV ★

On all the worlds of the Weave preparations were concluded, preparations that had been ongoing for some time. The vast net of troops and weapons, ships and supplies, was being drawn tight. It was a moment none among the select few who knew the ultimate objective of all the preparation had thought would come in their lifetime.

Though the ultimate goal remained secret to all but the uppermost ranks, it was clear even to the lowliest Lepar that something major was in the works. Too many ships and too great a volume of supplies were being sent to the same few assembly points: little-known, lightly populated worlds situated far from any ongoing conflict. A prodigious effort of logistics was under way.

As they gathered and waited, the thousands of soldiers speculated among themselves, wondering at the great mass of vessels and supplies drifting in organized orbit above them, waiting for assignment to Underspace transport. Massood came, with Hivistahm and O'o'yan technical support. The S'van were there, rendering a host of inconspicuously critical decisions.

And the Humans, of course. The most famous units, filled with veterans of many successful campaigns. Not even their officers could answer the continual queries of their curious troops except to say that they had been promised that all would soon be revealed to soldier and superior alike.

The movement of so great a force could not be kept a

secret, but expensive probings bought a curious media few hard facts. One thing no one could hide: The level of excitement and tension among the Human participants was building to an explosive pitch.

It was a uniquely primate phenomenon. To the Massood and the rest such preparations were no cause for excitement. They did not look forward to combat as Humans did. They assembled and waited quietly, marveling at the amount of energy their Human counterparts expended in anticipation.

One or two remarked on the absence of any Turlog in the burgeoning battle force. This apparent oversight remained a curiosity, but not an obsessive one.

Throughout the buildup Colonel Nevan Straat-ien stayed in touch with other Core members, monitoring developments and sharing information until he, too, was assigned to a ship orbiting an outpost world whose lengthy name he did not recognize. Observing and analyzing, the historian Lalelelang traveled in his company together with her voluminous store of notes and recordings. When they had time they would discuss her theories and, not infrequently now, matters of wholly personal interest.

When word of the great battle group's eventual target became official at Straat-ien's level, as it inevitably had to, they still found it as difficult to accept as did those who had been living in ignorance of the possibility all along.

"The Amplitur homeworlds," Lalelelang bobbed elegantly by way of emphasis. "Through you I knew they had been located, but I had no idea that the war had progressed so far."

"No one did."

Straat-ien regarded her approvingly. As near as he could tell she had been true to her word. Nothing of what she had learned of him and his relations had been communicated elsewhere, not even in the form of sealed storage.

What now of her theories? he found himself wondering. Suppositions that both of them expected to find a harmless place buried deep in volumes of research now looked to be put to the actual test. Or were they getting ahead of themselves? he wondered. Just because an assault had been planned on the Amplitur homeworlds didn't mean it was going to succeed, didn't mean that the end of the Great War was imminent. All it meant for certain was that a lot of warriors on both sides were about to embrace oblivion.

"When?" he heard her asking.

"That I haven't been told yet. Have you stood on the uppermost observation platform late at night and looked up at the sky? There's a ring around this planet. It looks like it might've been there for a billion years, but it's recent and artificial. Nothing but transports being loaded and positioned for Underspace insertion, with new ones arriving and departing all the time. I've seen a lot of attack groups in my time, but nothing like this. There are hundreds of ships up there, and other fleets being assembled off other worlds. It's the greatest logistical push the Weave has ever mounted.

"There's plenty of room in Underspace, but coordinating the emergence so two or three ships don't materialize in the same place is going to take some unprecedented preplanning. I'm glad I'm just a soldier."

"To anyone but a Human, Nevan, that would be a contradiction in terms." Both of them were quiet then, contemplating future possibilities that had unexpectedly and abruptly been brought forward by several hundred years.

The relentless preparations continued, as did fighting elsewhere. Despite the care taken to conceal the ultimate objective of the gathering fleets, it was doubted by those trained to ponder such matters that the Amplitur would be taken by surprise. They had always maintained an effective intelligence operation inside the Weave, and preparations on such a scale would inevitably draw more than the usual attention from their operatives.

Due to the diversion of so much Weave war material the enemy managed several small victories elsewhere, but if anything it was decided that this would make them even more wary. Still, the Weave High Command had hopes of achieving at least a modicum of surprise. If nothing else, the enemy would not know which of the twin worlds was to be struck first and would have to divide its defenses accordingly.

At the very least, if the Amplitur succeeded in staving off the attack, the use of forces drawn from elsewhere to defend their homeworlds should allow the Weave to roll up substantial triumphs in weakened systems. Weave tacticians were confident of the efficacy of their strategy even if they remained unsure of the actual outcome's direction. Victory there would be: it was just that no one could predict where it would occur.

Along with hundreds of other officers, Straat-ien eventually received formal orders. The only Wais in a battle group of human soldiers, Lalelelang enthusiastically continued her work, recording and analyzing the troop buildup and departure. So familiar a sight had she become to the milling troops that they no longer remarked on her presence and she was able to move among them with greater freedom and ease than ever before.

From Vecilan, from Nojong III, from Aulebebunda and Didone and a dozen other minor worlds the grand fleets departed. Preparations continued in Underspace right up until the moment of emergence. Little was known of the surface features of the Amplitur homeworlds, but no one doubted that they would conform to the norm for populated, civilized planets: a single extensive landmass surrounded by oceans, with a few scattered islands dotting the continental shelf. Only Earth deviated from that pattern. Ail and Eil were not expected to provide any such surprises.

Depending on the degree of surprise the Weave would be able to achieve, the Amplitur defenses would react accordingly. Yet despite arduous preparations, no one on any of the attacking Command ships was prepared for that which greeted them subsequent to their actual emergence from Underspace.

It took the form of a general communication that was repeated endlessly, in a dozen major Weave languages. It rose from both Amplitur homeworlds and effectively offset every variation in the elaborate plan of attack.

Naturally it was at first thought to be a trick, an outrageous subterfuge designed to buy the defenders time to mobilize and focus their defenses. Several commanders were all for ignoring the broadcast and proceeding with operations as planned. But the intensity of the presentation, the lack of flux by defensive orbital weaponry, and the concomitant communications from Mazvec, Crigolit, and other non-Amplitur forces in the vicinity only reinforced the original message.

It was still difficult for the High Command to countenance what they were hearing. Cipher specialists and other intelligence groups went to work, probing the depths of the communications as well as movement on the surface of Eil, around which the grand fleet had emerged. Fortifications were certainly present on the surface, but they were not active. Impossible as it seemed at first, specialists on board the grand fleet began to believe that the droning, repetitive communication might be genuine. Ampliturologists pointed out that if naught else it was supported by an important sociocultural precedent.

The Amplitur did not lie.

A bemused Lalelelang was searching the central assembly area for Straat-ien. All about her groups of Humans were screeching and howling, jumping wildly up and down while flailing joyfully at one another. Like everything else about their society, even their enjoyment was founded on violence. She kept to the fringes, hugging the wall lest she accidentally be crushed by the indiscriminate jubilation. She did not pay much attention to the activity, having observed and recorded it all before: what she was witnessing was a standard primate pack celebration.

She found him seated at the far side, contemplating the sweeping view of the Amplitur homeworld provided by a long, narrow port.

"What has happened? I have heard nothing about landings, or fighting. Meanwhile we sit in normal space, an easy target for the Amplitur's ground-based defenses."

Straat-ien turned to face her. "There isn't going to be any

fighting. No one believed it at first, but confirmation's just come down from on high.''

"No fighting? What do you mean?" She kept her recorder going. As always, his facial contortions supplied fascinating insights into Human thought processes. She could not easily interpret his present expression, however. He seemed dazed as well as contemplative.

"It's the Amplitur. They've surrendered.''

"Surrendered? But why? Have they suffered some noteworthy defeat elsewhere?''

"Nobody knows. Nobody knows much of anything, it seems. People still have a lot of questions. Meanwhile the Amplitur are allowing troops to land unopposed, and their orbital weaponry isn't reacting to our presence. The theory that's going around, and it's only a theory, is that once they got a good look at the extent of the forces arrayed against them, they simply decided to cut their losses before they occurred.'' He blinked at her. "Lalelelang, the Great War is over.''

Unable to reach the Human-scaled bench with her backside, she folded her legs beneath her body and squatted on the floor nearby.

All life had been circumscribed, if not defined, by the war. Generation upon generation had known nothing but the war, had been raised with its ponderous presence always dominating their consciousness. The origin of the conflict was ancient, commencing more than a thousand years ago with the first contact between the Weave and the Sspari. Could such a presence simply vanish?

"It's over,'' the Human colonel Straat-ien had said. How long before the real meaning of those words sank in? What would happen now?

"It hardly seems possible,'' she trilled, for lack of anything more profound to say.

The Human shrugged. "Possible or not, it's happened. According to the few reports I've been allowed to see, even as we sit here the enemy is turning over weapons, transports, communications facilities: everything. No more war. You don't have to fight anymore.''

"The Wais have never fought," she reminded him.

"You know what I mean," he responded restively. "The Weave. It'll probably fade away once the Amplitur have been completely disarmed. It came into existence specifically to counter them. Once they've been reduced and isolated, the Wais and the Hivistahm, the O'o'yan and the S'van and all the others will doubtless resume their individual paths.''

"I am not sure I agree with you. As a working organization the Weave has been around for so many centuries it may well linger long after the reason for its founding has passed.'' Her head cocked sideways as she regarded him. "Tell me what you think, Nevan. Is this capitulation for real, or are the ever-inscrutable Amplitur planning something?''

"I think it's some kind of trick, but Command is staffed by individuals a lot more perceptive than I am. Even if the Amplitur are trying to deceive us, they won't fool the S'van.'' He nodded in the direction of the gesticulating, hollering troops. "That's why I think this celebration is premature. No one's been ordered to stand down yet. But you can't keep people from reacting to the news.'' He shrugged. "I don't know what the Amplitur can do without ships or weapons, and with Weave forces stationed on their worlds.''

"Let us suppose it is for real and that it indeed means the end of the war. What do you imagine will happen now?'' she asked him.

"To what?''

"To you and your fellow Humans.''

"What? Oh, your theories.'' He smiled confidently. "I suppose some of us will stay here to assist in disarming the enemy and dismantling their orbital weapons. A discreet number will be stationed on both Amplitur worlds to keep an eye on their activities. The same may take place on the principal worlds of the Crigolit, the Mazvec, the Ashregan, and the other Amplitur-allied fighters.

"Those troops not needed for such duties will as soon as

is practical be released to return to their own homes. To Earth, to Asmaria, to Barnard's and the rest.''

''And then?''

''I know what you're thinking, Lalelelang, but I'm still convinced that you're wrong. They'll return to peacetime pursuits. Industry, the arts, education, agriculture: just living.''

''There are other species who do each of those things better than Humankind. If you venture to contend in such fields beyond the worlds you presently occupy you will find yourselves competing with the Hivistahm and O'o'yan in manufacture, the Wais in the arts, even the Lepar at simple labor.''

''I think you'll be surprised at how well we can redirect our energies, Lalelelang.''

''As I have often stated before, nothing would please me more.'' Inoffensive wide blue eyes bored into his own. ''You, for example. Have you given any thought to what occupation you might follow outside the military?''

He blinked. ''Not really, since I didn't exactly expect the war to end today.''

''I am certain it is the same with every Human. These reactions will be interesting to observe.''

''You never rest, do you, Lalelelang?''

''I have dedicated myself to this work. Why would I want to rest?''

He smiled understandingly, but deep inside his soul there was a persistent wisp of unease that all his confidence could not banish.

As soon as the word was passed through Underspace to the worlds of the Weave and its meaning began to sink in, the outpouring of emotion on board the transport was repeated elsewhere many billion times over. On non-Human worlds it generated less flamboyant but equally enthusiastic reaction.

Once the Amplitur homeworlds and those of their allies had been secured, the Weave military embarked upon a studied but steady reduction in strength. Whole units were still needed not merely to keep watch over the former enemy but to supervise the destruction of immense quantities of war material. A whole new industry arose simply to see to the recycling of vast resources originally designed for war and destruction.

On the Human worlds, the returning troops were greeted with elaborate parades and mass outpourings of relief and affection. Massood fighters dispersed to Massoodai and their own colonies, to be welcomed back less ostentatiously into family and clan. Support personnel of the Hivistahm and S'van slipped easily back into normal, civilized life-styles. Benumbed Lepar quietly returned to their few worlds as if nothing of note had transpired, while the Wais saw the termination of the great conflict reflected in an outpouring of art that was at once suave and restrained.

On the worlds of those who had been allied to the Amplitur—the Crigolit and Ashregan, the Segunians and Copavi and T'returia—returning soldiers mixed uneasily but hopefully into the general population. The first isolated instances of individuals casting off the tenets of the Purpose were recorded, though in the absence of an equally comforting alternative most continued to cling to that which had been the primary motivating force of their societies for many hundreds of years.

Lalelelang did not have the time or inclination to celebrate, nor did agitated outpourings of extreme emotion have a place in Wais society. She had returned to the somewhat guarded accolades of her colleagues, who were at once admiring of and unsettled by her work.

In sheer volume, however, it was breathtaking and unprecedented. Whatever another Wais personally thought of the distasteful, even morbid subject matter, it could not be ignored. She had accomplished all she had set out to do, which was reflected in the diffident but formidable honors that were bestowed upon her subsequent to her return. Never again could her academic standing be called into question.

She resumed presenting her seminars while attempting to prioritize the vast archive she had assembled. Without modern cataloging methods it would have been impossible just to digest the specifics, let alone provide for the thousands of critical cross-references. She was aided by the fact that there was no crush of scholars eager to delve into her discoveries. Her chosen field remained one in which fellow Wais were still reluctant to browse. In person, she was treated by colleagues and students alike much as they would have an award-winning artist possessed of a unique but unsettling viewpoint.

Exhibiting the utmost refinement in their choice of phrases and gestures, friends and acquaintances remarked that she appeared rather the worse for her experiences. There was no opprobrium attached to their observations. Nothing less could have been expected, considering what she had been through. Few could discuss combat in the abstract, much less envision what it must have been like to practically participate in it in the company of rampaging Humans, without suffering at least a modicum of digestive malaise. With the war over, her work would now truly be relegated to the realm of history.

She bore understandingly the affectations of those with whom she came in contact, suffering patiently even those whose obsequious attendance at her seminars was obviously nothing more than an attempt to curry academic favor. Otherwise she remained unchanged by her experiences, even to still neglecting to attend societal functions in the company of her triad sisters. She was too busy, she explained. Prior to her odyssey she had been too busy planning, and now she was too busy organizing. Her family and sisters despaired of improving her dismal social standing.

The longer she worked, the more she devoted herself to speculation and research, the less she saw of anything to disprove her original hypothesis.

There had been a brief period of social grace subsequent to the Amplitur surrender. That was already beginning to dissipate. Danger signs were cropping up on more than one Human world. They would not be recognized for what they were by anyone else, but to Lalelelang the historian their import was unmistakable.

A riot in Kendai City, on Edo. The rise of gang warfare

on Columbia. Conflict on Barnard's. And plenty of ongoing hostility on Earth itself, much but not all of it involving returning soldiers who were having the expected difficulties adjusting to a civilian, peacetime society.

To Lalelelang it was inevitable. What else could one expect from a species that had been encouraged by the Weave to devote all its energies for the past several hundred years to creating the most effective fighting force the galaxy had ever seen? What did the S'van and Hivistahm expect? They had made use of a patently uncivilized species. Now they expected it to react to a radical change of conditions in something approaching a civilized manner.

Men and women who had fought together tended to stay in contact by means of social clubs or traditional military service organizations. Such places were often the only readily comforting outlet for their confused emotions and suddenly restrained aggressions. Reading and interpreting these signs, she saw that the postwar explosion she feared was already building. If her theory was correct, then the question for all the civilized societies of the Weave including her own was not whether or not it could be forestalled, but if it could be contained.

The fact that there was no longer any obvious need or reason for other species to suppress their true feelings toward the smelly, discourteous, uncivilized Humans only threatened to compound the problem.

It was starting already.

★ XV ★

When the visitor was announced, she was sitting in her office, alternating her attention between two viewscreens, ignoring the bright sunshine that gilded the formal gardens outside. As she privatized her equipment she tried to organize her thoughts, only to find that it was not as simple as cataloging statistical information. Also, she was out of practice. Alien words and phrases trickled back to her slowly, rusty from long disuse.

She made sure the door to her office sealed behind her as she started down the corridor, heading for the official greeting center. It was a better place to meet. Her visitor would have found the connecting corridor too narrow, the ceiling too low.

Also, it would have been very upsetting for any Wais unfortunate enough to encounter him in such confined surroundings.

He waited alone in the greeting center, his legs crossed in front of him as he sat on the circular visitors' bench. Droplets of liquid cycled in stately precession behind him, constrained and manipulated by magnetic fields programmed by the artist, the glistening fluid avoiding the sprays of exquisite *kanda* blossoms that thrust upward in graceful loops from the central planter.

She noted the restrained glances that he drew from passing pedestrians. That was hardly surprising. Mahmahar had been far from the front, insofar as an interstellar conflict could be said to have a front. It serviced no military facilities. Humans were a rare sight even in the capitol. Here, in an academic conurbation, they were all but unknown. So everyone contrived to investigate the extraordinary visitor without appearing to look at him. They also kept their distance.

Several were unable to restrain themselves and stared unashamedly, however, when she strode directly toward the intruder and extended a wingtip to meet his fingers. Conscious of their lapse of courtesy they hurried away, trying to conceal their own faces with fluffed wing feathers. Not all succeeded.

"It is good to see you once more, Colonel Nevan Straatien."

Aware it could give offense to others nearby he was careful not to smile, not even for her. "It's still just 'Nevan' to you, honored historian." He indicated their surroundings. "I seem to have caused a bit of a ruckus."

"This university might see one Human visitor a year," she explained, "and it would be confined to administration. Your presence here has an effect comparable to that of one of your lions or tigers taking an unsupervised stroll through one of your schools for preadolescents. Be understanding of my colleagues. Fascination temporarily overwhelms their natural courtesy, not to mention the instinctive panic."

"I might have expected a little more discernment from the inhabitants of an institution of higher learning."

"Higher learning does not preclude the presence of lower minds. You're getting all the understanding they think you deserve. Come to my office. Mind your head; the ceiling becomes lower."

To the palpable shock of several of the mesmerized onlookers, she slipped the end of her right wing through the loop he formed with his left arm, having to stretch slightly to accomplish the maneuver. It was fortunate Straat-ien was of less than average Human height or she could not have managed it. He still towered over everyone in the room. More astonishing to the onlookers even than her obvious tolerance of the actual physical contact was the fact that she had initiated it.

A ledge ran beneath the window in her office, which overlooked the grounds outside. Pushing aside plants and other artifacts, he made himself as comfortable there as possible. It was either there or the floor, since his weight would have buckled her furniture.

"I've stayed in the military."

"I can see that," she murmured.

"I've never forgotten your theory. Couldn't have tossed it aside had I wanted to. Ever since the Amplitur capitulation I've paid a lot of attention to the general news in addition to running some follow-up probes and checks of my own. I don't much care for what they imply." He hesitated. "I'm afraid you may be right."

With a sweep of one perfumed wingtip she indicated her blank screens. "I, too, have seen nothing with which to contradict myself. But there is yet hope. The conflagrative index I designed has held steady for two months now. Perhaps it will not climb any higher."

"Do you really believe that?"

She exhaled musically, her heavily lashed, limpid eyes finally rising to meet his. "No."

"Neither do I. I can't, being as familiar with your work as I am." Rising, he removed a small instrument from his pocket and turned a slow circle, checking the compact device's readouts as he did so. Satisfied, he resumed his seat on the ledge.

"I've been in regular contact with my extended family." He did not need to explain. "They've all been made aware of your theories, but they're divided on their validity. In any case, there's not much they can do. As you know, we can't influence our own kind, not even to act sensibly. We *have* been able to defuse several potentially unpleasant situations by making appropriate suggestions to non-Human participants. In both cases Massood were involved. That's a bad precedent.

"Some of the people I've exchanged views with think that

several hundred years of contact with the Weave would have bred this kind of unbridled aggression out of us if not for the war.''

''I feel the same,'' she responded. ''How can you ask a people to produce the ultimate soldiers one moment and engineers and agriculturalists the next? It is too much to request of a civilized species, let alone Humankind.'' She was silent for a moment. ''What news of the Amplitur? Are they truly defeated?''

''Oh, they're defeated, all right. I'm just not so sure they're beaten.''

''I thought my mastery of your language was complete. Apparently this is not the case. Be so good as to explain, Nevan.''

''My position allows me access to a great deal of information. On the face of it, the war's definitely over. The Amplitur and their allies continue to turn over weapons for disassembly. Plants that have manufactured such materials for centuries are being rapidly converted to peacetime pursuits. Hivistahm technicians have begun work on techniques for undoing the extensive genetic manipulation the Amplitur have performed on races like the Mazvec. Weave inspection teams have even been allowed on their homeworlds.''

''What of their great and grand Purpose?''

''They continue to propagate it, but only verbally. They *say* they've sworn off using their singular mental abilities to forcibly manipulate others.''

''It would not matter,'' she murmured. ''Such things can be checked, and the Amplitur know that. Besides which they never lie.'' She considered the translucent blue sky outside the building.

''Among my kind there's an ancient saying to the effect that there's a first time for everything. Which is another way of saying that there are a lot of us who don't trust them.''

''But Humans don't trust anyone,'' she reminded him. ''Including each other. Given your perverse history it cannot be any other way. Which is why I have always been so concerned with what your people do. The task of monitoring the machinations of the Amplitur I leave to others. It is Humankind which worries me. Now that the war is ended, more than ever.

"The question is and actually has always been: Can your people overcome hundreds of years of persuasion on the part of the Weave and thousands of years of unbalanced social evolution on your own to develop a truly civilized society?"

"And not incidentally disprove your theories," he muttered. "To think that the first contact, William Dulac, believed we weren't naturally combative enough to be of help in the war!"

"Yet he eventually became a soldier himself," she reminded him.

"Sort of. The Weave has seen to it that most of the Will Dulacs have been bred out of Humankind. Now all of us, Human and non-Human alike, have to find a way to deal with the consequences." He rose and began pacing the small room, activity that any other Wais would have found intimidating in its power and aimlessness. The historian Lalelelang was not affected. She'd seen it plenty of times before.

He halted and leaned against her wallviewer. "My friends and I have been talking, postulating some hypotheses of our own. More than anything else, the Amplitur have been known for their patience. They think in terms of hundreds of years, not decades. What if they arrived at your theory independently?"

"What do you mean?"

"Suppose they saw that they couldn't beat the Weave. They must have realized they were losing badly even before the assault on their homeworlds was mounted. What if they planned their surrender as one last surprise?"

"In that event I should say that they succeeded."

"Maybe there's more to it than that. Let's say they decided they couldn't beat us, meaning a Human-led battle force. So they chose to preserve their worlds, their base of power, and themselves. To retire and exercise that endless patience of theirs, and wait. In the hope that eventually we'd do their work for them?"

''You?'' She was silent for a long time, eyes half-closed, upper and lower beak separated by a breathing gap of minimal politeness. ''I see. You think they will do nothing in the belief that your kind will eventually destroy the Weave for them?''

''That would be too obvious, and what's obvious to me and my friends has to be at least as obvious to the Hivistahm, for example. I think the S'van could take the steps necessary to prevent a Human–Weave conflict from growing to dangerous proportions.

''No, I think that what the Amplitur may be hoping for is for the Weave to continue to shun Humankind socially, shutting us off as much as possible from the main flow of galactic civilization. If that happens, my kind will once again be forced to turn inward. The result will be that the peoples of the Weave will be safe, but that we Humans will revert to fighting amongst ourselves, as we did before the Weave made contact with us.

''The result will be peace for the Weave for hundreds, maybe thousands of years. But eventually we'll weaken ourselves to the point where we can no longer be a factor in any interstellar conflict. That's when the Amplitur, ever patient, will renew their drive for dominance through the Purpose.''

She considered. ''Does that matter, if the ability of the Amplitur to wage war has been removed?''

''Of course. If Humankind destroys itself, it means that if the Weave and the Amplitur eventually resume their conflict, it will be on an even basis. Because now that the war is over the peoples of the Weave are going to revert to wholly 'civilized' behavior. Your own people won't let you contribute to a standing military force when there's no longer a demonstrable need for one. The Massood are already demobilizing with a vengeance.

''It'll start all over again. Long after you and I are dust there'll be another great war, only next time there won't be a world of congenital warriors waiting out there for the Weave to call on to help it out. And except for my kind, when it comes to warfare the Amplitur are better motivators than the S'van or the Hivistahm, or even the Massood.''

She made a gesture of acknowledgment. ''Then there is only one solution: Humankind must be brought into the mainstream of Weave development. Your aggression must be routed into other channels. While remaining true to yourselves, you must also somehow become civilized.'' She bobbed and dipped eloquently. ''Most of my colleagues would consider that an impossibility.''

''I'm not so sure I don't agree with them,'' Straat-ien confessed unhappily. ''It means undoing not only the conditioning of the past several hundred years but all of that from the previous several thousand, when Earth was an isolated backwater. We're talking about psychological adjustment on a colossal scale.''

''Nothing less than species therapy,'' Lalelelang agreed.

''I do know one thing. We can't do it without outside help. Without the assistance of the Wais, and the S'van, and all the rest. If out of dislike and fear you shun and ignore us, there's a good chance we will destroy ourselves. When that happens and you have to deal with the Amplitur again, we poor, dumb, homicidal Humans won't be there to bail you out. That's what I think the squids are counting on. I think that's what was behind their abrupt surrender.''

She was not sanguine. ''To convince Wais, for example, to become involved in Human affairs will be very difficult. I can think of only a few who might be willing, not to mention mentally and emotionally capable, to try.''

''That's a start,'' Straat-ien said encouragingly.

''A modest network to begin with, organized along academic lines.'' She was warming to the idea now. ''Dedicated to furthering Human–Weave understanding. It is a possibility.'' She eyed him evenly. ''There will be resistance. Perhaps even active discouragement.''

''That's where the Core can be of help.'' He stopped his pacing. ''I'm told that the Amplitur have a love of games. Of all those that they've ever embarked upon, this is probably their most complex and far-reaching. Certainly the stakes have never been higher.

"We have one great advantage. I don't think they're expecting anyone to recognize their early moves, much less anticipate them. We have you and your early work, Lalelelang, to thank for that."

"If we pursue this, we shall do so ignorant of its eventual outcome," she reminded him. "As you say, we will become dust."

He was nodding vigorously, energized now. It was a wonderful and frightening thing to see. "I know. But if we're successful it'll mean that our many-times-removed offspring will be able to look the Amplitur in their oh-so-inscrutable eyes and grin knowingly."

It was an image she found highly distasteful. "Speak for your own offspring, Nevan Straat-ien."

★ XVI ★

A slim, wiry man was the general; tall and gangly as a scarecrow, rough as recycled metal. From his considerable Human height he gazed condescendingly down at the clumsy, slow-moving being before him. It could advance but gingerly on its four squat legs. The ropy tentacles that extended outward from either side of the peculiar, four-sided mouth were not strong enough to raise the soft-bodied creature's own forebody off the floor, not even once. Though he knew the truth was otherwise, it was impossible to watch the thing's progress without interpreting its painful approach as an act of supplication.

The general took a bite of the enhanced chocolate wafer he held and regarded his visitor. "Excuse me if I stare. I've never seen an Amplitur before. In the flesh."

"Straight-go-Wise is pleased to satisfy your curiosity." A tentacle gestured delicately. "I am in charge of dismantling the military infrastructure on this world." Fascinated, he watched the Human eat.

"Thanks to you the Crigolit seem to be as efficient in defeat as they were in war. You've been very helpful."

"We hew to our word." The translator bungled the initial translation and the general had to wait for its second effort. Meanwhile the Amplitur admired the clean lines of the biped's uniform, stark beneath the floridly expressive face. "We are doing all we can to cooperate."

"I know. I couldn't have asked for better cooperation."

The general leaned back in his seat. "You know, I never understood why you started this war in the first place. It's one thing to try and promulgate a philosophy, quite another to fight a war over it."

"I sometimes wonder myself. Remember that this all began many, many hundreds of years ago." The Amplitur was as relaxed as it could be in the presence of a Human. "Perhaps you yourself may on occasion have wondered what might result if all intelligence could be brought together to focus on a single matter?"

"Never happen," the general declared curtly. "So I never wondered about it. Intelligence is too diverse. By that reckoning it's something of a miracle that the Weave stuck together long enough to defeat you. But I don't have to tell you that. You know now that you were wrong in your original assumptions."

A tentacle fluttered. "Perhaps our error lay not in our assumptions but in our methodology."

"Oh?" The general's eyes narrowed. Owing to his manner of speech, he sometimes sounded shallow, but he had a sharp, inquisitive mind. "Then you haven't entirely given up on your 'Purpose'?"

"When we surrendered we agreed to war no longer against the Weave, and to forgo trying to forcefully convince others of our beliefs. Nothing was said about abandoning them ourselves, or not providing information to those who seek it voluntarily."

"That's interesting." The Human stared boredly at the ceiling.

The Amplitur regarded him out of great, golden eyes. "You seem preoccupied."

The general lowered his gaze. "A little. Like most of my friends, I've spent my whole life in the Service. This may be my last active assignment. I'm too young for formal retirement and I don't know what I'm going to do next. Is it like that with you?"

"Rarely. We usually know what we are going to do next."

"Well, you're lucky. I have a cousin who owns a plant that manufactures shoes. He's invited me to come in with him."

"I have heard that for Humans choosing the direction of one's life can be an ordeal. We have no such problems. I am sure you will be content in your choice. Fortunately, there will soon no longer be any need anywhere for large military forces. Peace and tranquillity will everywhere reign. There will be no more fighting. A good thing."

"Yes, a good thing," the general echoed in lackluster fashion.

The Amplitur felt a surge of hope, which, of course, it strove to dampen. There was little reason for concern, since it was doubtful the Human could properly interpret the flush of bright yellow that appeared in several places on the puffy body, but Straight-go-Wise believed in caution.

By now it was clear that the Human was inclined to continue the conversation. Straight was equally eager to satisfy the biped's curiosity.

The Board was polite. Being Wais they could not be otherwise. But they were more polite than usual. It was a bad sign.

Restraining her impatience, she'd followed accepted procedures and had eventually been granted an audience. Because of her exalted scholarly status, the five senior academicians listened sympathetically to her application, but despite her best efforts they refused to countenance anything she had to say.

"Even if what you tell us is true," commented Grand Aumemenaht, "what can we do about it? Throughout the Great War the Wais were never more than peripherally associated with actual conflict. It should be the same in peacetime." Trills and whistles of concurrence emanated from her colleagues.

"Rightly true." The senior seated next to her preened his feathers as he spoke. Though elderly, he was still capable of mating.

Lalelelang's crest erected. "I am telling you that if we do

not deal with this problem now, then we will have to deal with it after it has spread. Even to us.''

''What you hypothesize cannot spread to the Wais.'' Grand Prewowalong sang confidence from between two exquisitely mounted sprays of fresh flowers. Behind the Board the elegant spirals of Famed Hotutidad's purple, green, and gold oil-suspension mural flowed in unceasingly pleasing patterns.

''We must at least make minimal preparations,'' Lalelelang insisted.

''For what?'' Grand Aumemenaht extended both wings and stretched, the quills quivering emphatically. ''We cannot alarm the government on the basis of a theory. You have no proof of anything. Only suppositions.''

''The proof is there for anyone not afraid to look.'' She was careful not to phrase her rejoinder in the form of an accusation, which would have been discourteous. ''Exchangeable media is available to anyone with the resources to access. I am not making this up. The Humans are already beginning to fight among themselves. How long before it severely diminishes them, or spreads to involve other members of the Weave?

''Don't you see? The Amplitur hope to achieve through peace what they could not in war.''

''The Amplitur,'' declared Grand Nauvenlileng, ''hope to achieve contentment. This laudable goal they approach with admirable and measured determination. Throughout the millennium we have fought each other, they have never been known to lie. What matters what the Humans do to themselves? If, as you claim it might, their internal dissension should spread to involve other peoples, the Weave will deal with it at that time. Until then they are, as Humans always are, better left alone.''

''If the Amplitur can adapt to peace, so can the Humans,'' Grand Prewowalong added.

''The Amplitur are civilized,'' she argued.

''As always, scholar Lalelelang, your theories are interesting but hardly conclusive.'' Grand Aumemenaht spoke affectionately. "You are a valuable asset to the university. Do not let yourself drift into iconoclasm and destroy what you have accomplished. How many other experts in your field concur with your findings?"

Her beak clicked. "There are no other experts in my field. Not at the level at which I am currently working."

"Precisely my point. You are a lone voice, one mated to worry. Return to your research, Exalted Scholar Lalelelang, and do not poison your life with concern for the future course of Human events. The victorious Weave has everything under control."

"Humans under control. A quaint idea," she murmured, but under her breath.

"Their confusion is understandable." Grand Nauvenlileng spoke with the quiet ardor of one who believes his qualifications impregnable. "Such occasional internal flare-ups are to be expected. They will burn bright but brief, only to fade as Humans settle into the kind of mature civilization that has heretofore been denied them. Just as the Weave encouraged them to become great warriors, so we will help them to appreciate the benefits of permanent peace."

"It will not be easy," agreed Grand Aumemenaht, "but everyone is convinced it can be done."

"That might have been possible if it had been implemented when contact was first made," Lalelelang argued, "but not now. Not anymore. We've encouraged their natural attributes for too long."

"They will find their niche within the grander orbit of Weave civilization, as have all species."

"*If* the Weave holds together. It was created for a specific purpose: to fight the Amplitur. Now that there is no reason to do so, will we retain close contact with the Massood? Will the Massood who privately despise the S'van continue to treat with them?"

"If naught else, inertia will preserve the Weave," said Grand Partouceceht. "A thousand years of association is not so easily dissolved."

Aumemenaht made a show of checking her official chronometer. "We have granted you more time than was scheduled. We have listened to your concerns; to your observations and theories. It is to be regretted, but others also have demands on our time." It was a formal dismissal.

"If we do not make a start at dealing with this problem *now*, in a shorter while than you can imagine there won't be any time to do so!"

At this extraordinary breach of courtesy several of the senior academicians regarded her with shock. Grand Nauvenlileng looked dazed.

Aumemenaht retained her composure. It was left to her to respond, which she did with as much equanimity as she could muster.

"It might strike some that you have been too long in the field, Exalted Scholar Lalelelang, and that you have through no fault of your own acquired certain aspects, certain overtones of a culture that is less than Wais. This is not unprecedented. It is known that you have suffered.

"I suggest, and take the liberty of suggesting on behalf of my colleagues—" Soft whistles of profound agreement came from the others "—that you consider taking some time to reintegrate yourself into the society from which you have been so long separated."

Stunned by the extent of her transgression, Lalelelang hastened to deliver herself of an elaborate apologia of words and gestures. It appeared to mollify the Board, which was as understanding as it was unperceptive.

The result was that she left the meeting dissatisfied and discouraged. She had hoped for, though she had not really expected, something more. Having thus damaged her academic social standing and gained nothing in return, she sought solace in her triad.

Her sisters managed to succor her somewhat, but they could not reassure her. They did not subscribe to her outrageous hypotheses any more than had the Board. Better, they advised her, that she should listen to the wise advice of the seniors and throw herself into systematizing the vast body of knowledge she had accumulated in the course of her daring travels.

She thanked them but declared to their dismay that she would continue to keep to her own counsel.

Part of the problem, she knew, was that any normal Wais would find the entire subject distasteful. She could hardly blame her people for that. Nor were her theories likely to find a more enthusiastic welcome among the S'van, or the Hivistahm.

The coming cataclysm was inevitable. There was no mistake. Her theories predicted it. At least, she mused in frustration, she would not be around to experience it.

She was in her office when the visitor was declared. The announcing code implied that it was not a student or fellow academic. For a brief while she bustled with excitement, remembering a similar visit of not so very long ago.

When her visitor finally arrived and was admitted she was as surprised as she was disappointed.

The female S'van searched in vain for a place to sit. Short and thickset, she could not fit into the simple untenanted seat intended for the much slimmer Wais pelvis, nor did she have a hope of reaching the ledge beneath the window, which a much larger visitor had at one time occupied.

In one corner sat a large potted plant whose slim, multiple trunks reached the ceiling before sending out overarching, spatulate leaves. She balanced herself precariously on the rim of the container, stroking the short, neatly trimmed beard that was a hallmark of S'van females. The thick black curls both front and back were heavily pomaded with a substance that caused them to flash iridescent beneath the overhead lights. Her clothing was traditionally garish in tone, with none of the subtlety or nuance of Wais attire.

"What do you want with me?" Lalelelang's S'van was smooth and accentless. Her disappointment could not completely suffocate her curiosity. "Do you represent an academic organization?"

"You could say that." The S'van was typically direct. "My

presence here is semiofficial, though as far as anyone outside
this office is concerned, this is an informal meeting.

"The organization which I represent has a long-standing
interest in your work. People have particularly been intrigued
by some of your recent publications, in which you harangue
like mad for one of your pet theories." The visitor shifted
her position on the planter. "It doesn't look like you're having much luck getting anyone to pay any attention to it."

"Until now, it would seem."

The S'van clicked her teeth. "You're unusually direct for
a Wais. I put that down to the amount of time you spent
working closely with Humans. By the way, my name's
Ch'vis."

"There is no question that I have been somewhat influenced by my studies," Lalelelang replied. "If you would
prefer to deal with traditional Wais politesse I can introduce
you to several colleagues who are familiar with my research."

"No, no. I think it's better that I talk to you." She
scratched at the back of her neck, where thick black coils
vanished down the collar of her jumpsuit. Lalelelang shuddered slightly. One of the differences between the humanoid
S'van and *Homo sapiens* was that the latter had no manners,
whereas the S'van had them but often chose to ignore them.
The S'van were also one of the few intelligent species the
Wais could physically look down upon, though the short,
hirsute bipeds were much heavier in body.

"What about my work interests you enough to prompt a
visit in person?" she inquired.

"Others have studied it in more depth than I, but the gist
of it seems to be your claim that now that the war is over,
unfocused Humans are going to go on the rampage: against
the rest of the Weave, against each other, or both. You predict
the rise of unmanageable conflict, to the general detriment
of civilization."

Lalelelang's neck dipped slightly forward and she blinked
one eye in an especially emphatic manner. "An unscholarly
but not inaccurate summation."

"The organization I represent is impressed with the research you've accumulated to back up your theories."

"Is it?" Eyelashes fluttered. "What organization might that be?"

"Doesn't really matter." Ch'vis leaned back against the multiple stems of the domesticated plant. It flexed alarmingly, and she hastened to straighten. "Nice place to work. Pleasant view, quiet."

"Are you offering me support?" Lalelelang asked.

"Call it mutual. You see, members of the group I work with have been observing Humankind pretty closely ever since they first joined in the war against the Amplitur. Some of our efforts parallel yours. Or did you think that your work was unique?"

She shuffled uncertainly on her work nest. "I know that it is not. I have had many contacts with non-Wais, off-world scholars with similar interests, but no such correspondence can be all-inclusive."

The S'van responded with a double clicking of her front incisors only. "It's not surprising that you wouldn't know of us. We don't seek publicity."

"Then if you people concur with my conclusions, you must realize that assertive intervention is imperative."

Ch'vis regarded her fingers. "Not necessarily. Many of us are of the mind that so long as Humankind's destructive energies are directed internally, there's no real danger to the Weave."

"That is not a civilized approach."

The S'van looked sharply at her. "Self-preservation takes precedence over civilized behavior. We agree with your analysis of Human nature. They've always fought and they always will fight. Contact with the Weave hasn't and isn't going to change that. So long as their conflict doesn't spread to non-Human worlds, we think they should be permitted to pursue their traditional forms of 'recreation' without interference.

"At the same time we don't ignore them completely because, as you correctly point out, we might need them again in some far distant, unforeseeable future to counter some unimaginable threat. So we try to manage them. Keep them aggressive but limit the damage. Let them slaughter one another but not allow them to weaken themselves beyond recovery.''

"Manage Humans? What a whimsical notion.''

"There are ways,'' the S'van insisted diffidently. "We think it can be done successfully as well as unobtrusively. Since they were first contacted we've learned a great deal about them. They're more malleable than you might think. Certainly the Wais, through no fault of your own, could not direct such an enterprise. We S'van, however, are a bit cleverer.''

"Devious and deceptive, you mean.''

Ch'vis screwed a stubby finger into her left ear. "Your mastery of my language is admirable, but not perfect. I must've misheard a word or two.''

Lalelelang eyed the S'van in disbelief. "So you could help them, but you're not going to. You will allow them to war among themselves within parameters that you will magisterially specify, without regard to their welfare.''

"Without our intervention they'd eventually destroy themselves altogether,'' Ch'vis argued. "That much of your research we accept implicitly. They were on the verge of doing so when the Weave first contacted them. Recall your Human history. They had actually gone as far as employing nuclear weapons against one another.''

"An isolated incident that was not repeated.''

The S'van sniffed. "Fortunate, but hardly indicative of a permanent change of behavior. If the Weave had not involved them they would probably have obliterated themselves by now.'' The visitor's attitude lightened. "Besides, where's the harm? They *like* to fight. We'll limit them but let them. Humankind has no proper civilization. They're a resource, to be managed. Help them to eschew their aggressive tendencies and you destroy that resource.'' She slipped off the planter and adjusted the folds of her suit.

"Why come all this way to tell me this?'' Lalelelang wanted to know.

"Your reputation extends beyond Mahmahar, and you make a lot of noise. Meanwhile your work on Human–non-

Human social interaction under combat conditions is pioneering. We think it deserves your full attention. You really need to concentrate on it instead of venting loud opinions on that which is already being brought under control.''

She fought to control her instinctive quivering. ''Ch'vis, are you threatening me?''

''Dear me, no!'' The S'van threw up both hands in mock alarm. ''How can you conceive of something so uncivilized? We are merely, as fellow researchers, suggesting that you narrow your field of endeavor and concentrate on the subspecialty in which your work is unparalleled.'' She waddled toward the doorway.

''We have extensive modeling facilities. We've plotted numerous possible futures for Humankind and we're pretty confident that the one we've chosen will be best not only for the entire Weave but for them as well.''

''Do you expect me to stand by and do nothing?''

''We don't expect anything of you, Exalted Scholar Lalelelang. I was not told to expect anything of you. I've made no demands here today, issued no ultimatums. It's a sign of the respect in which we hold you and your independent achievements that I was ordered to come here and deliver to you this information.''

''To induce me to retreat behind a veil of silence, you mean.''

''It's hard to convey bitterness in my language, but you do it very well,'' said Ch'vis admiringly. ''It doesn't become you, and it's not necessary. Sometime I hope to show you our models. Then you'd understand what we're doing is for the best, for everyone.''

''The S'van have never been noted for their altruism.''

''Nor have the Wais. We all have our own interests. Believe me, in this instance they coincide. You're a scholar, and a most remarkable one. Scholars are notoriously impractical individuals.'' She reached to activate the door.

''Wait! Are there other organizations like yours? Among the Hivistahm, perhaps, or the O'o'yan?''

Ch'vis considered. ''Interesting thought. Not to our knowledge. As you more than anyone should know, the in-

timate study of Humankind is not a popular subject." She
thumbed the door control, and the barrier slid aside. "We'd
like to share information with you, historian. We can help
each other."

"But not Humankind," Lalelelang shot back.

"Your attitude will change. It might as well, since there
isn't anything you can do about this. It has support from
quarters that would startle you."

With that Ch'vis excused herself. Not elaborately and floridly as a Wais would have, but in S'van fashion, with a click
of bright square teeth and a parting joke.

Lalelelang stared at the portal. If the S'van were as aware
of the problem as she was but wouldn't do anything to try
and solve it, what chance did she have? More than that, they
didn't *want* the problem solved. They just wanted to keep it
under control. That was not only unfair to Humankind, it was
dangerous. Nor did she share their optimism about managing
Human aggressiveness. That was something that needed to be
permanently modified, not administered, if Humans were ever
to be granted full Weave membership and take their rightful
and hard-earned place in the mainstream of galactic civilization. Only then could it be certain that they would no longer
be a threat to themselves or to any other species.

But if the Weave remained indifferent to granting that
membership, and a powerful S'van faction was arrayed
against her, what hope did she have of making any progress?

She would have to seek the aid of an organization of her
own, one powerful and shrewd enough to somehow contra-
vene the efforts of the devious S'van. Everything would have
to be carried out in a manner that would not alert Ch'vis and
her colleagues. Lalelelang knew of only one such group that
might have the requisite resources and determination.

Certainly they were powerful. The matter of their shrewd-
ness was still open to question.

★ XVII ★

"What's that?" Pila rolled over and tried to get a glimpse of the communicator that Straat-ien was watching as he sat on the edge of the bed. The compact screen he held was eight centimeters square and capable of mock-holo projection.

She leaned up against him, slipping her arms around his chest, resting her chin on his left shoulder. "A Wais! How interesting. I see she isn't wearing a translator." She listened intently.

"Her gestures are certainly emphatic. Is this the one you told me about, the one you've known for so long?" He nodded. They continued listening together until the transmission ended.

Straat-ien put the communicator on the end table and lay back down on the bed. His companion snuggled close to him, lying on her right side, her left hand warm on his chest. They were silent for a while, each digesting the contents of the alien's message.

"Do you think she's right about us?" Pila finally asked.

"I don't know." Straat-ien stared at the ceiling. "Sometimes I think she knows more about us than we do ourselves."

"So we're doomed to keep fighting forever? These S'van will keep us from destroying ourselves but that's it? No help to change old attitudes, no assistance in forging a peaceful civilization." She frowned. "I don't want to fight anymore."

"Nor do I," Straat-ien murmured. "But you and I have the benefit of Core insight. We're a very small, not especially influential minority. The bulk of Humankind still looks at things differently."

"It sounds like this Wais expects you to do something about it."

He shrugged and kicked against the sheets that clung to his legs. "She knows me better than she knows any other Human. She knows about the Core and that we're trying to find a way to make some changes in Human attitudes. That's going to be hard enough going without active opposition. From the S'van, no less. They're dangerously smart."

"You think she's safe?"

"She's managed okay so far." He looked thoughtful. "When the Core was deciding her fate, I argued that if we left her alone, she'd be useful to us someday. Here's the proof of it." He tapped the recorder. "If it wasn't for her, we wouldn't know about this S'van organization."

"Right enough." Pila was mature, and knowledgeable. "Now we can take steps to deal with that. A few suggestions in the right places and we can neutralize their influence without being obvious about it."

Straat-ien sighed. "I wish we could persuade our own kind as easily. There've already been outbreaks of fighting on several of the colonies. The Core Council expects it to spread to Earth any time now. Why people can't recognize the counterproductiveness of such regressive behavior is beyond me."

She patted his chest. "As you pointed out, we enjoy the Core perspective, darling. Most of Humankind doesn't . . . yet."

"If we're not careful, it never will. I know that the genome for the Amplitur-introduced neural nexus is dominant, but it'll take hundreds of years for it to spread deep enough into the racial pool to make a real difference."

"Until that happens we must do the best we can, Nevan. We have a great responsibility." She ran her fingers through the hair on his chest.

"I wish I knew for certain if Lalelelang's projections are right."

"We have to assume that they are. Assuming otherwise means leaving our fate in the hands of the S'van and the Hivistahm and all the rest."

"The S'van," he muttered. "I would have sooner suspected the Hivis, or even the Massood. But not the S'van."

"They joke and kid around to mask their intelligence," she reminded him. "They always have." She was silent for a moment, stroking him. "Nevan," she inquired somberly, "do you think we have a chance? To integrate ourselves into Weave society and enjoy a peaceful, participatory future? Or is your Wais right and we'll always be doomed to fighting and killing?"

"Lalelelang's a pessimist, but she hopes we can change. She thinks that because of our unique perspective the Core can be the instrument of that change, that we can be the renovating anomaly her statistics don't account for."

Pila raised herself higher and stared hard at him. "I didn't ask what she thinks. I asked what you think."

He was silent for a while. Then he turned to envelop her in his arms and draw her down to him.

"Right now I think I'm tired of thinking."

Cataloging the ocean of material she'd acquired, performing seminars, and designing course materials, all this left Lalelclang little time for promoting her theories or, for that matter, any kind of social life. Outwardly her triad sisters supported her efforts, but privately they despaired. Their brilliant, attractive, famous sister was wasting away, devoting her entire life to her studies. They told her repeatedly that her time was ill apportioned, but there was nothing they could do about it. Lalelelang would acknowledge their efforts on her behalf and proceed to ignore them, just as she ignored those males bold enough to approach her.

They could not know that she had much more than her own survival in mind.

Utilizing the university's far-ranging facilities, she scrutinized the interworld media with grim conviction, seeking out the kind of information that never reached the general population. One world, even a portion of one continent, generated more than enough news to satisfy their interest. Besides, now that the war was well over, who cared what Humans, or for that matter the Hivistahm or the Massood, did on their own worlds? The Weave had been created to deal with the Amplitur. With that ancient interstellar threat finally removed the frequency of interspecies contact was already beginning to abate.

Her files grew, and with them her concern.

On Human-settled Daccar, sustained fighting had broken out between the inhabitants of the eastern and northern portions of the landmass. Though not as severe as the explosive outbursts of violence that had marred the history of Old Earth, it was worrisome enough.

A trio of S'van interlocutors who just happened to be on MacKay working on another project energetically offered to mediate a dispute which ignited on that Human colony world. Their offer was accepted, but they had only limited success.

On Mauka IV dissension took the form of a group of offshore islanders who, claiming neglect, sought to distance themselves from the central planetary administration on the mainland. As the islands numbered among their inhabitants a large number of recently retired soldiers, the extent of their resistance was out of all proportion to their actual population. There were no S'van present to help dampen either the ardor of the islanders or the reactive resentment of those on the mainland.

The worst troubles flared on Barnard's, the first world to be colonized by Humans from Earth and one that was fast becoming nearly as urbanized. It was home also to a modest population of Massood, who did their best to remain aloof from their bipedal brethren's uncivilized and rapidly deteriorating behavior. The existence of a large class of Humans who'd grown wealthy from activities related to the war only exacerbated growing tensions, which threatened to involve the Massood in spite of themselves.

It was a situation sufficiently degenerative to inspire quiet jubilation among the Amplitur, but though she searched many sources Lalelelang could find no indication of even indirect Amplitur involvement in the growing canon of Human deviant activity. Nor was there any indication of regression or restlessness among their former allies such as the Ashregan and Crigolit. All blithely continued to disarm and to vocally embrace the new peace.

Lalelelang knew the Amplitur must be aware of what was happening on the human worlds, but she had no more proof of it than she had to substantiate her other theories. The tentacled ones continued to dismantle their extensive military apparatus while taking hesitant steps toward participating in unrestricted interstellar commerce and communication. If their activities were inspired by ulterior motives, the Amplitur kept them well hidden.

Then, near the end of the fourth year following the first such outbreak, and contrary to her ominous predictions, the fighting leveled off. It did not cease entirely. Some inter-Human conflicts continued, new ones flared, but others were settled. Not every potential confrontation reached flash point, not every argument erupted in violence. Several serious commercial disputes were settled by agreement.

Having learned a painful lesson on Barnard's, the Massood stayed out of such skirmishes. Any active S'van role remained invisible. Needless to say, the other members of the Weave ignored the ongoing Human preoccupation with violence as completely as was possible.

Maybe she'd underestimated the S'van. She wouldn't be the first to have done so. Maybe they *could* keep the Human disease under control without having to cure it completely. Or perhaps the lid was being kept on further outbreaks of violence thanks to the work of Colonel Nevan Straat-ien's mysterious Core. Or maybe *they* were working on the S'van. Whatever the cause, the results were encouraging.

Was there such a thing, even for an eccentric species like *Homo sapiens*, as a tolerable level of societal violence? She pondered the theoretical options.

Though distressed by the tumult, the rest of the Weave was more than willing to ignore it so long as it did not spread to their own worlds. Unlike the S'van, now that the war was over the general Weave population didn't much care if Humankind exterminated itself. In fact, there were many who would have thought such a denouement a good thing.

Several hundred years of association with the Weave had wrought some perceptible changes in the fabric of Human society. There were signs that perhaps the first contact, William Dulac, had been at least partially correct in his evaluation of his own kind. Now that the war was over, social interaction between some Humans and their colleagues on other worlds began to expand.

If the S'van could be persuaded to change their minds about continuing the cultivation of Human fighting abilities, such progress toward true integrated civilization might be accelerated. If not, she knew it was possible for Humankind to someday revert to the kind of uninhibited homicidal warfare that had originally characterized the species. Lalelelang checked and rechecked her work. The stocky, hirsute humanoids were playing a very dangerous game on an unimaginably grand scale.

In any event, the best she could do was observe and monitor. The visit she had received from the S'van years earlier remained clear and sharp in her memory, as did the implication behind it.

Occasionally she wondered how her old friend the colonel, Nevan Straat-ien, was coping with peace, or if he was involved in any of the violent flare-ups among his people. There'd been no contact between them for a number of years. Maintaining contact between individuals who lived on different worlds was a difficult, not to mention expensive, proposition. Like most Humans, he was doubtless frantically busy. With his own career, perhaps a new one, or with a family. He had never discussed mating in her presence, but then why should he? His rituals and dances were not hers.

The unusual friendship that had developed between them had been forged of necessity and immediacy. Neither condition any longer existed. Now and then she took a moment to wish him well wherever he was, and flattered herself that he might occasionally do the same in remembrance of her. She wondered if he gave much thought to her theories and decided he did not. Weave civilization was not after all on the verge of being overwhelmed by rampaging Humans.

She was greatly pleased that time had proven her wrong. So far.

⋆ XVIII ⋆

Lieutenant Tuan al-Haikim was as ignorant as his fellow officers of the reason for the meeting. Insofar as he knew, it couldn't have anything to do with the recent troubles in the southeastern provinces. Those had been settled weeks ago and there'd been nothing in the available media about any new flare-ups. Not that something couldn't have been kept quiet.

Perhaps the general wanted to congratulate them on their handling of the situation. Or maybe something new had come up. Al-Haikim hoped not. He didn't like shooting at his own kind. Of course, those damned impertinent southeasterners thought they were so much better than everyone else simply because their ancestors had settled the planet first, but that didn't give them the right to—

He caught himself. He'd been thinking like the average city dweller; not like one whose ancestors had suffered under the tentacles of the Amplitur on Cossuut. Such thoughts were unbecoming to one of the Core.

He studied his fellow officers. They stood or sat or sprawled around the comfortable room, chatting and joking. Several were due for demobilization next month. Even now, years after the end of the Great War, the military continued its inexorable shrinkage. Al-Haikim had worked hard to stay in the Force, just as he'd worked hard for his recent promotion. It was important that the Core remain well represented in the surviving military, if only to counter ongoing surreptitious S'van intervention in Human affairs.

He smiled to himself. While the S'van interfered with Humankind, unbeknownst to them the Core interfered with the S'van. Thus far it had been an equitable trade-off.

Though all but two of those present outranked him, he knew most of them personally. They constituted a significant portion of the general staff on Daccar. During the war they had been scattered across a great arc of space. When the troubles had begun on Daccar, they had been brought here. The colony was a particularly fractious place, a hive of innovation as well as a kind of sociological bellwether for the other Human worlds. It was a good place to spot new trends, bad as well as benign.

In his capacity as a communications specialist he'd met General Levaughn twice, and then only briefly. It was impossible to form an opinion of someone based on such abbreviated contact, and generals were not in the habit of confiding in or asking advice of their lieutenants. All he knew about his comparatively youthful commanding officer was that his record was distinguished. Levaughn was famed as a dedicated soldier and relentless fighter. It was rumored that he had helped to settle some of the more acrimonious southeastern disputes through personal intervention in the negotiating process.

Such musings were pushed into the background as Levaughn entered and waved. Those of his senior advisors who knew him best waved back. As none of those present were in uniform there was no need to maintain the strictures of military formality.

A colonel rose and did something at a wall panel. Al-Haikim watched as safeshields slid down over the windows and the single entryway. A couple of the officers acknowledged these defensive preparations with a low murmur, but no one ventured to question them. Surely everything would be explained, including the need for such security. To Al-Haikim's way of thinking it hearkened back to wartime conditions. He would have been even more surprised if he'd been able to see the armed guard that was taking up grim-faced positions outside the meeting room.

Levaughn halted in front of a bookshelf that, astonishingly enough, was full of books. Real books, made of board and glue and paper. A native of Daccar, the general came from a wealthy family. This had helped him considerably in his dealings with the obstreperous southeasterners.

Now he stood silently contemplating his hand-picked audience. He was a short man, though stockier than al-Haikim and many others. He wore his hair cut short and flat in the old military style, with his emblem of rank shaved into the sides. His eyes were large, black, and penetrating. They framed a nose that had been broken several times in combat. Below was a soft, rounded chin and an effeminate mouth. The ears were large and laid back, as if trying to hide within his hair.

Levaughn's rise through the ranks had been little short of meteoric. The man who had once commanded half a planetary invasion force was now reduced to overseeing the demobilization of troops on his homeworld while concurrently trying to deal with a string of small but bloody riots. The latter were limited in scope but persistent. Since the end of the war, urban Daccarans had developed a reputation for using old-style violence to settle local disputes.

"Please, ladies and gentlemen, be seated." Levaughn smiled at them, showing regenerated teeth.

When they'd complied he continued. "Before we get to the business at hand I want to congratulate all of you on your efforts these past months. The southeast is nearly at peace, a condition it hasn't experienced in some time. I'm told the education people down there are putting in overtime to see it doesn't get out of hand again. Maybe we haven't done as well as our equivalents on some other worlds, but after all, this is Daccar." A few knowing grins and guffaws greeted this sage observation.

"Sometimes I think it's harder to fight the peace than it was to fight the war." More chuckling, punctuated by a few

softly voiced obscenities. Al-Haikim automatically made note
of the latter for future use.

"Maybe some of you have noticed that demobilization
doesn't always go smoothly. It's hard when you and your
parents and your grandparents devoted their lives to fighting
for a great cause and then that cause is suddenly snatched
away. It's not easy to readjust." He smiled compassionately.
"I'm having a pretty tough time myself.

"It's hard to stand before units that have earned glory in
combat and tell them that tomorrow they have to learn how
to be statisticians or agriculturalists or assembly personnel.
I don't know about any of you, but I can't do that without
feeling a sense of loss. But let's face it: If it wasn't for the
occasional troubles that keep cropping up, the problem would
be even worse than it is." There was a substantial but by no
means universal muttering of assent.

"Those of us here are lucky. We're all still together, doing
what we've been trained to do. Performing that which we do
best." His tone turned regretful. "Pity it can't last. After
all, we're at peace now." He began to pace in front of the
bookshelf, his movements as measured and precise as his
speech.

"What I've always wondered about, soldiers, is what this
peace gains us. What do we, as fighting Humans, get out of
it?"

"An absence of death, sir," ventured a perceptive major
from the far side of the room.

Levaughn nodded. "Can't argue with that. What else?"
There were no other comments. "How about friendship with
the Weave? Except that we've never been invited to join that
august organization of noble noncombatants. Commercial
gain? Hell, the Hivistahm and the O'o'yan are better manu-
facturers than we are, the Wais better artists, the Massood
more disciplined workers, the S'van cannier innovators, the
Motar and Sspari more adroit growers. Where's that leave
us? And what happens when our former enemies get back on
nonmilitary tracks? Nobody can build anything more effi-

ciently than those damn bug-eyed Crigolit. Seems like anything we can do, some other species can do better.

"Course, we're still the galaxy's greatest warriors, its toughest fighters. Even our former enemies admit to that. So let me ask you something, ladies and gentlemen: What the fuck good is that gonna do us now?"

The assembled soldiers stirred uneasily. Al-Haikim made a show of participating, but his attention was devoted to recording the reactions of his colleagues. By now it was evident this gathering was intended as something much more than a casual get-together.

Levaughn let them bicker, and argue, and finally simmer down before raising both hands for silence. He had their full attention now. No one was laughing.

"I've known some of you since you began your careers, from Brigadier Higham there—" He indicated a nodding older man seated in a large overstuffed chair. "—to some of you junior officers." Al-Haikim was glad Levaughn didn't glance in his direction. "In turn, you know me. I'm no diplomat and I'm lousy at preplanning. Strike straight, don't deviate: that's been my motto since I was a field grunt. It's served me pretty well. I'm still here, still all original issue." He opened his mouth wide. "Except for these ceramic choppers." Several of those in attendance laughed in spite of themselves.

Levaughn lowered his voice. "O'o'yan manufacture." The laughing stopped.

"The war's over. *We* did that. We Humans. Oh sure, we had plenty of material aid from the Weave, and the Massood did their share of the fighting, but we're the ones who turned the tide. Can't no species take that away from us.

"The thing is, none of 'em want to give us anything in return. What's our place gonna be now that the service we perform best is no longer in demand?"

Someone else in the back spoke up. "I hear that the Mazvec have already petitioned to join!" There was a general murmur of surprise from the assembled.

Levaughn nodded sagely. "Former enemy. We beat the

crap out of 'em on Letant Three and Corschuuk. Now they're going be invited in and we're still standing around looking dumb, like the ugly wallflower waiting for somebody to ask 'em to dance.'' He put his fists on his hips and eyed them evenly.

"That's assuming that there's still a Weave around in half a century's time to ask anybody into anything. Without the Purpose to unite against, the whole system may fall apart. It's already starting to fray. Know what that means? Without any dependable, traditional interstellar alliances, like those existing between the Hivis and the O'os, for example, every Human-occupied world will become an instant galactic backwater. We won't have anything anybody else'll want, and they won't be compelled to have anything to do with us. Some thanks for a couple hundred years of blood and sacrifice.

"Oh, there won't be anarchy. They're all too civilized for that. Interstellar distances being what they are, things'll just become a lot looser. With us floating free on the fringes. No galactic empire for Humankind, like some writers speculated in the early days. Empire, hell! We won't even have a minor role. We'll go back to being ignored.

"Maybe there's worse fates than that, but I'm not so sure. Oh, Humankind'll get along okay. We'll have our own little association of worlds, centered on good old Earth. Provided we can keep from exterminating ourselves. The troubles are the first hints of that. Psychosocial specters from our claustrophobic one-world past. Meanwhile the rest of the galaxy will go back to spurning us, which is what they've always wanted to do.'' He was gesturing assertively with his hands now. For the first time al-Haikim noticed how they'd been torn, and scarred, and repeatedly repaired through regenerative surgery.

"As you may have guessed by now, I've given a lot of thought to Humankind's postwar future. Fact is, I've been thinking about it ever since the Great Surrender at Ail and Eil, observing and taking notes, and I can tell you that I don't much like what I see. I can also tell you that I, personally, after having helped to defeat the Amplitur and all their allies, am not prepared to passively accept that future.'' Jaws clenched in anger, he shook his fist at them.

''*We* put an end to the Purpose! We won the victory! And now we're expected to meekly hand it over and stagger off unprotestingly into oblivion.''

It was dead silent in the room when he finished.

A final protest against mutating times, al-Haikim thought uneasily. A last polemic raised against the changing order. Or was there something more?

A pensive Lieutenant Colonel Otumbo rose. He'd known Levaughn longer than any of them, even Higham. ''I assume you've got something in mind, Nicholas. Military dictatorship?'' A few nervous titters greeted this brazen query.

Levaughn's smile returned. ''You always did have a flair for the melodramatic, Rashidi. Even in combat.'' The lieutenant colonel grinned thinly. ''No, I'm not thinking along lines like that. Notwithstanding my stature, I'm no would-be Napoleon or MacArthur.'' This time the laughs came easier. ''I've no desire to rule any kind of empire, military or otherwise. I just want to see to it that after all we've done for the races of the Weave, Humankind gets back what it deserves.''

He had them now, al-Haikim saw. Most of them, anyway. Of course, the men and women in the room had been carefully chosen in the first place, presumably because Levaughn or someone else thought they would be receptive to his message. Al-Haikim wondered what he'd done to qualify. First explanation, then attack, then denial. A very effective technique, which Levaughn delivered persuasively.

''The Weave's been an effective organization for over a thousand years,'' Levaughn was saying. ''Now me, I dislike chaos. I think the Weave should be preserved. If necessary, in spite of itself. That's not too much to hope for. I think it can be done, and I think that we can help do it. I also think that we should be given our just place within the final structure. Not only us, but the Mazvec, and the T'returia, and all the others who used to be allied with the Amplitur. Hell, if the poor dim-witted *Lepar* deserve full membership, don't we?'' This time the chorus of agreement was barely restrained. Levaughn nodded in satisfaction.

''How is all this going to be brought about, General?'' someone asked.

Levaughn looked at her. ''I'm just a simple soldier. I started out with field armor and munitions and worked my way up in rank, if not in sophistication. I'm sure as hell no philosopher. I can give orders, but I'm not an innovator.''

''Got a S'van handy?'' someone quipped. There were a few desultory chuckles.

''No. I don't think the S'van would look kindly on any attempt to sustain the Weave by Human methods. But there is someone here, a guest of mine, who represents a school of thought that's their equal when it comes to implementing prognostication. Regardless of your initial reactions, or what you may think personally, I'd appreciate it if you'd give your undivided attention.'' He shrugged. ''Afterward everybody can decide for themselves how they feel about it.''

He turned to his right. People leaned forward curiously as the door leading to the next hallway opened. Though al-Haikim didn't see anything immediately, he heard clearly the astonished exclamations of those who could. Then he saw for himself as Levaughn's guest walked into view.

Waddled, rather.

It turned to face them and halted, tentacles curled formally against the sides of its face, slitted black-and gold eyes swiveling independently at the tips of short stalks to regard an entranced audience of former enemies. Silver blotches bloomed and contracted within the orange skin as chromophores reacted to shifting emotions. Container pouches were slung just behind the eyestalks, within easy reach of the flexible tentacles. A translator of unusual design hung below the recessed mouthparts. The Amplitur wore nothing recognizable as clothing.

There being nothing appropriate for it to sit or rest on, it stood. Looking at the creature it was difficult to see how the four stumpy legs could support the large, flabby mass. Those knowledgeable about the old enemy knew that it would have been more comfortable in a pool of shallow brine.

When it spoke, a lifetime of training caused many of those present to tense, even though they knew it could not affect them mentally the way it did the other races of the Weave. Facts, however, could not entirely banish old fears.

The horny mouthparts made a rasping, sucking sound that the translator struggled to transmute into comprehensible Huma.

"I bid you all greetings and good health. I am Cast-creative-Seeking, who is grateful to be this day in your company. You will excuse me if I have to leave suddenly. I find the atmosphere in here both too dry and too cool for comfort. This I will temporarily bear for the sake of viable communication."

"We could turn the heat up," someone offered, "and try to scrounge a watering can." Those sitting next to the officer who spoke laughed.

"Human humor," the Amplitur observed unemotionally. "A trait we do not entirely understand. Sometimes we feel deprived."

Al-Haikim rubbed his mustache, a nervous habit. This was the ancient enemy par excellence, and it was addressing them as matter-of-factly as a juvenile entertainment performer. No matter how much it or Levaughn attempted to put them at ease, al-Haikim still found himself considering the best means of escape and attack. He tried to make himself relax, telling himself firmly that there was no threat here. Only part of him would accept that.

What the hell was it doing on Daccar, as General Levaughn's guest, no less?

Gradually apprehension gave way to curiosity. It was inevitable. This Amplitur was the first of its kind most of those present had ever encountered in the flesh. The desire to listen and learn was irresistible. Al-Haikim was no less susceptible than anyone else in the room.

He told himself that the Amplitur could not mess with his mind because he was Human. It was not armed, it rasped words of friendship, and Levaughn had surely had it thoroughly checked out before allowing it into his home, much less onto Daccar. Without a Crigolit or Mazvec or similar armed escort to manipulate, it was virtually helpless.

Despite this, and the fact that the war had been over for years, not everyone present was prepared to be quite so understanding. Manifest anger prompted one officer to rise.

"What's this thing doing here, General? If I want to see biological curiosities, I'll go to the zoo. What's it got to do with us?"

Levaughn took no umbrage at the other's tone. "Maybe nothing. All you need to know right now is that Cast-creative-Seeking is my guest. We've been communicating, exchanging ideas and thoughts, for quite a while. Until now our relationship has been entirely private." His eyes narrowed just slightly as he scanned his visitors. "I'd like to request that knowledge of this meeting and what transpires here does not go beyond this room." Levaughn was polite, but insistent.

"Not long ago I reached the point where I felt that our dialogue had earned a wider audience. It'll be interesting to see if you agree. Some of it you've already heard from me."

Another lieutenant colonel spoke hesitantly. "General, are we talking here about some kind of alliance between us and the Amplitur?"

"Now, how do you think that news would be received?" said Levaughn. "The other members of the Weave wouldn't stand for it . . . not that they could do anything about it," he added darkly.

"Cast-creative-Seeking and his brethren are simply seeking common ground with their former adversaries, so that we can better understand one another and coexist peacefully. Nothing unnatural about that."

Tentacles unfurled and gesturing, the Amplitur addressed them anew. "For a long time your kind and mine were enemies. A regrettable state of affairs largely due, we now firmly believe, to ignorance on both sides. As you know, we the Amplitur abhor violence because it removes good minds from participation in the Purpose.''

"You didn't seem to abhor it when you attacked Earth,'' someone blurted accusingly. Mutters of assent rose from others in the room.

The alien was not fazed by the reminder. "That was a long time ago. It was what we felt had to be done at the time. We were panicked by the effectiveness of the first Human soldiers the Weave had recruited. As subsequent developments proved, our panic was not misplaced." Somewhat to their own surprise, this drew knowing smiles from several in the audience.

"We responded according to the directives formulated by our best minds, functioning in accord with the principles of the Purpose. What is the Purpose, after all?" Someone groaned. "I'm sure you know."

"Yeah, we know," said another lieutenant. "We just don't agree with it, that's all."

"I did not mean to provoke. This is, after all, an old argument we clearly cannot win. We hew to the Purpose, you do not. So it shall be. Please believe me when I say that though we have fought one another, the Amplitur have never had anything but the greatest respect for your kind. In your singular determination you are more like us than any other species we have ever encountered." A couple of those present made as if to object, but the Amplitur hurried on.

"You are the only species we cannot influence mentally, cannot persuade by projective suggestion. You possess a unique neurological defense of which you were completely unaware until you encountered us. What does this tell us? That we are the only two species whose minds operate on a different, higher plane, albeit in disparate ways. You cannot be suggested, and we can only suggest." Al-Haikim tensed in spite of himself, but the Amplitur paid no special attention to him. What would be its reaction, he wondered, if it learned of the Core and the Ampliturlike abilities of its constituents?

"What wisdom may astute analysts glean from this observation?" There was no immediate response and the Amplitur did not let the silence linger. It waved a tentacle high, the four flexible tips floating like so many airborne worms. "Does it not suggest that despite our disparate histories and evolution we may where it matters have more in common than any other two intelligent species?"

Shouts of disagreement and indignation rose from the gathering. "How can you say that?" someone sputtered.

"By now you have been exposed to galactic diversity long enough to know that where true interspecies compatibility is concerned, mere physical appearance counts for nothing. Like it or not, that is an ancient tenet of the Purpose."

"Even if our minds are similar," said the elder Brigadier Higham, "and being no biologist I'm not ready to concede that, our aims and ideals are still diametrically at odds with one other."

"Are they truly?" The Amplitur focused both eyes on him. "For a very long time we, too, thought that. When we first invited you to join with us you refused, as had a number of other species. But this is a disagreement with a long history, which we will not settle here.

"What is important is that you defeated us. We admit that, and as you know, we do not lie. I am here only as a supplicant, requesting and not demanding your consideration."

"Then you're not asking for some kind of alliance?"

"No. There can be no alliance between victor and defeated because they are by definition unequal. What I am here to do on behalf of my kind is to ask for you, as Humans, to take up the mantle of guidance from us."

Levaughn stepped forward to deal with the bewilderment and confusion that were the immediate result of the Amplitur's unexpected declaration.

"Ladies and gentlemen, we stand at a crossroads of history. Do we accept the irrelevant status to which the Weave would quietly relegate us, or do we step forward and grasp for ourselves the position of leadership which we have rightfully earned?" His eyes blazed. "A new age beckons Humankind. Why should it not begin here?"

The cynical lieutenant who'd spoken earlier didn't hesitate. "You speak, General, of leadership. Leadership of what: the Weave . . . or the Purpose?"

"You do not understand." The Amplitur entwined its tentacles. "Let me explain.

"Since you were buddings you have been taught to hate the Purpose. What, then, is the Purpose? Little more than a euphemism for sensible cooperation between intelligences."

"Cooperation dominated by you!" the junior officer shot back.

"We did not dominate: we led. Someone must lead. Some must give direction. For a very long time it was the Amplitur. Now it is clear that is no longer to be. This is not something that distresses us. Only the endemically foolish refuse to resign themselves to reality, and we are not fools.

"Leadership is a great burden. Even as it can weigh down a strong individual, so also it can an entire species. We are timeworn and tired. The thought of passing responsibility on to a younger, more vibrant species does not distress us."

"You want *us* to take over the *Purpose*? After fighting to obliterate it?" a major asked.

"Call it whatever you will. Galactic civilization, if it pleases you. Someone must assume leadership. Ignore the Purpose for now, if it suits you. As time passes you will find that the Purpose does not ignore you.

"Consider the Weave. Until they acquired in the Amplitur a common enemy to unite against, they were at best an indecisive association of mutually suspicious species with ambiguous aims and a parlous future. They bickered and quarreled endlessly among themselves. That is not civilization. Left leaderless as they were before, they will once again degenerate into mutual acrimony and fighting as each species goes its own way."

"That's your opinion," said the irrepressible lieutenant. "We call it independence."

"Yes, your vaunted independence." The Amplitur shifted its bulk. "There is a fine line, my young antagonist, between independence and anarchy. Bind together thinking beings in a real consolidation and you preserve civilization.

"What if someday another new species is encountered: one with our aims but your regressive behavioral characteristics? Would it not be better to be able to contest them from within the framework of a great and powerful Weave, instead of one riven and weakened by traditional internal dissension? The universe is a vast and dangerous place in which too much 'independence' might one day prove fatal.

"Listen to your own general! Who better to assume leadership than your kind? Not the reticent Hivistahm, for all their organizational skills. Not the S'van, for all their dexterous intelligence. Nor the Massood, fighters like yourselves. Who, then, but Humankind?"

"We don't want it," said the major earnestly. "No matter the rationalization, we're not going to fight our former allies."

"Who spoke of violence? Not I. The Amplitur spoke always of peace. Do you really think they would resist you as they resisted us, if it was made known that our two species were working side by side for the greater good? Perhaps only the Massood, and they would not resist long. They might challenge the idea, the O'o'yan and the Lepar and the rest, but they could not resist the reality. What sensible species would try to war against Humans assisted by Amplitur? There would be no fighting. It could all be done peacefully, and for the greater good."

"Okay So what do you get out of it?" the lieutenant asked sharply.

"Us?" Cast-creative-Seeking regarded the speaker mournfully out of ancient eyes whose depths could not be plumbed. "We see cooperation preserved between intelligences. We see it expanded and refined. Do not call it the Purpose. Call it common sense. In that is satisfaction enough.

"Remember that I cannot lie, and I cannot influence you mentally. We would not seek domination, or leadership. Always we will be present to offer help and advice, as those called viziers and cabinet ministers once offered counsel to individual rulers on your own world. A useful role for an aged, experienced people like ourselves. Or if you prefer, we will do nothing. We will retire to our homeworlds and let you proceed as you choose.

"But if you should opt for our assistance, we can begin by guaranteeing you the cooperation of all those who once were allied to us: the Mazvec and Ashregan, the Crigolit and T'returia, the Acaria and Segunians and Korath and all the rest. This I promise you: The true difficulty of your task will become apparent only *after* your ascension is no longer opposed.

"Presently you fight and argue among yourselves. That is because you no longer have an appropriate alternative outlet for your energies. Leadership of a new Weave will provide that. The present Weave only encourages your internal dissension."

"The Weave has nothing to do with it," argued the major.

"Precisely. They have nothing to do with it. They make no attempt to intervene to help because they are content to let you debilitate yourselves. That way they can keep you under control. They fear you. Bear in mind that we do not. Where friendship is concerned, respect is more to be desired than fear.

"Don't you see? Leadership is what you have evolved for. You are suited to the task. Now that we have been defeated, you are the only people who can hold a galactic coalition closely enough together to be useful, by enforcing cooperation amidst a multitude of fractious diversity."

None of those present had anticipated having to deal with matters of profound import when they'd received their invitations to gather at Levaughn's home. Now they had been given an immense amount to think about.

"I am not used to forming vocalizations," the Amplitur informed his listeners. "It is tiring, and I have said enough. But I will try to answer any questions you may still have. Bear in mind as you ask them that I cannot lie."

"You really have no intentions other than to act as our advisors?" one of the lieutenant colonels inquired.

"Nothing more. We seek stability above all else."

"But that's not your Purpose, the melding of intelligences

you've always spoken of and fought for," said a voice from the audience.

"True. You may be aware of our reputation for patience. In the absence of viable alternatives we will forgo active agitation on behalf of the Purpose because we firmly believe that in a thousand years, or two, or longer, all species will come around to our way of thinking, will see the universe as we see it. The additional wait is to be regretted, but because we have lost at fighting we must now seek to excel at waiting."

"How can we trust you? We still don't know very much about you," the major pointed out.

Cast-creative-Seeking spread tentacles wide. "We are disarmed. Come and study us. Our biologists will work side by side with yours. Learn all that you will. Nothing will be withheld, nothing concealed. We can learn from each other. Examine in depth our minds, as we have tried to examine yours."

It was a dangerous slip. Uneasy murmurs rose from the assembled as those present who were familiar with wartime incidents of Amplitur dissection and attempted mental manipulation of captured Humans had unpleasant memories jogged. But Cast-creative-Seeking spoke with such openness that the initial agitation soon passed. Except for al-Haikim, whose ancestors had been subject to precisely that kind of Amplitur experimentation. Nothing on his face betrayed what he was feeling at that moment, however. As a member of the Core he'd had to practice reaction restraint since childhood.

Levaughn surveyed his guests. "What've we got to lose here? If Cast-creative-Seeking is indeed telling the truth and his people want nothing but to help us take our rightful place in the scheme of things, where's the harm? If nothing else, we can learn a lot from them. Me, I think this is our destiny. It sure as hell beats fighting and killing each other.

"I'm not asking for a vote of confidence or anything like that now. I know this is a lot to think about. So return to your duty assignments, go home, and think about what you've seen and heard here today. All I ask is that you don't discuss it with anyone you don't trust implicitly. There are reactionary forces on Daccar and elsewhere who wouldn't understand what's transpired here today and who would take steps to try and prevent its recurrence.

"It's our future that's at stake here, ladies and gentlemen. Not just ours individually, you and I, but that of our entire species. I think our joint proposal," and he gestured in the direction of the silent Amplitur, "is a good template for future Human development." He smiled paternally.

"I know I can trust each and every one of you to be discreet as well as thoughtful. Otherwise you wouldn't be here today."

Cast-creative-Seeking waved a tentacle for attention. "I will remain here some time as General Levaughn's guest. If you would like to converse with me further, I look forward to such arrangements. Please take advantage of my presence. I am not a holo, not a projection. I think I understand you, your culture and your needs, as well as any of my kind."

"Weave xenopsychs have been studying us for decades and they don't understand us," said the major.

"I said I understood you as well as any of my kind." Cast-creative-Seeking regarded the speaker with both eyes. In the closed room those bulbous orbs seemed open and inoffensive. "It is quite true that no one understands you completely. I would be grateful if you would continue to educate me."

Obviously exhausted by the need to speak aloud while tolerating climatic differences well outside its comfort zone, the Amplitur turned to its Human host and murmured something beyond range of the translator, in its own language. Al-Haikim noted with interest that Levaughn appeared to understand. Clearly this was not an enterprise the general had embarked upon in haste a few weeks or months ago.

"I'll be available for questions also," Levaughn informed them. "Don't hesitate to ask. Discuss it among yourselves." The sealed door at the back of the room opened to allow the assembled to depart.

In twos and threes the officers rose to leave, conversing animatedly among themselves as they filed out. Levaughn watched them go, much pleased with himself. He felt it had gone well, and Cast-creative-Seeking concurred.

How many of them would throw in with him? How many had the vision? He'd chosen them carefully and he needed their support. One could lead the way to a glorious future, he knew, but one could not forge it alone.

Energetically ignoring Levaughn's strictures, al-Haikim cautiously but efficiently proceeded to disseminate the proceedings of the encounter to the rest of the modest Core population on Daccar. From there it spread both in person and via Underspace transmission to members on other worlds.

The reaction among those whose ancestors had been operated upon by Amplitur surgeons was predictably outraged, the more so when they learned that al-Haikim believed Levaughn's message had gone down well with his audience. Furious debate ensued on how best to expunge the infection before it could spread. Not that it was anything new. The symptoms were all too familiar from Human tribal history. Only the circumstances were different.

Dangerously different. No would-be Human despot had enjoyed the services of the Amplitur as advisors.

Pleading inexperience, al-Haikim called for assistance. He was more than willing to help carry out whatever plan of action the Core seniors deemed advisable, but felt incapable of fashioning one himself.

★ XIX ★

She knew what he was before she knew who he was. It was obvious from the manner in which students and scholars scattered with as much decorum as they could muster from the vicinity of the sinuous anodized fountain.

She was resting on one of the wading platforms that jutted gracefully out into the central pool, her unshod feet and lower legs dangling in the lightly carbonated water, enjoying on her face and feathers the cooling mist the fountain's jets propagated on a hot day. Triwinged Pligans roosted on the contorted strips of rainbow-hued metal, fizzing softly to one another as they diligently scanned the water below for drowned or drifting bugs, their equilibrium undisturbed by the fountain's sedately gyrating components.

Hydronacaleths bloomed fecundly in the backwaters of the pool, their star-shaped green pads covering much of the sun-dappled surface. Eyes flashing, bubble-faced Mokers used them for cover as they competed with the Pligans for the same chitonous meals. Naturally, only those whose skin color matched that of the paving which framed the fountain were allowed to reproduce.

Into this placid frieze strode the figure which had so unsettled everyone save for a single eccentric female scholar.

Strange to see him in civilian attire. That did not mean he had left the military, she knew. There were many who believed that a Human could never completely leave the military.

As he drew nearer she studied his face. Though many could speak the comparatively simple language, there were among the Wais probably fewer than a dozen individuals who could instantly and correctly interpret Human expressions without recourse to research materials.

Plumage ruffled, attitudes no less so, those who had been relaxing in the company of the fountain continued to retreat, putting as much distance between themselves and the approaching Human as possible. Those who knew about Lalelelang glanced in her direction and whispered to their companions when they thought she wasn't looking.

Since she was physically incapable of smiling outwardly, she smiled to herself. No doubt the Human had cleaved a path through the university grounds as cleanly as ancient ships had parted the waves of the Popememem Sea.

He was standing close now, gazing down at her through the self-darkening lenses Humans used to reduce the glare of Mahmahar's sun. Their eyes were sharper than those of the Wais, and correspondingly sensitive. The best of her friends would have shied fearfully from such proximity. She simply raised a wingtip in greeting.

"Been a long time, Lalelelang."

"Many years. Is your life filled with open sky, Colonel Straat-ien?"

He manipulated his facial muscles to show affection. As always, it was fascinating to watch them work. "You still have a hard time calling me Nevan."

"I've been long back among civilized Wais behavior. I can call you anything you want, Nevan, in as many languages as you can think of."

"And several times did, as I recall."

Edging to the far side of the platform, she described a descending curve with her wing. She didn't know if he recognized the gesture, but he took a seat next to her anyway. His bulk no longer made her nervous, but it provoked astonished commentary from those pedestrians who had not fled entirely the vicinity of the fountain.

"It must be something very important to bring you a second time all the way to my homeworld."

He let his gaze rove the surrounding manicured grounds, with their immaculately sculpted hills and strange trees and undergrowth. When it chanced to interdict any curious Wais, they hurriedly and uneasily looked away.

"What I have to say couldn't be trusted even to secured interworld communications. I may need your help."

She tensed visibly. "I gave my help prior to the end of the war. Now I pursue my research in peace and quiet, as behooves someone of my age."

"What about your grand hypothesis?"

"It troubles me less than it once did."

He nodded. "Some people think that though the war's over in name, it continues in spirit."

She pondered this, then drew her feet out of the pool. "Let's take a walk. I have been sitting in the sun too long."

Her head crest reached only to his lower chest. She led him to a green-and-yellow meadow shaded by broad-leaved trees. Brightly colored small ornithorps darted and danced in the air above the meadow, their range restricted by the shimmer of a delicate restraining field. A small group of students was observing the caged arboreals when they noticed the new arrivals and made haste to depart.

The war was long over. Life for her had settled into a comfortable, predictable pattern. Now here had come this engram from a difficult past, this Human, bashing his way back into her reality with demands the extent of which she could only imagine. Doubtless he didn't see it half so brusquely, but then what else could you expect of a hairy primate?

Folding her legs beneath her, she sat down beneath the nearest tree, dangling her feet over another pool that was a miniature of the one they had left behind. He made a temporary seat of a fancifully placed broken log.

"I'm ready," she sighed resignedly. "Tell me."

He explained, in depth and with quiet animation.

When he'd concluded she found herself staring at the hedge

that formed a greenish purple barrier on the far side of the meadow. It was rife with maturing black berries. She had a feeling she wasn't going to have time to pick any. The stones in her gut clinked.

In a nearby bush a hunting arachnid spat a minuscule globule of sticky mucus at a grazing honeyeater. Entangled and weighted down by the gummy blob, the larger bug spiraled to the ground, futilely fighting to free its wings. Having successfully expelled the combination of compressed air and mucus it stored in its special pouch, the arachnid pounced, smothering the body of its prey with its own striped, streamlined form.

It reminded her of something else.

"It has to be part of an official Amplitur covenant," Straatien was explaining. "This Cast-creative-Seeking can't be operating on its own, or on behalf of some small renegade group. Individual initiative is alien to its kind." Her friend's expression twisted. "Goes against the Purpose. The Amplitur do everything by consensus."

"If your information is correct in its particulars," she declared in measured tones, "then what we have here is nothing less than an entirely new and previously unsuspected Amplitur policy. The truth is sufficiently graphic. They want to help Humankind take control of the Weave and then they will try to control Humankind. They will use your people to gain what they themselves could not."

"They claim only to want to give advice," he replied.

She gestured actively. "As they advised the Crigolit, and the Mazvec, and all their other former allies." Her voice dropped. "You have to credit them. This is more subtle. Much more subtle. It is obvious they have devoted a great deal of effort to learning about you. What they have in mind is to appeal not only to your postwar frustrations but to your racial vanity." Her eyes widened slowly as she connected his presence with her assessment. "Surely you do not think it can happen?"

Straat-ien gazed across the grounds, idly trying to identify something hanging from a low branch. "Not among the educated. But as to the greater mass of Humankind, I frankly don't know. My people have always been tempted by dreams of absolute power. It's been a problem since the beginnings of our civilization. Would-be despots like this General Levaughn are usually the trigger."

Beneath brightly colored strands of metallic fabric, the feathers on her chest fluffed with her breathing. "You know that if Humankind resorts to violence to address ills real or imaginary, the Weave will be compelled to respond in kind."

"Wouldn't matter." He didn't look at her. "You wouldn't have a chance."

"The Massood would fight, and logistically you would be overwhelmed."

"Maybe," he admitted. "But with Amplitur help, and the aid of many of their former allies: I don't know. It could be a near thing."

"Regardless of the outcome, the Amplitur would emerge strengthened," she said bitterly.

"They couldn't control us."

She made a desultory clicking sound with her beak. "They don't want to control you. They want to organize you. You are great fighters, but you are not sophisticated in these matters. The Amplitur are ancient, and wise. If necessary I think they would go so far as to sacrifice some of themselves physically to convince you. They will do whatever is required to gain your confidence. Then in a hundred years, or a thousand, or longer, your species will find itself responding to their directions without even being aware of what is taking place.

"Because if you give them enough time, their neurological engineers will find a way to counter, or bypass, or otherwise defend against your peculiar mental defenses. When that happens, you will find them suggesting you even as they have suggested the Wais, or the Massood. You'll become their janissaries, and independence of intelligence will become no more than memory throughout the galaxy.

"Worst of all, you will believe that you are still in control."

"That's how most of us within the Core see things, but not everyone. Not yet. At such times it's valuable to have non-Human input."

"So you come to me." She watched a dark shape move gracefully through the pool near her feet, concerned with nothing beyond eating and procreation. At that moment all the weight of a lifetime of difficult work pressed down on her, as she envied the swimmer the smothering simplicity of its existence. She could not be so fortunate, being cursed as she was with intelligence.

"I am tired, Nevan. Though I fear no less for the future, I am less convinced that I should exert myself on its behalf. In my noninvolvement it neither tempts nor curses me. My surroundings please me, and occasionally I am even confounded by a student who seems genuinely interested in my socially abhorred subfield of expertise. The prospect of non-Wais activity exhausts me."

"How do you know I was going to ask you for anything more than your opinion?"

She peered straight at him out of large, round blue eyes. "Weren't you?"

This time it was the Human who looked away. "You have to help us deal with this threat. Your position is unique, Lalelelang. You know more about us than any non-Human alive. That makes your perspective invaluable."

She didn't reply. Instead she searched for the dark swimmer in the pool. It was gone, fled somewhere beneath the hydronacaleths. Where she knew that, despite her growing anxiety, she could not follow. She let out a long, lingering trill. Any casual Human listener would have thought it beautiful. Straat-ien knew better what it signified.

"How many important or influential Humans have the Amplitur thus far subverted?"

Straat-ien didn't waste time thanking her. "To the best of our knowledge, which is admittedly limited, this Levaughn and the few junior officers he's managed to convert are the only ones so far."

"That much is encouraging."

"Whatever course of action we eventually decide upon, we have to move very carefully. As you know, Lalelelang, we have our own secrets to preserve."

She remembered the simple Human gesture and nodded concurringly. "I know you cannot persuade other Humans," she said thoughtfully, "but could you not, in this instance, appropriately suggest the Amplitur involved?"

"That's a course of action we're considering, but it involves additional dangers. The Amplitur mind is similar to our own, but not identical. Unlike us, they have no inbuilt neurological defense against being suggested. But they're sensitive to intrusion. If we try to suggest to this one that it stop what it's doing and return to its own world and the procedure fails, they'll be made aware of the existence of the Core. They could bring Human allies like Levaughn to bear against us."

"I agree you must use caution in your dealings, but I had in mind something other than compelling them to abandon their attempts to subvert your people."

Straat-ien was confused. "Isn't that what we want them to do?"

"Ultimately. But why not make use of them first?"

"I don't understand your point." For the briefest of instants he wondered if Lalelelang's mastery of his language might be less than complete.

She flicked her lashes at him. "Instead of simply forcing them to withdraw their efforts, why not suggest that they explain the true motives behind their sudden offer of assistance?"

"That might be difficult to do if they really are, to their way of thinking, telling the truth. Besides, I'm told that among their Human supporters there are a fair number who still suspect the Amplitur's actual motives. They suspect, but they simply don't care."

Lalelelang could not hide her shock. "I have studied many of your kind, but I still find it hard to believe that among them are those who so desperately crave power over others."

"Believe me, Lalelelang, there are. I get no pleasure from admitting to it, but that's what we're dealing with here."

"These individuals must be stopped immediately."

"We agree. I think your suggestion about forcing the Amplitur to confess is good sense. It can't do any harm, and it just might rattle the equivocators in Levaughn's entourage."

"How do you plan to proceed?" she asked him.

"We're fortunate enough to have had someone on the inside from the beginning. He thinks he can get an operative close. Me."

"They would not suspect?"

Straat-ien shrugged. "I'm a senior officer with plenty of wartime experience and no obvious connections to Intelligence. Just the type Levaughn is looking to recruit. I think it can be managed. Once inside, I'll find a way to get close to the Amplitur. When I think the time's right I'll hit it with as convincing a piece of suggesting as anyone's ever attempted.

"As for your suggestion, it's a good one. I'll propose it to the Core Council. If they approve, then you know what kind of approach we'll be trying." He smiled fondly. "If you hear from me afterward, you'll know it went well. If you don't—" He shrugged again. "We can't foresee everything."

"I want to be there."

He blinked, turning away from the landscaped woodland and back to the elegant, fragile form seated by the side of the pond. "What do you mean, 'be there'? Levaughn's on Daccar. That's a Human world. More unsettling for a Wais than a mixed-species battlefield."

"Given my experience in these matters, you still presume to dictate limitations to me? The exercises and medications I originally developed to enable me to cope with combat have been refined. I would regard such a journey as merely an adjunct to my research."

"Every time I see you I think I know you, and every time you manage to astonish me." He rose, towering over her, and she fought back the natural impulse to sidle away from his overbearing, threatening bulk. "If you'd been Human . . ."

"Please, old friend, my insides are unsettled enough by the prospect before me. Do not contribute to the disturbance." She rose alongside him, disdaining his profferred hand. Turquoise eyes considered his from beneath lashes that today were tinted iridescent green. "If we are for purposes of amusement to speculate on might-have-beens, far better to imagine that you had been Wais."

"No thanks." He tried but failed to repress a smile. "Feathers make me sneeze. Why do you think I'm always wrinkling up my nose in your presence?"

Her beak clicked softly. "All these years I wondered about that and never thought to ask. Drawing upon my knowledge of Human expression I believed it to be a reflection of your distaste for my kind, which I politely ignored."

"No," he murmured. "Not distaste. At our first meetings, perhaps. But since that time, I've had nothing but admiration for you, Honored Scholar Lalelelang."

"That is kind to hear, however much it is delayed. Please start toward the building. Being confronted with both water and a Human is making me uneasy."

He hurried to make way for her, believing her implicitly. Not knowing it was an excuse she was using to avoid other thoughts, and other emotions.

★ XX ★

Six months passed before the communication arrived that caused her to take ship.

The ever disputatious government of Daccar was headed not by a single individual but by a duopoly consisting of a president and a premier. Such cross-checks extended throughout the body of the Daccaran government. While serving to prevent abuse, the system also unfortunately tended to foment constant disagreement and legislative stagnation.

For nine years the president, a tough but popular woman named Hachida, had dominated the Daccaran Executive. For seven of those years the premier, Daniel Cosgrave, had sought and failed to gain ascendance. Always he was a few votes shy of overriding her legislation, a trend or two behind her proclamations. At first it merely galled him. Then it be gan to fester. All of this was very much in keeping with Daccaran political tradition.

Levaughn and his clandestine intentions were not.

First there were calls offering support. These were followed by offers of credit, then several casual meetings, none of which attracted particular scrutiny from the popular media. Hachida and many other leading politicians had their own personal advisors. It was expected that Cosgrave would also.

The meetings were held in private, and only the two men knew what was discussed. The two men, and one that was something else.

Having been initially recommended by the lieutenant and subsequently made a member of Levaughn's inner circle, Straat-ien quietly kept the senior representatives of the Core advised of developments. Events did not bode well. With the help of General Levaughn and "unnamed" secondary parties, it appeared that Cosgrave was now finally poised to take control of the Daccaran government. If successful in his maneuvers, he would naturally be deeply indebted to his strongest supporters. Worse, he appeared to have fallen completely under Levaughn's sway. This was not a matter for concern as much as was the advice of Levaughn's own "advisors."

Contentious Daccar was particularly susceptible to reactionary philosophies. An influential world, it had made the standard attempts in the past to extend its influence beyond its orbit. If Cosgrave assumed control, it was probable that, like his voluble, volatile predecessors, he would try to promulgate his own philosophy elsewhere. The members of the Core had become greatly concerned with the direction events were taking.

At Straat-ien's suggestion Levaughn agreed that Lalelelang should be allowed to attend one of the political caucuses as an observer. The colonel's rationale was that her presence could do no harm and might generate some good publicity for the movement. Her reputation as one of the foremost Wais students of Human behavior duly impressed the general, and over the previous months he had come to value the bemedaled Colonel Straat-ien's advice. Furthermore, Straat-ien assured his superior that he would take personal responsibility for seeing to it that their visitor saw nothing she wasn't supposed to see.

Once Levaughn agreed to the proposal, he promptly put it out of his thoughts, which were presently inundated with events of far greater import.

The actual caucus was scheduled for the wealthy Cosgrave's private forest retreat, a sprawling complex of single- and two-story structures built on the side of a mountain high up in the great northern range. While Straat-ien found the setting attractive and invigorating, it made Lalelelang uneasy. Despite their avian ancestry the Wais did not care for high, steep places.

A fast-flowing river cascaded symphonically through the steep-sided gorge below the grounds, which had been creatively sited among the existing Daccaran evergreens. Higher peaks towered in the distance. Individual apartments were located in a pair of long, narrow buildings set apart from the main complex. One was assigned to Lalelelang. The appointments were recently modified and versatile, having been redesigned with the comfort of non-Humans in mind.

After greeting the newly arrived Lalelelang, Straat-ien remarked somberly that there appeared to be as many civilians present as active military. It was a bad sign, suggesting that Cosgrave and Levaughn continued to extend their personal influence among the Daccaran elite.

"Levaughn's very persuasive." Straat-ien spoke as they strolled along a winding cliffside path. Far below, the river ran its frothing, complaining way toward the distant sea. "And Cosgrave's vain and ambitious. Bad combination."

"Then it has begun." Lalelelang was wrapped in thin but warm multiple layers of clothing. Straat-ien found the alpine climate bracingly cool, but to Lalelelang it bordered on the frigid. "I had hoped circumstances would disprove my theories."

"They may yet." His expression was pensive and uninformative.

She stopped, keeping well back from the thin plastic guardrail. A waterfall thundered at the head of the gorge. "Do you recall the last time the two of us stood together at the edge of a precipice?"

He looked puzzled. Then recognition hit home and he turned away from her, letting his gaze drift out across the canyon. "It was a different time. I wasn't sure of you. There were a lot of things I wasn't sure about." He was silent for a moment before looking back to her. "You remember that?"

"Natural enough to recall the moment when someone you consider a friend was wrestling with the issue of whether or not to murder you. I am glad you made the choice you did."

Certain he was missing something, he found himself wishing he were more conversant with the elaborate Wais language of gestures and movements. "You're prejudiced in the matter."

"As the Hivistahm would say, truly." She turned serious again. "How dangerous is this man Cosgrave?"

"By himself not at all. Levaughn's still the one we have to watch out for. He needs a wider political base before he can make any overt military moves. If Cosgrave can wrest legislative control of the planetary government from the president, he'll have that. Daccar will become the springboard for Amplitur-inspired subversion of all the Human worlds."

She stepped farther away from the railing. "They're here, of course."

"Yes. At least, one of them is. Reported to have just arrived. I haven't seen it yet, but I think it's the same one Levaughn introduced to his original inner circle: Cast-creative-Seeking."

"That would follow. The Amplitur, too, understand the meaning of specialization." Her voice fell to an introspective murmur. "An Amplitur specialist in Human behavior. It would be interesting to exchange views with my mind-swaying counterpart. Our theses would be similar but not our objectives."

"How are you holding up surrounded by so many Humans?" he inquired solicitously.

"It is not so bad. There are additionally present a few Hivistahm on the engineering staff of this large facility. We have conversed. There are also several Lepar. We of course do not converse, but it is nonetheless refreshing to see still another non-Human face. I believe I have noticed a single Bir'rimor as well. So I do not feel completely isolated."

Straat-ien nodded. "Daccar's a pretty cosmopolitan world. Weave species mix freely here even though the population is predominantly Human."

"You breed so prolifically." Her comment was utterly nonjudgmental. "Do you know where the Amplitur is staying?"

"I have an idea. Premier Cosgrave apparently felt it necessary to install facilities suitable for other species."

"I know. My rooms are comfortable."

He encompassed the grounds with a wave of his hand. "You probably find all this chaotic compared to home. The Wais prefer to organize nature."

"We do not organize," she insisted. "Our aesthetics require that we aid nature in occupying the most amenable channels."

"Isn't that what the Amplitur Purpose wants to do with all intelligence?"

"It is all a question of perspective. Certainly the Human Levaughn has in mind rigid organizing as opposed to fluid channeling."

He looked meditative. "Now it's up to me to try and 'organize' one Amplitur."

As they walked along in silence something barked high up in a tree. A seedpod bounced at their feet. It was fist-sized, tapered to a point, and reminded Straat-ien of a beige turnip. He did not bother to try and locate the native animal that was responsible for its descent.

"When are you going to make the attempt?" she finally asked him.

"I'm not sure yet. If I try it while part of a group, I'll have some cover. The Amplitur may not be able to readily pick me out of a crowd. On the other hand, if I can arrange a private confrontation and the procedure fails and I'm discovered, I can still preserve the secret of my talent and of the Core's existence by killing it."

Unprepared, she quavered at the vision he'd conjured up. Having witnessed as much combat as she had, she was angry with her reaction. "You may yourself in turn be slain, and the Amplitur will only send another to take the place of the first. Your loss would deprive your colleagues of your valuable position here, and the information it provides. Having thus discovered one traitor to his cause, Levaughn will be thrice cautious about admitting newcomers to his circle."

"Then I'd better not get myself discovered." They turned

up a side path, away from the canyon and back toward what passed locally for civilization.

It seemed entirely too nice a morning for so momentous an enterprise. Without telling him, Lalelelang had quietly determined to help extricate Straat-ien in the event his attempt failed. How she might accomplish this once the alarm had been raised she had no idea. As a senior Wais academic, violent intrigues were entirely foreign to her. By the same token and for the same reason she knew that she would never be suspected of involvement.

Knowing he would ardently disapprove, she said nothing of her intention to Straat-ien. Instead she set vigorously to work making plans without his knowledge. Stealth-steered intelligence would have to suffice since despite her experience she was still, as unremittingly as the most sheltered Wais, quite incapable of wielding a weapon of destruction in her own defense, much less in that of another. Despite what some of her students and colleagues thought, she was not completely deranged. Only slightly.

Straat-ien had told her to wait in her own apartment in the residence wing that had been modified to provide for non-Human guests. The rooms that had been assigned to the visiting Amplitur lay at the far end of the same structure. As soon as it was over, he assured her, he would return to apprise her of how it had gone. If after a certain reasonable time he failed to call on her, she would be free to draw her own conclusions.

While she waited, she strove mightily not to fixate on the chronometer, throwing herself into the prioritization of the inevitable observations she'd been making since her arrival on Daccar. An obscure anthropological point managed to occupy her for nearly an hour.

After that she tried portable amusements, then made attempts to access the compound's library. She tried everything except leaving the apartment to press an ear opening to the door of the Amplitur's quarters.

Time passed sluggishly until the commotion in the hall

roused her from her self-imposed isolation. Stepping outside, she encountered a single, harried male Hivistahm. He wore a slightly paralyzed expression as well as the accoutrements and insignia of an energy engineer. Though she addressed him in calming tones in his own language, he failed to respond immediately.

"What happened has? What going on is?" she pressed him. A Human, she knew, would have grabbed the engineer and tried to shake him bodily out of his stupor. For a civilized Wais to engage in such an action was unthinkable. Had a Human done it, it would only have deepened the shiny-scaled Hivistahm's paralysis.

The double lids finally blinked in succession, and the dark slitted eyes turned in her direction. "There has," he paused, considering his position as well as his words, "an accident been." He shifted his attention back to the far end of the corridor. At the same time Lalelelang became aware of a distant, consistent whine. It might be some kind of Human alarm.

The passageway was empty now, but she was sure that only a few moments earlier she'd heard the distinctive clump of many Human feet moving fast past her apartment doorway.

"What kind of an accident?"

Unable to decide whether to stand or run, the Hivistahm opted to answer her questions. "There an important visitor staying here is."

"An Amplitur?" He clicked his teeth in a distinctive way, and she recognized the simple acknowledgment. "What about the Amplitur?"

The Hivistahm carefully mouthed a disbelieving reply. "It dead is. By assassination or combat."

"Details." She stepped in front of him so that he couldn't leave without forcing his way past her. The un-Wais boldness of her move surprised her, but it positively astonished her reluctant informant. "Details give me!"

Either as a consequence of her action or growing awareness of the violence inherent in the incident itself, the Hivistahm's paralysis continued to deepen. Whether he'd actually witnessed the purported violence or had simply heard about it didn't matter: the effects on his emotional stability were striking. Something was short-circuiting his ability to cope.

Leaving the engineer weaving slightly on his broad sandaled feet, she hurried down the corridor, feathers fluttering as she ran. She knew where the Amplitur's quarters were located; Straat-ien had shown her. But she couldn't get near the entrance. A milling cordon of Humans blocked the approach. Several carried weapons. All looked nervous and edgy.

One briefly noted her arrival and immediately peered past her. He was searching for potential threats, something that a dozen of her kind would not constitute.

Moving as close as she dared, she tried to peer between the milling bipedal masses. Other unarmed Humans were packed around a gaping double doorway. Fetid humid air issued from the exposed environment beyond.

Those blocking the entrance parted to admit a pair of Humans wearing anxious expressions. A single Hivistahm accompanied them, or rather, was swept along in their wake. Lalelelang thought the slit-eyed scaled one wore the uniform of a universal physician, but she couldn't be certain.

She astonished herself a second time by physically prodding the nearest Human to gain its attention. "What happened?" she asked in fluent, accentless Huma while keeping an instinctive eye on the biped's activated weapon. "What's going on?"

The youthful female regarded her indifferently. "I ain't sure. Some kind of fight or something." She glanced over her shoulder.

Lalelelang persisted. "You must know *something*."

The female soldier seemed to see her for the first time. "You speak awfully good Huma. Even for a Wais."

"It is my profession." Lalelelang took her time. "I am a scholar."

"Yeah, well; nothing here that I can see to interest a scholar. We've got some corpses in there. You know? Dead bodies? Slain violently. The sort of thing, if I ain't mistaken, to make a Wais faint. Better move along and let us deal with it.''

Lalelelang ignored the well-meaning if slightly condescending advice. "What kind of corpses?"

The soldier hesitated. "Listen, I don't really know who you are. This is a security situation. I ain't sure how much I can tell you."

"I have been a guest here for some days." Lalelelang fought to restrain her impatience. Fortunately the Human was quite incapable of correctly interpreting the subtle flickering of lashes and fluffing of underbody feathers. "I believe the rooms you are guarding were occupied by one of the Amplitur."

The woman held her weapon tightly. "I can't comment on that."

"But you will not deny it?" The soldier's expression was sufficient confirmation. "Nor that one of the corpses is Amplitur?" A slight but detectable twitching of facial muscles indicated that Lalelelang had again guessed correctly.

She retreated several steps, struggling to moderate her breathing. Good Nevan's strategy had failed. For whatever reason his attempt to mind-suggest the Amplitur representative had not worked. He had evidently been discovered, his ability revealed, and had been forced to fall back on violence to protect the secret of the Core talent. The scenario was entirely believable. Indeed, Straat-ien had more or less described it to her.

What she did not understand and could not imagine was how the Amplitur had in turn managed to kill its Human assailant.

It was possible that the guard was more worldly than she appeared. Perhaps she understood the meaning of Lalelelang's trembling. Regardless, she beckoned the Wais over, bent toward Lalelelang and lowered her voice.

"One of 'em's the squid, all right. The others are Human.''

Lalelelang cocked her head slightly to the left, expressing surprise. "Others?"

"Senior Human officers. One of them's General Levaughn himself. The other's a colonel I don't know."

She was remarkably composed. The ultimate component of self-control, she thought. Or the beginnings of paralysis. "You are certain both Humans are dead?"

The female gave a curious little shake of her head. Her close-cropped hair was so blonde as to be nearly white. "That's the report. Shot through. All three of 'em were apparently armed."

Lalelelang involuntarily dropped her lower beak. "The *Amplitur* was armed?"

"That's what the preliminary report says." The soldier's brow contracted with the stress of thinking. "Didn't know any of 'em carried arms. I always heard they hated violence. Course, there's still a lot we don't know about the squids. Guess there can be exceptions to any rule."

"Is there any indication as to what provoked the tragedy?"

"Not that I've heard. Somebody must've really holed it." She shook her head ruefully. "Bad business, this. Very bad. I got a quick look inside before they sealed it off. What a mess. Bodies are so badly shot up they can't tell who fired first, or even who shot who, much less why. Could be we'll never know."

"Although the war has been over for years, serious arguments between individuals of different species are not unknown," Lalelelang ventured lamely.

"You don't have to tell me. Daccarans like to settle things the old way. I been involved in a couple of scrapes myself. But nothing like this."

"You say all three were badly . . . shot up. Has the attending pathologist rendered any kind of preliminary report?"

"No idea. No reason to keep me and my buddies up on stuff like that. Having had a look, though, I'll give you my own opinion on one thing."

"What is that?"

The soldier's voice was cold. "None of 'em had a chance. Not even a Hiviphys could do anything with that mess. Got to be able to tell the pieces apart before you can try putting 'em back together again."

"I am certain you are correct." Lalelelang took a querulous step forward. "It may be that I can learn something if I am allowed in. Do you mind if I try? Those in charge can do no more than refuse me entrance."

Bone and muscle shifted to block her path. "Sorry, uh, ma'am. I'm afraid I can't do that. I'm sure you're a visiting scholar and all that, just like you claim, but it doesn't matter. Our orders are that nobody gets inside. 'Diplomatic incident,' violation of the integrity of the premier's compound: you understand."

Lalelelang did not try to press it farther. "Of course. Can I at least stand here and observe?"

The female shrugged. "Don't know how much you'll see, but as long as you don't get in anyone's way I guess it's okay. We've been ordered to keep everyone out, not to clear the building."

"Your kindness commends you," Lalelelang replied opulently. The finesse was lost on the soldier.

She stood and watched, and waited. After a while two shrouded shapes were wheeled out. The forms beneath the enveloping sheets were roughly Human in outline. Certainly neither of them was Amplitur.

The remains of that individual were brought out later, in many pieces. From what little Lalelelang could see the helpful Human soldier had been, if anything, conservative in her appraisal.

She remained a long while, wanting badly to talk with the attending Hivistahm physician. Besides, she had no desire to go anywhere else. But the Hivi vanished in tandem with the remains of the Amplitur, not to return, and still the guards refused to let her pass.

Subsequently she spent a horrible evening in her apartment, acutely conscious of the fact that she was isolated on a Human world, her sole friend having most unbelievably succumbed to the fatal consequences of a botched undertaking. She half-expected that at any moment her part in the enterprise would be discovered, whereupon strapping, stern-faced Human soldiers would arrive to carry her off to be questioned by methods she fought desperately against envisioning.

Her door stayed silent. As time passed undisturbed she began to feel a little more confident. After all, how much of a connection could anyone divine? She and Straat-ien had spent time in each other's company, but had been careful not to be blatant about it. They had arrived separately at the compound. There was no reason for anyone to suspect some sort of subtle connection between Human and Wais.

She knew she would be questioned eventually, though, if only because she had known him.

The following morning came and went placidly. An ominous calm pervaded the atmosphere of the retreat. She went for a walk simply to show herself, to prove that she was not being secretive or in hiding. By late afternoon the only one who had activated her door was a service Lepar performing its regular cleaning rounds. It silently freshened her room and changed her nesting material.

News of the general's death did not appear in the daily media. That was understandable. It would not do a politician like Cosgrave any good to have it known that an important guest had died in a firefight while at one of his residences.

No one came to confront her. As far as she knew she was free to leave at any time. That was what she desperately wanted to do: head for the nearest shuttleport and book passage homeward, there to retire to the tranquillity of the academic life once more and forever. Unbelievably, unaccountably, her old friend Straat-ien was dead. The Amplitur envoy was dead, and the invidious General Levaughn likewise defunct. It appeared that the manner of their passing was destined to remain forever a mystery to her. Fine and good. She had done all she could. It was time to have a care for herself.

Straat-ien's death had not been in vain. The Amplitur

would have to replace Cast-creative-Seeking with one of their own not so well versed in Human psychology. Cautious as ever, they would probably call a halt to their attempts to secure Human allies until they felt they better understood what had gone wrong on Daccar. As for the death of General Levaughn, it should put a serious crimp in the growth of reactionary political forces on Daccar. Presumably the Core would follow up on its complete, if blighted, success.

She realized that the supersecretive organization of which Straat-ien had once been an important member would also eventually want to question her. Inwardly she sighed. Try as she might to distance herself from what had happened, she could not eliminate what others thought she might know.

Sudden terror sent a ripple through her back feathers. What if the Amplitur also sought her out? A simple suggestion from any of them and she would find herself helplessly divested of all her secrets.

She forced herself to be calm. There was no reason for them to question her. She was a well-known Wais academic. Yes, she was a student of Human behavior, but so were a number of other non-Humans. Yes, she had known one of the two deceased Humans, but she had known many Humans. As far as the Amplitur were concerned there was nothing to connect her intimately with the incident that had occurred the previous night. The Amplitur were perceptive, but they were not prescient.

Still, she would take care to avoid them. On Mahmahar that should be a simple matter.

She regretted the loss of a friend. Over the years Straat-ien had certainly become that. He could not help his Humanness. Having forgiven him that while he was alive, she could do no less now that he was gone. His passing affected her almost, but not quite, as much as would that of a fellow Wais.

Her remorse did not prevent her from making arrangements to leave Daccar the next day. If any of Straat-ien's associates wanted to question her, they would have to follow the path he had previously taken to her homeworld. There she could arrange to meet with them in secrecy and some confidence.

She was able to prepare her nest without listening for the door, and her confidence continued to be justified. No one troubled or questioned her preparations for departure. She stayed up late, watching the local media and burying herself in the casual notes she had recorded prior to the disaster.

So relaxed had she become by the time she extinguished the apartment illumination that she fell immediately into a deep and restful sleep, from which she was abruptly and unexpectedly awakened in the middle of the night by the insistent buzzing of her door.

★ XXI ★

"Go away!" Tenuous uncertainties danced fuzzily at the periphery of her thoughts. "I am sleeping."

The words that reached her via the door speaker were not Huma, but she recognized them anyway. She wasn't quite as fluent in the guttural language of her nocturnal visitor as she was in that of the warrior bipeds or the Hivistahm, but even half-asleep she managed adequately.

"I reiterate: Go away!"

"Please," the voice pleaded. "It is urgent that I speak with you."

Considering the racial identity of the unseen speaker, the statement made no sense. Perplexed and by now more awake than asleep, she rose from the night nest and made her way to the door. The built-in scanner confirmed the species of the speaker but did nothing to alleviate her confusion.

The scanner showed an anxious Lepar clad in the shapeless, simple uniform they wore when on duty. Its tail hung motionless on the hallway floor, glistening moistly in the overhead night-lights. A maintenance case dangled from one thick-fingered, half-webbed hand.

"What do you want?"

"Some environmental controls were damaged in the big fighting yesterday. The monitors are just starting to light up. If the problem isn't fixed quickly, no one in this building will be able to adjust heat or cold or humidity to personal taste. It could get very uncomfortable. I know it is late, but if you will let me in I can fix a bypass in your room that will keep you comfortable while we replace the unit that failed.''

She leaned against the door, uncertain whether to try and wake up or go back to the nest. ''There is nothing the matter with conditions in here. Go work on someone else's room.''

''Please.'' On the scanner the Lepar's expression became more mournful than ever, the flat, wide-mouthed face frozen in a gaze of pitiable imbecility. ''I have been ordered to put a bypass in every room. If I do not, then I cannot sign off. I must remain here until everyone has let me in, even if I have to wait until sunrise. It will go on my work record as an incompetence and that means I will not get any sleep and will—''

''Enough! Don't whine. It is unbecoming to sapience.'' Irritably she unsealed the entrance and activated the room's interior illumination.

The heavyset male amphibian shuffled in, and she let the door close automatically behind it. Without a word it turned to the concealed control panel set in the same wall. Opening the case it carried, her unwelcome visitor began to examine the contents as if searching for a particular tool.

''I am sorry to disturb you so late at night,'' he gurgled.

''No matter. I am awake now.'' She was unclad and unadorned, but there was no reason to be otherwise in the presence of a Lepar to whom she would resemble nothing more than a large, flightless bird. The sight of her body would engender the same reaction in him as a view of an abstract sculpture.

Her visitor had insisted he wouldn't be long, but given his initial hesitation and knowing well the Lepar she decided she might as well make use of the time. Retiring to the viewer mounted just above the floor, she folded her legs beneath her and sat down in front of the screen. There were always notes to be organized, material to be reviewed.

She put the Lepar completely out of her mind until the throaty voice said from behind her, ''If I might have your attention for a moment?''

''What now?'' Grumbling, she turned to look up from the

viewer, and promptly received the greatest shock of her life. Which, considering everything she had experienced over the years, was a qualification of some magnitude.

The gun the Lepar held in one slick-skinned, dark green hand was small enough to qualify as toylike. Being far more familiar with such devices than the average Wais, she knew that its size in no way mitigated its potential lethality. Its presence in the hand of a non-Human or non-Massood was astonishing. To see it being wielded by a Lepar simply beggared belief.

Her dumbfounded gaze rose to the expansive face. The broad, toothless mouth was shut, the widely spaced, tiny black eyes glinting in the artificial light. She was too stunned to speak.

"Please do not be alarmed." The tone was polite and typically deferential. It gestured with the gun. "I can imagine using this only in the most extreme circumstances."

If he was trying to set her mind at ease, he wasn't succeeding. "You are Lepar. Your people have been civilized members of the Weave from its beginnings. While not particularly smart, you are no more inclined to violence than is my kind. I do not understand this." With twitching wingtip she indicated the weapon. "How can you stand there and threaten me with that?"

"It is a considerable emotional stretch, but I am managing. Know that I will make use of it without hesitation if circumstances require."

Her initial fear was slowly giving way to anger. This was simply too outrageous. "The people here are already trying to cope with one dead Amplitur and two dead Humans. Don't you think a Wais dead of a gunshot would be a little hard to explain?"

"It probably would be," the Lepar conceded. "If I am forced to kill you here and now, it is quite possible that my involvement would be discovered. Since that cannot be allowed, after killing you I will have to kill myself. That should be sufficient to put an end to any questions."

She thought she was beyond shock. She was wrong.

"So you intend to kill me?"

"No one wants to kill you, Honored Scholar Lalelelang. You are a unique and valuable individual. The knowledge you have gathered and distilled concerning how Humankind interacts with the other species of the Weave has proven very useful."

"Useful," she echoed. Her lashes jerked. "Surely not to *you*?"

"We have been accessing your archived material for a long time." That enigmatic visage seemed perpetually frozen in a skimpy, stupid grin. She reminded herself that the expression was a function of bone physiology, not emotion. "Lepar workers on your homeworld have ready entry to them."

She thought of the contract Lepar she had noted performing time-consuming, mostly menial tasks around the grounds of the university. The quiet, soft-spoken, obeisant Lepar. Like the rest of her colleagues she'd never given them a second thought. Mentally and emotionally they were suited to such employment, while the Wais and for that matter most other intelligent species were not. The Lepar had always been willing, even eager, to take on such tasks, recognizing their inherent limitations and taking quiet pleasure in carrying out their chosen pursuits to the best of their diffident abilities.

Nothing was making any sense. "What," she inquired dazedly, "are the Lepar doing accessing my files? What are the Lepar doing accessing *any* files? My work is complex and nonspecific. It is beyond the capacity of any of your kind to comprehend."

"Not beyond. Difficult certainly. But there are among us some of greater intelligence than is generally known. It is hard for them, but they are just smart enough to make sense of such things."

"This is insane," Lalelelang muttered aloud in her own sibilant language. "Crazy."

The translator he wore around his nearly nonexistent neck picked up her words. "The universe is a crazy place. I am told that the physics of it make no sense. Why should those who live within it be any more sensibly organized?"

Realization dawned gradually. There was the very real weapon her visitor held, the absence so far of any other suspect conspirators, and the fact that this creature was, if it could be believed and unbelievable as it seemed, ready to use it against her.

She had understood from the first how the Amplitur and the reactionary General Levaughn had died, but until now the cause of her friend Colonel Straat-ien's death had been a complete mystery. No Amplitur could overcome a Human in individual combat, nor could a single representative of any other species. Not even a Chirinaldo or Molitar. But Human fighters could sometimes be defeated by other, less obvious methods.

Complete surprise, for example.

"You were there," she said accusingly.

She recognized the simple, straightforward gesture, equally comprehensible above or below the water, that acknowledged her accusation. "I was there." It was conclusive that he did not ask to where she was referring.

"How did it happen? Can you tell me that much?" She did not add that it was gradually dawning on her that she probably had no future beyond the termination of the current conversation. Resistance was out of the question. In addition to everything else she was too numbed by the incredible reality of the situation.

It occurred to her that this might be an isolated condition, that the Lepar confronting her might really be clinically psychotic. As an unavoidable corollary to intelligence, insanity was found among every member of the Weave. Were the Lepar prone to it? She didn't know, having concentrated on Humankind to the exclusion of all else.

"It was . . . unpleasant," the Lepar told her unemotionally. "At the time of the confrontation I was attending to the Amplitur's quarters. You may know that our taste in environments is somewhat similar, so that I was at ease while carrying out my work.

"The human general was not. While oozing salt and water from his skin he engaged in much conversation with the Amplitur. Neither of them took any notice of me, nor did I of them, until the second Human arrived.''

"Colonel Straat-ien," she murmured softly.

"Yes. I heard him request entrance. As an associate of General Levaughn, he was admitted.''

"What ensued?''

The Lepar managed to look thoughtful. ''It was extraordinary. The Human Straat-ien made an attempt to mentally overwhelm the Amplitur. Though no sound issued from either individual it was plain to see that both were striving mightily toward some unfathomable end. The strain was evident in their expressions and gestures. The Human's face passed through the most remarkable series of contortions while the Amplitur thrashed about violently with its tentacles. The rapid color changes its skin underwent astonished me.

"As this silent struggle continued, the Human Levaughn grew increasingly alarmed. It was plain he did not understand what was happening, and neither of the mental combatants took the time to respond to his increasingly shrill inquiries.''

Lalelelang spoke very carefully. "Just a moment. How did *you* know there was a mental confrontation taking place? You might have guessed what the Amplitur was trying to do, but unless the Human Straat-ien tried to suggest you, there was no way you could know that he was actively involved in responding to the Amplitur.''

"You are owed an explanation. We are capable of detecting such activity.''

"Yes, yes. The Lepar are as suggestible as the Wais, or the Hivistahm, or any of the other sapient species except Humankind. But an Amplitur has to suggest *you*. You cannot by yourself detect the presence of such activity in them. And you claim that the Human was trying to suggest the Amplitur.'' She watched her captor carefully. "That is impossible. Humans can only resist such probing. They do not share with the Amplitur the ability to suggest.''

"The Amplitur does not have to suggest us. While we have

no projective talent ourselves, we can quite readily sense when others are using it, be they Amplitur or representatives of that Human group which calls itself the Core."

"The Core?" Her mind was reeling. "What is that?"

"We have known about it for some time. Collectively we know more about Humankind than any of the other member species of the Weave. Our knowledge is exceeded only by that of a few specialists, of whom you are prominent.

"Lepar were with the first contact ship. Lepar were among the first to speak and deal directly with Humans, and we are still the only ones who can interact effectively with them underwater. We were interested in them from the beginning, as we are interested in anything that threatens our security and safety.

"A Hivistahm was the first to encounter one of the captured Humans the Amplitur attempted to modify to look and think like Ashregan but fight for the Purpose with the strength and stealth of Humankind. His companion was a Lepar, who immediately recognized the significance of the encounter and made certain that the individual specimen was brought back alive for further study. It was the Lepar who was prepared to resort to violence to accomplish this aim.

"As for the Core, it was formed by the offspring of those Amplitur-modified children, whose unique abilities are an accidental and apparently inheritable by-product of Hivistahm attempts to surgically repair the alterations the Amplitur genetic engineers had made. We have been monitoring the activities of these gifted Humans since the time of the one called Ranji-aar."

Lalelelang was silent for several moments, carefully considering not only what the Lepar had said, but what it had not said.

"If you have done all this without interference, then it follows that you can not only detect attempts to suggest, you can, in the fashion of Humans, resist it."

"That is so. Your perception has not been overrated. Our nervous system acts differently from that of Humans. Theirs is an active defense that fights any attempt at intrusion or manipulation. Ours is passive. We simply are not suggestible.''

"But there have been many documented instances of captured Lepar being manipulated by the Amplitur."

"Those captured merely pretended to comply with the suggestions of the enemy. It is not difficult to do. Since we are a simple folk, we are given only simple tasks to do. Everyone knows we are no threat. Perceived ignorance is a surprisingly effective buffer. It is sometimes a good thing to be considered an imbecile.

"No Core Human ever tried to suggest us. There was no reason to. We had little to do with the conduct of the war. For the same reason the Amplitur have largely ignored us. Given a choice, ignored is what we prefer to be.

"This is a terrible shame. Everything was going so well. The war was ended, peace had come, and my people could go about trying to better themselves mentally and in other ways without having to worry about the destruction and disruption that war brings. We knew about the Core Humans and kept a watch on them, but they seemed concerned only with keeping the secret of their existence.'' He gestured idly with the gun.

"Not for the first time we underestimated the deviousness of the Amplitur. Who would have thought that having capitulated they would subsequently try to ally themselves with reactionary Humans? Or that some Humans would prove themselves even less civilized than anyone believed possible by agreeing to accept Amplitur assistance and guidance?

"We would have reacted sooner to this threat save for the fact that we are not very smart. It takes us a long time to see things clearly. Your research, for example, is very detailed and sometimes hard to follow.''

Having resigned herself to whatever might come, Lalelelang had grown calm. "If someone had come to me with such a litany as you have just recited I would have thought them addled.''

"We are little more than what we appear,'' said the Lepar

almost apologetically. "Helpful, subservient, and quite harmless."

"You will pardon my pointing out that you do not look very harmless just now."

"Believe me when I say that I am truly sorry for the way this has turned out. It is necessary, to insure the preservation of certain secrets."

"What happens . . . after?"

"I will not be suspected in the deaths. As you accurately point out, no one would suppose a Lepar capable of complicity in such violence. We will go on monitoring the activities of the Core, just as we will those of reactionary Humans and obsequious Amplitur. If it again proves necessary to interfere, we will do so as nonviolently and unobtrusively as possible."

"You appear to have thought everything out."

"We have no choice," the Lepar confessed. "We are not clever enough to resist the machinations of species like Humankind and the Amplitur. So we must act before they do."

"Having told me all this, surely there is no harm in telling me what transpired in the Amplitur's quarters?" The Lepar hesitated. "Please," Lalelelang entreated her captor. "The least you can do is satisfy my curiosity."

"Ever the true scholar. As you will." Tiny black eyes squinted with the strain of remembrance. "The Human Straat-ien and the Amplitur struggled silently. The Human Levaughn had no idea of the nature of the battle which was taking place in front of him. I did, and tried my best to pretend that I did not.

"Neither the Human Straat-ien nor the Amplitur could gain an advantage. The Human probed and the Amplitur resisted.

"When he could obtain no reaction to his entreaties from either his fellow Human or his guest, the Human Levaughn grew panicky and prepared to summon aid. Seeing this, the Human Straat-ien moved to stop him. There was a brief confrontation which resulted in the Human Straat-ien slaying the Human Levaughn.

"This momentary diversion of the Human Straat-ien's attention spurred the Amplitur to try and flee. As it had by now been made aware of the Human's suggestive capability, it was obvious Straat-ien could not permit this. Your friend turned the weapon he had just used on his fellow being toward the Amplitur and fired several times. It made terrible wounds on the Amplitur's body, butchering it beyond hope of resurrection.

"The Human Straat-ien then very cleverly placed his weapon in one of the dead human's hands, closing the deceased man's fingers around it. His intent was clearly to make it appear as if the general had slain the Amplitur and then killed himself. To make this strategy work it was necessary for your friend to resolve one final awkwardness.

"Me.

"I was a witness to everything that had taken place."

Lalelelang had followed the somber recitation in contemplative silence. Now she looked up again. "What did the Human Straat-ien do?"

"He placed himself deliberately between myself and the doorway, announcing with what I believe to be genuine regret that he was going to have to kill me. He was very surprised when I produced from inside a vest pocket a weapon much like his own with which I carefully shot him between the eyes. I am no expert at understanding Human expression but I am sure I am correct in this interpretation. Also, at the critical moment he projected involuntarily, and his consternation was clear in his thoughts. As he had conveniently put his own weapon in one of the deceased General Levaughn's hands, I was able to place mine in his.

"He seemed to me to be a very decent and concerned creature, for a Human, and I regretted having to kill him."

The inner edges of Lalelelang's beak ground slowly against one another. "Everything you have told me I believe, except that you killed him. You, a Lepar, slaying a Human?"

"It was unavoidable. It would have been better to leave Colonel Straat-ien alive, morally as well as for other reasons. But there are other members of the Core, younger than he, who will take up energetically the task of insuring that their own kind remains peaceful and does not succumb to cunning Amplitur blandishments.''

She appeared not to have heard the last. "You really expect me to believe that you shot a Human? A highly trained soldier like Nevan Straat-ien?''

"There have been times previous where it was nearly required, but not until this incident was it necessary to follow through.''

"The Lepar have never been fighters.''

"That is still so. We hate violence, and are not very good at it. We have to force ourselves. When you are sufficiently frightened you can do many things previously believed impossible, and because we are so insecure we are easily frightened.''

She gestured deliberately at the tiny gun. "Are you pointing that at me because I frighten you?''

"Yes," said the Lepar with portentous conviction. "The knowledge you possess frightens me terribly.''

"Enough to kill me? To cause physical violence to another intelligent being who means you no harm?'' When the Lepar did not reply she tried another tack. "How will you explain away my death by gunfire? No confrontation is taking place, no fighting. I am no Human whom others may imagine disposed to madness and fury. I am a peaceful scholar.''

The Lepar raised the compact weapon. "This is not like the weapon that was used to kill Colonel Straat-ien. It does not fire explosive or penetrating projectiles. It is a compressed gas injector that will leave no marks. The drug that will enter your bloodstream will make it appear as though your heart has failed due to natural causes. Though the toxin employed disperses rapidly into the system and breaks down into unidentifiable components soon thereafter, an in-depth forensic analysis performed immediately after death could possibly reveal the actual cause. I will therefore remain here after you expire, to insure that this does not take place and that your body is not disturbed for the proscribed period.

"The Wais are known for their delicate constitutions. Your death will arouse no unusual suspicion."

"What happens then? I will be dead, along with Colonel Straat-ien, General Levaughn, and the Amplitur representative. What will it have solved? Other Humans will take Levaughn's place."

"Perhaps not and if so, perhaps not for some time. The Human Levaughn evinced an unusual combination of capability and drive. Having failed spectacularly with him, the Amplitur will withdraw to contemplate their failure. This will give the peace time to further solidify.

"Meanwhile we will monitor political developments among reactionary-inclined Humans, and keep silent watch over the activities of the Core while they continue to oversee their own kind. Hopefully we will not soon again have to inject ourselves into the affairs of other species. The Hivistahm and the O'o'yan, the Bir'rimor and the Massood, the Yula and the S'van and Humankind and all the rest will be no more aware of us than they are now or have ever been. This is best, because we are and have always been frightened of all of them."

"If you truly are immune to Amplitur mind-manipulation," she said, "you could have been great fighters for the Weave. You could have fought alongside the Massood before we discovered and enlisted the Humans."

"I have told you that we are not fighters. Combat terrifies us, as it does any civilized species. Just because we are not as smart as some does not mean we are any less civilized."

"I'm not sure you are as dumb as you try to appear, either."

"We are. Do not doubt it. But it has sometimes seemed to those of us with the capacity to ponder such things that there are differences between being intelligent and being smart, and that too much intelligence may not be such a good thing. Where survival is at stake, sometimes instinct is better. Being stupid forces you to concentrate on what really matters and to live within your limitations.

"We do those jobs which more intelligent species disdain.

As a result we have prospered and multiplied within the framework of the Weave. While other species quarrel and sometimes even fight, we are ignored. Meanwhile we work hard, and watch, and listen, and try to become a little smarter. When you are given the lowliest jobs, when others ignore you as though you do not exist, you have wonderful opportunities to observe, and to listen. My people realized long ago that it is hard to learn when your own mouth is always open.

"Independence is better for such development. So the Amplitur cannot be permitted to resurrect the Purpose. Peace is a better framework for such an existence. So Humans cannot be allowed to resurrect war. Humans and Amplitur working together would result in the worst combination of possibilities. We are not so stupid that we cannot see that."

Lalelelang sensed that the Lepar was growing increasingly nervous and that she was running out of options. "If in spite of your precautions they find a lethal toxin in my body the local authorities are going to start looking for a murderer." She used the Human term, there being no exact equivalent in either the Lepar or Wais tongue.

"That is possible. No action is riskproof. However, in that unlikely event I do not think they will suspect or question me, a lowly Lepar maintenance worker. Even if they thought one of my kind capable of the act, they would not think us possessed of the necessary smarts.

"I do not want to kill you, Honored Scholar Lalelelang, any more than I wanted to kill the Human Straat-ien. But fear and insecurity are powerful motivators for such as my kind. They concentrate even limited abilities wonderfully well."

The greatest revelation in recorded history, she found herself thinking, more striking even than the existence of the Core among genetically altered Humans, and it was going to perish with her. All because she was dedicated to her studies.

"Besides which, we can help the Humans."

"You?" She was startled. "The Lepar?"

"Humankind knows that of all the intelligent species, the

Lepar represent the least threat to them. They consider us mentally as well as physically inferior and inoffensive. Therefore they will listen to us where their natural skepticism would make them wary of such as the S'van. That is the secret to dealing successfully with Humans. Challenge them and you incur their suspicion, as do the Hivistahm and Yula and all the others. Acknowledge their dominance and they become your friends and protectors forever.

"In addition, we are the only ones who can swim with them. Deep inside, they remember the water from which they sprang. It is a subtle bond, and it gives my kind an advantage in dealing with them.

"The Weave wants to perpetuate but control their fighting ability. We want to moderate it, for our own security. We can do that."

"By secretly monitoring them?"

"By offering them unthreatening friendship. Now that the peril posed by the individual Levaughn has been ended, the Core can probably deal adequately with lesser Humans of his persuasion. It will be left to us to deal with the species as a whole."

She knew she was almost out of time. "It's not for me to criticize your methodology or your goals, but is it really necessary to kill me to protect them? The modified Humans have trusted me with the secret of their Core. Can you not also trust me with yours? I can be useful to you as I have been useful to them."

"I am afraid not. We are not as clever as the modified Humans. You could deceive us without our realizing it. Better to be safe. You see, Honored Scholar, you know the truth about the modified Humans, and about the intentions of the Amplitur and the reactionary Humans, and now about us. You have accumulated so many truths that it has made you very possibly the most dangerous individual alive."

She blinked long lashes. "In an unusual life I have been called many things, but never dangerous."

"You underestimate yourself gravely. We do not."

"I am only a simple scholar, a plodding seeker after wisdom. It is all I ever wanted to be. Mere knowledge is not dangerous.''

The Lepar considered her thoughtfully. ''Perhaps you are not so smart after all.''

''I guess you are right, or I would not find myself in this position now. I am not even smart enough to hide all my notes in a safe place.'' She turned in the direction of the storage cube next to the nest. He followed her glance.

That's when she hit him with the recorder.

It wasn't very heavy, but it was made well. Cupped tightly within and propelled by the force of her right wingtip, it added just enough mass to make the blow effective. The actual wing motion was drawn from an adolescent mating dance, but it simulated a Human punch well enough. She was familiar with the physical mechanism from her studies.

As she made contact, pain exploded up the length of her wing, momentarily paralyzing her right side. The startled Lepar fared worse, the impact smashing a cheekbone and crushing an eye. He staggered on his short legs, the thick tail stiffening reflexively to provide additional support. She saw his fingers convulse on the injector, closed her eyes as she heard it emit a soft *phut*.

The high-velocity dose missed her chest and splatted harmlessly against the wall behind her. By then she was on top of the Lepar, knocking him to the floor. The impact further dazed him and she was able to wrest the weapon from his limp fingers.

Though it was designed for manipulation by bony digits, she was able to grasp the simple device with the flexible quill-tips of her left wing. Cyclically reciting her most dynamic control mantra, she rose and stood looking down at her reluctant assassin. The Lepar blinked up at her out of his remaining good eye, his tail twitching convulsively back and forth beneath him.

''How extraordinary. Had I not experienced such a thing, I would not have thought it possible. What are you going to do now?''

She was surprised to discover she didn't know. Everything

had happened very fast, and now sanity was returning with a rush. She started to shake violently.

Taking note of her reaction, the Lepar started to get to its feet. Blood trickled from the left side of its face, marring the sad, frozen smile. "You cannot kill me. You are Wais, who pride themselves on being the most civilized of all species." A webbed hand reached toward her. "Give back the weapon. The drug works painlessly. Let us put an end to all this, for both our sakes."

She stumbled backward. "You, too, are 'civilized.' "

"Yes. But we are just scared and simpleminded enough to get around it. Having attained a much higher level of civilization, you are not." The hand remained extended expectantly; fingers open, mottled green-black palm turned upward.

"You forget one thing. I have spent years working intimately with Humans. My friends, my family, my triad, and my colleagues have insisted all along that this has had a permanent and deleterious effect on me. Always I disputed them. Now I am afraid I must admit that they were right."

The Lepar blinked its remaining eye once as the little gun went off for the second time, making a sound like some small cuddly creature sneezing into its own fur. The capacious mouth gaped wide, showing a wet black gullet. No sound emerged.

It sat down heavily. "I was correctly informed. There is no pain." She eyed him insensibly. "What a pity that the toxin is not species-specific." Slowly it toppled over onto its left side. "Most interesting." The black eye gazed unblinkingly up at her. She wanted to turn away, to run, but she could not. Horrified fascination kept her transfixed to the spot.

"You should not have been capable of doing that." She had to strain to hear the weakly gargled words. "This will complicate things." The voice sank toward inaudibility.

After that the Lepar said nothing more, nor did any part of its body move again.

Shakily she walked around the corpse, not taking her eyes

off it for a second, and finally sat down on the edge of the nest. She watched the motionless form for over an hour. Feeling reasonably safe at that point, she put the deceptively innocuous-looking weapon down and walked to the apartment's hygiene alcove. Inclining her neck and head over the disposal, she proceeded to violently evacuate the contents of her stomach and crop into the pastel, scented receptacle.

When she'd finished, she washed and groomed herself as best she could and began to pack her belongings, not neglecting to include the deadly little gun. Whoever encountered the lifeless Lepar would discover that it had died of heart failure. The deception intended to disguise the true cause of her own death would serve equally well for her would-be assassin.

The medication that allowed her to work intimately and for extended periods with Human beings served to mask her nervousness as she departed the tense confines of the compound. Wholly absorbed by the inexplicable deaths of the Amplitur and two senior Human officers, none of the staff paid any attention to the decision of a visiting Wais scholar to depart. Amid the confusion she doubted if anyone would even bother to remark on the subsequent demise of a Lepar worker who had clearly died a natural death.

Except perhaps his fellow frightened, simpleminded Lepar. The Lepar who watched, and listened, and said little, but who occasionally acted. The Lepar who had never managed to master Underspace on their own and had to be conveyed by more technologically competent species from world to world. The Lepar who in that manner had succeeded in spreading themselves unobtrusively throughout the length and breadth of the Weave. Those Lepar.

What had he said? she reflected from the safety of her room aboard the Underspace liner hovering in orbit. That she, Lalelelang, was possibly the most dangerous individual alive?

The Lepar hadn't said anything about the traitorous Turlog. Was it possible the amphibians had never discovered that particular duplicity? Maybe it was true that only she knew *all* the secrets.

All she wanted was to be left alone with her work.

As the transship entered Underspace, she felt a pang of regret for the deceased Straat-ien, with whom she had shared many difficulties and much time. He had represented his species admirably. Now she would be forever deprived of his unique viewpoint.

No matter. Her research would go on without him.

Among the ship's crew were several Lepar. She kept a wary eye on them, but there was nothing to indicate that she was the focus of any unusual attention on their part or on the part of anyone else aboard. She had made her escape from Daccar with commendable speed.

Would they now seek her out on her homeworld? Lepar worked in the main cities, but they were not a common sight. None presently served at the university. How much would they dare, and how boldly? Or would they seek allies to carry out her assassination? A renegade Massood, perhaps, though a Human was a more likely candidate. Wasn't that how they had originally entered the war, as soldiers for hire? That would be ironic. A Human would be even more conspicuous in her environs than a lethally minded Lepar.

She was neither innocent nor helpless, and her distinctive experiences had taught her much. There were steps she could take to protect herself.

⋆ **XXII** ⋆

Much time passed and the Lepar did not move against her, nor did they send a homicidal surrogate in their stead. Perhaps it was because they had chosen to go slowly, perhaps because they wanted to be completely sure of themselves before taking such a serious and potentially maladroit step. Certainly they would have wondered, and worried, about the circumstances of their Daccaran agent's unexpected death. It hinted at a dangerous gap in their knowledge, which they would typically want to fill before acting.

She prepared as best she could.

Half a year passed from the time of her flight from Daccar before the two Lepar appeared. Attired as sanitation specialists, they went to work on the university's water systems, something they were uniquely equipped to do. Though she passed by in clear view, neither looked in her direction.

Though she harbored no illusions as to their true intentions, she did not vary her routine, maintaining her daily schedule in the face of the unspoken threat. Friends commented on her heightened state of alertness, on the tension she seemed to be under. She thanked them for their empathy even as she dismissed their concerns without elaboration.

The visiting workers remained cautious. It was not until the end of the season that her office door trilled one evening when she was working late. The external pickup revealed the simpleminded face of one of the two Lepar, black eyes doleful, its ingenuous expression wholly disarming. Responding to her query, it informed her that their work had brought them to this end of her building, and that in order to proceed they required a few moments' access to her office.

Which, she reflected sagely, was no doubt the truth.

"We will not trouble you for long," it said via the door speaker. Also doubtless a truthful statement.

Declining to comply would only delay the inevitable in addition to confirming anything they might suspect. She had completed a general catalog of her research, and both her personal and professional lives had been put in order. In a way she was relieved. She was very tired.

She passed a wingtip over a visual switch, and the door slid back to admit them.

They were attired for aqueous service. Long vests and belts held sealed pouches that bulged with equipment. The one who had spoken waddled into the office and without a word strode past her, making for the hygienic cubicle located in a rear alcove. His companion followed and adopted a casual stance close to the doorway, gazing with genuine interest at the depth images which decorated the walls.

"We will not be long." Its gurgling voice betrayed no ulterior motive. "We have to check out pressure and flow here before proceeding to the next office."

Lalelelang had not moved from atop the work nest behind the delicate, sculpted arc of her workstation. "You have to do nothing of the sort. You are here to kill me."

A flat, bulbous face peered out of the hygienic alcove, ebon eyes shimmering in the lights. Outside her single window a carnivorous *Vhastas* glider passed just below the rising moon, the fluorescent running lights of the nocturnal flier a flash of lambent green in the darkness. Within the office there was total silence until the Lepar at the door spoke anew.

"What a strange thing to say, Honored Scholar."

"Is it? You intend to murder me, but you want to be sure of yourselves first. I believe the Lepar never act without first making sure.

"Obviously you have sought an explanation for the death of your colleague on Daccar. He had been trying to kill me and instead he was the one who died. In my quarters. Whereupon I left Daccar rather hurriedly. I knew that despite your initial disbelief you would eventually settle on me as the cause through the simple process of patiently investigating and eliminating every other possibility. I am only surprised that you did not arrive here sooner."

The amphibian stared wordlessly. The first speaker emerged from the cubicle holding a weapon in one hand. She examined it with practiced detachment. Fashioned entirely of nonmetallic components, it was larger than the one she had been threatened with not so very long ago on Daccar. Nor was its shape as subtle. No attempt had been made by its makers to disguise its purpose. As the armed individual stepped to one side, his companion drew a similar device from a vest pocket.

What would be the method this time? More poison, shells, internally explosive pellets, or something she could not imagine? Not that it would matter.

"Your colleague was going to kill me. So I had to kill him."

"We are curious as to how you managed it." The second speaker was now blocking the sealed doorway with his body. "It was not believed that any Wais possessed such capabilities."

"I salute your ignorance." Death's proximity inspired her to flights of fatalistic wit. "I may be the only one."

The gun-wielder omitted a deep-throated grunt of satisfaction. The sound carried as well through the air as it did underwater. "We welcome your confirmation. Now I will kill you." The muzzle of the weapon rose.

"You cannot."

"Would you end your life on an argument?" But the Lepar at the door made a gesture and his companion paused.

"Why not?" he asked.

"There are a number of reasons. Did you think I would do nothing but wait quietly for representatives of your kind to locate and kill me at their leisure? Did you believe that having defended myself once I would never do so again?"

"Since our arrival on Mahmahar we have many times checked this entire building and especially this room. There are no protective mechanisms in evidence. No intricate alarms, no automatic weaponry, no voice or motion-activated transmitters. Nothing. Also, there are two of us and we are both armed. Whatever went wrong on Daccar will not be repeated here. You are defenseless."

"No, I'm not." Her beak clicked lightly and even her crest lay passively flat against the back of her head. The two intruders exchanged a glance. "You place much confidence in unsupported words," the one at the door declared.

"And you place too much in procedure and preparation. Ever since you arrived on my world you've been monitoring my movements. Did you think I was incapable of monitoring yours?"

She glanced to her right. The door to a rear storage alcove opened and a Human soldier stepped out. The Lepar blocking the door blinked slowly in the manner of his kind while his companion took an involuntary step backward. He carefully lowered his weapon. This was sensible, because the young Human female was fully armed and could go off at any moment. She towered over all of them.

"What do you want to me do, Scholar?" she growled in combat Huma.

"For now, nothing." Lalelelang regarded her visitors. "This is Pila. In addition to being a fully trained soldier, she is also a member of the Core.

"The Human Core member Nevan Straat-ien was for many years a good and true friend of mine. I knew very little about his family and relations, but I thought I at least owed it to them to relate the circumstances of his death. Furthermore, since I was informed that the Lepar can resist their probes as well as those of the Amplitur, and that your people were aware of their existence and suggestive abilities, I felt that it was only fair to share this information with the Humans of the Core." She paused to allow everything she had said to sink in.

When she felt sufficient time had passed, she continued.

"So now you know about them, and they know about you, and everyone concerned can deal with each other from a more equal perch."

"This is madness." The Lepar near the cubicle tried to divide his attention between the composed Wais and the edgily alert and very imposing Human. "Do you realize what you have done? This one will kill all three of us."

"I told you that the Human Straat-ien trusted me. In volunteering everything I know to his friends, I have gained their trust as well. Pila trusts me. If I were you, I would do nothing to upset her. She was very close to Straat-ien."

Noting that she wore one of the omnipresent translators, the Lepar at the door directed his attention to the soldier. "Don't your people recognize the danger that this individual represents? If we eliminate her we can still preserve our secrets among ourselves."

The Human only smiled. Both Lepar shuddered instinctively.

Lalelelang proceeded to try and reassure them. "There is no need for any more uncivilized bloodshed. The Core does not trust you, and I know that you respect but do not necessarily trust the Core."

"How could we?" opined the door guard. "They are Human."

"Precisely. But they do trust me. If you will only grant me equal respect, then both sides will have gained something of great value: a mediator."

"You?" The would-be assassin goggled at her. "You are a scholar, not a diplomat."

"What is diplomacy but experience mated to common sense? I am Wais. I favor neither Human nor Lepar. I am better prepared to assume such a role than any representative of any of the intelligent species. Not that I wish it. I do *not* wish it. But it has been thrust upon me and I do not see how I can turn away." She paused for breath. "There are rare, isolated moments in one's life when one devoutly wishes one could act in an uncivilized fashion. For that much, if naught else, I envy Humankind.'' A long, melancholy whistle escaped her.

"All I ever wanted was to study. To accumulate knowledge and from that distill wisdom. I do not want to play diplomat or go-between or peacemaker. Circumstances have thrust this on me.''

The Lepar at the door addressed Lalelelang while warily eyeing the soldier. "Are you going to have her kill us?'' He made no movement with the handgun he held, knowing that the slightest suggestion of a hostile gesture would visit instant death upon him and his companion.

"No!'' The violence of her response startled everyone in the room, including her Human protector. "I have been directly responsible for the death of another intelligent being only once in my life. Even though I acted only to preserve my own, I found it an extraordinarily disagreeable experience that I will never forget. I have no desire to endure it again.'' Her heavily painted lashes fluttered.

"What are the goals here? You wish to ensure your own security and keep your secret from as much of the Weave and our former enemies as possible. You have no reason to fear the Core Humans because you can resist their suggestions. If you moved to reveal their secret they would turn on you. Maybe you can resist them mentally, but you would still have to deal with their more blatantly Human capabilities.''

"See,'' the first Lepar said to the Human. "She is trying to play us off against one another to preserve her own life.''

"My *life*? My life?'' she repeated more softly. "For the sake of knowledge I have voluntarily put my life at risk of death by violence from actual combat, something no Lepar has ever done. I have been now twice threatened by your kind. I have given up on my life many times over. I am not afraid to put it at risk in this cause.''

"Kill her.'' The Lepar at the door addressed the soldier earnestly. "She is a complication. We can work everything out between us without need of a dangerous intermediary. While she lives she holds the threat of revelation over both our kind.''

Never taking its eyes off the two amphibians, the Human spoke for the second time. "No. She's useful. Nevan . . . Colonel Straat-ien thought so, and my superiors concur. She's played linear with us, and she's fixed things neat." The soldier regarded the nesting Wais with a mixture of awe and admiration. "You don't know everything. She's fixed things so that it's more dangerous to kill her than keep her alive."

"I do none of this out of altruism," Lalelelang explained coolly. "Everything proceeds from necessity."

"I do not understand all of this." The door guard wheezed. "We are not clever, and you must explain slowly and carefully so that we will comprehend."

Lalelelang took a deep breath. "It is not that complicated. After I—killed—your agent, I knew that you might someday try to eliminate me, as a safety measure. I have subsequently caused to have placed a number of high-density storage beads containing everything I know, everything I have learned, in certain locations throughout the Weave. These worlds shall go unnamed." The Lepar neither spoke nor reacted, listening quietly.

"If I die without sending to these locations certain specific transmissions at regular intervals, the scheme I have put in place will be activated. As a result, the beads will be forwarded to a number of incorruptible organizations noted for their independent dissemination of information. The secrets of the Lepar and of the Core will become known to all."

The Lepar at the door responded. "What happens if you die accidentally? If you are struck by an out-of-control vehicle or expire of natural causes?"

"Eventually I will send a transmission to terminate the procedure. This will also wipe clean the storage beads. I am in good health—" She stared at the door guard in a most un-Waislike manner. "—and I expect to remain so. Meanwhile it would behoove the representatives of both the Core and the Lepar to see to it that I do not meet with any unforeseen accidents."

"You ask us to do nothing, to react to this not at all."

"You have no choice."

"We are not happy about this," commented the other Lepar, "but I must express my admiration. You defy all of one species and part of another."

"I do not do this because I am so enamored of life," she replied. "I have lived long enough to be displeased by much of what I have seen. But things are better now than when I was born, and may through understanding and awareness of the methods of the Amplitur and the potential regressive nature of Humankind become better still.

"I say again that I dislike all of this. I am by nature a solitary researcher." She indicated the Human. "Pila's people want the same things as you. It will serve the Lepar well to have a faction among Humankind they can trust. I think you can help each other, work well together. In any event, now you will have to."

The assassins deliberated. Out of considerable bravery—or stupidity—the Lepar at the door said, "You cannot trust a Human."

It was the soldier who responded. "You can trust us. We're different. And we can't mess with your minds. You're more equal to us than anyone else, even the Massood."

Careful to employ its empty hand, the first Lepar gestured toward Lalelelang. "Why do you not simply suggest her? Order her to reveal the details of the transmission scheme and the location of the threatening storage beads so that we can render it all harmless?"

The soldier grinned. "Don't you think we thought of that when she first came to us? She set everything up in advance so that we can't touch her. Any more than you can. Suggesting her would activate special redundancies she's installed. That's assuming it would work in the first place. She's strong-willed. No, playing with her mind at this point is too chancy.

"Besides, what she says makes sense. We *can* use each other's help. From my own standpoint as one of the Core, I know how hard it is to be isolated all the time, to always be looking over your shoulder." She chuckled tersely. "We won't show yours to anybody else if you don't show them ours.''

"I believe I follow your meaning if not your syntax," the Lepar replied. "You will keep the secret of our ability to resist Core and Amplitur mind-probes?''

"Yes. Provided you do the same concerning our existence. Together we'll monitor my own rowdy kind as well as the activities of the Amplitur. You have easy access to people and places that are often denied to us, and vice versa. I think you'll find us good friends as well as valuable allies.'' She shrugged. "Anyway, it's the only rational course of action the canary's left open to us.''

The Lepar looked at one another. "We do not have the authority to sanction such an agreement.''

"Didn't expect that you did. Convey everything that's happened here to your superiors.'' She nodded toward the contemplative Lalelelang. "You know how to find us, and we certainly know how to find you.''

"We are putting up our arms now.'' Very slowly, the two amphibians returned their weapons to their respective pockets. When this was done the door guard performed a strange little bow in Lalelelang's direction.

"You work great things here, Scholar. I personally would not have thought it of a Wais, much less of an academic.''

"Generalization is always dangerous," she responded. "I am not your ordinary Wais.''

"On this point we are all of us present agreed," the Lepar replied fervently.

"We are all something else," she added, "or had you not noticed?'' This time the Human as well as the Lepar eyed her questioningly. "The four of us here are all female.''

"What of that?'' wondered the other Lepar.

"In addition to our professions we have the added responsibility of procreation. Leastwise the three of you do. I am too old, and sometimes I mourn for lost opportunities. As you go your separate ways I ask you to consider the future you will be leaving to the offspring you have not yet birthed.

Do your utmost to bequeath to them a civilization of diverse peoples that is peaceful and true.''

"It seems we have little choice," said the door guard.

"That's right." The Human soldier nodded by way of confirmation. "It's no longer a matter of whether she lives or dies. She's pushed everything beyond that. She's taken herself out of the equation by making herself extraneous."

"I understand you." The Lepar at the door considered the Human. "Is it really true that your species has never known happiness or contentment?"

"Not from what I've seen of my history," Pila responded. "We've always been good at war, but we've never been able to handle peace. Maybe you can give us some pointers. Bearing in mind that we have to keep a wary eye on the squids."

The Lepar hesitated, then stepped forward and extended a lightly webbed, slick-skinned hand. "While not binding, I believe this is the proper mode of signifying agreement."

Smiling, the soldier lightly gripped the proffered fingers with her free hand. Unlike the Lepar, she did not put aside her weapon, but this was to be expected and the Lepar was not offended.

Lalelelang briefly closed her eyes tight. No one had died, there had been no fighting. All had gone more or less according to plan.

"That is better. One thing I have learned from a lifetime of studying Humans is that peace is not a gift. It is like a building that is never finished. Such things are difficult to do without assistance. You will each contribute different talents to the process of construction."

The Human and the Lepar turned to her as they parted. "What of you?" asked the amphibian. "Will you help?"

"Not in that process. You do not need me and there is little I can do."

"You can teach us. About Humans. You know more about them than any other non-Human."

Lalelelang trilled lightly. "Perhaps, perhaps. I am very fatigued. We will see. Meanwhile the Lepar are welcome to continue accessing my research. None of it is hidden."

"You can interpret it for us," the Lepar insisted. "Remember that we are not very smart."

"Only if there are no other options," she insisted wearily. "Only if you have no other choice."

"I understand. We will try not to impose on you."

"Same here," said the Human. She turned back to the amphibian. "I am not alone on Mahmahar. Now that you and I have established a basis for cooperation, there are others of my organization who would like to talk to you."

Human and Lepar departed in tandem, making extensive use of their translators.

Lalelelang sat on her work nest in her silent office for a long time, not moving, meditating peacefully. After a long while she rose, turned out the lights, and left the building, looking neither to left nor right and not very intently straight ahead. If some Human or Lepar with homicidal thoughts on its mind lay waiting in ambush there was nothing she would be able to do about it.

She walked through the covered, soaring atrium with its fountains and flowers, deserted at this time of night, and exited onto the blue-green ground cover outside. Creamcolored night-blooming alarias filled the air with sultry perfume. An occasional worker or student sauntered past in a fog of undulating attire.

After a while she reached the crest of a rounded knoll. On her left, carefully trimmed fluel bushes formed a low hedge florid with phosphorescence. Tiny glittering bugs no bigger than dust motes danced among the leaves.

Activating the tiny player she carried in her side pouch, she stood perfectly still and listened to the music. The volume was set low and personal. The music was several hundred years old and had been composed by a Human. A very special Human. The first contact Human, William Dulac.

It rose and fell, rushed forward and slowed uncertainly. Very much like Humankind itself, she mused. Everything that infuriating, wondrous, terrifying, remarkable species was could be found in their music.

Eventually the neurotic cacophony grew subdued, the

composition concluding in a whisper of woodwinds and muted strings. Fascinating sounds. Maybe someday she would be able to understand them completely. Emitting a soft, exhausted trill, she let her neck arch backward with a flexibility no Human, constrained by its powerful musculature and heavy bones, could match. Mahmahar's lone moon had set and the constellations of her homeworld were at their most brilliant.

She had no way of knowing what the future would bring, but she did know that she'd done her best. Core Humans and Lepar would cooperate to keep watch, and to protect one another's secrets. In light of that accomplishment the preserving of her own life seemed very much an afterthought. What matter one Wais more or less?

Her research awaited further codification, annotation, categorization. A lot still to do.

At least everyone had been polite, she reflected. Even the Human. Manners were indisputably the one great Wais contribution to galactic civilization.

She straightened and stretched, flexing and relaxing her crest and neck feathers before continuing on down the far side of the knoll in the direction of the university internal transport that would carry her home. She walked confident in the knowledge that she had left in her wake if not peace, at least a little understanding.

That, after all, was what scholars were for.

Don't miss the other intriguing volumes of *THE DAMNED* series by Alan Dean Foster.

A CALL TO ARMS

For millennia, the alien union called the Weave had been at war with the Amplitur. Will Dulac was a New Orleans composer who stumbled upon a scouting party for the Weave. The Weave was looking for allies among the uniquely warlike Human race, but Dulac knew the dangers of Human involvement. And then the Amplitur discovered Earth.

THE FALSE MIRROR

In the handful of centuries since the Earth had joined the Weave in the struggle against the Amplitur, it began to look as though the Weave might finally prevail. Then an elite Amplitur combat unit designed to look like Humans threatened to tear the Weave alliance apart and pit the entire galaxy against the Human race.

Published by Del Rey Books.

Also by
ALAN DEAN FOSTER